****

Into the Calm

Book Six of Rise of the Republic

By

James Rosone

****

Illustration © Tom Edwards
Tom EdwardsDesign.com

****

Published in conjunction with Front Line Publishing, Inc.

Manuscript Copyright Notice

©2022, James Rosone in conjunction with Front Line Publishing, Inc. Except as provided by the Copyright Act, no part of this publication may be reproduced, stored in a retrieval system or transmitted in any form or by any means without the prior written permission of the publisher.

All rights reserved
ISBN: 978-1-957634-40-1
Sun City Center, Florida, United States of America
Library of Congress Control Number: 2022909296

Table of Contents

Prologue.. 5
Chapter 1: Supply Run 15
Chapter 2: The Honeypot 21
Chapter 3: The Gray Man 30
Chapter 4: Hands Tied... 43
Chapter 5: A New World.. 49
Chapter 6: Top Gun 57
Chapter 7: What Neutral Zone?.. 64
Chapter 8: Phase One – Terror 81
Chapter 9: Reorg.. 86
Chapter 10: Digging Deeper... 98
Chapter 11: Spies Like Us 105
Chapter 12: Too Big to Fail... 114
Chapter 13: The X 120
Chapter 14: Change of Command 125
Chapter 15: Found 'Em 130
Chapter 16: Routine Patrol 136
Chapter 17: Cruisin' 140
Chapter 18: Never Forgotten 144
Chapter 19: The Summons 151
Chapter 20: Many Faces.. 160
Chapter 21: My Laktish... 164
Chapter 22: Our World, Our Future..................................... 172
Chapter 23: Domestic Affairs.. 176
Chapter 24: Project 970 184
Chapter 25: Consequences... 190
Chapter 26: Mum's the Word 207
Chapter 27: Storm Clouds 209
Chapter 28: Rags to Riches.. 218
Chapter 29: Seat of Power 221
Chapter 30: Evolution of the Terminator.............................. 227
Chapter 31: Those Who Enter, Lead 230
Chapter 32: The Gray Lady 236
Chapter 33: Spies From Afar... 245
Chapter 34: The Web... 253
Chapter 35: Biscuits and Gravy 268

Chapter 36: The Code.. 279
Chapter 37: Why Alfheim 290
Chapter 38: The Burden of Command.. 292
Chapter 39: Shifting the Balance.. 298
From the Authors... 304
Abbreviation Key 307

Prologue

2107 AD
Eight Months Post Dominion War
Jacksonville, Arkansas
Earth, Sol System

"Subject is approaching. Stand by."

Hosni felt his body tense. He stepped out of the coffee shop, joining the sea of bodies. The morning rush of pedestrians moving in unison on the sidewalk was heavy as usual.

Ten seconds, the voice said over their neurolink.

I'm ready, Joe replied over the same system, falling in next to Hosni.

Glancing toward Joe's hand, Hosni saw the edge of the autoinjector. He looked up—the van was approaching. Hosni quickened his pace; the subject was just a few feet in front of them now.

Five seconds.

An attractive blond-haired woman at the wheel of a BMW i8 steered her hover car out of her parking spot and into traffic, creating an instant opening for their van to slide into.

We're ready, the occupants of the van announced. *Take him!*

In a blur of action, Joe surged forward, the autoinjector briefly connecting with the side of the man's neck. Hosni reached up, grabbing the man's arm as his body went limp. Joe and Hosni held the man's body upright as they turned toward the van, its side door now opened. Moments later, the three of them were in the vehicle, the door automatically closing as their driver pulled out of their parking spot and into the morning traffic.

****

Five Hours Later
Undisclosed Site

"You got this, Hosni," Major Royce assured him. "Assess if he's willing to play ball or if we're going to have to let Tom work on him for a while."

Hosni nodded. "Got it. He'll talk…I doubt he'll want to go a few rounds with Tom. Speaking of Tom, here he is," Hosni said, motioning to the Synth. "Tom, have you completed your examination of the subject? Are we ready to proceed?"

Tom was the name they had given the Unit's T200 Human Domain Medical Specialist synthetic. Unlike the C200 combat-variant medical Synths, this civilian version had been crafted specifically for covert intelligence operations. The T200s had been programmed with the psychological knowledge and other skills needed to interview suspects and prisoners. The suspects were questioned softly, yet pointedly. The prisoners, on the other hand, were offered only a short courtesy window to talk before enhanced interrogation techniques were introduced. Use of the T200s was restricted to "Special" units within the Republic Armed Forces.

Tom's emotionless voice answered, "Major Royce, Lieutenant Hosni, the subject has been stripped and searched. No weapons or false teeth were found. Medical scan did not detect any other foreign objects or materials that pose a danger to Republic personnel. The subject's vitals read normal; his sedation should wear off soon. He will be ready shortly to commence interrogation."

"Thank you, Tom. I'll join you inside in a moment," Hosni replied. Tom returned to the room where the sedated prisoner was being held.

"I'll be in the observation room, Hosni. Good luck," Royce offered, moving to the room adjacent to his.

Standing in the hallway, Hosni watched Tom through the door of the interrogation room and couldn't help but shudder slightly. The combat Synths were beasts on the battlefield, tearing through Zodark warriors with a fury that matched the Zodarks' own. The specialist models, the ones like Tom…those gave Hosni goose bumps. Devoid of human emotions, morals, and ethics, they were the perfect interrogators.

Entering the room, Hosni looked the unconscious man over. He glanced at the tablet, reviewing the information available. It wasn't much; the man had immigrated to Earth from Sumer a few months earlier—his trail of information wasn't very deep.

Interrupting his thoughts, Tom announced, "When you are ready, we can begin interrogating the subject." It was a reminder to get the show on the road. They had a lot to discuss, and God only knew if he'd be cooperative. If Tom had to take over…it could take a while. Extracting information a subject didn't want to reveal required time.

Taking a breath in, Hosni looked at the medical Synth before briefly making eye contact with Royce.

Using their neurolinks, Royce encouraged, *You got this, Hosni. Just like we practiced…*

"OK, Tom. Let's begin."

Grabbing the frigid glass of water from the counter, Hosni splashed it against the chest of the naked man, who instantly woke from the cold bath. "Aghhh!" the man briefly yelled as his eyes suddenly popped open, the bright light momentarily blinding him.

"What? Where am I?" he stammered, confused.

His eyes darted around the room, taking in the sights. A bright light hovered over him, making the edges of the room dark and out of focus.

Squinting at Hosni, the man demanded, "Who are you?"

Fear shone in the man's eyes, his body shivering as goose bumps rose on his skin. Looking down, he realized he was naked, restrained to a chair.

"You can call me… Smith."

The man seemed confused at first. Then his facial expression changed. Almost instantaneously, he went from nervous and scared to calm.

Hosni smirked at the change in demeanor, catching the subtlety others might have missed. The man had been trained for interrogations.

"Why don't you tell me your name?"

"Sure, I've done nothing wrong. My name is Tobin Swerve," the man said evenly, like he was introducing himself at a cocktail party.

Walking to the right side of the man, Hosni bent down close to his ear. "OK, Tobin…why don't you tell me your *real* name so we can move on?"

The man scrunched up his eyebrows at the question before repeating, "I told you my name. It's Tobin Swerve."

Moving to the man's other ear, Hosni whispered, "We both know that's not true." He shifted around the man, pulling a nearby chair closer, his legs touching the man's as he leaned in, his face invading the man's private space. "If you'd like to play games instead, we can do that. I promise it's fun. It goes like this. I ask you questions, you answer them truthfully. Each time you lie, though, a consequence is introduced. The more you lie, well…you get the picture. It's like my mother used to say: 'the truth shall set you free.'"

Staring into Tobin's eyes, Hosni saw a look of confusion, then fear, then abject horror washing over him at the realization of what awaited him. Tobin squirmed in the chair, clearly not liking the direction this conversation was headed. His eyes glanced at the restraints. His arms, legs, and chest were firmly held in place by a series of one-inch straps.

Leaning against the chair's back, Hosni canted his head to the side. "Yes, Tobin, I think we should play this game. That is, unless you want to answer my questions truthfully."

Tobin's eyes narrowed, a determined look replacing the confusion from moments ago. "What do you want…Smith?"

Hosni grinned. The facade was gone, replaced with acceptance of his situation.

"You know what I want. I've already asked you. What's your *name*?" he repeated, tapping the prisoner's chest with his finger.

The man stuck his chin up as he countered, "I'm afraid you have me mixed up with someone else. My name is Tobin Swerve. I'm a logistics specialist for Yale Industrial Goods. I've done nothing wrong. In fact, I demand to speak with a lawyer. I have *rights*." The restraints tightened the more he tugged at them.

Hosni motioned for Tom to bring the medical cart. Beads of sweat formed on the man's forehead as he saw its contents. The contemptuous scowl crumbled at the sight of two clear vials with different-colored lettering, syringes, and other mysterious tools.

"Please!" the man pleaded. "I don't know what you think I know, but you have the wrong person. I'm just a logistics specialist."

Hosni grabbed the vial with red lettering and loaded 10cc of liquid into a syringe. Holding it toward the light, he nudged the plunger, pushing out any air bubbles and causing a very small amount of the liquid to escape as a mist.

"We're going to play a game, you and I."

Sweat now streamed down the sides of Tobin's face.

"At every step in this process, I'll give you a chance to answer my questions honestly. But each time you lie or attempt to deceive, your pain will increase exponentially."

A stream of urine ran down the man's leg, pooling at his feet.

Hosni continued to calmly explain, "No matter how bad the pain gets, I assure you, death will not find you—no matter how loud you scream for it. My assistant, Tom, he's a medical humanoid, highly trained in this. If your heart gives out, he'll bring you back. You will find no escape in death. We'll just keep reviving you until you answer our questions."

The man's eyes had drifted, causing Hosni to snap his fingers. "OK, then. You know the rules—it's time to start the game. This should be fun. Answer my questions readily, and you might even make it home for dinner. So, let's try this from the beginning, shall we? What is your name?"

The man hesitated for a moment before his resolve stiffened. He barked angrily, "Who do you think I am? Who the hell are you to question me like this?"

Hosni slapped the man hard across his face and lurched from his chair, his face right up against his prisoner's. "Stop playing games! We know you aren't a logistics specialist for Yale Industrial Goods. Tell me who you really are, who you work for, and what your real job is!"

"I swear, you have the wrong person."

"Wrong answer. Time for round one." Hosni motioned for Tom to administer the first dose.

Inches from his prisoner's face, Hosni stared into his eyes, searching them for the look—the look that said *I'm caught; I'm not getting out of this*. Then he saw it, fractions of a second before the drug took over.

He's our guy, Hosni thought as the drug transformed the man's eyes and facial features almost instantly.

As the pharmaceuticals attached to the prisoner's nervous system, they would trick him into believing his body had been set on fire. As the substance spread throughout his body, it caused every pain receptor to flood the brain, initially overwhelming his ability to respond. Once he could, a violent scream roared from within his body. Then he violently convulsed, testing the limits of the restraints as his mind deceived him into believing his very being was on fire.

"What is your real name?" yelled Hosni over the man's agonizing screams.

"Make it stop! Make it stop!" he begged desperately, the straps tearing into his flesh the more he struggled against them.

"Tell me your name and it'll stop!"

"Enki! My real name is Enki Enuma," the man shouted through tears.

Hosni countered with rapid-fire questions. "Who do you work for? What is your mission? How many others are with you?"

Through gritted teeth, he hissed, "The Mukhabarat. I work for the Mukhabarat! Now give me the antidote!"

"You're still not answering my questions, Enki!" Hosni countered, using his real name for emphasis. "What is your job? What is your mission? How many others are with you?" He wasn't about to turn the drug off until those questions had been answered.

"Stop this pain and I'll tell you what you want to know," Enki railed, the restraints becoming bloody as they tore further into his flesh.

Hosni shook his head. "Wrong answer, Enki. I keep giving you chances to tell the truth, but you keep holding back on me. Now we're going to move to the next round."

Hosni motioned for Tom to administer the second dose. This amplified things to an entirely new level as the prisoner's muscles spasmed and contracted while the fire drug continued to rack his body and brain.

Enki howled and cursed Hosni, shouting in Sumerian and English before pleading for mercy, begging him to make the pain stop.

"What is your job? What is your mission? Who else is working with you?" Hosni repeated the questions a third time.

"My job is logistics. I'm supposed to prepare the way for others. I work alone. My job has me working alone. There, I've answered your questions. Now turn it off!" he begged, eyes bloodshot, his face contorted in agonizing pain.

Getting back into Enki's face, Hosni shouted over his cries, "I still have more questions!"

"Turn off the drug and I'll tell you whatever you want to know. Just turn it off. Turn it off and I'll tell you everything," Enki pleaded, snot running down his face between sobs and muscle contractions.

Hosni nodded to Tom; it was time to move to the next level.

Tom administered the counteragent, which was not just a designer pain reliever but also functioned as a truth serum when given after the fire medication. The drugs flooded Enki's body. His facial expression relaxed, and his eyes became glassy.

Enki has arrived in La-la land. Now he's ready to talk…

Hosni snapped his fingers to gain his prisoner's attention. "Isn't this better, Enki? If you keep answering my questions, you can stay in this happy place for as long as you want," Hosni explained as he shifted to a softer, mellower tone.

Enki smiled happily. "Water," he stammered. "Can I please have some water?"

"Sure. I'll have some water brought in." Turning to look at the one-way mirror, Hosni used his neurolink. *Juan, can you please bring a glass of water in?*

Hosni smiled at Enki. "There we go, water is on the way. Now, let's try to stay in this happy place and not have to go back to the bad place we just left. How about you tell me about this neat job you have with the Mukhabarat in logistics?"

Enki looked through him for a moment, nodding in compliance. "Yes, my job with them is logistics. When the new people arrive, it's my job to secure the safe house they'll use, provide their new identity, and establish the necessary bank information and credits to get them established. If a front company or legitimate cutout needs to be purchased, then I take care of that as well."

"Enki, you said when people arrive…who are these people? How many people have you settled on Earth?"

Enki looked confused by the question. He began to speak like he was talking in his mind, not realizing he was vocalizing his thoughts. "I said people? Did I tell them about the assets? Did I mention the watchers? Oh, Lindow, I didn't mention the Ani, did I? Only a few have come so far…it's not their time yet…"

Damn it. He's having a much stronger reaction to the drug than we want to see.

Hosni spoke to Royce and Juan over the neurolink. *The drugs are hitting him harder than expected.* He'd seen something like this before— the fire drugs caused prisoners to perspire heavily, and it affected some more than others. *We need to get some fluids in him, or we'll lose our ability to guide his mind to the answer we want.*

Royce responded, *Good call. Get in there with the water, Juan. Hosni, come out here and let's talk for a moment.*

Hosni stood as Juan walked in with a pitcher of water and a plastic glass.

"I've got it from here. See what the boss wants," Juan said softly, out of Enki's earshot.

Hosni turned to his prisoner. "We've brought you some water, Enki. I need you to drink as much as you can. We'll talk some more in a few minutes."

As Hosni left the room, the electronic noise scrambler in the hallway kicked back on, and the door sealed the room up tight, the harmonic vibrations of what was happening inside now fully blocked off from the outside world.

Royce approached him with a grin of satisfaction. "Good job in there. That's some good intel you're getting out of him. Press him more on what he meant by those three groups he mentioned: asset, watcher, and Ani. We also need to find out how they're creating these new identities. That last piece is critical if we're going to figure out how to find the others."

Hosni felt elated at the praise—this was his first human intelligence operation, and he'd already found some blockbuster intelligence.

"Hey, Hosni. I know you feel like you just hit the jackpot with this guy, but it's not over yet," Royce said, apparently reading his mind. "You have a lot more to ask him. He's pliable right now, but that's not to say he won't figure out what the drugs are doing and find another way to resist. Stay focused; keep your head in the game. Now get back in there and get us answers to those questions," Royce explained, his tone reminding Hosni who was the boss.

"Sorry about that—you're right. We have a lot more to press him on. I'll get it out of him."
****

What kind of drugs have they given me? I didn't just tell them how many have arrived, did I? Enki questioned himself, finding it nearly impossible to focus. Then his eyes saw the water.

Oh, Lindow. I can't focus…this won't work. I must make this work…I've said too much.

"Water. Water, please," Enki rasped to the soldier who'd looked away.

"All right, give me a second," the man replied, waiting for the door to fully close.

As the overwhelming sensation of thirst swept over him, Enki reminded himself, *OK, now hold some back.* He fought through the drugs clouding his mind, melting his ability to resist despite his training. If he couldn't focus, this wouldn't work.

The soldier approached, glass in hand. Enki held his mouth open, waiting for his moment.

Too bad Smith isn't in here with me...

Taking the water in, Enki gulped some down, then turned his head to the side, indicating he needed a moment. The soldier picked up on the cue, stepping back, waiting to see if he'd ask for more.

This is it; it's now or never...

He gave a slight nod to the soldier that he was done. When he turned away, Enki closed his eyes, pushing through the chemical haze and focusing on a single thought, a single word. He thought of the word *mya*, and then an image appeared. He focused on the image until it disappeared. He thought of the word *troya*. A new image appeared. Moments later, it was replaced with a final image containing two words: *yes* and *no.*

When the moment arrived, Enki didn't hold back. He focused on the word *yes*. It blinked three times, then disappeared. For a moment, there was nothing—no reaction, no big reveal like he'd thought there would be.

Then Enki felt something along the roof of his mouth. The water he'd held in his mouth began a radical transformation as the substance reacted to its presence. He'd been told it would react the same with saliva, but a mouth full of water would make you a greater vessel of death to anything nearby.

As the reaction reached critical mass, the water transformed rapidly into a gas that filled his mouth and lungs until the pressure was too much. Like a kettle releasing pent-up steam, the gas shot out his mouth and nose in a rapid gush of aerated poison that filled the room.

In those final moments, Enki saw the face of the soldier he'd just sprayed. The man's expression changed from anger at being spat on to horror as his throat began to constrict. The glass hit the floor, spilling its contents as the soldier fell below his line of sight.

Before his brain shut down from lack of oxygen, Enki faced the mirror and forced a smile. The blackness enveloped him, leaving him with a final thought before it vanished.

I win.

****

By the time Hosni and the others knew something had happened in the room, the building's AI had sealed the room and quarantined its HVAC system from the building. Nothing was getting in or out until a hazmat team determined it was safe.

Hosni raced into the observation room. Juan's body lay still on the floor, and a crooked smile was frozen on the face of the prisoner he'd spoken to just moments ago.

Major Royce shouted commands at the building's AI and the synthetic humanoid Tom, who remained devoid of any type of emotional reaction.

"Damn it!" Hosni shouted as he pounded a fist on the mirror, anger boiling over at the sight of his friend lying dead just a few feet away. They'd survived years of war, only for him to die while questioning a prisoner.

Major Royce placed a hand on his shoulder. "This isn't your fault, Hosni. It's mine. I'm the commander. I'm the one who failed to detect whatever killed them. Once the bodies are rendered safe, we'll figure out what the hell that was and make sure this can't happen again."

Hosni stared at his friend's body, then glanced at the prisoner before commenting, "They'd rather die at their own hands than talk." He shook his head and turned away. "If that doesn't convince you we have a serious Zodark problem on our hands, I don't know what will. That last comment, though…assets, watchers, Ani…I think we're in for some serious trouble soon. Let's hope the brass figures out what to do next."

Royce grimaced at the comment. They could only hope the Senate and these new agencies they'd created would let them do their jobs before things got out of control.

"Juan was a damn good soldier, Hosni. Like that prisoner said, more are on the way. This war isn't over. They've just changed how it'll be fought. Let's go brief the boss and round up the rest of the team. We've got a new enemy to hunt, and it's time we get ready for what's coming next."

Chapter 1
Supply Run

Magnussen Orbital Station
Above Planet Alfheim, Sirius System

Dakkuri entered the cantina, keeping his head low as he made his way to the bar.

"What'll you have?" asked a man with a dirty towel draped over his shoulder. Bottles of alcohol and assorted drinks lined the glass wall behind him.

"Whiskey, neat," was all Dakkuri said, turning slightly away from the bar, surveilling the scene around him.

Dakkuri caught some movement to his right before a glass appeared from beneath the bar, a bottle of brown liquid filling it to the halfway point.

"Let me know if you need anything else," the man said before turning to walk toward another patron.

Lifting the glass to his lips, Dakkuri sipped, almost wincing as the liquid ran down his throat. *Damn. How do these people tolerate such strong drinks?* he wondered.

His eyes continued scanning for the man he knew only as TJ. When Dakkuri didn't see him, he sighed. A song played in the background, the lyrics and their meaning unfamiliar to him—something about whiskey and reaching the bottom of the barrel, only to be rescued by love.

This is what they call music? he marveled.

A man in coveralls with a forgettable face walked in, standing at the entrance for a moment. When he spotted Dakkuri, he made his way toward him.

Sliding into the open seat next to Dakkuri, the man caught the bartender's attention and ordered a drink of his own. When the barkeep left, the man pulled his Qpad out and proceeded to watch some sort of video clip, adding to the noise happening around them.

Dakkuri turned to face toward the bar and away from the man as he pulled his own Qpad out. He composed a short message using the holographic keypad, hit send, and waited.

A voice spoke, intermixed with the noise and chatter of whatever show the man behind him was watching. "You have the money?"

TJ was late—something that made Dakkuri nervous. Still, he needed the goods.

He held the Qpad up like he was sending a video message. "If you still have the product... I do." If this guy didn't have it, he'd walk and find another dealer who did.

"I got it. It's still on our ship, ready to transfer to yours." TJ drained half his glass. "You know, I love this song. It's an old one—came out damn near a hundred years ago. Guy's got a voice, and those lyrics...they speak to a simpler time."

Dakkuri snorted. *This whiny crap is making my ears bleed*, he thought privately. "What do they call this kind of...what music is this?"

"Country music."

The lyrics continued on, talking about alcohol and romance. "Country music? What is it? Why do they call it that?" There was so much Dakkuri didn't understand about the humans from the Republic— they were still so...*alien*.

The man laughed briefly before finishing off the rest of his drink. "It's about life, my man: the happy and sad moments and everything in between. That's life in its truest form."

"Huh, OK. Maybe it'll grow on me in time," Dakkuri replied with a slight smile. TJ seemed to relax a bit as they both faced the bottles staring back at them from behind the wall.

"Before I show you the product, let me see that you have the money."

Dakkuri tapped a couple of keys, pulling a recent picture up. There were four crates, their tops held open to reveal their contents. He angled the screen slightly for TJ, who caught the glimpse he needed and let out a soft whistle at the sight.

TJ got up, and Dakkuri waited an appropriate amount of time before exiting the bar and walking toward the station's warehouses and docking ports. Dakkuri closed the distance between him and TJ as he walked through the promenade. In his peripheral vision, Dakkuri noticed that two figures casually followed them.

When they approached docking slip 31B, Dakkuri entered a pass code used to secure the warehouse and docking port. The door opened, revealing a cavernous warehouse filled with palletized cargo. When a freighter docked, it transferred cargo to and from these docking warehouse slips along the edges of the station.

Dakkuri called to his enforcer, "Orchamus, bring the crates. He wants to visually inspect them."

"Sure thing, boss," the man replied as he turned to grab them from just inside the ship.

TJ grinned as they approached the cargo entrance to the *Wawat*. "That's an interesting ship. Would love to see the inside of a Sumerian ship one day. Don't think I've ever seen one before now."

Dakkuri shrugged at the comment. The only human to have seen the insides of their ship was a station cargo inspector, and he'd been watched like a hawk. "A ship is a ship. It ain't a fancy passenger ship, but it can haul cargo and we're able to scratch a living from it. What more can you ask for?"

"Amen to that. With the war over, you civilian haulers are bound to stay busy now."

Orchamus reappeared, pushing the crates toward them on a hover cart. Stopping in front of them, he opened the top one. "It's all here. Go ahead, pick one up if you'd like."

TJ looked down and smiled at what he saw.

"Wow, you really do have the money," he exclaimed, picking a brick up to examine it. Each brick bore the seal of the former Sumerian government. Below the seal, the weight was listed in Sumerian, reading 12.4 kilograms, or 400 ounces of 99.99 percent pure gold.

"It's all there—five million Republic credits in physical gold. That's one hundred bars to be exact," Dakkuri explained as TJ marveled at the feeling of holding physical currency, not a digital credit.

"Now it's your turn. Let's see the product and make the exchange."

TJ placed the gold bar in the crate. "Yes, sir. We need to bring the crates to 48A—it'll show as being closed for maintenance. We do that to keep the inspectors and the lookie-loos away. Come on, I'll show you."

They made for the exit with Orchamus pushing the hover cart behind them. Dakkuri saw him nod; he was ready if this went south.

As they left the warehouse, walking down the transfer corridors, TJ tapped the side of his smart glasses, telling his people they were on the way.

As they approached 48A, Dakkuri saw figures materialize from the shadows nearby. The three men looked tough, like they had seen a few bar fights in their time. After they'd been ushered inside, the lead figure motioned for Dakkuri to check the packages.

A figure from further in the warehouse moved toward them, pushing a hover cart with four large rectangular crates evenly stacked on it. Dakkuri unsealed the first one, and a hissing sound escaped from within. He lifted up the top, revealing a single warhead for a Havoc II high-explosive missile.

TJ spoke from behind him. "I've got four of them, just like you asked for." Then he ordered his friend, "Show him the rest of it. Let's get the transaction complete; then we can talk."

Another guy pushed a hover cart toward them and opened it to reveal its contents. The crate was packed with blasters and two hundred Republic Army pistols, still fresh from the factory. A second crate was opened, revealing fifty M1 battle rifles. The third crate had one hundred neatly packed fragmentation grenades. When Dakkuri saw the fourth crate, his heart skipped a beat. Staring back at him were twenty M-12 multipurpose launchers or MPLs.

TJ responded to his look of surprise. "You didn't think we could find 'em, did ya?"

"Honestly, no. You got the missiles? 'Cause launchers won't do me any good without them."

"Every one of 'em. It's all there, mate, just as you asked. We good to make our swap now?"

"Yeah, TJ. We're good," Dakkuri replied happily. "Hey, TJ, before we leave, how are you guys acquiring this stuff, and could we acquire more if we want?"

TJ gave him a sideways look, sizing him up before answering, "Let's just say there's more than a few Republic freighter wrecks floating around out there. And there's plenty of other places with leftovers from the war. But as to acquiring more from us...that all depends."

"Oh? On what exactly?"

"On what it is you're looking for and whether you can afford it, my friend. Good stuff ain't cheap, and hard untraceable currency like that gold...that's hard to come by."

"Ah, well, I don't think that'll be a problem on our end," Dakkuri assured.

TJ snorted. "The war's over, man. What exactly are you needing all this stuff for?"

Dakkuri scratched the stubble on his chin. "We're Sumerians. The war may be over for some…but we have long memories of the Zodarks. Who's to say they won't return one day?"

TJ grunted. "Yeah, I suppose you're right. Zodarks, though…that's the Republic's problem, not mine. As to buying more, that all depends on when you purchase. In our business, we like to move around—maybe we'll be here, maybe we'll be back in the Belt. If you do place an order, once we've gotten what we want, we'll let you know where to meet."

Orchamus walked up to TJ, leaning in so only he could hear. Seeing TJ's facial expressions told Dakkuri all he needed to know.

Time to go, he thought as Orchamus traded hover carts with them.

Dakkuri extended his hand to TJ. As he took it, he told him, "We'll send you another order when we're ready. Good working with you, TJ. Oh, and don't forget, like that sad song said, life is about the ups and downs, the good and the bad. Let's try to keep things good. I see a lot of hard currency headed your way soon. I like this arrangement—don't mess it up."

****

Eighteen Days Later
Free Trader *Wawat*

Dakkuri silently observed Sadat as he finished packing the explosives in the cylindrical device. Chryssoula took the cylinder next and went to work. She attached the detonator cap and the top of the cylinder together before doing a quick systems check. Once the device was assembled, they placed it in the suitcase.

Dakkuri felt good about their progress. Things were moving along as they got closer to Earth. It had been nearly a year since his teams had dispersed from Sumer. They'd nearly completed phase zero—Republic integration.

With the minions working on their tasks, he had responsibilities he could only complete in his quarters, away from his people. When he entered the room, he locked it, ensuring no interruptions.

Reviewing the special data pad only he could use, Dakkuri brought up the set of reports they'd downloaded prior to FTL jump. It wouldn't be long before they reached Earth, and he had plenty to catch up on. Alfheim truly was located at the end of nowhere.

Before Dakkuri had left Sumer, NOS Heltet had given him and a few others the same P2 devices used by the Zodark NOSs and others within the Groff, the security service within the Zodark Empire, and the Malvari, the command element within the Zodark military. This would allow Dakkuri to receive and send secured communications with the Groff.

The first report Dakkuri checked was from his logistics team on New Eden. They'd been busy, and things looked productive. They'd established a series of front companies or cutouts based out of the Emerald City. The cutouts would allow them to establish a series of apartments and safe houses across New Eden, Earth, Mars, Sumer, and Alpha Centauri. He opened another file labeled "Watcher Reports." He skimmed the reports—since he didn't spot anything unusual, he moved on.

Dakkuri thought about Sol as they neared it. He'd be handing this logistics team a challenging task. They'd be the ones to distribute the packages they'd just acquired to the safe houses for the Ani. He already felt uncomfortable having one of them on his ship—the last thing he wanted was for them to find fault with his operation. He'd seen the way Orchamus looked at him, assessing him.

They may be Ani, but I'm still the one in charge of this operation, Dakkuri thought, pushing any doubts out of his mind. He saw the clock on the wall…it was time to sleep. Tomorrow was a big day. Time to begin phase one.

Chapter 2
The Honeypot

Earth, Sol System

After Ashurina Zidan had arrived on Earth from Sumer, she had spent the next few months learning everything she could about these humans that constituted the Republic. Of particular interest was a place called Nasiriyah, a city that straddled the Euphrates River as it flowed to the Arabian Gulf not far away. Nasiriyah was in a Republic state called Iraq. She'd learned it had previously been part of another alliance called the Tri-Parte Alliance before the governments of Earth had consolidated to form one government. Had this place not been selected as the home city of her new legend, she doubted she'd ever have given it more than a fraction of a second's thought. But the Kafarr she worked for had carefully crafted her new legend, and now she'd have to assume this persona if she had any hope of accomplishing her assigned mission.

Ashurina Zidan would now become Ashurina Hamoud, built around the professional skill sets she'd honed as a deep-cover agent for the Mukhabarat. The cover story she'd been given closely matched her own skill set as an engineer who'd worked on power generation reactors. The employment history of Ashurina Hamoud would show that she'd previously worked for the Iraq Ministry of Electricity. It would also show that, during her time in university and in her professional work, she'd earned credentials and gained experience working on the dominant reactors used for power generation throughout the Republic.

Sometime during the 2050s, a switch had been made in nuclear power generation and the globe had radically changed with the integration of the new Gen-IV reactors. Some regions had gone for the sodium-cooled fast reactors or SFRs and other regions had adopted the molten salt reactors or MSRs. She'd been chosen for this specific mission because both of these concepts were similar to the more powerful and efficient Arkonorian reactors she'd worked on, the type that were used by the Zodarks and Sumerians.

As she immersed herself in understanding of her new legend, Ashurina found the people of the Republic to be incredibly interesting—yet also insanely wild. They lived life like every day was their last. Sure, they had plans for the future, but they didn't live in fear of the Zodarks like the humans on Sumer had. On Sumer, the wrong word or thought spoken aloud against the government in power or the Zodarks could land one in an off-world mining camp or worse.

To her, it appeared these humans of the Republic lived in unfettered freedom. The society she came from was so controlled—every choice was curated from the moment of birth. And yet, despite the threat the Zodarks and the many other races within the Dominion Alliance presented, the Earthers were more or less allowed to live their lives as they chose. Her first inclination was that the humans just didn't understand who and what the Zodarks were or how vulnerable they were to the whims of more powerful nations than them. Then something changed.

When Ashurina moved to the John Glenn Orbital Station, the target location for her mission, she started to meet the groups of humans she'd heard so much about—the ones who lived and traveled amongst the stars. But it wasn't until the large groups of warships and troopships began to return home from afar that she came to understand why their Zodark masters considered them such a threat. The tens of thousands of soldiers and spacers passing through the gateway to the Republic had been eye-opening.

These were the warriors returning from the front lines, the ones who had fought her Zodark and Orbot masters and lived to tell about it. She'd found it hard to believe that a group of humans had somehow defeated both races she had thought impossible to overcome. This was hard to accept given she had known little about the Republic and its capabilities until their ships had appeared in orbit and liberated Sumer. But the more she spoke with these soldiers and fleeters, the more she realized the little information the Zodarks had told her was patently false. These humans might appear vapid and lighthearted, but beneath that exterior lay a warrior ethos she suspected the Zodarks had greatly underestimated.

Ashurina put aside this newfound information. The Mukhabarat had assigned her to the John Glenn for a reason. If she wanted to see her husband and kids again, she'd find a way to accomplish the mission she'd been hand-selected for. Her assignment was to infiltrate a company called John Bentley Reactors. JBR was the company that managed the Arkonorian reactors being used to power the giant Republic Naval Shipyard and the John Glenn station. For weeks, Ashurina had done her best to blend into the background of the bars and restaurants on the station, applying the tradecraft she'd been taught throughout years of training.

When a shift of workers changed over, she saw a pattern emerge. Groups of employees would spend an hour or two at some of the bars or restaurants on the station. When she'd spot a JBR employee or two come in after work to grab a drink or a bite to eat at the bar or a nearby table in one of the establishments, she'd take note of which ones and how many would frequent each of them. In time, she knew which bars were most likely to attract the kind of employee she was angling to find.

Knowing the bar and the time to find the most JBR employees, Ashurina would arrive shortly beforehand and stealthily get herself and the tiny parabolic microphone set up and ready to listen in on their conversations. She knew exactly what to wear and how to behave to make herself appear almost invisible as she observed. Nearly all of what she heard was useless chitchat. Then she'd hear about a money issue, problems at the plants, supply chain issues, or, more importantly, a retirement or resignation of an employee that would likely result in a job opening.

When she'd learned about the pending retirement of Irene, a reactor engineer, Ashurina had gone to work identifying the right employee she could use to get her foot in the door. Having surveilled many of the JBR employees already, she'd had a good idea of who to target. She'd heard that the Republic Intelligence had a term for this, a useful idiot or UI. The Mukhabarat called them playful idiots or PIs—individuals you could ensnare through vapid temptations. This was where Burt Schumacher came into play. He was someone who'd been through two divorces and was working on his third, a nice guy who liked to drink too much and chase pretty skirts in his off time. As a PI, he was perfect.

Having surveilled him for a little while, she had his schedule down pat. He was, if nothing else, predictable. Ashurina developed her plan and received approval to move forward with it, putting things into motion. If all went according to plan, she would gain access to the target location of her primary assignment.

Knowing Burt's pattern, she waited for Thursday to approach—his usual night on the town. Reviewing the notes she'd taken while assessing the man, Ashurina recalled the kind of makeup and specific tight, body-hugging outfit that always drew his attention. If this oaf was anything, it was boorish. Having choreographed every step of the evening, Ashurina made sure that when he walked into the bar that night, she would be the first thing her PI saw. She'd even managed to keep the seat next to her free, just for him.

Like clockwork, Burt showed up at his usual time with his usual friends. A couple of steps into the place, he saw her. From the moment she locked eyes with him, she knew she'd gotten his attention. He waved his friends on as his eyes stayed focused on her. In typical fashion, he made the pass he always made—but instead of her blowing him off like women usually did, Ashurina invited him to sit and talk. His eyes lit up like he'd just won the lottery as her silky words washed over him. As she introduced herself, it became clear she was the one who'd struck gold. The lusty way he looked at her meant she'd have him eating out of her hand in no time. Yes, Burt would be her PI, and she'd extract everything she could out of him.

For several hours, she let him talk about himself, his job and how important he was. The longer they talked, the more he drank. As the compliments and alcohol flowed, her tentacles continued to find hard-to-get information about JBR and his role there. She mentioned in passing that she had seen a position there and had applied, sharing her own expertise working for the Iraq Ministry of Electricity and her knowledge of the difference between the reactors used in the Republic and the ones they'd recently begun integrating since their discovery of New Eden. The more Burt learned about her, the more intoxicating she became—she was foreign, exotic in his eyes, having originated from the Middle East. Leveraging a lifetime of knowledge gained from infiltrating hard-to-get places, Ashurina worked Burt for all his worth, eventually suggesting they ditch this place for a more private conversation. Whether it was the liquor or thinking with the wrong head, she gave him the thrill of a lifetime before he passed out.

With the brute finally out, Ashurina went to work. Searching the apartment, she found what she was after: the JBR-issued tablet she'd seen Burt use during her surveillance of him. Sitting at the desk with it, she pulled the snoopy from her clutch and placed it on the table before turning both devices on. Once she'd activated the small black device, which was similar in appearance to the jack for a wireless mouse, it synced with her NIP, the Zodark-issued neurolink she'd had implanted, giving her functional control of the snoopy's tools and the login screen to Burt's device.

Ashurina glanced to make sure the oaf was still passed out before she closed her eyes and worked the tools necessary to gain access to the JBR tablet. When the snoopy broke through the encryption, she activated Fireburn and Deepreach, letting them run the preprogrammed infiltration files she'd created months ago in preparation for this very moment.

Fireburn was the keylogger malware that would track everything Burt did on the device. As he typed his login credentials, she'd capture them for future use. But Deepreach...now that was her masterpiece. Aside from establishing a remote access program or RAP, it would allow her to access not only Burt's device but soon just about any device her malware had interacted with.

With her eyes still closed, Ashurina navigated through Burt's emails, looking for items to flag for later review. She noticed that the download status for Deepreach already read eighty-seven percent. It moved rapidly, entrenching itself in the device's firmware, not just its software. It was also transferring a copy of the device for her to remove later. Given the quantity of data being scraped, she was proud of how fast it moved. Ashurina thought about the time and a clock appeared in her mind, telling her that the snoopy had been running for a little more than four minutes.

Ashurina verified what she'd collected already—she had access to all of Burt's personal and professional email accounts, his login KPIs and credentials for JBR, and the four other projects Burt had worked on in the past. Then a message popped up, letting her know Deepreach was fully installed. She hit the execute button, knowing her work was done. She'd be able to access his accounts whenever she wanted while the keylogger would continually update her remote version of his tablet and JBR profile on her own system whenever she wanted, and nobody would be the wiser.

As Burt continued to go about his daily business, corresponding via email, the malware she'd inserted in his digital profile would attach itself to every email he replied to or sent. With her hooks in the email server, it wouldn't take her long to co-opt her way into many other accounts as she deepened her access within JBR and, soon, the clients they worked for.

Before signing off, she opened Burt's email and composed a message to the head of HR with her résumé attached. She titled it *Possible Replacement for Irene, Recommend Interview.* Pausing before she hit send, Ashurina made a mental note—*Don't forget to thank him in the morning.*

Once her task had been completed, she disconnected the snoopy and placed his tablet back where she'd found it. Then, like nothing had happened, she slipped into bed naked and went to sleep, the first steps in her infiltration of JBR now complete.

The following morning, Ashurina made sure to show Burt her heartfelt thanks for giving her a shot at the job opening. He groggily stumbled through his reply, not remembering the email but obviously seeing he'd sent it shortly after they'd arrived. He just smiled stupidly and enjoyed the morning exuberance before breakfast.

A few days later, Ashurina received that interview and was hired on the spot. During her discussion with the senior engineers, she demonstrated new ways to make the reactors run more efficiently and produce more power than they had even thought possible. She explained how she'd studied every report she could get her hands on about the reactors used on Sumer and the Zodark warships. To say the engineers were impressed would have been an understatement. They offered her fifty percent more than they had paid Irene and said she'd be fast-tracked for management, pending her obtaining a Republic security clearance and completing a one-year probational review.
****

John Glenn Orbital Station
Earth Orbit, Sol System

"Good job today, Ashurina. I'm really glad to have you on the team," Burt Schumacher complimented as he approached her workstation.

A chime sounded over the PA, letting everyone know their shift had ended.

"Well, thank you, Burt, for helping me get hired. I'd been wanting to find an off-world job that allowed me to still put my expertise to good use," she responded with a mischievous smile.

"Hey, finding a reactor engineer with practical skills and an understanding of these new Arkonorian reactors felt almost too good to be true. I'm just glad we were able to snag you before some other company did," he said with a wink.

"Hey, are you two heading over to the X Bar?" a coworker asked as he walked past the two. "It's Irene's going-away party. She's finally heading off to Alpha Centauri in a couple of days."

Burt smiled that million-dollar smile. "You want to go? Join us in saying goodbye to the gal you're replacing?"

Ashurina hesitated, not sure if she should; she really didn't know Irene. Then her training kicked in. The party presented an opportunity for her to learn more about her coworkers and begin the process of ingratiating herself with others besides just Burt.

Seeing her hesitation, Burt offered, "It'll be all right. I'll buy you a drink and we'll introduce you to more people. It's good for you to learn who else works for the company outside of our plant. We just won a huge contract to take over the power generation plants in the Republic's new shipyard. That place is enormous."

She smiled coyly, then relented, nodding that she'd go.
****

The X Bar

Irene's eyes lit up when she saw her friend Burt arrive with the rock star replacement they'd found to fill her position. Walking up to them, Irene said, "Burt, I'm so glad you could come, and thank you, Ashurina, for coming as well. I'd love a chance to become better friends during your training before I head off to my next adventure."

"I couldn't miss your going-away party, Irene," Burt said with his usual charming smile. "I'm excited for you—finally heading on your next adventure, leaving Sol and heading off to Alpha Centauri."

"I know. Me, leaving Sol—can you believe it? Burt, would you be a dear and get me and Ashurina a couple of orbital martinis? I want to show our friend here my favorite drink," Irene asked, winking at Ashurina.

"Anything for you two ladies."

As Burt trotted off to the bar, Ashurina was curious to know why Irene had asked Burt to give her a few minutes alone with her.

"Ashurina, I'm so glad they found you. I've worked hard over the years to learn what I can about these Sumerian-Zodark reactors. It hasn't been easy to learn how to use a technology so different from our own, but you—wow, I feel like I should be learning from you. If you aren't careful, you'll find yourself being loaned out to all kinds of universities to give lectures and consult on all the JBR contracts. The company likes to tout itself as the world's leader in these new Arkonorian reactors by having their best engineers speak at various events or collaborate on some high-profile projects," Irene explained, seeming a bit jealous about the potential opportunities that awaited Ashurina.

"Eh, wow, that sounds amazing," Ashurina replied before falling back into her cover. "Maybe I should try not to stick out until I'm more comfortable working outside of Earth. My transition here…well…it's been an adjustment. I've always wanted to leave Earth and explore the stars. I just need to get used to this whole concept of living on a station in space before I think about being on a ship for days or even months," she replied nervously.

Irene smiled warmly at her as she clasped both of her hands in her own.

"I felt the same way when I first left Earth. There is always this segment of our population that longs for adventure. The explorers of our society, the risk takers, the ones who jump at a chance to spend months, even years, cooped up on a starship to travel to some unknown planet. But not everyone is like that. Before we discovered New Eden, I looked at space as risky. The thought of being trapped on a starship for years was more than I could handle."

"My parents were like that. So was my ex-husband. What changed for you? What made it easier for you to push aside those fears and just go for it?"

"The discovery of New Eden," she replied.

Ashurina lifted an eyebrow at the response. "How did that change things for you?"

"Are you kidding me? This was the first time we had discovered a real, honest-to-goodness planet that could sustain life. We now had proof they really did exist; we just had to leave our own system and begin to explore the stars. That's when I knew I had to overcome my fear of living in space to be part of this next chapter in human history."

"Wow, that's really inspiring, Irene. Thank you for sharing. It's encouraging to hear I'm not the only one who has struggled with these types of feelings. You see all these stories about millions of people clamoring to be settlers on the new moons and planets of the Republic—

it almost makes you feel like there's something wrong with you for not wanting to be a part of that."

Irene nodded. "Change can be hard for people to accept. It was for me. Now that I have embraced it, I can't believe I used to let it hold me back. Now, I'm not afraid of that change. I'm not even scared of these Zodarks or those creepy cyborg things—Orbots."

"How can you not be afraid? They seem terrifying, if you ask me."

Ashurina had spent months trying to grapple with this question. Most people she talked with had a healthy fear of them, like a normal person would have of a snake or wild animal that could kill you. Something about these Earthers was different. Fear of the unknown didn't deter them. In fact, she felt it almost drove them.

"At first, I was afraid," Irene admitted. "The Zodarks are hideous beasts. But like all fears, like all demons that secretly haunt us, if you face them head-on, you can defeat them. It kind of reminds me of a saying my dad used to tell me when I was little. He said, it's not the size of the dog in the fight, it's the size of the fight in the dog that matters. I made the fight inside the dog more fierce than the size of my fear."

Burt showed up with two orange-red fruity drinks, causing the conversation to turn to more casual chit chat.

Ashurina pledged to stay in touch with Irene, saying she was eager to hear about life on Alpha colony. Conversing with her colleagues during the party, Ashurina found that Irene's perception of the Zodarks wasn't a minority viewpoint. She needed to write up a more detailed, nuanced assessment on the Earthers' view of the Zodarks and Orbots. Based on the briefing she'd received prior to leaving Sumer, her superiors in the higher echelons of the Mukhabarat and the Groff had seriously miscalculated in their assessment of the Republic. She was starting to better understand how these Earthers had managed to defeat an adversary she thought it impossible to win against.

As she sipped on her orbital martini, a slight smile almost slipped past Ashurina's facade…she was in. Now her true mission started.

Chapter 3
The Gray Man

2108 AD
Jacksonville, Arkansas
Earth, Sol System

Dakkuri glanced up, noticing the change in the dreary sky above. With little more than an hour until sunset, a rainy drizzle had started. He hoped it didn't turn into a full-on rainstorm that would obscure his view of the alleyway. He thought about the time, and his implant displayed it. He had two minutes—then he had to leave.

Dakkuri brushed the reminder aside; he'd give his man no more than five extra minutes. If the information wasn't so valuable, he'd never risk staying beyond the agreed-upon time. As it was, his agent had lost two sources acquiring it, and he'd lost one person already himself— Enki, the first of their team to have arrived. But it was a critical piece of intel for the next step in the plan.

Then a noise snapped him out of his thoughts. It reminded him of a metal door creaking on its hinges. He tensed up, his body ready to react. The sound came from his left, down the alleyway. Risking a look, he inched his head around the corner and breathed a sigh of relief when he saw a man in an apron tossing a trash bag into a nearby dumpster. The man likely worked for the nearby upscale restaurant, Beijing Delight. Just as Dakkuri was about to look away, the employee pulled a vape pen out.

Dakkuri cursed under his breath. *Of all the times to take a break...*

After about a minute, the light drizzle turned to a steadily increasing beat of rain. The man pocketed his vaping device and turned to head inside. Then Dakkuri saw a shadow advancing down the alleyway, heading toward the trash cans next to the restaurant.

Dakkuri observed the figure cautiously as he walked slowly past a large dumpster. The man's left hand briefly ran across the side of it as he kept walking.

As Dakkuri depressed a tab on the side of his glasses, he felt his heart sink. The hidden mark, only visible when seen through a special layer of light, was a signal. His operative was warning him—he'd been made, and he likely had a tail.

Damnit, this can't be—not after Enki, he thought, a sense of dread washing over him. *Bitner just arrived two months ago.*

Staying in the growing shadows as the rain hastened the darkness of the evening, Dakkuri watched as his agent made his way toward the other end of the alleyway—walking past their meeting location.

Dakkuri turned his head slightly. A new sound had caught his ear, and it was approaching quickly. Voices sang a foreign tune loudly as they staggered, bumping into trash cans in the alley. Pegging them as harmless drunks, Dakkuri turned and saw Bitner. He'd reached the edge of the alleyway.

A hover van suddenly swerved out of traffic and swooped in, blocking the alley. In a swirl of motion and speed, two individuals jumped out of the van's side doors and reached for Bitner. One attacker lunged for him, a small cylindrical device in hand, as his companion raised a stun gun.

No, not another one, Dakkuri thought angrily as he saw Bitner transform from an elusive gray man into a gladiator fighting for his very survival.

The Mukhabarat spy reflexively stepped back as he flicked his wrists, activating the nanotubular batons in his bracelets. In an instant, the batons sprang from the bracelets, giving Bitner semiflexible twelve-inch weapons to fight his attackers.

With precision honed through years of training, the baton in Bitner's right hand swung through the air before crashing into the face of the man closest to him. When the baton connected with the man's flesh, an unseen puff of a paralytic toxin enveloped the attacker. The man staggered before the toxin caused his body to collapse.

As the first attacker went down, the man with the stun gun fired as he reacted to Bitner's sudden counterattack. Having anticipated the likely shot from the stun gun, Bitner spun to the left just as the electrical darts sailed through where he'd been only fractions of a second earlier. Pivoting on his left foot, the spy turned gladiator sprang forward as he closed the distance on the man still holding the stun gun. The baton in his left hand crashed into the side of the man's head with a sickening *thwack*, releasing another dose of the paralytic toxin. The man staggered backwards from the hit before the toxin's effects dropped him.

As Bitner fought his attackers, a blur of motion swooshed past the shadows Dakkuri had taken refuge in. The men he'd assumed were drunkards moments earlier had sprung into action, racing down the alley toward Bitner. The lead man, wearing a black sports jersey of some sort, collided first, hitting Bitner in the back with his shoulder and throwing him off-balance as the second man, in a red jersey, managed to hook his elbow around Bitner's neck before he twisted his body in such a way that they both ended up on the ground.

Once on the pavement, it became a grappling match. The red jersey attacker managed to get his legs hooked around Bitner's and establish a rear naked chokehold. During Bitner's fall, he'd lost his grip on the batons and they'd clattered just out of his reach, leaving him weaponless as he tried to break free of the chokehold before his brain blacked out.

Screw it! I'm not losing Bitner too.

Pulling his ball cap low to obscure his face, Dakkuri stepped out of the shadows, moving swiftly to end this fight and retrieve the information from his agent.

Racing down the alleyway toward the grappling match on the ground, Dakkuri reached into his jacket. His grip tightened on the pistol as he withdrew it.

"Damn it! Grab the autoinjector! I'm losing my grip on this guy," Dakkuri could barely hear the red jersey man yell as he ran forward.

The guy in the black jersey reached for the autoinjector.

"Got it," the man declared.

Dakkuri watched in horror as Bitner thrashed about wildly before he suddenly went limp, losing consciousness from the chokehold.

"Hit him with the injector—we don't want this guy waking up in the van," the red jersey man ordered as he loosened his grip on Bitner's neck.

Just as the man with the autoinjector approached Bitner, Dakkuri figured he'd gotten close enough and raised his pistol. "Drop it!" he ordered.

Suddenly, the van's driver popped out from behind the vehicle. His eyes met with Dakkuri's, and Dakkuri pointed his pistol at him. Before the man could intervene on behalf of his comrades, Dakkuri fired his weapon, sending a pair of blaster bolts into the man's chest. Pivoting back toward Bitner, he fired several shots at the man holding the autoinjector, hitting him multiple times before he could react.

Zip, zip.

The man in the red jersey fired a couple of shots as Dakkuri dove to the right, putting a large dumpster between him and the final attacker.

A couple more shots hit the dumpster and the wall above and behind his head as the assailant continued to react to Dakkuri's sudden appearance. Somewhere in the background, the sound of police sirens approached, an indication that any number of the bystanders on the nearby street had seen the fight taking place and called the police.

Acting quickly, Dakkuri used the cover to his advantage as he peered around the dumpster. The shooter had been aiming toward the top of the dumpster when he was hit by Dakkuri, who'd appeared from the side, not the top, to return fire.

Seeing the man fall, Dakkuri held still for just a moment to assess the situation. The sound of emergency sirens grew louder, a reminder that he didn't have time to waste.

Dakkuri raced to Bitner, reached down and slapped his colleague hard across the face.

Bitner's eyes popped open, his body tensing up to resume the fight before he recognized the face of Dakkuri.

"Huh? What happened?"

"You got choked out. We don't have time to talk. We need to get out of here before the police arrive." Dakkuri tucked his pistol back in his jacket and helped Bitner to his feet.

Looking around at the bodies around him as they ran down the alley, Bitner commented, "You shouldn't have done that. They'll know there are two of us here now."

"You're right. But I couldn't let them capture you before obtaining your information. Come on. We need to go."

Before they stepped out of the alleyway, the two men adjusted the fiberoptic mesh on the shirts and pants they had been wearing—their outfits now appeared to be a completely different color and design. Dakkuri pulled a couple of new hats out of a small satchel he'd been carrying and they put them on. When they left the alley, their appearance had radically changed from the images any CCTV cameras would have caught of the fight.

With the cover of the rain and the growing darkness, they moved between the shadows of the alleyways between city blocks and the nightly crowds of pedestrians on the sidewalks in front of the skyscrapers. When they passed a mirrored window, they scanned for possible tails. They maintained a zigzagging pattern of turns and counterturns to put distance between themselves and the fight while also running their countersurveillance protocols. Throughout it all, Dakkuri and Bitner maintained overwatch distance of each other, never coming closer than twenty feet apart. As the rain continued to fall, Dakkuri thanked Lindow for providing them with precipitation to aid in their escape. With the materials woven into the clothes they were wearing, added to the rain, it would be nearly impossible for surveillance cameras to follow them.

Forty minutes into their escape and evasion on the surface, they changed course and descended the escalator to the subway station connecting them with the Red Line.

Joining a throng of evening commuters heading home from work, they got into the same car, using different entrances. Both continued to watch and observe, making sure that, despite all the ducking and dodging, neither had somehow picked up a tail they hadn't previously seen. When they didn't see any, Dakkuri determined it was time to get to the safe house.

When they reached the fourth stop on the Red Line, they changed over to the Green Line. Four stops and twenty minutes later, Dakkuri signaled to get off. If someone had been following them, they would have spotted it by now.

The two men exited the subway station and crossed the street. Dakkuri led them to a four-story parking garage, where they walked toward a gray utility van, an inscription saying *Ready Electricians* on the side of it with contact information to make an appointment.

Dakkuri hit the unlock button, and the two of them climbed in, breathing a momentary sigh of relief. Dakkuri turned the van on and drove them out of the parking garage. They turned onto a crowded road, heading away from the downtown capital of the Republic into the sprawling suburbs.

For more than two hours, neither spoke a word. Finally, Bitner asked, "What do we do now?"

"I don't know yet. I need time to think."

Dakkuri ran through the events in his head again. He was certain their surveillance detection route would have spotted a tail if they'd had one. Then again, they'd just killed multiple agents, or whoever those men had been—he doubted the Earthers wouldn't try to lock down the city on them. They'd likely attempt to kill them if they couldn't capture them.

"Those batons really work," Bitner commented.

"I wish we could have kept them a secret longer. You did good, though, you fought them off."

"I still can't believe the toxin didn't take me out."

"You had the counteragent. It wouldn't affect you, you know that," Dakkuri reminded him before adding, "Right now, I need to think. Just give me a minute to formulate my thoughts."

Keeping his eyes on the road, Dakkuri tried to unravel what the hell had gone wrong.

"Bitner, when did you know you were being followed?"

A pause ensued as Dakkuri observed his operative look out the window, likely trying to figure that out.

"It was right before I was supposed to meet you."

"Go on. What tipped you off? This is important, so try to remember every little detail."

"Ah, I saw one of those self-driving taxis pull up and let those guys in the jerseys out. They stumbled along, acting drunk. At first, I didn't think much of it, but then when I made my first turn, they followed me.

"At this point, I suspected something odd was happening. I knew I needed to get a look at the guys on the sidewalk. When I crossed the street, they followed again. For the rest of the block, I kept tabs on them by using the store windows to look behind me. By the way, these glasses we're using—wow, they really work great."

Mukhabarat field operatives made heavy use of a specially designed set of eyeglasses that enabled the lens to separate, or in some cases, add in, different spectral layers of light or sound frequencies all around the wearer. In an instant, specific types of energy waves would be layered in to give an operative in the field a tactical advantage, either identifying surveillance equipment being used to track or identify them or assisting them in penetrating the security of a facility they needed to gain access to. In this case, the lenses were allowing them to use the glass windows of storefronts as mirrors to monitor what was happening behind them.

Dakkuri interrupted, "Enough about the glasses; we can talk about them at the safe house. Keep telling me what happened next."

"Sorry, you're right. When I turned down the alleyway leading to our meet, I saw—via the mirror—that the same individuals continued to follow me—and I knew for certain I'd somehow been discovered."

"OK, that's good. That makes sense. But if you knew you'd been made, why'd you still head to the meet location?" Dakkuri inquired, trying not to let his frustration show.

Bitner hung his head low as he shook it from side to side. "I guess you're right. Looking back on it, I probably should have gone into my escape and evasion protocol. With the meet location just a block away, I knew we couldn't meet. Still, I also knew I had to somehow warn you that they'd managed to figure out who I was. My thinking was you might be able to warn the others to be more vigilant." Pausing for a second, Bitner continued, "I may have been discovered, but you shouldn't have risked yourself like that, Dakkuri. You're too important and you just exposed yourself to Republic Intelligence."

Dakkuri didn't respond right away; he was deep in thought. He knew Bitner was right, but at the end of the day, he didn't want to lose another operative like he had Enki. When their vehicle stopped at a traffic light, he turned to face Bitner. "You're right. If I'd stuck to the SOP, I would have walked away as soon as I saw your sign. But here's the deal. Every member, every operative, is critically important. This isn't like Sumer, or our own home worlds—we can't easily get replacements if one of you gets captured."

"I understand—that makes sense. Just so you know, if I had gotten captured, I would have self-terminated before giving them anything."

"I have no doubt you would have, just as Enki did. But based on the information you told me your source had sold you, the risk of even my own exposure was worth it. So, let's talk about what your source found. Was my assumption right?"

"Yeah, it was. I don't know how you figured that out, but according to what my source delivered, the Earthers are still preparing for war—a fleet of even more powerful warships is being built."

Dakkuri smiled at the confirmation. He had a few sources of his own, so he wasn't entirely dependent on his team for everything. "This is good—it means we're establishing more than one source providing the same kind of information. Now, tell me, were you able to get your hands on the plans—the schematics? Was your source able to come through for you in the end?"

Bitner nodded. "He wasn't at first. I pressed him for it and even doubled our agreed-upon rate. But looking back on it, I think the fact that I was attacked today could probably be linked back to my source's discovery shortly after I paid him his credits."

"Oh, really? That's interesting. How do you figure?"

"A week after I paid him, he asked if we could meet again. There was something he needed to tell me, but only in person. I knew we had our scheduled meet soon, so I arranged for us to meet last night. I figured if he had something big, then I could include it in our handoff today. Thinking back to last night and what just happened, I think this is when I likely got made," Bitner explained glumly.

"OK, well, let's put aside what happened and focus on why he wanted to meet and what led you to believe you were found out after meeting with your source."

"My source told me his company was participating in the design and engineering team responsible for building a new class of Republic battleships. Apparently, this new iteration of warships now included some kind of armor improvements—I don't know what exactly that means, but he said something about how the new armor would be similar to the armor used on the RNS *Freedom*. Supposedly, it would give their warships the same kind of toughness in battle the *Freedom* had."

Dakkuri tried to hide his excitement at this new information. Any information about the RNS *Freedom*, that Titan-class behemoth of a warship the Gallentines had given Viceroy Hunt to use as the alliance flagship, was a priority collection requirement.

"He also told me that his engineering section had been assigned to work on integrating this new armor. But due to the risk of discovery, my source wanted more credits. I don't know anything about metallurgy or armor, but I do remember that anything to do with the *Freedom* was part of our primary PCRs, so I offered double for the information, and he readily agreed. But as I left the bar, that's when I think I first spotted a tail," Bitner explained.

Scrunching his eyebrows, Dakkuri pressed, "You were right to chase after the PCR—if it turns out your source isn't compromised, then I'll need to assign someone else to work him. But let's focus back on what you said about being spotted. Remember, whatever you can tell me about what happened will hopefully help the others avoid getting caught."

"Yes, of course. If I had to guess, I'd say my source got discovered after I paid him. Maybe he did something stupid and made a large purchase that raised some red flags—I don't know, but chances are that when we met last night, they placed me under surveillance, not knowing who I was just yet. But as I ran through my countersurveillance protocol on the way to our meet, I probably unwittingly confirmed to them that I wasn't who my legend said I was. That's probably when they opted to try and bring me in for questioning."

Dakkuri listened intently, trying to figure out what to do next. Bitner's legend was burned. No way around that. That also meant he was essentially useless for operations within the Republic until they could arrange to have his facial biometrics changed. Depending on how well that worked, Dakkuri might just have to send him back to Sumer for reassignment.

As they drove another hour to the safe house, Bitner shared the files and information of the sources he'd recruited up to this point. With his cover blown, it was important the next handler had everything he needed to keep running them as sources. It took time, patience, and money for a handler to get a source network producing a steady flow of valuable intelligence. Losing Bitner as a handler was going to hurt. Dakkuri hadn't deployed to Republic space with all his handlers and operation specialists at once. NOS Heltet had told him it was necessary for him to infiltrate a small team first to get things going and establish a base of operation. Once that had been achieved, he'd start to receive the rest of his operatives as they arrived on Sumer. Heltet had told him it wasn't impossible to infiltrate operatives from Zodark-controlled space to Sumer, but the process was slow and delicate.

When they reached the safe house, Dakkuri validated the information Bitner had collected. Then they compiled a detailed report, with the source material attached, that would get sent back to Sumer and handed off to the Zodarks.

Now that Republic Intelligence was aware of their presence on Earth, it was time to give them a shiny object to take the heat off Dakkuri and Bitner.
****

Republic Capital
Jacksonville, Arkansas

Earth, Sol System

Sitting on his speeder under the fifth-story apartment balcony, Zudolly hovered above the scene of the attack as his suite of electronic tools continued their collection of the marshals' activity below. His cloaking device made it nearly impossible for the untrained eye to spot him. On two occasions, the rain had nearly blown his cover. Thankfully, he'd been able to slide in under the balcony of a nearby apartment building, close enough for him to see what was happening below.

Hours into observing how the Republic's counterintelligence service was handling what had transpired had done nothing to improve his opinion of their ability to detect or counter foreign espionage activities.

And this is the society from which the Emperor chose his new Viceroy, Zudolly thought. The Gallentines' decision to remove Admiral Grigdolly as the Viceroy had stunned his agency, the Kraxmer, when it had been announced.

As he sat on his speeder, watching the investigators below, Zudolly was thankful his electronic detection equipment and surveillance cameras captured the entire event as it unfolded. It gave him a chance to add some commentary around what the video showed. It would also validate the Kraxmer's assessment of the Earthers' unpreparedness and lack of skills necessary to govern and lead the alliance. In his mind, if a picture was worth a thousand words, as the English saying went, then a video with supporting commentary was priceless.

Zudolly was fortunate to have recorded the lead-up to the Republic's planned abduction of the Mukhabarat spy and the subsequent fight between the two groups. It was only a matter of time until these spies began to appear in Altairian territory. Knowing how they fought and the personal weapons they used would aid in taking them down.

While Zudolly was frustrated with the apparent incompetence of the marshals, the spies' escape was honestly a blessing in disguise. They'd led him right to their safe house. Now that he'd discovered the place and had it under surveillance, he would soon be able to identify who else was part of this spy ring. Like a dangling thread, once you pulled it, the whole thing would eventually unravel.

As he observed this new Interstellar Marshals Service grow, what surprised Zudolly most beyond their lack of preparedness to take on their new counterespionage role was that they had access to what he'd come to learn was a specialty organization within their Special Forces and intelligence service but that they couldn't use them for operations on Earth. He'd been told the citizens within the Republic valued things like personal freedoms and the right to privacy. Try as he might, he couldn't understand why any government would give its subjects such autonomy. They had the ability to handle this Mukhabarat situation better than the marshals, but some law prevented them from doing so.

Thankfully, Zudolly wasn't subject to such nonsense. When he'd seen the Sumerians flee the area, he'd followed them. Per his own agency's protocols, he'd deployed a pair of surveillance drones to assist him in tracking them. The men had some new technology that gave them the ability to change the color and style of their clothing right before his eyes—he'd never seen such a thing before, and it would make tracking these guys harder.

Twenty minutes into their escape from the ambush, Zudolly had almost lost them. However, one of his drones had been able to tag them with a tracking device. Moments later, they ducked into the subway station.

Not being able to follow them into the subway without revealing his presence, Zudolly had to trust the tracking tag to do its job. The tracker showed the two of them had boarded a train and used it to put some distance between themselves and the operatives who had tried to capture them. As they moved about the underground system, Zudolly used his speeder to stay somewhat close to where they might eventually exit once they got off the train.

For two hours, he followed their movements, observing their countersurveillance patterns and tactics both above ground and on the subway system, how they carried out checks for tails and changed subway lines and directions. He documented and recorded everything.

These Mukhabarat are far more lethal and capable than the marshals, he thought.

Eventually, they did leave the subway and headed for a nearby parking garage. When Zudolly saw them climb into a van, he tagged the vehicle with a couple of surveillance drones, having them attach themselves to the top of it. Once they reached their destination, he'd direct the drones to infiltrate the safe house and begin his own penetration of their organization.

The Kraxmer used microdrones the size of a grain of rice—a little smaller than similar ones the humans used, plus they were immune to electronic detection. Once in place, they were sheathed in a translucent material that could mimic its surroundings, effectively cloaking them and rendering them invisible to the naked eye. With the tracking drones nearly impossible to detect, the Kraxmer could place them wherever they wanted. Their only drawback was their travel speed. Given their size, they could only move so fast, hence his reasoning for attaching them to the van.

For three hours, the van drove a couple of different routes, making more than a few cutbacks to check for tails. Eventually it came to a halt in a nearby suburb of Jacksonville, near the back of a small storefront that read *Ready Electricians*. As the men walked into the store, they intentionally hid their faces, making it all but impossible to capture a solid image of them. Before the door closed behind them, Zudolly's three microdrones followed them in, relaying everything they saw back to his device. Ten minutes later, he'd identified the best locations to place the drones and had them go into stealth mode, leaving their electronic collection suite on and routing everything they collected to his device.

Half an hour later, he spotted movement near the building. A synthetic humanoid worker exited and climbed into the same van the men had arrived in earlier. The Synth drove off in the vehicle, likely to handle a service call.

Zudolly smiled—he had to give the Mukhabarat credit. They were running a legitimate business as a cover for their espionage activities. It gave them cover to move about the city, handling whatever activities they were up to without drawing undue attention.

Clever, he thought. *Exactly how I'd run this kind of operation.* The Mukhabarat's skill level was far better than they had initially assessed. He shook his head as he thought about it. An unsettling thought kept running through his mind. *These Earthers are operating way out of their league. They aren't ready for this…*

Once his drones were in the safe house and actively collecting information, Zudolly returned to the scene of the crime in his speeder. He covered the distance in no time, speeding along as he zipped between buildings and down crossroads. With his cloaking device still active, he was able to stealthily move about the city, no one the wiser that he was there.

Back at the scene of the attack, the humans had the place roped off. A few individuals were taking some pictures. A synthetic humanoid looked to be analyzing how the attack had gone down. Zudolly stayed under a balcony while the rain continued to fall. He might still be in active cloaking mode, but that didn't mean he couldn't be spotted. Stealth, cloaking, none of that prevented rain from falling on you and eventually rolling down your sides to drop below. As the water landed on you, it spread itself out around your form. If enough water was able to do this, then your silhouette became easy to spot.

Within an hour, the humans wrapped up their investigation. They'd collected the bodies and taken what they thought was of value. When the investigators left, Zudolly began to compile his detailed report of what had transpired. He checked in with his surveillance drones and added their information to his report.

When he'd finished compiling everything and written his own assessment of the marshals and the Mukhabarat, offering some recommendations for how their agency might spot the Mukhabarat on their worlds and how the marshals could improve their own efforts, he sent the report off to the Altairian embassy in the city. They'd review it and ask him follow-up questions before it would finally be sent to headquarters.

Zudolly turned his speeder around—it was time to head back to Ready Electricians. He'd continue to observe the Sumerians, see what else they might be up to and wait until they led him to the rest of their cells on Earth and throughout the Republic.

Chapter 4
Hands Tied

Galactic Empire Headquarters
Alliance City, New Eden
Rhea System

Major Brian Royce looked up from the report the marshals had provided, shaking his head. "I thought we'd made it clear to the Jacksonville office that they were only supposed to observe and report. They weren't supposed to intervene until our liaison was on scene to assist them," he growled in frustration.

"We did," Lieutenant Hosni replied. "Someone in their chain of command decided they wanted to try and make a name for themselves, uncover and bust up a foreign spy ring in the capital city all on their own."

Royce placed the tablet on the desk. He was pissed off that his orders had been ignored. The marshals' incompetence had likely just cost them their best chance at learning more about this Mukhabarat cell operating in the capital. *The boss isn't going to be happy about this*, he thought. He was going to have to get Bates involved. The Interstellar Marshals Service or IMS was outside military control, so there was only so much influence Royce could exert on them.

"Do you want me to assemble a team and head to Jacksonville? Maybe we can piece together what this operative was up to—find some new leads that might help us reestablish surveillance on the agent or possibly find the person who helped him."

Royce rubbed the bridge of his nose as he thought about that. He knew Hosni was trying to help. *Maybe he's right. Maybe we need some of our own people directly involved in this.* Looking up, he replied, "All right, go ahead and get your team ready. When you get there, report to JSOC headquarters to let them know your team will be operating in the area. I'll get General Bates to provide you with orders and a blanket authorization for support from any local military and civilian agencies you may require."

Hosni looked pleased that his idea had some merit and had been approved. This would be his second time leading a team in the field since Royce had recruited him into Task Force Orange. "Sir, what do you want me to do about the IMS? If they find out we're in the area, they'll likely make a fuss about it."

Grunting at the question, Royce countered, "Let me worry about the IMS. Get your team put together and prepare to leave for Sol. I need to go brief the boss and get you those orders."

****

Major General Alfred Bates took a sip of his coffee as Major Brian Royce finished briefing him on what had happened. He shouldn't have been surprised by the marshals' actions or their outcome. They were a brand-new organization still trying to figure themselves out.

When the war had ended, the Republic had had colonies on multiple planets across several different star systems. It had been obvious that a unified law enforcement agency to assist the central government in managing and maintaining the rule of law throughout the Republic was needed, particularly when the people of Earth were still coming to grips with the reality of dozens of new alien species—some of which were now establishing businesses in the Republic and immigrating to some of the new colonies, to include the Republic home world, Earth. Unsurprisingly, the rapid growth and ever-expanding scope of responsibility of the IMS meant they were woefully underprepared for the challenges being thrown at them.

General Bates looked at his operations chief and sighed. "Unfortunately, you're right, Brian," he responded, dropping the formalities and calling him by his first name. "This is going to be complicated. It's going to require a diplomatic approach if we're to avoid ruffling any feathers or creating new problems for ourselves. Damn those marshals—this could have been avoided if our liaison officer hadn't been cut out of the loop. We need to get them to understand that they need our involvement in these matters, whether or not they like it or want it."

Bates could tell Royce was still fuming at how everything had gone down before his protégé replied, "That's the plan. We're steadily moving forward with getting them trained up to eventually handle these kinds of operations on their own. Learning to walk before you run seems to be a learning objective they like to repeat a few times."

Bates paused for a second, studying Royce. At the end of the war, Bates had been given the job of reorienting Task Force Orange from the direct-action arm of Republic Intelligence to an advisory group to the

44

marshals until they could effectively take over and manage the domestic counterintelligence and spying program on their own. It wasn't ideal, but as a byproduct of the Senate reasserting more control over Sol from Space Command, they no longer wanted the externally facing Republic Intelligence Service to be in charge of domestic operations as well. They were nearly eighteen months into the transition. The jury was still out on whether it was actually going to work or not.

When General Reiker had tasked him with reorienting the group, he hadn't anticipated how difficult it would be to find the right soldiers to fill these specialized roles. Not everyone was cut out for the kind of surveillance and espionage work TF Orange was now tasked with. Even when they did find the right person, they still had to go through a two-month course in surveillance and countersurveillance with the RI, followed by a three-month course in human and identity intelligence—training necessary to know how to spot and assess people and then recruit them to spy for you. Needless to say, it was taking time to get people through the required training to eventually become operational agents or operators in TF Orange.

"Brian, I know your focus has been on building our intelligence apparatus on Sumer, and to a lesser extent here on New Eden. But this report"—he held up his tablet for emphasis—"clearly demonstrates the need to start prioritizing our efforts on Earth. The Emerald City is going to become the new headquarters for the alliance, but Earth is still the capital planet of the Republic.

"Brian, you're a good officer and leader. Your problem is you're allowing the perfectionist side of you to morph you into a control freak. You're not doing a good enough job of delegating important tasks or missions to your subordinates, which means you've become laser-focused in some areas and you're completely dropping the ball in others. You need to learn to trust your officers and senior noncoms and start assigning ownership over many of the tasks you're trying to do yourself. This whole liaison issue with the IMS is a case in point. You've gotten so tunnel-visioned with priorities out here that you've neglected to nurture our relationship with the IMS and get those people spun up and ready to handle this job," Bates explained.

"General—"

"Brian, please call me Al or Alfred unless we're in some sort of military or formal setting. We may still be soldiers, but in this task force, we're all gray men—ghosts, or as close to them as we can be."

Bates didn't want everyone calling each other by their ranks when they didn't have to, and he preferred them all to be on a first-name basis. If they were to blend into the background of society, as their jobs often required, then they couldn't be heard addressing each other by their ranks or surnames when in the field.

Royce blushed slightly at the correction. "You're right, Al. I haven't done a good enough job of letting my captains and lieutenants take charge of many of these tasks. I suppose you're right; I've become a bit of a perfectionist lately and that's kept me from letting others take charge when they should have." He leaned back. "If you approve, I'd like to refocus more of our people back to Sol while we look to get the marshals better prepared. This last operation clearly shows a need to readjust our approach."

"I think that would be a wise choice, Brian. I suppose you've cooked something up for me to consider?"

"I have," Royce acknowledged, and Bates smiled. Not only could this guy take constructive criticism well, he always seemed to have a plan to rectify any challenges that came up.

"If you approve it, I'd like Hosni to reengage the marshals with a fresh team. I'm not sure what happened other than to say I'd like to bring in a new team to try and reestablish some new relationships with the marshals," Royce explained.

"That sounds like a good plan, Brian. I approve. It sounds like you have something else you'd like to ask. What is it?"

"I do. I'd like Hosni to interact with the marshals, and I'd like to have his team perform two functions. First, they'll start aggressively training some marshals and getting these guys better prepared to handle these kinds of missions. Clearly something didn't work with the previous team in place, so I'd like to restart that effort. Second, I'd like to have some of his team disappear off base and look to reestablish our own surveillance operation to find these bastards. When we do find them, we'll loop the IMS in and make sure we have our own people involved in the capture this time. This should prevent another slipup like this last one. I know we're dancing on the edge; I'd like to wager our guys are good enough to do their jobs without the IMS being the wiser. If you approve of our new approach, then I'll need a letter of authorization from you and authority to request any additional help or resources they may need once we're on Earth."

Bates turned his chair toward his monitor and drafted something up, essentially granting Royce what he wanted while providing him the appropriate top cover they'd need to get it done. Hitting send on the file, he heard Royce's tablet buzz, letting him know he'd received it.

"I just sent you the authorization letter you asked for. I also just sent a copy to JSOC, the Defense Attaché Office in the capital and the Director of the Marshals Service. Oh, and before you leave, I'd like you to travel with Hosni back to Earth, at least for a day or two. You'll probably have a bit of a tussle with the marshals. They're likely going to want to stay in control of things, especially after losing several agents. There's also something else I'm assigning you to personally check on."

"Oh? A special mission?" Royce asked, a mischievous smile spreading across his face.

"Yeah, you could call it that. I got a request from Republic Intelligence to see if you, in particular, could help them with something. I don't have the specifics on it. I was just told you'd receive a message with more details about it once you landed back on Earth."

Smiling at the vagueness, Royce replied, "Well, you know I love a good mystery." As he got up to leave, he added, "I'll keep you apprised of what we find and what's going on. Thank you for the opportunity to let me get this situation fixed."

Once Royce had left his office, Bates placed some calls to Earth, giving them a heads-up that one of his teams was on their way. He also spent a few minutes bringing the fleet admiral up to speed on the discovery of the Mukhabarat and what had happened. Admiral Bailey said he'd reach out to Chancellor Luca, letting her know he might need her to intervene on their behalf if the IMS didn't want to work with them. The head of the IMS wasn't particularly fond of their organization's way of doing business, particularly if he had any say over it.

With his call to Admiral Bailey finished, Bates turned his attention back to catching up on the latest FID or foreign internal defense assessments he was finally starting to receive. TF Orange had thirty-eight twelve-man ODA or Operational Detachment Alpha teams scattered across the home worlds and core planets of the alliance. Slowly and steadily, they were gaining a comprehensive picture of their allies' strengths and weaknesses. Now if they could just get a handle on this web of spies the Mukhabarat had managed to set up surprisingly fast, he'd be able to shift their focus toward the Zodarks. Rumor had it they were staging all sorts of ships and soldiers near the border lands. God only knew if they were just beefing up their defenses or preparing for renewed hostilities and an invasion of the Republic's side of the neutral zone.

Chapter 5
A New World

New Berlin
Alpha Centauri

When Yani Yanukovych had been elected Governor, he'd had one major priority—housing. For the better part of fifteen years, there had been a steady flow of immigration from Earth to the new world in the Centaurus system. The planet had been discovered nearly twenty years ago, a year before the Zodarks and New Eden—before humanity had been plunged into an interstellar war it hadn't been prepared for.

Resources needed to grow the planet and make it self-sufficient had been scarce in those early years. The colony had nearly collapsed a couple of times from a lack of food and supplies it couldn't readily recreate on Alpha. That first decade had been tough, but they had gotten through it. The delivery of Altairian food replicators had solved one crisis, and the arrival of a few thousand industrial-grade 3-D printers had solved the next. In those early years, Alpha had had to compete for supplies from Earth with New Eden. Given the latter's military importance and proximity to a stargate, they'd received the lion's share of supplies. Still, the people of Alpha had found a way to make it work and grow Earth's first off-world colony.

With the war finally over, the supply spigot that had been trickling for years was suddenly thrown wide open. Freighter after freighter arrived at Alpha Station, the gateway connected to New Berlin on the surface by a space elevator. The supplies started arriving so fast and in such volume that it began to cause problems. They were running out of room to store all the unloaded materials. Dozens of new warehouses popped up to take in the cargo.

Next came the immigrants. The passenger ships that had been used to transport and shuffle the hundreds of thousands of Republic soldiers across the vast distances of space to where the battles were being fought had now been returned to civilian use. Suddenly, the opportunity to immigrate from Earth to the colonies was no longer restricted to the lottery system or those with great financial means. With the floodgates opened, a rush to leave Earth and participate in humanity's expansion into the stars began in earnest.

Where before, Alpha had been inundated with freight as everything started arriving all at once, the unsustainable waves of immigration now followed. Thousands of people were arriving daily and there was simply nowhere to house them. The influx of supplies and sea of incoming humanity had overwhelmed the last administration, just in time for the next planetary election.

Yani Yanukovych had been among the first groups of settlers from the former Greater European Union. Having been a civil engineer, he'd been selected to join the second of four groups of settlers sent to Alpha. His group was bringing with them the necessary tools and materials to begin construction of humanity's first city beyond its solar system. He'd been involved in nearly every aspect of growing the colony—yet he'd never been in a position of power to influence its growth or really solve the multitude of problems that kept expanding.

When the election had approached, Yani had seen this as his moment. He felt that, with him in charge, the challenges facing the colony could finally be dealt with. When he'd made housing and immigration the center of his campaign, he'd managed to sway just enough voters to give him a shot at solving the problem.

Five months after he was sworn in as the new Governor of Alpha Centauri, reality began to set in. Apparently, winning an election was the easy part. Trying to solve a crisis getting worse by the day had given him a new appreciation for what the previous governor had been dealing with.

Placing his coffee down, Yani reached for his tablet. He began reviewing the latest report on one of the eight major housing development projects they had underway. Everything was looking good until he reached the project in the capitol district. Apparently, one of the hyperloop construction teams had found something that was now bringing the project to a halt. When he clicked on the report to view the details, a red warning popped up.

CLASSIFIED – AUTHORIZED PERSONNEL ONLY

What the hell? I'm the Governor. How do I not have the authorization to see what this is?

Contacting his office's systems administrator, Yani said, "Morning, Troy. Hope all is well on your end. I've got a problem I was hoping you might be able to help me with."

"Morning, Governor," his tech whiz replied. "All's good here. Why don't you tell me about this problem?"

"I tried to click on an engineering report about a hyperloop project and got a warning. Actually, can you remote in? It'll probably be easier to just show you."

"Um, sure. One moment."

A second later, a little icon let Yani know Troy was in.

"Ah, I see the problem."

"Good, so you can you fix it, right?"

"Um, no," Troy replied flatly. "This looks to have been classified by DARPA. That's the Defense Advanced Research Projects Agency. They're outside our government's control. You'd need them to give you a high-level security clearance to access what's in the file."

Yani grunted at the explanation. "Great. DARPA—that's military. In case you forgot, Troy, we're not exactly on good terms with them since they handed control of the planet back over to the civilian government. Is there a reason why DARPA would classify something at a construction site?"

Troy took a moment to think. "If I had to guess, Governor, I'd say they likely found something they thought was worth guarding. But before you get too excited about it, they classified a lot of really stupid stuff they thought was interesting or of value too. I think some of it was to prevent the Zodarks from finding out about whatever it was."

Damn, this might complicate our new housing development. This needs to get resolved ASAP.

"OK, thanks, Troy. Looks like I'm going to have to reach out to the military attaché and see what the deal is."

Twenty minutes after requesting a meeting with the attaché, Yani got one. The man's response wasn't the one he was hoping for. He was leaving to travel to the other colony nearby and would be back in a few weeks. When Yani brought up the security issue, the attaché said it'd have to wait until they could talk in person. He wouldn't discuss the nature of this kind of material over a nonmilitary communications system.

Great, another delay…fine, the project's on hold. We'll focus on the others…

****

Archaeology Dig Site
Alpha Centauri

Dr. Katō Sakura hit the alarm next to her bed with a little too much force.

"Time to rise and shine, sleepyhead," called Jack cheerfully from the kitchen.

She groaned as she pulled herself into a vertical position. Sakura was still getting used to living with someone—she'd spent so much of her life alone, entrenched in her work, that her whirlwind romance with Jack Walker, one of the excavators at her dig site, had really caught her off guard.

When she entered the kitchen, Sakura found Jack's newest attempt to replicate her favorite tea sitting out for her. She took a sip and breathed out slowly. "Not bad," she admitted. "This one is less bitter, more harmonious."

Tea wasn't exactly on the priority list of imports from Earth just yet. There were a lot more pressing supplies that had to make the journey to the new human colony. Jack had been experimenting with local tea options to find something acceptable—and he was getting close.

Jack kissed Sakura on the cheek. "Good morning," he said, wrapping his arms around her.

"Good morning," she replied, allowing herself to relax into his hug. Jack was strong and smart, thoughtful and funny—everything she'd ever hoped for in a partner. Of course, her father wouldn't have approved of his less-than-prestigious upbringing, but Sakura had decided that she didn't care about that anymore. Out here in Alpha Centauri, everyone was making their own path; there was no entrenched social hierarchy based on who you were related to. Sakura preferred it this way.

"So, what's on the docket today, boss?" asked Jack.

"Well, it's just a Tuesday morning in paradise," she replied. "I think we're getting closer to entering the next layer of the underground structure."

He smiled. "Sure are. Several of the guys have placed bets on us hitting a door today."

"So they're gambling over our work now?" she chided, poking Jack in the ribs playfully.

"Can't stop human nature," he said, tickling her.

"Hey, cut that out," she laughed.

Jack looked at the clock. "We have time."

"Well, in that case, I guess I better make time," she replied with a flirtatious wink.

****

Several hours later, the equipment at the dig did indeed hit a door. Jack's friend Li held out a hand. "You owe me twenty bucks."

"Fair enough," Jack replied, reaching over to his tablet to transfer the funds.

Sakura's assistant, Arjun, waved his arms to get their attention. "Hold up!" he called. "I want to examine the markings on the door before we go any further."

"Sure thing," Jack answered.

Arjun and Sakura grabbed their brushes and tablets and went to work. After uncovering more of the doorway, they took lots of photographs with their tablets and ran the pictures through their databases. Although the Humtar language had not been decoded yet, the more images they collected, the closer they could get to creating some sort of key.

Sakura thought she recognized one of the markings. Her gloved hand glided over a groove near eye level. Suddenly, a rim of light outlined the door. It hissed before parting wide.

"Crap!" she squealed, backing up rapidly.

Arjun smiled. "After all this time here, you're still kind of jumpy," he teased.

"I just wasn't expecting that," she explained, pushing a few strands of hair from her face.

They'd known for years there were rooms down here, but this was the first time they'd made it past the exterior. Sakura and her team had been making progress in understanding the Humtars, but she had a feeling they were about to make a giant leap forward.

"Uh, ma'am," said one of the security team, tapping her on the shoulder. "I think you should let us clear the space, just to be safe."

"Oh, very well," Sakura answered impatiently.

Two of the government contractors entered the open space before her, blasters at the low ready. As soon as they walked through the doorway, lights began to illuminate throughout the room.

"Oh my God," Sakura gasped. "This is incredible." She turned to Jack and Li. "Is there any way to tell where that power is coming from?" she asked.

"Well, provided the security team comes back alive, we could use our FLIR devices to visually see if there's any wiring or conduits and follow where it leads," Jack explained. "I'll go grab mine."

It took a moment, but eventually the overpaid government bodyguards returned to the doorway. "It's all clear, Dr. Katō. There were some additional doorways that we couldn't open, but everything in the accessible space appears to be safe."

Sakura entered the well-lit room cautiously and looked around. The air was a bit stale, but it reminded her very much of a modern office space. The walls were a light gray, bedecked throughout with diagrams or charts of some kind. There were individual workstations or desks with oddly shaped chairs that Sakura imagined had been designed to reduce strain on the body. She examined the arms of one of the seats—there were a series of buttons where the right hand would naturally rest, and a series of symbols marked where the left hand would go.

"There's so much of the Humtar language here," Sakura said softly to herself.

Arjun heard her. "It's probably time to bring in Dr. Audrey Lancaster," he suggested. "If anyone can help us decode all this, it's her."

"Excellent suggestion, Arjun," Sakura agreed. After all, Dr. Lancaster and her software had essentially been responsible for decoding the Sumerian language during their initial discovery of New Eden. "Can you see if you can get in touch with her? Last I heard, she was actually on Alpha Centauri, working on another research project. I don't think it would be very hard to entice her to take a break from that."

Arjun chuckled. "I'll see what I can do," he said and left to try and coordinate some assistance from Dr. Lancaster.

Sakura continued her exploration of the new space. In one room was a large metal table with a screen on the surface, possibly some type of computer or image projector. She didn't touch anything yet, busy documenting her discoveries with photographs on her tablet.

Jack walked up next to her. "Do you want to come with me while we see what turned all these lights on?" he asked.

"Yes. Definitely," Sakura replied. "I think it was motion-activated, and I'm really curious."

"All right. Let's fire this thing up."

Jack flipped a switch and the screen turned on. The image that propagated reminded Sakura of early-twenty-first-century artwork she'd seen in museums—a simple network of lines with no particular meaning.

"Can you explain this to me?" she asked.

"Yeah, so they upgraded these devices to be able to detect electrical currents as well as heat signatures. From what I'm seeing here, the power from this overhead light connects to wiring of some type down that wall," he explained, pointing. "Let's follow the yellow brick road."

"Yellow brick road?" Sakura prodded, confused.

"Oh, that's from an old classic American movie. Maybe we can watch it sometime."

"OK, but for now, let's focus on those squiggly lines," joked Sakura.

"All righty, then." Jack walked around the wall and followed the power source into a path along the floor. After tracing it for a while, he stopped at a circular disk inlaid in the flooring. "The power's coming from below, but if we want to see that, we'll probably have to figure out how to open this hatch."

She stopped and looked at the markings beneath her. Suddenly, one stuck out to her. "I think this might be the same symbol that opened the outer door," Sakura announced. She slid her gloved finger over the marking, and just like before, a light illuminated around the rim of the hatch. There was a hissing noise, and then the door opened.

One of the security team members wasn't too far away, and so she obliged them their few minutes to make sure the new space wasn't booby-trapped. When she heard the all clear, she and Jack climbed down the ladder.

The ceilings were a bit taller in this space. The room they were in was most likely some sort of canteen, based on the seating arrangements and the presence of a long bar with plates or bowls on the end and machines lining the counter.

These are probably their replicators, Sakura realized. She suddenly became really curious to know what the Humtars used to eat.

Down the hall to the left was an open area with various machines that weren't all that different from what you might find in a Republic gym. Sakura reasoned that the people who worked here must have spent a lot of time here, and possibly even lived here.

"This way," said Jack, motioning back in the other direction.

They passed a few rooms along the way. Sakura posited that one was most likely a bathroom, given the proximity to the canteen. She'd have to check it out later. Jack was walking quickly, almost racing down the hall.

They stopped at the end, and he announced, "This is it. The power is definitely coming from here. I need you to work your magic on that door."

Sakura searched the markings, but she didn't see what she was looking for. "I think I'm going to have to wait for Dr. Lancaster to arrive," she finally admitted.

Chapter 6
Top Gun

Altairius Prime
RNS *Freedom*
4th Fighter Group – Death Rattlers

A string of laser bolts zipped right past his cockpit as Paladin pulled up hard on the flight controls. His Hellcat had nearly completed a 180-degree pivot as he looked for his prey. *There you are,* he said to himself as the enemy fighter appeared on his HUD. Nudging his positioning thrusters just a bit, Paladin saw his blasters acquire a lock and depressed the firing stud. A dozen shots raced after the fighter before Paladin jinked and banked away from another fighter shooting at him from behind.

Paladin adjusted his angle for an attack on the guy trying to shoot at him. His computer said his previous shots had scored a kill. Craning his neck to see where the guy shooting at him had gone, he lost him but saw the battle had moved closer to home, the *Freedom*. Checking his scanners, Paladin saw he was down half his squadron.

"Paladin, Spike. I'm showing another wave joining the mix. Orders?" came the call from Lieutenant Vivaan "Spike" Khatri, the Blues Squadron commander. The 18th Fighter Squadron or 18th FS Blues was among the best squadrons in the group.

"Spike, Paladin. I seem to have lost my tail. Let's try and finish these guys off and regroup for the next wave."

"Affirmative," came the quick response.

For two hours, Commander Ethan Hunt, call sign Paladin, had the Blues flying a screening mission for the *Freedom* while Commander Tommy Rens, "Old Man," was the acting group leader in charge of the fighters given the job of attacking the giant carrier. His squadron, the 15th FS Yellowjackets, were the first fighters to mix it up with Paladin's single squadron. Thirty minutes into the fight, the 16th FS Greens joined in, leaving the Blues outnumbered two to one. They'd held their own for most of the battle, but once the 17th FS Reds joined the fray, it was over.

For a little more than two hours, the four squadrons fought a valiant battle, testing dogfighting skills and evasive maneuvers against multiple adversaries. They'd learned some hard truths during that final battle in the Sirius system—namely, that they sucked at dogfighting and coordinating large-scale fighter operations. They'd gotten lucky during that battle, but one didn't depend on luck if one planned on living to see retirement.

Patching into the group coms, Paladin announced, "That was some good training today. Once we land, I want those AARs finished before anyone leaves. Squadron commander, have your summaries on today's outcome ready for review by COB Monday. Enjoy the weekend; you all earned it. Paladin out." Hearing a few excited calls, he knew he'd made the right call giving them the weekend off. They needed to blow some steam if he was going to keep pushing them hard the way he had been.

I love these new fighters, he said to himself.

Built into the Gallentine fighters was a training function that allowed them to fire low-yield laser shots at each other. The shots weren't powerful enough to damage each other, but they did allow the ship to register simulated damage that forced the fighter to respond accordingly. In some cases, you'd be marked as killed. In other cases, the pilot might be forced to learn how to fly or fight a damaged fighter. The unique features built into the Gallentine fighters allowed them to train aggressively and use their fighters exactly the way they would in a battle.

Since the war had ended a few years back, Commander Hunt had been relentless in training his pilots. In his mind, the war might be over, but that didn't mean it couldn't restart. They'd learned during the final years of the war that training was their key deficiency. It'd taken them almost two years and a lot of effort, but the *Freedom* could now field most of its fighter and bomber air wings.

Ethan powered down the Hellcat once it had been moved to its parking place, then climbed down before pulling his helmet off. The maintenance crew approached, asking a few questions before thanking him for bringing it back in one piece. It was a running joke between the pilots and the crews. In space, the fighter belonged to them; in the hangar, the crew owned it.

Heading to the office reminded Ethan of the one thing he hated about command—the paperwork. It was a never-ending battle. One would have thought with a PA implant, it would have gotten better, but the implants just made it easy for higher-ups to assign more busywork.

After a few hours of wanting to gouge his eyeballs out and having an internal battle with his PA, Ethan abandoned the office and headed for the Hellcat Bar, the preferred hangout of the ship's pilots and flight crew when not on duty. The Hellcat had become the go-to place to blow off steam, eat, drink, and occasionally settle differences in a less-than-diplomatic manner. Many a tall tale and war story was told by the pilots who virtually lived here when not flying. With a ship that ran twenty-four-hour operations, there was seldom a time when it wasn't hopping with activity.

Surveying the place as he walked in, Ethan spotted the person he was looking for. He wound his way toward the far side of the bar, where a small crowd had gathered around one of the pool tables.

Rear Admiral Aaron Blade, or Warhawk to his pilots, was bent down in one of his unique pool shooting positions, lining up a shot, when Ethan approached the edge of the table. "Hold that thought, Paladin. I'm about to finish destroying this pup's attempt to hustle an old man."

Ethan had to stifle a laugh at the comment. No one hustled Warhawk at pool. If anything, the old man was a pool shark, hustling his subordinates out of their hard-earned pay.

Warhawk drew back for his shot and let it fly. To Ethan's continued amazement, the cue ball hit the pool balls with incredible accuracy and speed. One of the balls hit the sidewall at the exact angle the old man had aimed for, connecting with another ball behind his opponent's striped balls and sending only his into the pocket. He casually walked around the table as he rubbed some chalk on the stick's tip before lining up for his next shot.

Ethan looked over at the young lieutenant holding his pool stick, a look of shock and dismay on his face at how the opening shots were turning out. They'd received a new batch of pilots from flight school last week. This young lieutenant was still learning the ropes, like who the pool sharks were and when not to play at a cash table.

During the past year, batches of newly trained pilots had continued to filter into their ranks. Even with a steady flow of pups showing up every two weeks, the *Freedom* was still down four-hundred-plus qualified pilots across the different platforms the ship carried. They still needed fighter pilots, bomber pilots, and a whole lot of cargo and utility pilots before the ship's entire air wing would be fully operational.

Crack.

In a shot that looked impossible to make, Warhawk hit the cue ball, sending it hard to the side of the table, where it bounced back at an equally crazy angle to sink another one of his balls into the opposite side pocket.

"Hot damn! How does that guy keep making shots like that?" someone commented loudly.

"He's Warhawk. Nobody knows how he does it, he just does it," another person commented in amazement.

Three more shots and the game was over. The crowd cheered and jeered as the master of the pool tables walked over to the "pup" who fancied himself a hotshot pool player and extended his hand.

"Good game, son. Keep at it, you might beat me one of these days."

Instead of taking the pilot's money, he picked it up and placed it back in his hands, then leaned in and whispered something too quiet for the others to hear. Whatever he said made the young lieutenant smile and changed his entire demeanor.

Warhawk walked toward Ethan, a serious look on his face. "I heard you ran your guys pretty hard today."

"No harder than I do any other day," Ethan countered. Everyone knew he ran his squadrons ragged.

They walked toward the bar, taking a seat as the synthetic humanoid manning the bar poured them each a cold beer. A group of flight crew workers called out for another round, summoning the Synth away, leaving them alone.

"You said we needed to speak?" Ethan inquired. Warhawk's message had been somewhat cryptic.

The admiral nodded, then took a long couple of gulps from his glass, draining half of it. "Ethan, I need to talk to you about something—something I need your thoughts on."

Now Ethan's interest was piqued. The admiral didn't usually address him by his first name, not unless he was truly looking for some advice on something—which was happening more and more since the war had ended. Steadily, he was being brought into the man's circle of trust, and not just because his last name was Hunt.

Turning in his chair, the admiral leaned in. "You know this shortage of properly trained pilots we're facing? I think I may have come up with a solution."

Ethan nodded grimly. It was a serious issue the Fleet was grappling with. The brass had been unable to come up with a better solution than what they were currently doing.

"Hey, I'm all ears. If you've got an idea that might work, you know you can count on my help."

Warhawk nodded approvingly. Ethan knew he'd earned a lot of respect from the man during the battle of Alfheim and since.

Leaning in, Warhawk explained, "I know I'm preaching to the choir when I say this, but it's important to have context for how we've gotten here so we can better understand how we're going to make improvements. Peace may have returned, but let's not kid ourselves into believing the Zodarks are going to leave us alone or not look to restart hostilities. The war caught us by surprise. You know as well as I do that the kinds of pilot losses the Fleet took were unsustainable, particularly during the latter half of the war.

"Despite what the brass at Space Command says publicly, switching the Fleet's starfighter doctrine in the middle of the war proved to be an epic disaster—one that cost us thousands of pilots during the second half of the war," the admiral explained.

Ethan had heard many senior officers say this same thing during and after the war. He also knew to just let Warhawk paint the big picture for him, so he stayed silent and nodded along in agreement.

"As you already know, Ethan, when the Republic became a spacefaring military, we took our drone and autonomous fighter platforms from Earth and developed a replica program for our starships. The idea was simple—a starfighter drone was something that could be easily replaced during combat. Pilots, as we've come to learn, not so much. When the war with the Zodarks started, our starfighter drones held up pretty well in combat. When we did take losses, our support ships fabricated new ones and our drone pilots were back in the fight. Hell, even I lost something like fourteen drones over the years, but each time I lost one, a replacement was almost always available. That's not something we can do with pilots.

"Somehow, someway, we got convinced by the Altairians that manned starfighters like the ones they flew were more effective in combat than what we'd been using. While that may have been true for them, given they'd been flying manned starfighters for God knows how long, we had not. This change instantly meant our pilots had to relearn how to anticipate and deal with extreme g-forces the body had to endure with manned flights and extreme combat maneuvers. That wasn't something you had to contend with as a drone pilot, which allowed us to fly with reckless abandon and without the fear of crushing our bodies or blacking out.

"Ultimately, this radical change in how we fought in the middle of the war was the single greatest reason our fighter corps was getting hammered with a thirty percent loss ratio. We still had plenty of people wanting to be pilots. But without an adequate advanced fighter training program, we were just throwing pilots fresh out of flight school into battle and hoping they survived. I can't change the decision to use manned fighters, at least not right now, but if we could create an advanced fighter training school that could give our pilots the necessary skills to become real dogfighters, then maybe they'll be better prepared for the next war."

Ethan interjected, "You don't think the training programs the ship's air wings are responsible for are enough to fill that gap?"

The admiral shook his head. "No, not at all. You saw how things worked out in Sirius. It was a complete mess. Every air wing had their own way of operating and training their pilots. Once they were all thrown together in one giant fleet and had to work as a single unit, it all fell apart. That's what I'm getting at, Ethan—we gotta come up with some new ways to fix this. If a war restarts with those Zodark bastards and we don't find a way to fix our screwups from the last war, we may not win."

Ethan saw the concern and worry on the admiral's face and knew he was right. When he'd been able to talk with his father, he'd mentioned a lot of similar concerns. For all the successes the Republic had managed to eke out during the last war, Earth, for better or worse, had found itself thrust into an interstellar war it had had no idea how to win. It was only the Altairians' direct intervention that had saved humanity from becoming a subjected people like the Sumerians. His father had told him in confidence that direct foreign intervention to save the Republic was not something that could be counted on happening again. The Republic would have to stand on its own if it was to maintain its sovereignty in the future.

"That's a sentiment my father shared with me as well. So, what's this solution you wanted to talk to me about?" Ethan asked, bringing the conversation back to where they'd started.

A smile spread across the old man's face. "Well, we weren't the first people to struggle with the transition with new technology introduced during a conflict," Warhawk began. "During the Vietnam

War, the Americans lost well over three thousand fighter aircraft and over five thousand helicopters. The introduction of surface-to-air missiles and other radical technology shifts in the middle of the war ultimately led to severe casualties. But that led to the creation of Top Gun and Red Flag. These training programs would ensure future aviators had the skills to fight and win future wars as the technology of aviation warfare continued to evolve."

Ethan placed his now-empty beer on the table. "So, you want to create a similar type of Top Gun program for our own pilots. Right?"

Warhawk chuckled. "Well, believe it or not, I just got permission to create such a program. But before we announce it to the Fleet's air wings, I wanted to get your opinion of it. As a group commander, it's going to be guys like you that are going to benefit from it most. But if the group commanders don't see the value in it, it'll be hard to get them to buy into supporting it and sending their pilots."

"Well, I can tell you this—I think every group commander on the *Freedom* is going to be for it. Once the pilots start talking about it, you'll have a long line of people wanting to attend it," replied Ethan encouragingly.

Warhawk smiled, excited to see his enthusiasm. "Excellent, that's exactly the kind of feedback I was looking for. Now comes the hard part. Who do I appoint to head this up and how do we create this program without stripping the *Freedom* of its best pilots and commanders to become the cadre of this new program?"

Chapter 7
What Neutral Zone?

Mid-2108
Bravo Company, 3rd Battalion, 126th Infantry Regiment
Neutral Zone
Alfheim, Sirius System

In some ways, every week that Corporal David Roberts had been left on this desolate, frozen planet called Alfheim felt like a year. Once he'd recovered from his wounds sustained during the initial invasion of Alfheim, he'd been assigned to a new unit slated to reinvade the planet. Shortly after he'd participated in the second invasion to retake the place from the Zodarks, the war had ended.

In a way, he was glad it had ended the way it had. He'd seen limited combat during the war, and that was fine by him. Having been shot once, he wasn't eager to experience it a second time. He'd hoped their unit would head back to the Primord planet of Rass, where his new battalion was home-stationed. But as more units left Alfheim for home, his battalion got the dubious honor of staying behind.

In total, sixteen battalions had been identified to stay on as the new planetary garrison. Making matters worse, because Alfheim was at the far end of the Republic's logistical chain, this first occupation tour was going to last four years. The Army was intending to establish it as a permanent duty station, just with Zodarks and Orbots staring at them from across the border. To say there was some wailing and gnashing of teeth coming from the soldiers being left behind was an understatement. The only real compensation the Army offered to try and assuage all the ticked-off soldiers and officers was first choice of anywhere they wanted for their next two duty assignments or one ten-year duty assignment of their choice. They also doubled their pay for the duration of the four-year tour. It took a few months for people to eventually learn to accept it, but it wasn't like they had a choice or a ride off the planet.

The units chosen to stay behind had undergone a complete reorganization. Roberts's battalion had been folded into the 34th Infantry Division; the 34th ID and the 40th ID would become the garrison divisions. The 38th Sustainment Brigade, the 225th Engineer Brigade, and the 185th Theater Aviation Brigade were among the unlucky support elements selected to assist the two divisions and begin the reconstruction of the local infrastructure and establishment of permanent bases and outposts along the neutral zone. Roberts had been told the parent organization in charge of the planet was called IX Corps, or just the Unlucky 9C or U9C as they'd come to call themselves.

Over time, Roberts had mostly learned to deal with the cards he'd been dealt. It hadn't been easy at first, but after the reorg and his initial acceptance of the situation, he'd tried to make the best of it. For instance, he was now part of a famous unit, one that traced its legacy all the way back to the First World War between the years of 1914 and 1918. The 32nd Infantry Brigade Combat Team or "Red Arrow" Brigade was a unit steeped in history, and if there was one thing the soldiers on Alfheim loved to do, it was read.

As Roberts watched the snow continue to drift downwards, he could feel the cold taking a toll on him as it bit through his clothes. The last four hours of darkness couldn't end soon enough. Clenching his jaw, he tried to stop his teeth from chattering as he shivered. He'd be racked out in a warm bunk if these Zodark bastards hadn't started breaking the terms of the truce.

He sighed as another shiver ran through him. *At least this is our last night ambush for a few weeks…*

Roberts looked in the direction of the Peace Bridge, the official demarcation line between Zodark and Republic territory. A breeze caused him to clench his teeth, the wind only further adding to the misery index. Balling his gloved fist, he muttered a few curse words in the direction of the Zodarks.

"You say something, Roberts?" Private First Class Trisha Denk asked in a hushed voice, just above a whisper.

"Nah, just talking to myself."

She laughed. "You do that too much and they're liable to think you've lost your mind."

"Ha, what are they going to do? Send me to Alfheim?"

They both laughed. It was a running joke among the grunts—"What are they going to do, send me to Alfheim?"

Roberts glanced at the clock in the corner of his helmet HUD. Dawn would be approaching. *Just have to hold out ten more minutes*, he thought.

Once the light supplanted the darkness, the temperature change would make the day far more bearable than the evening. It would still only be twenty-eight degrees out, but it was a far cry from the minus sixteen his helmet showed him right now.

Then a voice interrupted his thoughts, intruding on his melancholy of the moment.

"What are we doing here, Dave?" Denk asked in a quiet voice, just above a whisper.

He shook his head in the dark, not that she could see his frustration. It was a question they were all asking, especially once they got past the halfway point. No one wanted to get hurt or killed when they weren't even at war.

Turning his head slightly to face her, he said, "Two words, Trish: Delta Company. It seems these Zodark bastards don't want to accept they lost to us. After what happened to Delta, the brass wants to make sure the neutral zone is locked down tight. That's what we're doing here."

Roberts hoped that would satisfy her for the moment. He knew Denk was a smart soldier; like the rest of them, she was nervous about getting killed. It was one thing during war—you expected you might die then. But the war was over, or at least it was supposed to be.

The battalions of Alfheim went on a rotation of one month guarding the mines, two months on-base duty, two weeks guard duty along the neutral zone either patrolling the forest and hills or in one of the fortified combat outposts, then base duty before the cycle restarted. It was like a never-ending sequence. It did break up the monotony, though.

Right now, their battalion was on neutral zone duty. Given what had happened to Delta Company, the unit that had swapped out for them at the mines, he hoped they'd be all right. This last attack had been a huge escalation, something they hoped wasn't a sign of things to come.

Delta Company had gotten hit hard. They'd just finished their first week on rotation when the Zodarks had carried out their first attack on the mines. It had also been the largest attack since the end of the war.

The way things typically worked at the mines, on Monday, Thursday, and Saturday, a twelve-vehicle convoy hauled the mined materials some forty miles away to the refinery. Two weeks ago Saturday, the convoy had gone twenty-two miles into the drive when the lead Cougar infantry fighting vehicle had been blown to hell and gone by an IED. As the vehicles had come to a halt, a group of Zodarks had materialized from the tree line along the highway and torn into them. They'd shredded the convoy with smart missiles and blaster fire, destroying all twelve cargo vehicles.

The remaining two Cougars with the security element had dismounted their infantry and collectively countered the ambush as they called for the quick reaction force. The combat outpost the soldiers stayed on had dispatched the QRF just like they had trained. The six Cougars had roared out of the base to rescue their comrades, only to get slammed by a series of IEDs and missiles just a few miles outside the base.

As the QRF had come under attack, the base itself had been attacked by missiles and small-arms fire from multiple directions, while a fourth attack had occurred at the mines themselves. By the time reinforcements and close-air support had arrived on the scene, the Zodarks had broken contact and done their best to slip away. When it was all done, fifty-eight workers from the mines had been killed, and some hundred and sixty-two synthetic workers and other machinery used in the mines had been destroyed. A sapper team had torn the mines and equipment up while the main attack pinned any chance to protect the mines. The attacks had lasted a total of four minutes. In that brief time, fifty-nine soldiers of Delta Company had been killed.

After more than two years of relative peace on Alfheim, something had changed. The uneasy détente with the Zodarks appeared to be ending. Their captain had said the diplomats and the brass would get it all figured out. In the meantime, they were Republic Army soldiers, and by God, if those Zodarks wanted a fight, they'd give it to them.

Thinking back to what the captain had said, Roberts chuckled. *Yeah, negotiating with a Zodark. Like that'll work…*

"Sun's finally up. Should begin to warm up soon," Denk commented as the predawn light pushed the darkness of the evening aside.

"Thank God, I'm freezing. You'd think I'd get used to it by now, but damn, it's hard to get used to this weather."

Denk laughed at his comment. "Eh, it's not so bad. I mean, it's not nearly as bad as Fairbanks."

Roberts had forgotten that Denk had grown up in Alaska. This kind of cold was second nature to her.

"I hope this latest skirmish with the Zodarks doesn't become the new norm. The war's over—they should accept that. What do you think? Is this what we have to look forward to for the remainder of our time here?"

Roberts sighed. *God, she asks a lot of questions...*

"Trish, I'm just a corporal. What do I know about what's going to become the new norm or not? I'm like a mushroom, just like the rest of you. They keep us in the dark, feed us crap."

Denk laughed at his analogy. "You crack me up, Dave. You're probably right. Hopefully this doesn't get any worse. Eighteen months, then we're out."

Roberts nodded in agreement at that. Despite her questions, he did like her. No, scratch that—if he was being honest, he was starting to develop some feelings for her. If he hadn't, he wouldn't have put up with her second-guessing their orders and constantly questioning everything. No one liked leaving the perceived safety of the FOB now. Not with the Zodarks getting more and more bold.

Roberts turned to face her. "Trish, we're just soldiers," he said. "We do as we're told. If they want us out on patrol doing this kind of stuff to our last day, then that's what we're gonna do."

Hearing the annoyance in his voice, she scooched closer to him, attempting to snuggle next to his warm body. "Ah, don't give me that, Davy, you know what I mean," she said playfully.

Why does she have to call me Davy? I hate that name. Oh great, now she wants to get playful, he thought as she gave him that look he'd come to love back in the barracks. *This is not the time or place to try and get laid, Trish*, he grumbled in his head.

"I was talking with Angie from supply," Denk commented. "She told me a new brigade from Earth arrived two weeks ago. I'll bet they'll swap battalions like ours out of these field rotations with the fresh meat. Start givin' 'em some practice and training to take over for us. Then we can play FOBIT while the clock runs out."

Snickering at her persistence in finding a way to duck field duty, he replied in a sarcastic tone, "Yes, General Denk. Let me issue the orders to the troops right away, General Denk!"

She punched his shoulder, sticking her tongue out for mocking her. "Come on, Davy...think about the barracks." She winked flirtatiously.

When she mentioned the barracks, his mind drifted to what he and Denk could be doing if they were there right now. He sighed. *Nineteen hours, then we can follow our instincts and forget about this place for a few moments.*

Trying to distract his mind from the barracks, Roberts put his rifle down and pulled his helmet off. He'd let his hair grow too long and now it itched like crazy in his helmet. Looking at Denk as she watched him, he blew some air past his lips. "I'm just a corporal, Trish. You know I have no say in what we do."

The look on her face told him she finally realized her questions were starting to drive him nuts. He had no control over the situation.

Lying next to her, he stared into her eyes as she searched his. He wasn't sure why, but something about seeing her kitted out in body armor and weapons was strangely attractive.

A mischievous smile spread on her face. She reached her hands out for him, attempting to unbutton his trousers.

"Dude, Trish. We'll be back at the FOB in like nineteen hours. You need to wait, girl."

Undeterred, she took her helmet off, shaking her short-cropped blond hair. Closing the gap between them, she kissed him savagely while her hands moved down his trousers.

Unbeknownst to them, as she'd removed her helmet, her finger had accidentally tapped the speaker button, allowing her helmet to detect and broadcast whatever noise it heard happening near it.

"Come on, Davy—that bulge in your pants says you don't want to wait either. We're hidden under a blanket. No one's going to see or know what we're doing. You can make it a quickie if you want," she whispered, kissing his neck and face.

Suddenly the unthinkable happened. Roberts's greatest fear about their tryst came true. The squad net chirped to life, with a voice declaring, "Oh yeah! I knew it. Way to go, David!"

"Oh, Davy...we can make it a quickie," someone imitating a woman's voice proclaimed before making some moaning sounds.

Through fits of laughter, a female soldier exclaimed, "Just lay back, Davy, let me do all the work for you, baby."

A loud, angry voice broke through the laughter and jabs, sending a chill down Roberts's spine. The voice of their platoon sergeant barked, "For God's sake, Corporal! We're sitting on the neutral zone watching the very bridge these Zodark bastards regularly use to cross. You all can mate like rabbits back on the FOB for all I care. When we're outside the wire, looking for a fight with the Zodarks, you best have your head in the game."

Their platoon sergeant was pissed. Roberts looked at Denk. She was clearly mortified by what had just happened. Her eyes started to water and she fought not to utter a sound. Roberts grabbed for her helmet and smashed the speaker button, cutting off the broadcast.

She burst into tears the moment no one could hear them anymore. Roberts pulled her close to him, embracing her in a strong hug. His emotions were racing between embarrassment and anger at being caught. The stinging rebuke by their platoon sergeant hurt. He'd just let his mentor down and failed to lead by example as a junior NCO.

He wiped a tear away from her cheek with his thumb and he opened his mouth to say something to her, but an urgent call stopped him. Then a shiver ran down his spine as he realized who it was and what it meant.

"Ghost Actual, Ghost Ten. I've got movement to our front. Looks to be three tangos, approaching marker Delta Six. How copy?"

Staff Sergeant Howell barked angrily, "Cut the chatter, everyone, and get ready for contact!"

Their platoon leader jumped in, taking charge. "Ghost Ten, Ghost Actual. Good copy. Three tangos approaching Delta Six. Do they appear to be headed toward the bridge?"

As Roberts listened to the radio, he handed Denk her helmet. Before she put it on, he leaned in and kissed her softly. "It'll be OK," he whispered. "Let's get our war faces on and prepare for whatever this may be."

She looked at him, nodding as she fastened her helmet. Moving to her spot under the camouflage blanket, she readied her M1 rifle and the squad's M-12 smart missile should they encounter any sort of Zodark ground or aerial vehicles. He was glad Staff Sergeant Howell had ordered the squads to bring an M-12 with them.

The M-12 multipurpose launcher or MPL was the twenty-second-century version of the FGM-148 Javelin man-portable fire-and-forget antitank missile. Through many upgrades, the Javelins had stayed in service through their discovery of New Eden but had been phased out a few years later in favor of the more versatile MPL.

With Denk set up, Roberts looked at the sector of fire his fire team was responsible for. He did a quick check on his two soldiers hidden ten meters to his right in a similar position. They were manning the squad's lone M91 heavy blaster. In a fight, the M91's rapid rate of fire was especially effective at laying waste to whatever was in front of it.

"Ghost Actual, tangos have advanced to Delta Five. They appear to be some sort of scout element. Break. Requesting permission to deploy the Beatles. My gut says the main force is somewhere nearby. How copy?"

The Beatles were microdrones that mimicked the appearance of insects. The small devices would attach themselves to trees and other objects, and had a wide angle lens that could provide standard images as well as night vision and infrared. They had an exceptional range of three to five kilometers, depending on the terrain, and they could also sync up with a local wifi or coms system to transmit their images to rear elements hundreds of miles away.

"Ghost Ten, negative on the Beatles. Not enough time to emplace them. We don't want them knowing we're here. Attempt visual observation if possible."

The longer the radio stayed quiet, the more nervous Roberts was becoming. They knew three Zodarks were attempting to stealthily approach the Peace Bridge. They could just be another sapper team trying to infiltrate across. If that was the case, then this was exactly why the brigade had ordered a permanent rotation of units to observe the bridge and a narrow, shallow section of the river a couple of kilometers downstream. In the three weeks since this new rotation had started, five Zodark teams had been intercepted and destroyed. Ironically, not a single mention of these teams had been made during the quarterly meetings between the Republic-Primord envoys and their Zodark-Orbot counterparts.

"Ghost Actual. Tangos have reached Delta Three. You should have visual ID. Please confirm you have the eye."

"Confirmed. We have the eye. We see 'em—"

"Break. Enemy force identified. Approaching marker Echo Eight. I count…sixteen tangos. Wait. Stand by, I have additional movement."

Listening to the play-by-play between the scout team and their platoon leader was killing Roberts. Everything was moving incredibly slow and fast all at the same time. It was obvious the Zodarks were moving soldiers in their direction. The question was how many, and in how many groups? Was this a probe or were they looking for a fight?

"Ghost Actual, we've detected two separate groups. Group one, now Zebra One, has passed marker Charlie Seven. Count fifty-six tangos. Break. Group two, now Zebra Two, has passed marker Echo Five. Count sixty-one tangos. Break. There could be more groups further away. UGS Two detected eight vehicles in the vicinity of grid Kilo-five-five. Break. Requesting Hawkeye for aerial assist. How copy?"

Damn, if those underground sensors are detecting vehicles, then they could have offloaded a ton of Zodarks, Roberts thought pensively. He hoped they'd get approval to tap into Hawkeye. It was part of a group of keyhole satellites that could give a ground unit a real-time image of what it was seeing around your position.

"Stand by, Ghost Ten," came the voice of Staff Sergeant Howell.

If Roberts had to guess, their green, baby-faced lieutenant was probably crapping puppies as the scouts' report came in. It was still possible the Zodarks were doing what they had done—setting up a position to observe the bridge and watch for activity.

"Ghost Ten, good copy on all. Continue to observe and report any changes to the enemy disposition or changes in movement. Out."

Peering through the optics of his M1, Roberts looked in the direction the Zodarks were coming from. Time seemed to slow to an agonizing crawl as he waited for the first signs of the blue beasts. Then he saw them. *Damn, these guys are jumpy.* The three-man team approaching them was moving slowly, cautiously, like they sensed they were being hunted, not like they were the hunters.

Staff Sergeant Howell's voice cautioned, "Everyone, stand by. Don't fire and don't make any sudden moves. I need to contact the captain and see what he wants to do."

While their platoon was directly observing the bridge, the rest of their company was observing the nearby river crossings. The Kiltium River was the official demarcation line between the Zodarks' territory and that of the Republic. The neutral zone encompassed a kilometer on either side, leaving plenty of separation between the parties.

While the higher-ups worked out the platoon's next moves, Roberts looked their position over on his helmet's HUD. The platoon had good interlocking fields of fire covering the "Peace Bridge," as it was called. It was a large structure, some one hundred meters from shore to shore.

Before the war, it had connected a four-lane highway, linking several major cities in the region. Roberts wasn't sure what it was made of. Both sides had tried to destroy it at one time or another. Like a monument to its builders, it still stood despite their best efforts to drop it.

While their position was good, there was a weak spot Roberts didn't like. A kilometer downriver, the raging water calmed once it got past a series of rocks. It narrowed to twenty meters and got shallower. If Roberts had to guess, the Zodarks could ford this section, bypassing the bridge altogether if push came to shove. The rest of the company was set up in an ambush, ready to hit them if they tried to cross. Unlike at the bridge, if the Zodarks got around behind them here, they'd be in serious trouble. Then again, if the Zodarks threw a large enough force at the bridge, they might overrun their own positions. This was one of those times he wished they had a detachment of C100s.

"Listen up," Staff Sergeant Howell barked. "We've got reinforcements inbound. A company of C100s and the QRF, Charlie Company, are loading into transports as we speak. Close-air support has been granted should we need it; a flight of AS-90 Reapers is getting ready to fly. With help inbound, if the Zodarks move into our kill zone— we've been ordered to engage."

Roberts turned to Denk. "Well, there you have it. If those bastards try to cross the bridge, we're going to light 'em up."

"Maybe we'll get lucky and they're out here just like us, watching the neutral zone. Maybe they won't try to cross and pick a fight." Denk sounded nervous.

Roberts looked at her a moment longer, taking the sight of her in. He could tell she was terrified; so was he. Anyone who'd fought the Zodarks held a fear of those blue bastards. Trying to assuage her concerns, he smiled. "Yeah, maybe. Nothing wrong with hoping they're just on a patrol and not looking to cross the bridge."

Turning back to the Zodarks, Roberts watched them with rapt attention as they steadily moved closer. It wasn't often he got to see them operate like this, so it was fascinating to observe, yet terrifying, knowing what they were capable of.

When the three scouts got within two hundred meters of the bridge—they froze. To the untrained eye, they might have looked like they'd just paused for a break, but Roberts knew then that, like a coiled snake, they were taking in their surroundings, preparing to strike. The lead scout stood still, his eyes searching, his ears listening; he knew they were being watched. He raised one of his right hands, gesturing with his fingers. Without speaking, the three of them slowly lowered themselves to a kneeling position, their blasters raised in the direction of Roberts's platoon.

Peering through his optics, Roberts looked past the scouts to the larger group following further behind. None of the soldiers were saying a thing, yet they moved with a sense of urgency, changing their formation from a forward V-shape to a line formation with everyone abreast of each other. Roberts sensed trouble. This wasn't some small raiding force. These were soldiers on a mission. The shift in formation brought the bulk of their firepower online to point directly at his platoon. When they got close to the scouts' positions, they'd started taking cover behind the sides of trees, fallen logs, pretty much whatever was available, like they knew they were being watched and a fight might break out in moments.

As that reality set in, Roberts felt his body tensing, his hands becoming sweaty, his heart starting to race. He hadn't seen years of combat or fought in multiple campaigns like some others in the platoon had. His only serious combat experience was the first day of the Alfheim invasion, when he'd gotten injured—then three days of limited fighting during the second invasion to liberate their comrades who'd been left behind. What he did know, and respect, was that the Zodarks were fearless in combat.

Looking back at the Zodark scouts, Roberts saw one of them take a pack off his back. Aiming his rifle at it, he attempted to use its optic to see what it was. He sighed. *I'm too far out*, he realized. He wasn't going to be able to tell what they were doing, at least not with the optics on his rifle. Some of the sharpshooters using better optics probably could.

Roberts could see that the Zodark pulled something out of the bag and held it in one of his upper hands for a moment. His two lower hands typed away on a tablet. Moments later, the small device lifted off his hand, gaining altitude above their position.

It dawned on Roberts what they were doing. A sudden jolt of adrenaline shot through his body. *Oh, this is bad news…*

Staff Sergeant Howell urgently yelled through their coms, "Activate your blankets and get below them *now!*"

Roberts reached for the device near the edge of the blanket, activating it. "Trish, help me with this."

They pulled the blanket down, covering the front of their position facing the Zodarks.

Denk whispered, "What's wrong?"

"The scout—he's launching a recon drone. The little bastard will scout our side of the border looking for potential heat signatures. If it finds one, they'll know to look for more, plotting our positions for a mortar or missile to hit all our positions once they're ready. They can also use 'em like kamikazes and just slam into us, blowing us to kingdom come."

"How the hell is this blanket going to protect us?" she asked anxiously.

"I'll tell you how. This is a digital, IR, and thermal protective camouflage blanket. It's a damn cloaking blanket, Trish." Roberts tried to remain patient—she was still really green and didn't know certain things. "Special Forces started using it halfway through the war. In theory, this should make our entire presence disappear."

DARPA had developed the semitranslucent blanket—weaving together tiny clear wire-like tubes that allowed the blanket to mimic and blend into its surroundings. It was standard-issue for Special Forces midway through the war. As the regular army looked to add them, they prioritized them to the forward-deployed units, like the troops on Alfheim.

Roberts and Denk looked through the mesh of the blanket in time to see the Zodark launch a second drone. The first drone appeared to have risen just below the bottom canopy layer of the forest, hovering in place. The other moved slowly toward the Republic's position. It was clearly scanning the area, seeing if it could spot anything out of place.

"Hey, David, those other Zodarks are on the move."

Roberts heard the terror in her voice. He just wanted to get this ambush going, smoke 'em while they still had the element of surprise on their side. Despite being heavily outnumbered, he knew they had reinforcements inbound and Reapers on their way. Clenching his rifle, he readied himself for the fight he now felt was about to start.

"Is there a signal for when we should fire?"

"Ah, yeah. Once they enter the kill box, Staff Sergeant Howell will tell us when to fire. If it's just these three guys approaching the bridge, we'll likely wait until more of 'em expose themselves."

"OK, I'll just fire when you start firing," she commented.

As Roberts watched the three Zodarks advance toward the bridge, he suddenly felt a lot less confident in his battle buddy. *What the hell, Trish? Have you not been paying any attention during the briefings or did you forget all your training until today?*

The three Zodarks moving toward the bridge were likely the sacrificial lambs their sergeants were using to draw out any potential ambush before they brought their main force forward. Once the lead Zodark advanced ten or fifteen meters, he'd take a knee next to a tree trunk as he aimed his rifle toward their positions. The other two would rush forward ten or fifteen meters before seeking cover, readying themselves for an attack. The lead Zodark would then leap up and run past his two comrades until he found a new position. As the scouts steadily moved closer to the bridge, the larger force further back went into action. The entire group of nearly seventy of them began to do the same thing, knowing they were about to make contact but wanting to close the distance before they did. In Roberts's mind, the enemy was executing a textbook covering/bounding tactic he'd learned during infantry advanced school.

Then a single magrail shot broke the silence of the moment.

Crack.

A gush of blueish blood, bone and braided hair exploded as the high-velocity magnetic rail slug popped the head of a Zodark like a balloon. The soldier had been attempting to sprint across the bridge when it had taken the headshot. The Zodark's now-limp body collapsed forward, crashing hard into the ground in an awkward position from its forward momentum.

Roberts wasn't sure who had fired the first shot. All he knew was it was game on; the fight had started. Rapid streaks of light raced across the bridge as the platoon's heavy blaster MGs began spitting death in a sweeping pattern across the Zodarks' positions at a stunning rate of speed. Scores of Zodark soldiers were cut apart as they found themselves caught within the interlocking fields of fire. The two grenadier soldiers in the squad began raining 20mm smart grenades amongst the Zodarks as they scrambled for safety from the ambush.

Roberts wasn't sure when he had joined the fray—he'd zeroed in on a Zodark shooting at them and pulled the trigger several times. His eyes registered the blaster hits against the upper torso of the giant blue beast. It staggered briefly to the side before collapsing against the side of a tree, dead.

To his left, Denk had joined in. She was doing what she'd been taught, focusing on taking one target out and then moving to the next. It didn't do you any good to fire wildly or shift from target to target if you weren't taking the threats out.

The Zodarks rallied after the initial shock, bringing their own weapons to bear. The second group of soldiers further back rushed forward to join their comrades. The volume of return fire coming from the Zodarks was becoming overwhelming. Close to half the Zodarks preferred to fight using two blasters, one in each upper hand, as opposed to their larger assault rifles. The rate of fire they could deliver was incredible, though it wasn't always as accurate as it would have been if they'd just stuck to their rifles.

Cries for medics started almost as soon as the fighting began. The medics and their C200 medical Synth darted to various fighting positions, doing what they could. Roberts heard some calls over the platoon leadership net for air support. He was glad to know some Reapers were still inbound. Their reinforcements weren't far off either.

BOOM, BOOM.

A pair of large explosions rocked him and Denk. A missile had slammed into the fighting hole next to them, killing its occupants. Looking across the river, Roberts spotted a couple more missiles racing toward their lines. Two more explosions, two more positions gone. Six of their platoonmates were dead.

Damn, if that air support doesn't get here soon, they'll pick us apart with those missiles.

A loud guttural yell broke out from somewhere in the forest. The sound sent a chill down Roberts's spine. The last time he'd heard that yell was the day he'd been wounded. He had to force the memories of that day out of his mind. That was the past; this was the present.

"I wish they'd just charge already. This bloody screaming is driving me insane!" Denk commented.

"Here they come!" was his reply.

Hordes of Zodark soldiers emerged from the tree line as they broke out into a full sprint toward the bridge. They were going to try and overwhelm their defense of the bridge, the convenient kill box it funneled them into, and get across at all costs. Then they'd work to outflank and encircle their positions, all while the second or even third wave of soldiers sprinted across the bridge.

"See if you can get some grenades on that bridge and don't let up. They're going to overwhelm us!" Roberts ordered, desperately hoping their two remaining MGs might be enough.

A missile streaked through the air, slamming into one of the heavy blaster machine guns. Its absence was immediately felt as the first wave of Zodarks reached the bridge. A second missile emerged from the trees, hitting their final MG position. All they had left was a handful of grenadiers and their M1s.

"Covering fire!" Denk yelled to Roberts's surprise.

He turned and saw she'd risen above their position, exposing herself to the withering fire trying to take them out. Resting on her right shoulder was their man-portable M-12 missile launcher. She fired the missile, sending it right down the throats of the charging horde.

Boom!

It landed in the center of the group, exploding its powerful warhead where it could do the most damage. A couple of Zodarks had been blown off the bridge from the concussive blast, landing in the river. Many others had been knocked to the ground, dazed and confused. One Zodark had apparently lost two of his four arms. He seemed to be stunned, unaware of what was going on around him. He found one of his severed arms, then the other. With bluish blood squirting from the wounds, the Zodark stumbled back across the bridge, heading toward the tree line, bringing his arms with him.

"Hot damn, Davy! You see that hit?!" Denk yelled excitedly.

"Hell yeah. God, I love those MPLs. Keep 'em coming, Trish! You just might save our bacon today," Roberts congratulated her. The volume of fire being directed at them doubled. He and Denk were barely able to escape as they hunkered low in their fighting positions.

"Trish, when you get that thing reloaded, we need to move before they hit us with a missile," Roberts directed.

"I need ten more seconds," she replied, hastily attaching the reload to the launcher.

Somewhere inside Roberts's lizard brain, he felt the overwhelming urgency to move, to get the hell out of this fighting position. He yelled at Denk, "Get out! Don't wait another second. Move!"

Roberts turned and started crawling. The underbrush and tree branches above him were being cut apart. The intensity of the blaster fire whizzing over his head covered his body in foliage and tree debris, yet he kept crawling through the snow, the muck, the tree limbs falling around him. He needed distance—distance from what he knew was going to happen.

BOOM.

The explosion behind him was powerful. The concussive blast and shockwave had bounced him off the ground before slamming him back into it. He almost blacked out. Lying still, his brain tried to assess for injuries. A sudden panic took hold—he couldn't breathe. He'd gotten the wind knocked out of him. Attempting to regain control, Roberts felt like his lungs were on fire. His brain was screaming for oxygen his lungs weren't bringing in, and his vision was starting to narrow.

Breathe, damn it! he yelled at himself.

Like a switch had been flicked, his lungs turned back on. He gasped for air, taking several deep breaths in, coughing a couple of times. As the fog lifted, his eyes caught images of blaster fire over his head. The battle wasn't over. The Zodarks were still coming. Feeling around for his rifle, Roberts grabbed the familiar weapon, bringing it close and glancing where their hide position had just been. All he saw now was a smoldering ruin.

Trish...

Ignoring the battle raging around him, Roberts crawled, then stumbled in the direction he'd last seen her. Then he stopped. Collapsing to his knees, he screamed out in agony and anger. The missile had ripped her body apart, likely killing her instantly. A wave of emotions washed over him, but one emotion began to take over—rage.

Tightening his grip on his rifle, Roberts turned to the bridge, to the animals who had killed Denk. The first groups of Zodarks had nearly reached his side of the river, another wave following quickly on their heels. He aimed his rifle at the horde as a series of explosions blossomed across the bridge, consuming the charging horde in flame and shrapnel. Roberts blinked, trying to figure out what had just happened, when a pair of Reaper ground-attack fighters swooped overhead.

Roberts shouted in excitement. The attackers on the bridge had been wiped out. The fighters clawed for altitude as they circled for another pass. A pair of missiles flew out of the forest, giving chase to the

Reapers. A string of missiles flew over their position, slamming into the tree line approaching the bridge, hammering the Zodarks still firing at Roberts's platoon. Another barrage of missiles hit multiple positions further into the Zodarks' territory.

Then Roberts detected a new sound—*Ospreys*. Roberts saw six of the assault transports go into a hover as soldiers began rappelling down. The C100 combat synthetics simply jumped from an altitude of fifty to a hundred feet right off the rear ramps, their ankle thrusters slowing them down as they landed. Once on the ground, they charged straight into the fight, guns blazing.

Three hours later, after the battle had ended, Roberts stood near Denk's remains. A pair of medical Synths were placing what was left of her into a body bag before moving on to the next fallen soldier.

Walking up behind him, Staff Sergeant Howell rested a hand on his shoulder. "I'm sorry about, Trish, David. She fought bravely."

"If that air support had gotten here just a few minutes sooner…she'd still be alive."

"Maybe. Don't beat yourself up, David. This was out of your control. Nothing you did or didn't do would have changed what happened. When it's your time, it's your time."

Roberts grunted at the comment. He knew Howell was right. The enemy always gets a vote. Still, that didn't make accepting it any easier.

"Come on, our ride's here. Time to head back to the FOB."

Roberts nodded, turning to walk toward the Osprey. "I hope what happened today was just a big mistake. I don't want to go back to war. Not after today."

"Time will tell, David. Time will tell."

Chapter 8
Phase One – Terror

Republic Capital
Jacksonville, Arkansas
Earth, Sol System

Shirin stood patiently on the platform with the rest of the morning commuters, waiting for the next car to arrive. Like clockwork, every six minutes during the morning commute, a five-car link would arrive to drop off one set of commuters and collect the next. When Shirin had arrived on Earth, she'd thought the hyperloop system was incredible. It wasn't a normal train like she was used to on Sumer, with an engine that powered it along. Instead, it consisted of a string of cabin cars linked together that moved rapidly through a clear vacuum-sealed cylindrical tube. Hovering in the tube, it was propelled by a magnetic levitation field, providing a fast, efficient way to move large numbers of people or vast amounts of cargo rapidly across vast distances or through a densely packed city.

"Next car arriving. Please watch your step," an automated PA announced to the people on the platform.

When the car arrived, the doors on the opposite side opened first, allowing those who wanted to get off to do so without facing a rush of people trying to get on. A moment later, those doors closed and the doors facing her opened.

"Please watch your step," the PA announced again as the passengers climbed aboard.

Spotting an empty seat, Shirin made her move. She slid in just before another person could. The would-be seat grabber shot her a dirty look. Shirin just smiled, causing the person to look away.

She sat through two more stops before she lowered her shoulder bag between her feet. Reaching inside, she grabbed the small cylinder and held it tight, gently turning the cap once. Then she withdrew her compact and began to apply some powder. Reaching back into her bag, she turned the cap two more times before withdrawing her eyeliner. From time to time, a person would glance in her direction before moving on as she continued to apply her makeup. Reaching into her bag yet again, she turned the cap a fourth time before holding it down for three seconds. Glancing down, she saw a red light appear. Smiling, she pulled her lipstick out and applied it casually to her lips, smacking them twice to make sure it looked nice. When she bent down to place it and her compact back in her bag, she gently pulled the cylinder out and held it briefly under her seat as it attached.

Pulling her shoulder bag back onto her lap, she prepared to get off at the next stop. She smiled, recalling that each turn of the cap added five minutes to the device's timer. She'd given herself twenty minutes—more than enough time to get off the train and hop on the next one before the bomb would go off. Seeing the next platform approaching, she got up and made her way toward the exit, smiling flirtatiously with anyone who looked at her.

Once she'd exited the first train, she made her way down another level and climbed aboard a different line that would take her through another section of the city. Her assignment was to plant three devices on three different hyperloop lines, then disappear to her apartment and lie low away from the prying eyes of everyone in the city. Tomorrow, she'd sanitize the place as she'd been taught and head to the address of the next apartment. Then, assuming her cover hadn't been blown, she'd carry out whatever assignment Dakkuri had for her next.
****

Same Time
The Egg & I
The University District

Grabbing his ham-and-cheese croissant, Orchamus made his way to an open table near the back of the coffee shop. The place was hopping with college-age students and thirtysomething-year-olds as they grabbed a bite to eat or a morning coffee on their way to class or work. Weaving his way through the crowd, Orchamus did his best to keep his head low, avoiding the surveillance cameras. He'd bought a ball cap of a local sports team, allowing the cap's bill to obscure his face while not drawing undue attention to that purpose.

Taking a seat, he kept his face somewhat low and let his shoulder satchel slide forward across his chest to rest on his lap while he ate. Next, he placed a napkin on his leg next to the satchel's opening. In between bites, he'd move his hand down to wipe it on the napkin, establishing a pattern of his hands moving between his food and his satchel. With each napkin wipe, he turned the slide on the cylinder top one notch. As he did, a memory of the training he'd received flashed through his mind. He'd wondered why they were to activate the device at the scene, as opposed to coming with it already armed. His instructor had said that once the device had been armed, you couldn't add or take away time from the sequence. You were stuck with whatever you had programmed. Also, once the device had been armed, a mechanism needed to mix the chemical compounds was activated. The energy signature of that arming sequence was just high enough that it could be detected by a Zodark scanner. The theory was that if a Zodark could detect it, then so could your enemy.

I still wish I could just arm these things in advance, he thought as he continued to turn the slide until he'd turned it six times. Once it was armed, he activated the device. Doing his best to act as casual as he could, he pulled it from his satchel and slid it into the now-empty sandwich wrapper.

Glancing around at the tables and rush of people, Orchamus stood confidently like he had nothing to hide as he made his way toward a garbage bin near the store entrance. Depositing his trash as he left, he walked across the street and down the block before briefly ducking into an alleyway between two buildings.

Making like he was tying his shoes, Orchamus pulled a round floppy hat from his satchel and placed his ball cap inside. He donned a pair of glasses with colored frames and stood like nothing had changed as he walked to the opposite end of the alleyway. Sliding into the morning rush of people, he walked a few more blocks before ducking into another breakfast bar. Having ordered an apricot Danish instead of an egg croissant, he repeated the process of arming and activating the next bomb.

Nearly thirty minutes had gone by when he left the third breakfast bar of the morning. With his tasks for the day complete, Orchamus began to run his countersurveillance route, heading toward his new apartment. He'd sanitized his old place, knowing he wouldn't be returning after he left. It was assumed his current identity wouldn't take long to uncover. His new legend and assignment would be waiting for him at the new place.

BOOM!

Orchamus instinctively turned his head left, just like everyone else. His eyes caught sight of a tongue of orange flame as it licked past the side of a building. Thick gobs of ever-expanding black smoke followed behind the orange flames, spreading further from the concussive blast of the explosion.

A woman nearby screamed in horror, causing Orchamus to nearly jump out of his skin. Another person began to sob while others cursed in shock. The onlookers didn't know what to do. Should they run? But where? For the moment, they seemed to be paralyzed by the events.

Orchamus excused himself as he moved through the crowds of people. He wanted to put more distance between himself and the breakfast bar he'd placed a bomb inside. As he moved through the crowd, Orchamus asked himself why he'd assumed his bombs would be the only ones going off today. As a second explosion rocked the city, he knew for sure he wasn't the only bomber who'd be striking fear in the capital of the Republic.

Orchamus saw that the smoke from this latest blast rose nearly a hundred feet in the air, and a slight smile crept across his face. As compartmentalized as they were, he had no idea how many others might be operating on Earth, let alone in the capital city. Somehow, it comforted him to know he wasn't alone in this city after all.

Pulling the timers up on his smart glasses, Orchamus saw he didn't have much time left before his own bombs would join in. Two minutes remained until the lives of dozens if not hundreds of people in the most popular breakfast bar in the University District would change forever.

Orchamus continued to run his countersurveillance route; he felt reasonably sure no one was actively following him. When he approached the door to his new apartment, he entered the key code he'd been given. After entering the apartment, he did a quick search to make sure he was alone and then swept the place for electronic devices. Feeling secure, he headed to the bathroom.

As he stared at the face in the mirror, he marveled at the mask he wore. He pulled a small electronic device and held it near his face. A shimmer occurred as what had just been his face dissolved into a grayish liquid that was pulled into the small device near his cheek. When the mask had come off, he smiled at the sight of his real face.

It wasn't something Orchamus got to wear often. In fact, it was likely that only he and Dakkuri had been issued this new piece of gadgetry. The nanobot technology allowed an operative to change their appearance temporarily, but it did have problems of instability in bad weather. He was sure that when they worked the remaining kinks out of this technology, it would change the world of spycraft forever.

Walking out of the bathroom, he headed toward the small box on the countertop. It was a messaging tool that likely held his next assignment. Holding the device so its scanner could see his face, Orchamus activated it. A scan of his face, irises, and both index fingers and thumbs verified his identity. A holographic message from Dakkuri appeared.

"If you are reading this message, then your last mission was a success. Congratulations on striking a blow against our enemies. This next mission will test your skills and, if successful, may alter the course of the coming war."

As the details of the mission unfolded, a mischievous smile spread across his face. *This will change the coming war...if it doesn't kill me first*, Orchamus thought as he began to analyze exactly how he was going to pull this off.

Chapter 9
Reorg

Altairius Prime

"Have you seen the report from Earth?"

Pandolly had. It was not flattering. "I received the communiqué. I am not sure what you want me to do about it."

"How about the report from an apparent battle on Alfheim?" Jandolly pressed.

"I have. Again, I am not sure what your point is, Jandolly."

"My point?! My point is they aren't ready for this. They can't handle the role the Emperor has given them. This is further proof of their weakness."

"Jandolly, are you second-guessing the Emperor?" Pandolly didn't like the direction this was going.

The other Altairian huffed at the comment, offended by its implication. "I am not questioning the Emperor. I am questioning the Earthers' ability to represent his *will* in our galaxy and alliance."

"This is not for us to question. The Emperor chose them for a reason. We must trust that he knows what he is doing."

Jandolly shook his head dismissively. He'd previously held the ear of Grigdolly, their fleet admiral and the Altairian Viceroy for the Gallentines. He was used to having direct access to the Viceroy and being heard; now he didn't have that kind of pull, and the change had not sat well with him. The real problem was that the Earthers weren't prepared for their new position. They didn't have the knowledge or technical expertise to suddenly be the conduit between their alliance and the Gallentines.

"Pandolly, I am not questioning the Emperor's wisdom. I am suggesting that maybe the Emperor does not have all the facts about these Earthers. Perhaps if he knew how unprepared they are and how poorly they are handling their new role, he might restore our position. Maybe he could be convinced to allow us to act as advisors, coequal viceroys if you will, to help mentor them until they are ready."

Pandolly looked at his friend. He knew Jandolly had ulterior motives in all this. But he wasn't entirely wrong about the Earthers' miscues, at least this latest one with the spies in their capital. It was embarrassing, their seeming inability to capture two men that had been outnumbered.

"Jandolly, I understand your reluctance to embrace this new change. But we must. The Emperor has spoken. It is not our place to challenge his decision. We must now work to implement the plan he has given to Viceroy Miles Hunt. We are fortunate that he has continued to seek our guidance and help. We still have the ability to influence the direction of the alliance. In fact, I will be meeting with him shortly."

Jandolly was not satisfied. He countered, "Admiral Grigdolly is not pleased either. He's directed the Kraxmer to create a dossier, a documented history of their failings to provide proof they are not ready to assume the role they now find themselves in. You do not rush a Tindolz to run when they only know how to crawl."

Pandolly thought the Tindolz argument too apt. When a young Altairian first learned to crawl, it took them a little while before they had the strength to stand on two feet. Then they learned to balance before they took those first steps. Pandolly conceded his point—the Earthers had learned to crawl, but even crawling was something they still struggled with. Asking them to run, as the Emperor had done, might be more than they were capable of.

Jandolly continued as he saw his friend starting to agree with him. "The Kraxmer's spies across the alliance are reporting dissatisfaction with Viceroy Hunt. They question the direction he is leading us in and the reforms he is trying to push through. The Kraxmer are also reporting disturbing information on the Zodarks' pets, their human spying agency, the Mukhabarat. When the Republic made Sumer one of their colonies, Sumerians became Republic citizens. Using the freedom of travel that entailed, they have spread their tentacles across the alliance. That was unheard of when the Viceroy was one of ours. We never faced the threat of foreign operatives infiltrating the members of the alliance as we are now."

Jandolly held up his tablet as he exclaimed, "You have seen the report. These Zodark spies are carrying out terrorist attacks across the Republic's own capital city. How much longer until this spreads to our capital? Or the others in the alliance?" He shook his head in disgust. "You must speak to them, Pandolly. This is making all of us look weak in the eyes of the Zodarks and the Orbots. Mark my words, this will be used as a point to place us back in charge of the alliance."

Shaking his head dismissively, Pandolly pleaded with his friend, "Jandolly, the Kraxmer need to tread carefully with the Republic. We cannot afford for our spies to get caught by them."

Jandolly scoffed at the suggestion. "Caught by the Republic's security service? Is that some sort of joke, Pandolly? You need to read the reports on how they operate. Our agents have reported that they are so ineffective, the Mukhabarat has already managed to carry out more than a dozen terrorist attacks and not a single person has been taken into custody."

"Jandolly, you had better warn our spies about the Republic's Special Forces," Pandolly insisted. "They are very effective at sniffing out spies. If they are brought in to help the civilian government, then our spies may get discovered. Please make sure they know to steer clear if the Republic's Deltas are brought in to assist the civilian government."

Jandolly didn't look pleased with the suggestion but agreed to pass it along to the intelligence service. Their spies needed to be reminded they were there in an observational role only. They were not to get caught and they were not to intervene or do anything to compromise their positions. Excusing himself, Pandolly headed off to his meeting with the Viceroy—a meeting he valued immensely.

He hoped Jandolly and his cronies wouldn't eventually screw things up with the Republic.

▪▪

Alliance Headquarters
Altairius Prime

Viceroy Miles Hunt was reading a status report from New Eden. For now, he was satisfied with the progress being made in building the alliance's headquarters village. It was an enormous project he'd ordered built almost four years ago. The alliance village was going to be connected to the Emerald City via hyperloop trains and a massive ground and air highway system. Emerald City was rapidly growing into a megacity with millions of inhabitants. The village was being built to integrate as many traits and functions as possible to meet the needs of the different races that made up the alliance. Once completed, the village, or rather city, would be able to accommodate up to three hundred thousand people, with ample room to grow and expand beyond that.

If Hunt had a gripe about the project, it was the time it was taking to build. He knew they were moving mountains getting this city built; still, he was eager to get the seat of power moved. With the war over, Hunt was placing a heavy emphasis on reorganizing the alliance both economically and militarily, so it would be in a better position should hostilities with the Dominion restart. Ultimately, he knew they'd have to fight them again. The Emperor had made that clear. The Collective would likely demand the Dominion restart the war at some point if they didn't. While they waited for that day to arrive, Hunt was determined to whip the alliance into shape so they would be ready when it finally came.

A chime sounded, breaking Hunt's train of thought. The AI let him know his Altairian friend, Pandolly, was waiting outside. He told the AI to let him enter.

Swiveling in his chair, Hunt turned to see his friend approach. He stood and offered an Altairian greeting, which Pandolly returned. Hunt gestured for him to take a seat as he walked around his desk to sit next to his friend.

"It's good to see you, Pandolly. When did you return from the neutral zone?"

Pandolly had recently become one of the Altairian senior fleet commanders. His fleet had just returned from a four-month deployment along the neutral zone between their space and the Orbots'.

"It is good to see you as well, Viceroy. My fleet returned three days ago. I would have come sooner, but I had some business I needed to handle. As you know, when a fleet action is complete, we demobilize until our next rotation. I needed to finish some administrative functions and leave instructions for the ship commanders. But I am here now, ready to discuss some items of interest with you," Pandolly explained in the direct manner the Altairians were known for.

"I'm glad you had a successful, and hopefully uneventful, trip— and please, call me Miles in private."

Pandolly bowed slightly. "Yes, Miles. Thank you. Any deployment that does not result in battle is a good deployment."

Hunt chuckled at the comment before turning serious again. "Pandolly, I summoned you because I need your advice."

Pandolly's facial expressions, such as they were, seemed to light up. He very much enjoyed being a confidant to the Viceroy over many other Altairians who felt they should be the ones advising him.

"What can I assist you in?" Pandolly asked, head slightly bowed.

"As you know, we're going to move the alliance seat of power to New Eden—to a village specially designed to meet the needs of the alliance. This is all part of my overall effort to reorganize us into a cohesive force made up of species that, while uniquely different, can still function as a unified body when the need arises. What I'd like to know from you is how these changes are being received by the Altairian government and everyday people."

Pandolly didn't respond right away. He made his customary response, taking a minute to evaluate the question before replying. Finally, he explained, "Miles, in general, the average Altairian is pleased you ended the war. This is truly the only time they have ever known peace given how long our society has been fighting with the Orbots and then the Zodarks, among other species in their alliance. The government, however, is not pleased. Many are still bitter at losing their leadership role in the alliance. Senator Jandolly, for example, is not pleased with this new arrangement."

"I've gathered that about him. He's always had kind of an adversarial relationship with me. What's his deal, Pandolly?" Hunt interrupted. He'd clashed with Jandolly for years. Ever since he had first taken his seat on the council, there had been friction between them.

Bowing slightly, Pandolly explained, "Jandolly is a complicated man who uses his family's extreme wealth to exert influence on those in charge. He has a thirst for power. When you became the Viceroy, he lost some of that power. If I am not mistaken, Miles, I believe there is an English term for this—how do you call it? A plutocrat."

Hunt snickered at Pandolly's pronunciation of plutocrat. Thinking of Jandolly in those terms put their interactions over the years in a whole new light. "Sorry for the interruption—that's a good description of the man. Please, continue."

"Yes, of course. It is good that you understand the dynamics in place right now. As I was saying, for hundreds of years, our King and his descendants have retained the Viceroy appointment and been the Emperor's voice in our galaxy. As you can imagine, across the centuries and throughout both the expansion of our territory and the admission of new species into the alliance, a plutocracy has arisen within our Senate, especially within the war council. As the alliance grew, it had been our vision, our voice, that guided and led the alliance. For King Grigdolly, our fleet commander, to be suddenly replaced by a new spacefaring species, one that is vastly inferior to us, has not gone over well with our civilian or military leadership. It is likely being viewed the same way by the other alliance members, particularly the ones that are still militarily superior to the Republic," Pandolly explained as delicately as he could.

Hunt listened attentively, trying his hardest to keep an emotionless face. What Pandolly said hurt him, but in reality, it was the kind of brutally honest feedback he'd missed while he was gone. The last thing he wanted was to surround himself with yes-men—people who would tell him what he wanted to hear and not the hard truths of the reality on the ground. There was still so much he didn't know about the inner workings of the alliance he now had to lead.

Hunt then asked, "What about the coming war? During recent meetings, I've detected some resentment toward military proposals I've opened for discussion. It feels like there may be something more to it."

"Ah, that is a wise assessment, Miles. Yes, there is some deep-seated resentment on the part of some of the admirals on the war council. It stems from your unilateral end to the last war, which forced us to abandon our invasion of Orbot space. That decision created a lot of animosity. We had spent more than twenty years preparing for this massive campaign, and suddenly it was called off without any warning or consultation. That kind of impulsive decision only reinforced their belief that you were not ready to be promoted to such an exalted position.

"I, more than my fellow Altairians, understand why you made the decision you did to end the war. You Earthers, the Prims, and likely the Tully believe you have been fighting this war on your own. That we Altairians and even the Ry'lians, with whom you have had minimal contact, have used your species in this conflict. What you were not aware of, Miles, is that the Ry'lians were going to participate in a campaign with us that we believed might have ended the war with the Orbots completely. Our strategic goal was to force them into surrender or wipe them out. Once they had been removed as a threat, the entire alliance could have turned our attention to the Zodarks and the lesser powers in their alliance and destroyed them. We had worked with the Ry'lians for nearly twenty of your Earth years to train the soldiers needed to capture their planets and build the ships needed to invade and defeat their navies. But this is not how things turned out. This, Miles, is why our government and military have not been very supportive of your new initiatives or proposals."

Hunt was about to speak in his own defense when Pandolly held a hand up to stop him. "Please, Miles, let me finish."

"You're right—I asked a question, I need to let you fully answer it." Hunt felt like he should have known this was happening. Perhaps if he'd spent more time leading the alliance council and less time traveling on the *Freedom*, he would have known that these kinds of issues were simmering below the surface.

Pandolly continued, "Miles, it is true that we Altairians have not fought many battles with you Earthers or the Prims during your brief participation in the war. This was not because we wanted to use you, um, how does your language describe it…as cannon fodder…I had to look that word up. I was told by Ambassador Chapman that people on Earth and within your military believed this was what we Altairians thought of your people. I want to apologize on behalf of all Altairians for allowing this perception to grow among your military. In retrospect, I now see this opinion has colored your military's view of us.

"This was not how we viewed your people or your contributions to the war. In fact, your military prowess was what allowed us to focus exclusively on our invasion plans against the Orbots. We knew we could count on your people to fight and defeat the Zodarks with minimal help from us. In hindsight, we should have made you aware of our invasion plans—that would have dispelled this belief that has taken root within your people and now sows division and mistrust between us. Had you known, then it is likely you would not have proposed a cease-fire in Alfheim. You simply did not know the bigger picture and how that decision likely changed the course of the new war the Emperor is pushing us to start."

Hunt sighed audibly in frustration at the frank admission. He was finally realizing the full impact of his decision and the rift it had caused between him and the Altairians. He was going to have to work at healing this rift.

Looking at Pandolly, Hunt said, "Thank you for sharing this. I understand now why your people are hesitant to move forward with many of the plans and strategies I've issued and been slow to implement them."

"Miles, our admiral's skepticism is also rooted in past attempts to do the same thing you are trying to do. Across many hundreds of years, many of these approaches have been tried before and failed. They are not convinced your approach will succeed when theirs did not. Keep in mind, our alliance has many different species in it. Not all of them get along. The Primords and the Ry'lians, for example, despise each other. They will not work together. It is the same with the Tully. They and the Ry'lians had, at one time, been mortal enemies and fought a few wars against each other. Now they find themselves in the same alliance, having to see each other at the alliance council. It took nearly seventy-five years to get them to speak civilly to each other during sessions. Trying to manage a growing, sprawling alliance like ours is not easy."

Hunt shook his head in amazement at what he was being told. He knew from his own conversations with the Tully and the Primords that they did not trust or like the Ry'lians. Hunt had never really had a problem with them. Then again, his interactions with them had been minimal.

"You will see, Miles. You may be the Viceroy, but trying to integrate multiple species, all with different technological levels and understandings, is not going to be as easy as demanding it be done. Creating an integrated alliance navy is going to be nearly impossible to accomplish overnight. I think in your language, you have a word that groups segments of years together—decades, I was told. Yes, it will take decades before such a force can be fully realized, but you are wanting this to be done instantly, before the next offensive. It simply does not work like that, Miles. Even now, your own people are struggling to implement the technology we have given you, let alone what the Emperor has given you—hence our admirals' wait-and-see approach to this unified alliance fleet you have proposed."

For years before the war had ended, Hunt had been advocating for the Altairians to help create a series of standardized warships the alliance members could use. This would make coordinating ship tactics during the heat of battle more efficient and lead to a more streamlined logistical support system. Going into battle with a hodgepodge of human warships plus Prim, Altairian, Tully, Ry'lian, and now Gallentine ships, all with different capabilities, made it nearly impossible to coordinate their efforts during a large battle. Now that he was the Viceroy, his suggestions were becoming policy, not merely ideas.

Looking at Pandolly, Hunt steepled his fingers. "Hmm—OK, you've brought up some fair points. I can understand their skepticism and I've clearly done a poor job myself in understanding this problem and addressing it. I own that, that's something I need to fix." Hunt then placed his hands flat on his legs as he leaned forward. "Pandolly, what I need you to convey to your counterparts is this—I won't tolerate intentional foot-dragging or sabotaging the implementation of my directives from them or anyone else in the alliance. I want to ask you something and I need an honest answer. Do you believe the shipyards are slowing production of these alliance warships because they're short on materials, or do you believe they have been given guidance to deliberately slow things down?"

Pandolly didn't reply right away. Hunt knew he had just placed him in a tough spot. Still, he needed to know what the holdup was.

"Viceroy, I think this is a complicated question that has several answers. The yards are taking the basic versions of warships we helped your people build—the frigates, cruisers, battleships, and even the star carriers. Then they are transitioning the interiors and operations of the warships to meet the varied needs and requirements of the Prims, Tully, Ry'lians, and other alliance members. Despite the vast automation throughout the ships, this is still not an easy task. My understanding is that the shipyards are working on these new warships as quickly as they can. It will still take years before many of them are completed. Then it will take time to get the crews trained and ready to use them. My humble suggestion, Viceroy, is to develop some patience and allow this process to move along at a natural pace."

Hunt bit his lower lip as his face pouted. Pandolly was likely right, of course. But patience was not one of his strong suits. It was a character trait he was continually learning how to master.

Conceding the point, Hunt moved on. "Pandolly, as you know, my people are still looking to learn as much as we can about the Orbots and Zodarks. We're interested in knowledge about their culture, history, politics, military, pretty much everything you can think of. Do the Altairians possess any medical journals, histories, or anything like this about the Orbots and Zodarks that my people might be able to obtain that can further our knowledge of these species?"

"As a matter of fact, yes. I will have a detailed summary of everything we have accumulated about their species sent to your office immediately," Pandolly said before he paused briefly. "If I may, I was asked to inquire with you to see if it might be possible for our government to obtain more work and residency visas for our people to live on Earth and your other colonies?"

"That is a good question, but this falls outside of my authority. I may be the Viceroy, but I'm trying not to wade into the domestic affairs of the individual races. I'll bring this up directly with Chancellor Luca along with my own recommendation to allow for more visas."

"Thank you, that would be helpful. If I can ask, why do you believe there is some hesitation in allowing for more alien immigration to Earth and your other colonies?" Pandolly inquired. "We have not placed any limitations on the number of humans who can live and work within our territory."

"That's a complicated question, Pandolly. Please keep in mind, eighteen years ago, we humans had never encountered an alien race before, let alone the more than a dozen that we know of so far," Hunt began. "Our government is doing its best to educate and inform our citizens about the friendly and nonfriendly alien species. Some of our people have not taken well to having aliens living on our planet or our newly acquired colonies. Fortunately, this is a very small fringe element of our society. Still, we want to make sure any alliance member citizens are treated fairly. Let me find out if there are certain regions or cities that might be able to handle more Altairians settling in them than other regions."

"Viceroy, before our meeting ends, I was asked to inquire about two other items. The first is the Zodarks' breach of the peace agreement governing the planet Alfheim."

"All right, what is your question about Alfheim? Let me speak to that point first before you ask your second question," Hunt replied. He'd had a feeling this issue and likely the terrorist attacks happening on Earth would come up before their meeting ended.

"Miles, King Grigdolly and our other military leaders would like to know what the Republic is going to do in response to the Zodarks' latest acts of aggression. Not that long ago, the Zodarks began launching a series of complex attacks on Alfheim. The terms of the neutrality agreement governing the partition of Alfheim are simple: if one side breaks the agreement, then their continued claim to the planet is null and void. They lose the right to remain on the planet and can be forcibly removed without triggering a restart of the war between our two alliances. What our people want to know is will the Republic enforce the consequences for these violations and move to evict the Zodarks and Orbots from the planet? Are your people moving to enforce the terms of the treaty?"

"That is a good question, Pandolly. It deserves an honest answer. As you know, I am not the ruler of the Republic. I am traveling to the Republic soon to meet with our leaders. I will bring this up to them and get an official government response. Until I have that for you, please, ask me your second question. This way I can provide your people with a full response when I return."

"Yes, that would be good. The second question is about a series of terrorist attacks occurring on Earth. Do you have any information about what is going on and when this matter will be brought under control?"

Hunt grimaced at the question now that it had been formally asked. "I was recently informed about them as well. Obviously, this is a sensitive matter the Republic is trying to handle internally. From what I've been told, it looks like it may have been carried out by the Sumerian Mukhabarat organization."

Pandolly let the information hang there for a moment before responding. "Viceroy, the Zodarks are an insidious species. The Sumerian secret police have been a highly groomed, highly trained force they have cultivated and mentored for hundreds of years. The police state they enforced on Sumer was not kind. I fear the Zodarks have now unleashed this force on your own people. You would do well to hunt them down quickly before they are able to spread further into your society and burrow themselves within it. Once that happens, you'll be dealing with these kinds of attacks on a regular basis."

Hunt sighed at the comment. He had the same feelings. Still, he had too many unanswered questions about the Sumerians. "Pandolly, if I may—we liberated the Sumerians from the Zodarks. Why would this secret police continue to work for them and obey their orders now that they're free of the Zodarks?"

Pandolly canted his head to the side as he countered, "Viceroy, you may believe you have liberated the Sumerians, and you have in the physical sense. But you have not freed them mentally or emotionally from the Zodarks just yet. Not everyone on Sumer believes they are truly free from them, despite whatever assurances you may have given them.

The Mukhabarat are likely reminding the people that the Zodarks will return."

Pausing for a moment, Pandolly continued, "Miles, there is something more you need to understand. Nearly all the Mukhabarat members train extensively across the Zodark Empire, including on other Zodark-controlled human worlds. It would not surprise me to learn that many of them have families on these other planets. Their ties to the Zodarks are not going to be easily severed. You will have to hunt them down and eliminate them. If you do not, they will only entrench themselves in your society. In fact, I would not be surprised if the Zodarks had tasked them with mapping out the location of Earth and all your important military and industrial centers. If they have, then when the Zodarks restart the war, they will know exactly where and how to attack the Republic and the rest of the alliance."

Sitting back in his chair, Hunt suddenly felt sick to his stomach. *What have we done, allowing Sumer to join the Republic?* he asked himself. *I've allowed the Trojans to roll their wooden horse right into the heart of our empire...*

Chapter 10
Digging Deeper

Archaeological Dig Site
Alpha Centauri

"Well, Dr. Katō, you sure do know how to make an offer I can't refuse," said Dr. Audrey Lancaster. "You must have some serious pull, because after thirty seconds on the phone with you, I've been given indefinite leave to spend as much time as I want on this project."

"Please, call me Sakura. I have a feeling we'll be working together quite a bit."

"OK, Sakura." She stepped to the side and lowered her voice. "Just so you know, I did reach out to Viceroy Hunt for the work that was previously done on the Humtar language. Apparently those files are highly classified, though, and we will be lucky if we ever get a chance to see them. We're going to have to go about this the old-fashioned way," she explained.

"Well, I hear you're the best," Sakura countered.

Audrey's mouth curled into a half smile. "So, how about you show me what we're working with?" she suggested.

"Right this way."

The two women walked down to the entrance of the newly unearthed Humtar building. As they prepared to cross the threshold, Audrey took a deep breath in and closed her eyes for a second. When she opened them, she let out a low whistle. "Well, this is going to be fun."

She walked around without saying anything for a while, just taking it all in. When she reached one of the walls with some of the diagrams, she stopped and tilted her head to the side.

After a moment, Sakura couldn't hold back her curiosity any longer. "I'm sorry to interrupt your train of thought, but I really want to know what's going through your head right now."

"Well, you know how the Japanese have two alphabets, hiragana and katakana, in addition to the Chinese-derived pictograms called kanji?"

"Yes..."

"Well, alphabets morph over time," Audrey explained. "If you give a cursory look to Proto-Sinaitic script and Modern Hebrew, you might not initially see them as related, but they are."

"I'm sorry, but I'm not following you," Sakura replied.

"Yeah, it's hard for me to distill this all into a short explanation, but I think I'm seeing connections between these Humtar writings and the Sumerian language. They aren't the same, but I'm almost certain my software will be able to decode a significant portion of it."

"So, is there anything we can do to help?" asked Sakura.

"Yes, we need to upload every available language input we can into my system. Have you tried to access any of the panels or screens?" Audrey inquired.

"No, we were waiting for you."

"All right—well, then, I think it's time to see what happens. What do you think?" Audrey asked with a wink.

"Hell yeah," replied Sakura.

Audrey laughed. The two of them walked over to the large metal table situated in what might have been a conference room. "Let's get a couple of different people ready to record with their Qpads before we do anything," Audrey directed. "Sometimes a different angle can really make a difference."

Sakura and Jack readied themselves at opposite ends of the table and nodded when they were in position.

"Here goes," said Audrey.

She reached out a hand and touched the table. It lit up like a Christmas tree. Around the spaces where each person would have sat, there were several lines of the Humtar language.

"I think this is a menu," Audrey observed. "Let's see what happens when I click on one of these items."

A 3-D map of the facility was displayed before her. Most of the areas were indicated in blue. The room where the power supply was located was framed in gray, as if it were an empty box that needed to be uncovered. There was a third floor below the two that had already been uncovered; part of that area was marked in blue, some in gray like the power source room, and one room had three yellow indicators in it.

"What do you think that means?" asked Sakura, pointing.

"I don't know yet," Audrey admitted, "but zoom in on any text, and then let's see what other data we can collect."

After finishing the collection on the map, Audrey moved to the next item, which had various color-coded lines of text.

"If I had to hazard a guess, I'd say this was probably their supply inventory. Several of the items are in flashing orange, and my guess is they were either out of certain things or running low. The blue items are probably the ones that are within a normal range, and this gray box at the bottom is probably classified information I would need a pass code to unlock."

"You figured all that out from a few colors?" asked Sakura in amazement.

"Well, I'm seeing patterns," Audrey replied. "I can't really read it yet exactly, but you know how if you learn Spanish, you might be able to read some Italian? It's the same concept. The computer will do a much better job than I will."

In the next line item, a star map was pulled up. Various planets had notes near them, but they were all in black. Audrey tried clicking on one of the notes, and a message popped up, but they didn't understand what it meant yet and had to move on.

Audrey thought that the next item in the menu used to be a communications interface, but of course there was no one to communicate with.

Finally, there was just a screen with a flashing set of squares. "I think it's asking for a pass code," Audrey remarked.

"I wonder if it's the same one that opens the door to the power source room," said Jack.

"I guess we'll have to find out."

****

Hours went by collecting data. It was tedious and slow. There were data pads near each workstation, but the information available without a pass code was pretty limited. There were a handful of workbags in the office, filled with the kinds of things you might take with you if you had to be at the office for a while: changes of clothing, shoes, and small containers that Audrey figured must have held food or toiletry items at one time.

"Let's put those in biohazard bags, just in case," Sakura remarked.

Jack chuckled.

"She's not wrong, though," Audrey shot back in defense. "We can analyze this at the lab."

Jack marveled at the shoes, which were a shiny off-white cross between a sneaker and a boot. "I have no idea what these are made of," he remarked. "They're over a thousand years old, and they look brand-new. And these fasteners seem like they adjust themselves."

Sakura held up a jacket in wonder. "The fabric is still in good condition. I've never seen fabric last this long at a dig site before. The air filtration system must have been extremely powerful, and the seals on the doors would have had to be completely airtight."

On the sleeve of the jacket was some kind of marking. Sakura took a picture of it with her Qpad. There was also some kind of button affixed to it with a Humtar word printed on it, faded colors behind the lettering.

Audrey waved to get their attention. "Check this out," she exclaimed. One of the screens near the desk appeared to activate a holographic photo album.

"Oh my God," whispered Sakura. "They had digital frames even back then."

Images of a man were displayed with various other Humtars. "I think this is his family," said Jack when he saw a photo of the man with a woman and two small children. "This is incredible, they really do look just like us."

They watched the images with rapt attention until they repeated. Sakura noticed that in the photo with his children, the little boy was wearing a button just like the one on the jacket she'd found. She wondered in fascination if this little handmade adornment had been a school craft project.

They continued on, cataloging everything they could access, from the charts to the cafeteria. Finally, they reached a stopping point.

"I think we can call it a day," Audrey announced. "Send everything you have to me, and we'll let the computers do their thing. Time to get some rest."

****

Next Day
Archaeological Dig Site
Alpha Centauri

Dr. Audrey Lancaster was extremely chipper as she approached Dr. Katō Sakura and Jack Walker. "So, do you want the good news, or the really good news?" she asked.

"Dealer's choice," Sakura replied with a laugh.

"First, the software was able to translate the vast majority of the text available to us. As I suspected, the Humtar and Sumerian languages are related."

"And the really good news?" asked Jack.

"I have a few very good guesses for some passwords."

"Really?" Sakura pressed. "How in the world did you manage that?"

"The language software looks for patterns, but it also recognizes elements of human psychology. We have a tendency to use something that's connected to us in some way when we create a password. The software examined all the personal items of any significance, and based on that information, I have about twenty word and number combinations that seem to be the most logical choices."

"Wow," Jack remarked. "Well, what should we unlock first, Sakura?" he asked, turning to her with a wry smile.

"Let's see if we can't make it into the power room," she replied.
****

A few moments went by, and the first several pass code combinations yielded no results—Sakura was starting to grow nervous. She reached for Jack's hand as Audrey continued her work, waiting with bated breath.

And then, miraculously, the door opened, just as easily as the front door had when she'd first discovered it.

Jack walked into the enormous room, and his jaw dropped. There was a bright window along a cylinder in the middle. Inside were brightly glowing crystals. "I have absolutely no idea what this thing is, or how it works," he admitted.

"Well, I guess we'll have to bring in the experts on this," Audrey remarked. "Maybe the Sumerians or the Gallentines can shed some light on it."

"I think we're going to have to collect what we can and then send it off to Dr. Katherine Johnson," said Sakura. "This all might end up being highly classified information at the end of the day."

"Good point," Audrey admitted. "Well, do you want to see if this code gets us in downstairs?"

"Definitely."

A few minutes later, after yet another security sweep, they were climbing the ladder down to the third and final floor below.

The rooms that had been marked off in gray definitely appeared to be laboratories of some kind, although they would have to wait on some further analysis from the computer to fully understand what all the equipment was and what was being researched.

One room remained. The door opened without a code. Two rows of five beds filled the room, spaced out with small spaces for personal belongings.

"Is that…?" asked Audrey, horrified. "Are those…?"

"Mummies," Jack finished.

"Yes," said Sakura matter-of-factly. "We have found ourselves three mummies."

****

Governor's Office
New London, Alpha

Yani stared at the attaché officer, a colonel in the Republic Army. His dislike for the man only grew the more they talked, or rather, the more he kept giving Yani the runaround.

"Colonel, you're saying that, despite being the Governor, I don't have a need to know, so therefore you can't let me access information on why this dig site is off-limits and classified?"

With a smug smile, the colonel nodded. "That about sums it up, Governor."

Yani canted his head to the side; he wasn't done yet. "OK, fair enough. Since we don't have a need to know, according to you, here's our need to know. Unless I'm given a reason why that location is off-limits, we're going to continue building our hyperloop line through that area and we're going to proceed with building the next housing spoke that happens to encompass part of that area. How's that for your need to know?"

The smug look left the man's face. The colonel blushed slightly. He obviously didn't like the civilians being back in charge and not the military. *Well, he'll just have to get over it*, Yani thought. The war was over and so was martial law. Civilian authority was back.

Attempting to regain his composure, the colonel replied, "All I have been told, Governor, is that some sort of alien artifact was discovered at the dig site. I honestly don't know more than that. What I was told in no uncertain terms was that neither I nor any of my garrison on the planet are allowed anywhere near there. If I'm not allowed near it, I can guarantee that you won't be either."

Now Yani's interest was piqued. *Why'd he have to put it like that?* Yani wondered. "Colonel, if you and your men aren't allowed to protect it or see what's there, who is guarding it and what's to stop any of us from venturing out there to look for ourselves?"

The self-assured look returned as the colonel responded, "A company of Deltas are camped out there, and so is an entire battalion of C100 combat synthetics. Whatever they found, they don't want anyone seeing or knowing about it. Maybe it's nothing, maybe it's a holdover from the war. What I do know is this—if you try to venture out there, you'd be lucky if they only stop you. I'd wager those killing machines have shoot-to-kill orders if you breach whatever perimeter they've been assigned to protect. That's how those toasters work—I saw them in plenty of action, killing Zodarks. You don't want to cross those machines, Governor."

Bollocks. We're going to have to change this entire housing development now. War's over and the military still runs the show, Yani stewed. He dismissed the attaché; there wasn't anything left to talk about. *This isn't over…*

Chapter 11
Spies Like Us

Space Command
Republic Headquarters
Jacksonville, Arkansas
Earth, Sol System

"Stand by for final approach," announced the pilot flying the blacked-out Type-003 frigate.

The sleek obsidian warship settled near a parking ramp near the Special Forces hangars. It wasn't very often one of the highly classified and rare 003 models touched down on Earth. Its presence, even in the wee hours of the morning as the dawn was starting to break, had attracted more attention than the JSOC operators had intended.

As the ship settled on the ramp, Lieutenant Hosni said, "You really didn't need to come, sir. I think Bates's letter would have been all the cover and support we needed."

Major Brian Royce looked at his top lieutenant. "You're right. I have absolute confidence in your abilities and know you'll leverage Bates's letter appropriately. I decided at the last minute to join you to follow up on a potential lead on the John Glenn. It's likely nothing, but the tip came from an old Delta buddy, so I thought it was worth checking out."

Now Hosni was intrigued. He'd assumed the major had tagged along to provide some overwatch and cover for him if he got in trouble. But a lead on the John Glenn—now that was big stuff if it panned out.

"Ah, that's good to know, sir. I was hoping we hadn't done anything to bring into question our ability to handle this, ah…situation with the marshals."

Smiling at Hosni, Royce countered confidently, "You have my complete and utmost trust until you do something to lose it. I have no doubt in my mind about you or your team's ability to handle this mission. I fully anticipate you'll reacquire the leads our beloved marshal service so lovingly blew up for us."

The sarcasm from Royce's comment wasn't lost on anyone. Several people soon joined in on the ribbing at the marshals' expense.

"Ha, that's one way to call what those clowns did," heckled one of the operators.

"Damn amateur hour if you ask me," mocked another.

"Not only did they blow the operation, they've had fourteen bombings in a week and still no leads," another chided angrily.

"Well, boys and girls, that's why we're here," said Royce. "Time to clean this situation up and reacquire the targets. So let's go ahead and get everyone suited up in your armor and the rest of your gear. Keep your visors in one-way mode as well. I don't want one being able to ID who arrived on this ship or what we're likely here to do. Head straight for the JSOC compound. We'll store our kits and gear there and go plainclothes from here on out unless you hear otherwise from Lieutenant Hosni here or myself. Got it?"

"Hooah," came the proverbial rally cry.

Royce stood and looked at them all. "I largely won't be involved in what you guys are doing. But keep in mind, for this op, you guys are gray men. You're shadows that don't appear unless you have to. This city is crawling with spies: marshals, Altairians, Tully, Prims, and of course the Mukhabarat. Never forget, you're always being watched. Blending into the background and becoming just another face in a sea of faces is the name of the game. You only kit up in your armor suits when it's time to bring our war faces out. Listen to Hosni. He knows what he's doing. Hooah?"

"Hooah!"

"Good, now get off this ship and start earning your pay," Royce said. He motioned for Hosni to stay behind for a second. When the others were out of earshot, he said softly, "If you run into trouble, do not hesitate to contact me. I'll drop whatever I'm doing to get back here. This isn't like the war, when nothing was off-limits. Since it ended, Earth…is behind enemy lines for us. Forbidden territory. Bates's letter will be the only thing standing between you and the marshals should they discover your guys. The only way you can be here is in an official liaison role. That's why it's imperative they only know about *your* presence here. This means you're going to have to place a lot of trust in your platoon sergeant. Trust him; trust his instincts. He won't lead you astray."

Hosni nodded grimly. He knew what the stakes were. His last mission on Earth had taught him that.

As the operators exited the frigate in their exo-combat suits and gear, a ground chief walked up to them, waving his hands to get their attention. "Hey, hold up there, hotshots. Someone's going to need to explain to me why a Spec Ops ship just landed on my ramp without prior authorization."

Using his neurolink, Royce told the others to ignore the man and continue to the compound. He'd handle the bureaucrat.

Stopping his stride, Major Royce turned around to look at the lieutenant commander from base ops. He took a step toward the man, towering at least six inches over him. Keeping his visor shade in its one-way view mode, he kept his face hidden as he handed the man a data pad. "Commander, I think you'll see our paperwork is in order. If you have any further questions, there's a point of contact you can reach out to." The POC was Major General Alfred Bates, JSOC Deputy Commander.

The man took the pad, stuttering for a second as he quickly looked it over. He sheepishly stammered, "Ah, thank you for this. But who are you guys?"

"That's a question you aren't allowed to ask. That'll be all, Commander. Thank you for assisting our flight crew with whatever they may need." Without a further word, Royce turned on his heel and walked away, beaming from ear to ear.

"Damn Fleeters," he mumbled under his breath.
■■■

JSOC Headquarters

Lieutenant General John Reiker had taken over command of Joint Special Operations Command or JSOC just as the war had ended. Most SOF officers would be thrilled to take command of the secretive yet highly sought-after position—especially now that the war had ended. But not Reiker. Unlike those officers, he knew he'd just been handed a pile of crap and was being told to eat it with a smile. With the new rules for how SOF would have to operate in Sol, his hands were being tied just as he was being tasked with developing a critically important mission that would necessitate the use of SOF operators inside Sol. With the war over, martial law had ended. The politicians wanted to rein in the military, at least inside Sol. There was a big effort to return life to a semblance of normalcy after fourteen years of war.

Not ready to retire or give up when facing a unique challenge, Reiker had managed to create a soft workaround with the newly created Interstellar Marshals Service. That was where Bates and Task Force Orange came into play.

The IMS, in addition to becoming the new law enforcement agency across the Republic, had somehow gotten saddled with creating a domestic spy agency. Prior to the passage of Senate Rule 902, the Republic Intelligence Service or RI for short had covered both foreign and domestic surveillance and countersurveillance activities. When a more direct or heavy-handed approach was needed, they'd turn to JSOC: the secretive group within the Special Forces community, specifically the intelligence support activity group otherwise known as Task Force Orange.

The challenge for the marshals was that they lacked experience working with the allies within the alliance and performing this kind of covert and, at times, aggressive kind of intelligence work. Their inexperience made them clumsy, often leading them to be discovered by the very people they were supposed to watch.

This growing embarrassment created what Reiker liked to call "a unique opportunity to circumvent some troublesome rules." Through an unofficial drug deal of sorts, the IMS agreed to accept liaison help from JSOC if and when the need should arise. The IMS was gaining access to surveillance tools and expertise they didn't have, and JSOC was able to circumvent the Senate rules governing military intelligence activity within Sol. It was one thing to have millions of uniformed soldiers spread across Sol. What the Senate didn't want was Special Forces gray and black teams running around, causing trouble with the new alliance immigrants arriving by the millions each month.

It was now 0700 hours, and standing in front of Reiker was a man carrying orders that represented trouble to this newly established partnership with the IMS. In all his wisdom, that damn old goat Bates had authorized a covert capture-kill team to do exactly what they were forbidden to do. Then again, after the recent string of terror attacks, something had to be done.

Holding the tablet with the mission op order and details, Reiker looked up at the lieutenant standing in front of his desk, still at attention.

"At ease, Lieutenant. Take a seat."

"Yes, sir," Lieutenant Hosni responded as he sat down opposite the general. Not knowing what to say, Hosni offered naively, "I believe everything is in order and clearly spelled out."

Staring daggers back at him, Reiker didn't say anything for a second. "No kidding, Lieutenant. Anything else you want to tell me I don't already know?"

Hosni's cheeks turned beet red. He gulped and shook his head ever so slightly.

"Good. I've been at this game since decades before you were born, Lieutenant. Al has made a compelling case to justify this mission. But the situation here on Earth is a bit more complicated than I believe he's aware of."

A brief silence settled over the room as Reiker looked over the tablet and read it again, then placed it back down. "OK, Lieutenant. We're going to go along with Al's op order. But I'm going to modify a few things, make some introductions for you with the IMS, and then I'm going to watch you like a hawk to make sure you don't mess things up. Got me?"

Hosni gulped again and nodded. Reiker knew there were all kinds of stories circulating about his time as an OG badass from the days of America. But it was a fact that one screwup with him watching you and your career would go down the toilet, at least in the SOF world.

Steeling his nerves, Hosni asked, "How would you like me to proceed, and how would you like my team to begin our infiltration and surveillance operation?"

Shaking his head, Reiker said, "Cocky little bugger, aren't you?"

Hosni sat up a little straighter. "Sir, you know my file. I used to be a slave to a Zodark NOS. They don't tolerate hesitation and they require complete obedience."

Reiker laughed briefly before shaking his head. "Damn. I think I'm going to start liking you after all, Lieutenant. Maybe there's a place for you in JSOC. You know we're the elite of the elite. You don't apply to get in. You're handpicked. You're here because I respect the hell out of Brian Royce—best damn operator in SOF. Don't screw this up for me or Brian. Got it?"

"Yes, sir!"

"All right, here's what's going to happen. Hang out in the team room with your guys. Brief what you want and put together your plan for how they'll support you in your liaising with the marshals. I'm going to work on getting us a meeting with the Director, and we'll begin our delicate dance of being here while not being here, if you know what I mean."

■■■

John Glenn Orbital Station
Earth Orbit, Sol System

Once Royce had dropped his gear in the team room, he changed into civilian clothes and swapped out his Special Forces ID for his newly updated credentials that read Republic Intelligence. These credentials were still tied to the legend he'd originally operated under prior to being blackballed from JSOC, way before the war with the Zodarks. It was still intact despite him having not used it in nearly twenty years. His intelligence file showed he'd been working on a lot of black projects with more language that said "above your pay grade" to anyone who tried to ask around.

Strapping a compact blaster to the inside of his trousers, Royce left his shirt untucked to further conceal the weapon while making it readily available should he need it. Standing in front of a mirror, Royce had to admit, he looked jacked from years of physical training and the augmentations his body had been given. He didn't look like the kind of guy you wanted to pick a fight with in a dark alley. It only added to his legend and kept the wrong people from asking too much about him.

Once he'd flagged a Tesla hover taxi to take him off base, Royce directed the autonomous driver to take him straight to the hyperloop station downtown. The ride gave him a chance to see how the city had grown and changed over the last few years. No matter how many times he'd seen these armies of construction Synths crawling over the skyscrapers and towers, it was still amazing. The speed at which they worked was simply incredible. The Republic's new capital wasn't on par with New Eden's capital, the Emerald City, which had grown into a megacity unlike anything within the Republic. However, at this rate, it might not take many more years to catch up.

"We'll reach Grand Central in five minutes," the humanoid driver informed him.

"Thank you," Royce said before realizing he was thanking a machine. It didn't reply; it wasn't programmed to do more than receive instructions and drive.

The humanoid driver sitting in the front seat wasn't a true synthetic like the ones Walburg Industries built. The Tesla autonomous drivers essentially had a human-like upper body to give the appearance of a person driving the vehicle, while in reality, the vehicle's AI leveraged all the complex sensors and maps that drove the vehicle.

Royce leaned back in his seat, observing the vehicles and people passing by. He'd spent so much of the last thirty years in Special Forces, he'd hardly had time to see how much normal daily life had changed. The blinding speed with which synthetic humanoids had replaced human workers was incredible. It had started out with just a few jobs, easy ones that could be automated away. Steadily, that had grown into more complicated jobs as the Ais' ability to learn and master tasks had improved.

There were still plenty of human jobs a Synth couldn't or wouldn't be allowed to do—how much longer that would last was anyone's guess. The damn Synths were just more efficient than human workers. Royce had been told the biggest drawback to expanded use of the Synths was their inability to operate beyond their programmed limitations. Royce's concern was the possibility of a war between humans and the AI, like they had fought some eighty years earlier. That war had nearly ended humanity. The thought sent a shiver down his spine.

The taxi changed lanes as it approached the station. Once it came to a halt and parked, Royce debited the credits from his burner card and exited. Standing on the sidewalk, he checked his Qpad for the anonymous message he'd received as his taxi had approached the station. Transferring the message to his neurolink, he pocketed his device and headed in.

The newly built Grand Central was an engineering marvel. The station had multiple hyperloop platforms that connected travelers to other transportation hubs, letting them reach nearly every major city on Earth. For travel inside the city, there was another set of platforms connecting the city tram system to most buildings.

Royce surveyed the station as he walked in, looking for the sign that would lead him to the storage lockers. Finding it, he made his way toward the locker facilities and located the unit he was after. Using his neurolink, he entered the pass code, opening the unit to see the items inside waiting for him. He grabbed the two burner credit cards, noticing they had the name of his assumed legend on them. Pulling his Qpad out, he linked the cards to the device. This would ensure his legend had plenty of money and the ability to transact as needed. Then he grabbed the note. It was on one of those thick papers that allowed you to encrypt the message on it. On the right corner of the note was a semivisible X. Placing his thumb on the X and holding it there, Royce watched as the paper changed color and a message appeared.

"Meet me at the X, 1900 hours sharp."

Looking at the internal clock his PA brought up, Royce saw he had twelve hours.

Walking out of the storage area, he bent and destroyed the burner card he'd used with the taxi. After purchasing a cinnamon roll with a new card on his way to the ticketing kiosk, he tossed the destroyed card with the trash from his cinnamon-sugar rush and looked to get a ticket to the John Glenn in orbit.

The ticketing kiosks were nice. Royce entered where he wanted to go and how fast he wanted to get there and poof, it gave him a couple of options to choose from. Royce entered the John Glenn and selected urgent, and a ticket for a commercial shuttle was suggested. It asked if he wanted to purchase a first-class or coach ticket. Remembering the phrase *gray man*, he selected coach. His electronic ticket was transferred to his Qpad.

∎∎∎

Six hours later, the shuttle docked at the John Glenn. Once the shuttle doors had been opened, the passengers dispersed quickly and went their separate ways. Travel between the orbital station and the Earth below had become as routine as taking a flight or hyperloop to another city. It was a regular occurrence at this point.

Finding his way to the cheapest hotel on the station, Royce checked himself in for a week at the Hilton. It wasn't the Ritz-Carlton, but there weren't any dive hotels on the station either.

"Here you go, sir, your room key," said the Hilton humanoid number 30247. "Will there be anything else I can do to increase the satisfaction of your stay?"

Royce bunched his eyebrows at the question. It kind of caught him off guard. "Actually, 30247, there is. I need to know if my plans were to change in a few days, could I extend my stay a few more weeks?"

Without looking down at a computer display, 30247 replied, "Unfortunately, your room is booked two days after your stay ends. There are also three separate wedding parties and a conference checking in, so the hotel will be fully booked. If you would like, I could place a room hold for you at the Marriott or the Ritz-Carlton if they have availability?"

"That would be great. Thank you, and have a good day," Royce said, smiling, though he didn't know why he'd thanked another humanoid. Chuckling to himself, he thought, *Jane's politeness is rubbing off on me.*

Reaching his room, he dropped his bag on the bed and emptied the contents. He'd traveled light. He fiddled for a moment with the bottom of the bag until it unlocked. Pulling the false bottom aside, he retrieved the four pieces that constituted the blaster. The shielded compartment that spoofed the scanners to appear to be a part of the bag was the only way to get it through security unless he declared his presence to the authorities. If he had to, he would. But until he knew why he'd been summoned to the John Glenn, the less people knew about him and why he was here, the better.

With his blaster reassembled, he tucked it in his trousers and headed off to the bar known as the X. He was a man on a mission, ready for the hunt. Soon, Royce would learn who the prey was—he only hoped it was a worthy adversary.

Chapter 12
Too Big to Fail

Interstellar Marshals Service
Higgins Federal Building
Jacksonville, Arkansas
Earth, Sol System

Reinhard Gehlen had been the top Senate candidate for the newly created postwar agency. Before the Altairians had forced the governments of Earth to merge, he'd had been the director of the only globally recognized independent law enforcement agency, Interpol, one of the few institutions to survive the last Great War. When the Greater European Union had merged with the Republic, he'd essentially stayed on in that role, only now his agency was backed by the Republic. When the war had ended, it had become clear Interpol had to expand not just beyond Earth but beyond Sol to the other colonies and worlds now under the Republic's control.

Recognizing the need for a new organization that could grow with the Republic and continue to serve its people and needs as it expanded further into space, Reinhard had proposed transforming Interpol into such an organization. That was when he'd conceived of the Interstellar Marshals Service. When he'd pitched the idea to a couple of senators, it had taken off. The Senate and the Chancellor had pounced on the idea, crafting Senate Rule 902 and transforming Interpol into the IMS.

Reinhard celebrated the transformation of his beloved agency. As he read deeper into Rule 902, he realized the IMS would not operate like previous interagency organizations. Instead, it would take on the intelligence roles previously held by Republic Intelligence and the Fleet's JSOC unit. It hadn't taken Reinhard long to realize his agency lacked the skills to assume these roles. The Senate had tasked the IMS with creating a domestic spying program focused on internal threats in the same way his counterparts at Republic Intelligence focused on external foreign threats.

Reinhard thought the RI program could be splintered off to seed his program. He also hoped they could retain some personnel to help them build this capability out. What he hadn't known at the time was how the intelligence service was collecting its data or how those operations were carried out.

That was when he'd learned they'd been relying on the small but incredibly capable unit called JSOC. They were an offshoot of Special Operations Command, handling the counterterrorism-counterespionage tasks for the intelligence service. The Unit, as it was sometimes called, handled the RI's dirty work, from capture-kill missions and interrogations to surveillance operations deep behind enemy lines or even among allied partners. As augmented supersoldiers, their skills and capabilities were unmatched by nonaugmented operatives, giving them a huge advantage.

The problems Reinhard faced as the head of this new organization were many. With no assistance from the RI, he had no idea how to create such a vast and complicated program from scratch. The RI wasn't going to detail off hundreds of their best people to help him build this program when their own postwar mission had grown exponentially. After he'd floundered for a year and suffered some high-profile embarrassments, Lieutenant General Reiker, the JSOC Commander, quietly reached out to have dinner. It was during this meeting that he'd pitched a workaround that might address both their needs.

The urgency of some sort of agreement came to a head when it was discovered how vast and deep the Zodarks' Sumerian spying program, the Mukhabarat, had become. When the Republic had liberated Sumer, the Mukhabarat had gone to ground and blended back into the public. Six months after the establishment of the new Sumerian government, the Mukhabarat had reemerged. With their newfound freedom of movement within the Republic and the alliance writ large, there was an immediate urgency to begin identifying who they were and what they were doing and seeing if they could be flipped. If they couldn't, then they had to be eliminated.

The more Reinhard learned about the true nature of the threat, the more overwhelmed and trapped he felt. He couldn't break the very Senate rules he was being expected to enforce; he also couldn't protect the Republic by ignoring the help he desperately needed. That was when they created a joint classified memorandum between the IMS and JSOC to create a liaison role until the IMS had a mature enough program to handle the threat. JSOC, via Task Force Orange, would help train and advise his people until they had an effective force that could handle this mission. That said, Reinhard wasn't about to turn a blind eye, breaking the rules to let them operate on his turf without supervision. The IMS was first and foremost a law enforcement agency. That meant people had certain rights that had to be protected even while they were being policed. This applied to JSOC, who was notorious for violating such rights through invasive surveillance tactics. If his agency wasn't failing so spectacularly in this mission right now, Reinhard wouldn't have even considered this deal with the devil. But if he didn't right the ship soon and stop these terrorist attacks, he'd be replaced by another director who could.

In six months, this drug deal was already starting to bear fruit. His agents, under guidance from a JSOC liaison, had uncovered half a dozen different spy rings from various allied worlds. With key operatives identified, it was just a matter of time until they uncovered everyone involved. Then a case built on evidence could be levied against the culprits and the spy ring eliminated along with its collaborators.

That was the plan—until eight days ago, when everything had blown up in their faces, literally. After uncovering a defense contractor stealing plans for a Republic battleship, they had started to surveil him to see what he was doing with the plans. After weeks of surveillance, he had finally met with someone—a figure that had set off alarm bells, a person whose identity was both too perfect and strangely limited. Until six years ago, that person had had no social media accounts, pictures, posts, or anything. He'd just suddenly appeared, which wasn't really possible given the interconnected world everyone lived in.

"What a mess we've found ourselves with these Sumerians. How can they still be so tied to these Zodarks after we liberated their planet?" Reinhard said aloud as he shook his head in frustration.

He had a meeting about this subject shortly. Frankly, at this point, he'd accept just about any kind of help he could get. Looking at his coffee cup, he stood and walked toward the replicator to get a refill. *I love that replicator*, he thought. At least something was there to cheer him up.

Thinking back to the mission that had blown up in their faces, Reinhard sighed. "I never should have agreed to that mission. Krzysztof was so sure it'd work," he muttered as he sat at his desk. Talking out loud to oneself might sound weird or crazy, but he found it helped him work through tough problems. Sometimes just hearing an idea spoken out loud could help him figure out if it was worth pursuing.

Looking back at the lead-up to that ambush, Reinhard chided himself for not adhering to the very rules and policies he'd put in place for operations just such as this one. Their JSOC rep had been able to verify that the person in question had arrived on Earth from Sumer two months prior. With this knowledge, he'd advised them that this individual was likely a Mukhabarat operative. What Reinhard and his chief spy found incredible was their liaison rep's ability to dismantle the suspect's cover and designate him a likely spy so quickly. He recommended the marshals keep them both under surveillance while he worked on getting a capture team to take the spy into custody once the suspect had led them to the rest of his cell.

While the liaison rep was off-world chasing down a possible lead connected to the suspect, an urgent tasking from Republic Intelligence had directed his office to coordinate with their rep to take him into custody immediately. He'd been told they had some information that led them to believe a domestic terror attack was imminent.

"If I hadn't let Krzysztof bypass our JSOC rep, this likely would have turned out differently," Reinhard said aloud.

When he'd called Krzysztof Waclawek, his spy chief, to his office and told him of the request and the possible terrorist attacks, Krzysztof had insisted they act on it immediately. He'd told him the team their JSOC rep had been helping to train was more than ready to handle this on their own, and he'd recommended grabbing the guy right away, while they had eyes on him, rather than waiting for their advisor to take charge of the situation and letting the military handle it.

Krzysztof had made a good case for letting his guys handle it. If it had worked, it would have been a huge PR boon for the marshals. In hindsight, Reinhard never should have gone along with it. Instead of having a PR win they could tout to the Senate, he had a high-profile slaughter of five agents during the evening rush hour. Worse, the target had escaped. Adding salt to the wound, the terrorist attacks they'd hoped to ward off had happened anyway. Less than sixteen hours after the botched apprehension, a series of bombings had rocked the capital. A total of fourteen bombings had hit the city over a five-day period of sheer terror for the millions of people in the city, unsure of what other locations might later be hit.

By the time the attacks had subsided, the government and people were on edge. People didn't know if it was safe to stop at a coffee shop or ride the hyperloop or the subways to work or get around the city. All told, two hundred and sixty-eight people had been killed, with nearly five times that number injured. If Reinhard didn't stop these attacks and soon, his agency might be brushed aside in favor of the military.

He sighed as he saw the time; his guest would be here momentarily. No sooner had he had that thought than a chime sounded. Looking at his office door, Reinhard was informed that General Reiker had arrived for their impromptu meeting. If he had to guess, the man was furious with him for blowing a major operation that might have thwarted the recent terrorist attacks.

Let's get this over with.

Speaking loudly, Reinhard called out, "Let General Reiker know he can come in. I'm ready to see him."

To his surprise, when the general came in, he had a much younger man accompanying him. Reinhard stood, walking around his desk to greet them, and then guided everyone toward a set of couches where he liked to conduct his meetings.

Breathing heavily, Reiker got right to the point. "Reinhard, I didn't come here to pick a fight with you or dress you down for your agents blowing this operation. What's done is done and the past can't be changed. Right now, what's critically important is that we reacquire the operative and move to disrupt any additional attacks they're planning. I obviously can't do this without your help, so I'd like to introduce you to someone I believe can help us accomplish it."

Reiker turned to face the man to his right. "This is Lieutenant Hosni. He's one of the best Delta Operators I've got, and he's uniquely qualified to take lead in hunting this group. Hosni is Sumerian. He was among the prisoners we liberated on Sumer some sixteen years ago. He was also part of the pathfinder group that infiltrated Sumer before we invaded. If anyone is going to understand how these Sumerian operatives think and act, it's going to be him. If you'll allow it, I'd like you to accept Hosni as our liaison rep for this operation. I think it also might be in both our best interests at this point if you let him lead this mission and direct your people as he sees fit to stop further attacks."

Reinhard nodded casually as he took in the information and looked Hosni over. He had that Sumerian look to him. Piercing dark eyes, dark hair, brownish-olive skin tone, and a slight Chaldean accent when he introduced himself.

"You want to send a Sumerian to hunt a Sumerian." It was more of a rhetorical statement. Reinhard sighed deeply, not seeing another alternative. In fact, it was kind of brilliant bringing in one of their own to hunt them. "You make a compelling argument, Reiker. One I can't easily dismiss. We have to stop these individuals swiftly, so I'll agree to this request. But under one condition."

Reiker and Hosni leaned in.

"It still has to be my people that ultimately bring this guy in," Reinhard insisted. "You can take lead in finding him, but my IMS agents need to apprehend them. After that, he's all yours. But if you can't flip him or he's no longer of value, then you need to hand him over so we can prosecute him. I know you may not see the merit in a prosecution, but in the eyes of the public, the Senate, and our allies, these kinds of prosecutions have meaning. In time, it'll become a deterrent to others who may try similar acts. Are we in agreement?"

Reiker turned to Hosni. "You think you can live with those rules?"

The Sumerian let slip a devilish smile. "Absolutely. When can I start the hunt?"

Reinhard stood, forcing the others to stand too, and extended his hand to Hosni. "How about right now? I'll walk you down to meet Krzysztof Waclawek. He's my spy chief, the head of our counterintelligence division. I'll let him know that for this case, he'll be working under your guidance. If you have a problem with any of my people, I want you to report it directly to me and General Reiker. No one else. Understood, Lieutenant?"

"Understood, sir. We'll nab this guy and get you a head for prosecution."

Reinhard liked Hosni's optimism. He seemed to grasp that this was as much about politics as it was national security. If this worked, then maybe he'd have found a possible permanent liaison rep. Time would tell.

Chapter 13
The X

The X
John Glenn Orbital Station
Earth Orbit, Sol System

Sitting at the bar, Royce took another bite of his half-pound bacon cheeseburger with all the trimmings. As he swallowed, he washed it all down with a cold beer and smiled like a man who'd just won the lottery. *God, I missed beef and thick-cut black peppercorn bacon*, he thought. Beef was a rarity on New Eden. There were the Andorran ranges, but for Royce, it just wasn't the same. New Eden had a small population of cattle that had been imported there, but it would take time to grow their herds before the price of *real* beef would come down. In general, food was cheap now that food replicators had been introduced. But sometimes, you just wanted the real thing, and the real thing was *rare* and *expensive*.

When he thought about the time, Royce's internal clock appeared. The meet time had arrived. Moments later, he received a neurolink ping from an old friend. If this had been a real hello and not a neurolink hello, his friend's thick southern drawl would have been unmistakable.

Damn, Brian. You look good. What's it been, nineteen years since you left the Unit? asked Drew.

Yeah, something like that, Royce answered. *Got stuck with that BS drill sergeant duty as penance for the Mars fiasco.*

Yeah, I remember that, Drew replied. *Shame how they blamed you for your team leader's screwup. Hell, none of us would have lived if it hadn't been for you and that idea about swapping our oxygen tanks for those prisoners we captured.*

Yeah, well, it's not like the leadership was going to accept the blame for things going sideways on a mission that didn't exist, Royce scoffed. *Whatever, Drew, it's led me to where I am now, so I can't complain too hard.*

True, true—hell, you're a damn war hero, Brian, Drew said. *Done got that Medal of Honor not once but twice. Our old squadron talked about you like you were a living legend back in the Unit before I left all that behind.*

Royce had to chuckle at that. He'd been a good operator back in those days. He'd also had a bit of an authority problem and a temper. He hadn't suffered fools well, and sometimes, fools were all you had to work with.

Well, enough about me, said Brian. *How's life on the outside, Drew?*

You know, that's the strangest thing, Brian. I thought it'd be different when I crossed over. Guess I should have known fellas in our line of work...well, you never really leave, do ya? I mean, the name signing your paycheck changes, but it's all the same money coming from the same pot.

Royce grunted at the blunt assessment. Drew Kanter always was the philosophical one on his old team. *Is the pay at least better? Tell me I have that to look forward to, Drew.*

Oh yeah, Brian, the RI treats me well, and the pay is substantially better, so I can't complain about that. The benefits are nice—you know, a credit card with no limits can be fun on vacation. In fact, when you're ready to hang that uniform up, you let me know. I'll put in a good word for ya with my peoples. Then you can come play soldier with me, wearing 511s instead and fancy clothes and all.

Royce had to stifle a laugh. Putting his burger down, he finally looked around the bar for Drew. He was eight seats down and opposite him on the other side of the bar as he nursed a beer of his own, pretending to be doing something on his Qpad, everyone else oblivious to the conversation they were having.

Well, I suppose we should get to it, Drew. I'm here and I got your message and the package—what do you have for me?

Aw, that's all the foreplay we get after all these years, Brian? OK, if it has to be that way, I guess we should start talking about why you've been summoned. Let's say we've got something that's piqued our interest. It might be nothing, but it might be something. But before I tell you more, let's ditch this joint. Let's go back to your place, have ourselves a little talk, maybe establish a little quiet place of our own, ya know what I mean? Surely there couldn't possibly be more than two gray men walking around the John Glenn at the same time...could there?

Without saying another word, Drew downed the last of his beer and headed for the exit.

Damn, he's concerned there might be other spies nearby, Royce thought as Drew left the bar. *Well, this burger cost me a fortune, so I'm finishing it. He can wait another few bites.*

As Royce walked through the Hilton, the hotel's AI detected his presence. When he approached his hotel room, his door automatically unlocked, letting him walk in seamlessly. Unsurprisingly, Drew was already sitting at the table waiting for him.

"Thanks for coming, Brian. Let me get the device turned on."

Drew pulled a small black puck out of his pocket and placed it on the table between them. Once activated, it created a ten-foot electronic bubble that would be impervious to electronic surveillance, allowing them to share highly classified information without the fear of being discovered.

"What's the issue the vaunted *Intelligence Service* needs my help with?"

Smiling at the slight dig, Drew explained, "Oh, we don't need your help with it—we just thought we'd throw you orange guys a bone and let you play in your old yard again before Mama finds out."

They laughed, which broke the tension of the moment. Two old friends, uniting after nearly two decades.

"As I was saying," Drew resumed, his southern drawl amusing Royce, "a few months ago, we discovered a security incident at a sensitive government contracting company. You may have heard of them—some outfit called John Bentley Reactors. They provide the personnel that manage all the stations' reactor rooms across the Republic. They also build all the reactors for our warships. So you can imagine something going on there would catch our attention. It would appear a piece of foreign spyware has been detected on their email server during a routine surveillance sweep performed on their systems."

"Really? Was this something they alerted you guys to, or something you discovered on your own?"

Drew shrugged. "Does it really matter, Brian?"

Royce chuckled. *They must have had their own backdoor into JBR.* "OK, I'm intrigued. Tell me more; you know I like a good mystery."

"Hmm, indeed you do. See, I told my peoples you'd find this interesting. As it turns out, we're still trying to evaluate the depth of the breach. It would appear whoever inserted the software has likely obtained extensive credentialed access across the company at this point.

What we're doing now is trying to ascertain whose spyware this is and what they are doing with it."

"Any ideas on that front?"

"Not yet. It has some similarities to what we've seen on Sumer, so it's likely it's Mukhabarat. But it also has similarities with what we've seen with the Altairians, the Zodarks, the Primords, and the Orbots. If I was a wagerin' kind of man, I'd say it's possible the real culprit has laced their software with the fingerprints of others to mask who it really belongs to," Drew explained casually. "It's what I would do if I was running this kind of an operation, so why shouldn't we assume they are as well?"

Thinking about it, Royce started to run through a few ideas in his head. "Have you guys identified when the initial breach took place?"

"Ah, now that's the crux of the problem, Brian, and wouldn't you know it...that's why I've asked for your help."

Royce smirked at the subterfuge going on between him and Drew. They had been thick as thieves back in the day, when they'd both been part of Task Force Orange before the war.

Drew smiled as he explained, "As much as I want to dig into this myself, Brian, I simply do not have the time or ability to do so. Then I thought, well, my good friend Brian has a predilection for mysteries. That's when I thought we could rope you in on this. Ya see, when the war came to an end, our mission never slowed down—in fact, they grew our mission, and then Section 902 chopped us off at the knees. So as you can imagine, the espionage game has gotten rather unique and overly complicated. Hell, Brian, if you can believe it, what's happening at JBR is just one of a dozen similar incidents and threats we're trying to monitor.

"Obviously, I can't work them all, so I'm trying to prioritize the ones I can. This, however, needs a more hands-on approach than what I can provide. Hence why I reached out to you. I know we technically can't task you with this, but I'd like to know if this is something ya think you might wanna take on? I don't know what your current responsibilities are—maybe you're tapped out like me, but given your love for the enigmatic, I thought I'd ask."

Royce rubbed the bridge of his nose, thinking about it. "I'll be frank, Drew, this likely isn't something I can spend weeks or months being heavily involved in, personally. I could dig into it and see how serious it looks. If it really is a big problem, then I can assign additional assets on my end to run with it. If that's cool with you, then let me poke around JBR, see what I can find."

"See, I knew you were the right guy for this," said Drew. "Anticipating your response, I had some of our folks give your legend a good look. It's still intact, and we've made a few modifications to help cover some of your time during the war. I'd recommend checking some of those deets before you go snooping too far. If you need some help or want a modification, just let me know."

"I do see that. I looked over the changes on the shuttle here. It all looks good, should be easy enough for me to maintain. I'm assuming you want me to run with my old RI credentials—you know, since I'm technically not allowed to be here."

Drew laughed at the comment. "Oh, the complicated world the Senate made for us all, didn't they? I mean, wow, these politicians couldn't manage their way out of a paper bag. Yeah, use your RI credentials. If anyone investigates you, that should be enough to stop 'em, and it'll alert us so we can alert you. Now that that's settled, good luck, ma friend. Stay in touch if you find anything, will ya? I'm off to go solve the next problem."

When Drew left, Royce looked at the packet of information he'd sent him. The more he saw, the more he realized this was going to be a problem.

Whoa...this is bad...this is really *bad...*, he realized. This was the groundwork for something much bigger... *But what? An invasion?* Would the Zodarks really look to restart the war so soon?

Royce composed a short message to Major General Bates:

Al, this looks much worse than you thought. I need Lisa from the wizard shop. Tell her to meet me at the Hilton on the John Glenn. We've got our work cut out for us.

Chapter 14
Change of Command

RNS *Victory*
Naval Shipyard
Altairius Prime

Admiral Abigail Halsey was impressed. She'd just spent the last five days being given a thorough tour of and briefing on every section of the Republic's first star carrier. This was the warship the Altairians had been building for the Republic. Technically, it had been completed a few years ago. If Halsey or Hunt had had their way, it would have been used in the war. The Altairians, on the other hand, would not release the ship to the Republic until it had a fully functional and operational crew. *That* had taken a lot longer to sort out than it should have given the sheer amount of automation built into the ship.

Ironically, it was the automation that had taken so long to figure out. If a system broke, the crew needed the skills to fix the repair bots or do the repairs themselves. The crew assigned to a ship this advanced had to undergo years of difficult technical training—including preparatory training before they could even start learning how to maintain the ship. Once underway with a trained crew, the ship became a self-contained city, fully independent of any kind of logistical support.

Sitting on the couch in her quarters, Halsey had almost dozed off when a chime sounded, letting her know she had a visitor.

"Enter," she said aloud, letting the AI know to open the door.

A smile spread across her face when she saw Hunt. "Hi, Abi. It's good to see you in person again."

They hugged briefly, exchanging pleasantries.

"This…is an impressive ship, Abi. I'm really excited for you."

"It's incredible, Miles. What this ship will be able to do…it's going to be the flagship and backbone of the Republic."

"Agreed. That's also something I want to talk with you about," he said almost cryptically, motioning with his head for them to sit and talk.

"Why do I get a sense something bigger is going on?"

Hunt smiled at the comment. "Oh, Abi, something bigger is *always* going on. It's just some things actually require immediate attention while others can wait."

She nodded, waiting for him to explain more.

"You've heard about some of the terrorist attacks happening back home?"

"I did. I only learned of it the other day. News from home is a little slow to reach us this far away."

"The Altairians have been sharing some information with me about how the Zodark intelligence apparatus works, giving me some new insights into how the Sumerian secret police, the Mukhabarat, are likely being used and directed by their former masters."

Halsey raised an eyebrow at that. "You think the Zodarks are orchestrating these terrorist attacks in preparation for renewed hostilities?"

Hunt shook his head slightly. "Yes and no. First, I do not believe the Zodarks are going to launch an invasion in the near term. However, now that Sumer is an official Republic colony world, the Altairians believe the Zodarks are leveraging the Sumerians' newfound freedom of movement to establish cells across our territory and that of the rest of the alliance."

"Damn. I was hoping that old goat Walhoon was wrong. I thought it was fearmongering to say that the Zodarks would find a way to leverage their Mukhabarat spies to find Earth. I'll bet he's secretly giddy at being proven right. Please tell me you've got some secret squirrel plan up your sleeve to deal with?" she responded.

"Yeah, it's created a bit of a problem for us, especially after they pushed that Senate Rule 902 on us," Hunt admitted. "He really doesn't like having the military in so much control of every facet of the Republic."

Halsey grunted.

"I believe I may be able to get the Altairians to help us," Hunt continued. "They've been increasing their own surveillance of anyone that leaves Sumer or has recently traveled from Sumer to any of their own worlds. But that's not what I wanted to brief you on. I'd like the two of us to focus on the larger strategic picture of what's going on. When you leave in a few days, I'd like you to start thinking about how we can employ and use the *Victory* in a future battle with the Zodarks. Those new frigates and missile boats that debuted during the Sirius campaign caught us by surprise. We need to figure out what kind of fleet composition will work best in defending the *Victory* while still being able to leverage its full gamut of weaponry."

Halsey nodded. "You're right, Miles. Thankfully, Admiral Bailey agrees with you as well. We're making this a top priority. When I get back to Republic space, I'll start developing some new battlegroup compositions. We're finally starting to get a steady flow of warships coming out of the shipyards."

As the Director of Fleet Operations, Halsey was responsible for getting the Navy ready to fight the next war. She also had to make sure the fleet they had was strategically positioned across the Republic so it could respond to any incursions. It was a daunting task, one she frankly reveled in after having spent nearly a year on Sumer.

"Miles, when I return to Sol with the *Victory*, do you have a system in mind you'd like me to homeport her out of? I obviously won't be retaining command of her once I get back to Earth, but I can station her where you think she may be needed most."

"Hmm. OK, let's pull up some stargate maps and take a look."

The two of them talked for a few hours, looking at each of the stargates connecting Republic space to either Zodark space or nearby allied stargates that connected to Zodark space. The advantage the Republic generally had was that most of their colonies were in systems that didn't have direct stargate access. It was a dual-edged sword—they were better protected from the Zodarks and had more warning about an enemy fleet headed their way, but it took the Republic longer to get ships and soldiers sent where they needed to go. They had to travel through a lot more standard space as opposed to jumping from one gate to another like so many other allied and Zodark worlds could.

Eventually, they settled on homeporting the *Victory* out of the MOS or Mars Orbital Station. Two and a half years after the second battle of Sirius, Rear Admiral Fran McKee's *George Washington* battlegroup was nearly done with their battle damage repairs in Kita, at the Primords' shipyard facilities. A hundred-year basing deal had been reached with the Primords to let the Republic maintain the battlegroup in Kita. If Alfheim was invaded again, the *GW*'s battlegroup would be a few days away. If they had to rely solely on forces from Sol or Centaurus for help, then it would take two or three months to get reinforcements there. Alfheim was at the edge of Primord space, a long way from help if it was needed.

"Abi, before I leave, I wanted to ask you something about the older *Rook*-class ships."

"The *Rooks*? They're about as old as the *Voyager*. What do you want to know?"

"I know they're old ships, but I think there's a gap in our battlegroup composition that they could fill—a gap that was clearly identified during the fleet action in Sirius," Hunt began to explain. "That battle was the first time we really saw heavy use of attack fighters and bombers against our fleets. During my after-action analysis, it became clear we must address this. The Zodark and Orbot carriers overwhelmed us—they were saturating our ships' point-defense systems, keeping them from protecting us from their missiles and torpedoes. If we hadn't had the *Freedom* there with our Gallentine fighters, and the refitted *Rook* flak ships, it's very likely we would have lost that battle. I'm not sure what your plans are with the few remaining *Rooks* we have left, but I'd like to propose you consider converting the remaining ships into flak ships, then integrating them with the battlegroups. I think the concept of covering a ship with point-defense guns and having them screen for the battleships, cruisers, and troop assault ships proved decisive during the battle. What do you think about this?"

Halsey held a hand up for a second as she got up and walked to her desk. She retrieved a tablet and brought it over, handing it to Hunt.

"I'm way ahead of you, Miles. We're going to phase the *Rooks* out and place them in the reserve fleet once we get these little bad boys completed. When the war ended, I asked Blue Origin if they could come up with a faster, better-equipped version of the same ship that wouldn't take a decade to design and build and could rely heavily on automation instead of a large manned crew."

Flipping through the schematics, Hunt was thoroughly impressed by what he was seeing. "This is incredible, Abi. If I'm understanding this, the idea they proposed was to take the Type-003 frigates and turn them into flak ships?"

Nodding, Halsey explained, "It is. I wasn't sure at first, especially with the limited armament of the original ship. Given the size difference between the 003s and the *Rooks*, this new ship would have roughly half the number of PDGs the *Rooks* carried. To offset the difference in PDGs, they're incorporating ten duel-barreled turbo laser turrets and four missile launchers. The laser turrets will allow the flak ships to engage enemy fighters and missiles much faster and from further out than our current PDGs can. To support the increase in energy demand for the laser turrets, they're removing the added troop compartment the Special Forces soldiers would normally use. This will double the size of the engineering compartment, allowing them to integrate a more powerful reactor. It'll also have a redesigned magazine storage for the missile launchers."

Hunt flipped through the rest of the schematics, taking it all in, then looked up at her. "This is going to be awesome. Great job getting ahead of this, Abi. I have a feeling we're going to need these in the future."

Chapter 15
Found 'Em

Interstellar Marshals Service Headquarters
Jacksonville, Arkansas
Earth, Sol System

"Hold up. Go back three seconds," Hosni said excitedly.

"Sure. What are we looking for?" senior analyst Pierre Brochand asked.

Hosni pointed to a figure stepping out of the crowd toward a side alleyway. "Zoom in on that woman; see if you can capture an image of her face. Then rewind three more seconds, let it play forward, and let's see what we can spot."

Krzysztof Waclawek pushed his chair slightly closer to Hosni. In a hushed tone, he asked, "You think this might be one of the attackers?"

"Possibly. I'm not sure. Something just seems off about her. Let's watch the video and see what we find."

"Wait. Before you start the video, were you able to grab a facial image we could use, Pierre?" Krzysztof asked.

A second later, an image of the suspect appeared on the screen. It wasn't a very good image. The woman was wearing a ball cap with the bill down low. Her face was somewhat obscured further by a yellow-framed pair of glasses.

"Eh, this isn't a high-quality image. We can likely run the video feed in reverse and see how far back we can track her. It's possible we can find a better angle."

"Let's let the video play first before we do that."

"Sure thing, Hosni."

As they let the video run, they saw the woman in question walking casually with the morning crowd. As she neared the alleyway, she effortlessly slipped out of the crowd like a shadow. If they hadn't known to watch the alley, they would have missed it. While a steady blur of people walked nearby, a new woman appeared to emerge from the same alley. This woman had a different-colored shirt on, a floppy hat, and a standard-looking pair of black-rimmed smart glasses. Her hair was different too—a cropped blond cut instead of a jet-black ponytail.

"Stop. That woman—the one with the floppy hat and the blond hair. Follow her for a few minutes and let's see if we can get a facial image. Start collecting information on her gait as she walks, too. I think our subject may have just swapped disguises on us."

Pierre made a face, replying, "That can't be the same person, can it?"

He kept the video rolling as they watched her walk a couple of blocks until she made her way into a breakfast bar.

"Wait—that bar, that bar was hit—um, thirty-six minutes after she walked in. I think that might be our girl," Krzysztof said excitedly. This might be their first solid piece of intelligence on who had been leaving these bombs behind.

"Pierre, watch the entrance and grab an image of every woman that exits the bar. Cross-reference it with this image and the data on her gait. I'm betting this lady changes disguises on us again," Hosni explained. A few analysts had joined them, intently listening to Hosni.

Observing the café for six minutes after she had entered it, they got a hit. Sure enough, the target had altered her appearance once again.

Pierre looked at Hosni in disbelief. "My God, you're right. It's her. She barely looks like the same woman." She now had gray hair and a different color of shirt once again.

Pierre and his team of analysts had spent more than a week trying to piece together clues about who was leaving these bombs behind, with no luck until now.

"OK, Pierre. Here's what I want you to do next," Hosni directed. "Backtrack all the way to the first coffee bar that blew up and start tracking everyone entering the place up to one hour before the first bomb went off. See if any of the people match any of the disguises we've seen. If you can't find a match, then cross-reference them against our suspect's gait. We'll use that as a secondary means of identifying her. Once you find her, continue to follow her and let's make sure she visited all three places. *If* we can do that, then I want you to see if we can back-trace her to where she first shows up on a surveillance camera. Maybe we'll see if she's staying in an apartment in the city. Once you've done that, let's follow her after the third attack and see if she leads us back to the same apartment or someplace new." As he was speaking, Krzysztof placed a few calls, asking for some others to assist Pierre. This was a lot of data they were about to start sifting through.

Four hours into their AI-assisted analysis, they'd filtered through footage from thousands of cameras, following the suspect from the apartment building she'd left in the morning and back to the same place later that day. When they found the apartment, Krzysztof wanted to raid it immediately, but Hosni held them back. He wanted to figure out who'd leased the apartment and then dig into that information. He also had them fast-forward the CCTV video of the apartment now that they knew the suspect was in it. Six hours after arriving, the suspect left, a large bag on her shoulder being the only thing she took. They followed her for an hour; then she managed to give them the slip when she traveled beyond the continuous drone and CCTV surveillance coverage of the city.

Hosni directed the marshals to dig into the company that leased the apartment, see if they had leased any others, find out who owned the company and what financial institutions it was tied to. With a handful of images, disguises, and the suspect's gait as reference points, they created a search profile and placed it on their watchlist. Now it was just a matter of time before the AI algorithm would find the woman. Then the hunt would continue.

In the meantime, Hosni asked Krzysztof to organize a team to apprehend the suspect. He was going to start teaching these guys some tactics to aid in taking down the Mukhabarat agent. The last attempt hadn't gone so well, and unless Reinhard let him use his own team, he needed to get these guys ready to do the job themselves.
****

48 Hours Later

"Here's the lease for the apartment," Pierre said as he displayed the documentation on the monitor. "Before any of you get excited, you need to know it's a dead end. It was bought through a company some fourteen months ago and then leased to another company before being leased to a third company four weeks ago. I've already investigated the identities of the people on the lease, the owners of the companies, and the individuals who signed for the different leases—ghosts, every one of them."

Krzysztof looked furious. He cursed a few times. "That can't be possible," he insisted. "You can't just create a company with a fake identity." He started making some calls to see if there was any kind of banking or tax information on the companies, something that might give them some additional leads to track down.

Pierre turned to Hosni. "Sir, if I may, using the various images and videos we've captured of our mystery woman, I've been running a search pattern against the video archives we have of each bombing location. I specifically narrowed it down to roughly one hour prior to the explosions."

Hosni perked right up at this. Pierre was finally starting to piece together how to track individuals like this down. "Let me guess. You found a few matches to our suspect…and…you now know we're dealing with more than one bomber."

Pierre looked surprised. "Uh, yeah. How did you come to that conclusion too?"

Krzysztof had finally gotten off his calls and was now paying rapt attention to this realization as well.

"Truthfully, I think we're likely dealing with not just one or two bombers. I think it's likely we're dealing with up to four."

"OK, Hosni, why don't you help us understand how you're coming to that conclusion?" Krzysztof asked, a serious look of concern on his face.

Hosni nodded, taking a breath in before explaining. "All right, Krzysztof, Pierre. While we've been chasing this information down the last couple of days, I've had some members of my team back on the base looking into this as well."

"Whoa—you know your guys can't operate here, right?" Krzysztof interrupted defensively.

"Yes, I know. They haven't left the base. I'm having them use our own tools and resources to help speed things along for us. As I was saying, this first set of bombings that took place in the capital—they happened too far apart to have been carried out by just one person. That's our first indication there was more than one bomber. Second, when my guys ran our one known suspect from this bombing—her biometrics, her gait, her facial images, such as they are—against the bombings in Canberra two days later, we matched her to half of them, just like we did here. But here's the kicker. When we looked for the same details in Nagoya and Surat—those occurred three days apart from each other—we couldn't find any matches to the previous bombings. That likely means we're dealing with a separate cell carrying out attacks in those cities."

"Great, so you're suggesting we're likely dealing with at least four suspects?" Krzysztof said hesitantly.

Hosni nodded.

"OK, Hosni, I'm trying to understand something. How is your team of soldiers, who are confined to your base, able to figure this stuff out in less than two days while my guys are struggling to keep up and still hadn't made this same connection yet?" Krzysztof pressed, not sure if something else was ultimately going on.

Hosni tried to explain. "Krzysztof, I know this may seem frustrating on your end, trying to figure out how to track these bastards down. Before that frustration can be directed at me or my soldiers, I'd ask you to consider this—you're approaching this from a law enforcement perspective, just as your people have been trained to do. But *we're* not law enforcement. We're Special Forces, and we have been at the forefront of this conflict from the beginning.

"During these past fourteen years of war, our tactics, technology, and experience have grown exponentially. When we invaded New Eden, we fought a multiyear insurgency campaign against the Zodarks and a small cadre of Mukhabarat agents. During the Intus invasion and subsequent liberation, we fought another multiyear insurgency to root out various Zodark holdouts. What we didn't know prior to that campaign was how long the Zodarks had occupied the planet. During their occupation, they had established a Primord version of the Mukhabarat. That was a huge surprise for us. It added another layer to the insurgency—it was something else we had to overcome.

"What I'm trying to say, Krzysztof, is we have extensive experience in combating insurgents and waging our own kind of counterinsurgency operations. In contrast, you're trying to transition from a law enforcement–driven agency, where rights and privacy matter. Now you're suddenly having to create a counterintelligence organization from scratch—against alien species you have never worked with or fought against. How can you be expected to succeed when you've had everything stacked against you?"

Hosni took a breath in, adding, "The Mukhabarat are not the only alien intelligence apparatus you have to be concerned about. They're just the one that is causing you the most problems right now. I'm hoping you'll allow me, and maybe the rest of my team, to help get your guys ready to take on these current and future threats. This spying and insurgency stuff...it's tough work, Krzysztof. It's something you guys are going to get good at, but it's going to take time and a lot of training."

Krzysztof and the others began to realize how underequipped they were to handle this mission. Hosni and his soldiers had done more to identify and counter these foreign agents in two days than his entire department had in the six months since they had been created.

Standing, Krzysztof extended his hand to Hosni. "Thanks for the explanation, Hosni. If I had my druthers, I'd have your entire team embedded with our teams so we could speed up this training. Since we can't, or until it can be made possible, what's your suggestion for how we should locate the remaining suspects still on the loose?"

Smiling, Hosni replied, "Well, since you asked...here's what I suggest we do next."

Chapter 16
Routine Patrol

Bravo Company, 3rd Battalion, 126th Infantry Regiment
Forward Operating Base Takata
Alfheim, Sirius System

Come on, Roberts, you can do this. Eleven months and twenty-eight more days until this nightmare is finally over, Roberts thought pensively as he hugged the ground, blaster fire zipping over his head. A Zodark shouted something, and the blaster fire shifted from him to another target.

Keep it together, Roberts. They're shifting fire; it's OK, he mentally yelled at himself.

He'd charged forward, his team hot on his heels, but when he saw Jordy's body, his lower half ripped apart from the mine, all he saw was an image of Denk. It momentarily caused Roberts to freeze, to drop to his belly and search for cover when he should have kept charging with his team.

Boom!

An explosion tore through the trees, raining dirt and debris on the Zodark positions.

Zip, zip, zap.

Roberts lay flat, fighting to regain control of his mind and actions as clumps of dirt and broken tree limbs rained down around them.

Voices sounded nearby. A soldier was yelling—one of *his* soldiers, he realized.

"Frag out!" came the warning before another crump as the grenade detonated, followed by a Zodark yelping in pain from the shrapnel.

"Splash out! Splash out!" warned their lieutenant urgently. The artillery rounds landed moments later, adding a new layer of chaos, assaulting Roberts's mind as he fought to regain control.

BOOM, BOOM, BOOM.

"Yeah, baby! Take that, you bastards!" shouted one soldier, a few others cheering as well.

"Heads up, I got movement to my right! Shift fire to our right! They're trying to flank us!" someone yelled from further away.

Roberts was about to rush forward when a string of laser bolts zipped overhead once again, keeping him pinned where he was.

"I want that damn MG laying down suppressive fire!" Sergeant Ado roared to the soldiers manning the Pig.

The blaster fire shifted, pivoting away from his direction to somewhere else. Roberts knew he had to move—he had to regain control of his mind and body or he'd die in minutes if they got flanked. Reading his grenade launcher, Roberts flicked the setting to proximity. He wasn't sure where they were, but if the grenade got close enough, it'd go off and hopefully take 'em out.

Taking one deep breath in, Roberts let it out as he jumped up just long enough to find the position the Zodarks were shooting at them from. Spotting their blaster fire, he pulled the trigger, sending the six grenades his magazine held down their throats before ducking and rolling to his left. A couple of laser bolts slammed into his previous position moments later.

Don't forget, your grenades don't fire as fast as your blaster. The words of his drill sergeant echoed in his mind. He'd exposed himself longer than he should have—a mistake he hadn't made since basic training. This thought was broken by the crumping sound made by the detonation of the 20mm smart munitions he'd launched.

Screams erupted moments later, drowning out parts of the battle. Roberts knew they weren't human cries. The hideous screams assaulting his ears were coming from more than one Zodark. He'd wounded them, hopefully taking them out of the fight so they couldn't kill him or his friends anymore.

Dropping the spent mag, Roberts slapped a new one in its place, ready to move, his eyes searching for what to do next. Looking to his right, he saw Staff Sergeant Howell and three other soldiers bounding forward into the swirling snow, their rifles firing as they did. It was a sight to behold, yet he was too far away to join them.

Noise to his left caught his attention in time for Sergeant Ado, pointing to several soldiers and yelling for them to move forward, to close the distance on the group of Zodarks Roberts had wounded earlier with his grenades. Awestruck in the moment, Roberts watched as the soldiers ran right into the Zodark positions, blasters raging.

Intermixed with the swirling snow and lights of the blasters, an object flew out of the trees—flailing as it crashed into the ground.

Roberts was unsure what he'd just seen, but the HUD identified the soldier's tracker, illuminating the name PFC Gonzo.

He blanked at the name initially, until his mind found the information he was looking for. *Gonzo, the guy from supply filling in for Lindy...*

As Roberts stared at Gonzo writhing on the ground, movement near the bushes caught his attention. He turned just in time to see a blur of motion and speed as the Zodark burst through the shrubs, a cloud of snow erupting around the warrior charging toward Gonzo.

"Oh crap," Roberts yelled to himself. Pulling his rifle up, he brought it to bear and squeezed the trigger wildly at the beast as it closed the distance faster than he thought possible. His shots went high, missing the Zodark as he pounced on Gonzo, swords in his lower hands and blasters in his uppers.

"No, you animal!" Roberts yelled in a blinding rage, leaping to his feet and running right for the Zodark.

The beast lopped Gonzo's head off his body and, in the same motion, hurled the helmet-encased head right at Roberts, slamming it into the center of his body armor like a sledgehammer. The force flung him backwards through the air until he landed flat on his back.

Shaking off the stars he was seeing, Roberts gasped for air, his mind screaming at his body to breathe. His lungs filled, the blackness he'd felt moments earlier fading. *Gonzo—that bastard is still out there*, came the horrifying thought, his hands searching for his rifle.

The roaring scream of the Zodark got louder, closer to him by the time he clutched the grip of his rifle. Swinging it forward, Roberts leveled it at the face of the beast that was almost on him. Squeezing the trigger, he saw the beast's eyes, the unfiltered hate and rage that filled them, the muscles of its arms gripping the weapons about to kill him.

The animal grunted as its body collapsed to the ground, skidding to a stop right in front of him. Roberts had killed the beast; he'd live a moment longer.

As he fought his own battle, oblivious to his surroundings, a familiar sound filled the air, approaching rapidly. Looking to the sky, he saw the shadows moving against the clouds. The shadows brought help, images of Ospreys arriving just in time.

An Osprey flew over his position and leveled above the trees not far from the remaining Zodarks. The gunners on the transport fired like mad, shooting at anything threatening their bird of prey as it released its deadly cargo.

Roberts looked to the rear of the flying tanks, waiting for their avenging angels to descend...waiting for the help they'd begged for nearly an hour to arrive before it was too late. Then he saw the instruments of death leaping to the ground below.

As scores of C100s landed on the ground, they raced headlong into the battle still raging, still trying to keep them from going home. With a fearlessness only found in the killing machine they were, they tore into the remaining Zodark positions, blasters firing, swords out as the melee turned medieval in those final moments.

Then the sounds of battle petered out, a silence enveloping the forest. In that moment of serenity and silence, Roberts knew he'd made it. He'd live a little longer...and maybe, just maybe, long enough to get off this rock before the Zodarks killed them all.

Chapter 17
Cruisin'

Celebrity Cruise Ship *Infinity*
Rings of Jupiter

Seeing the redhead at the end of the bar, Ashurina spotted her mark. Walking confidently toward the bar, she took a seat. "Is that drink any good?"

The woman, who'd been scrolling through her Qpad, briefly looked up. "Actually, it's not bad."

"I'll have what she's having."

"Yes, ma'am," the humanoid barkeeper replied as it went to work creating her drink.

Ashurina turned, looking at the woman next to her. "That's a pretty blouse. Did you find that here on the ship or is it something you brought with you?"

Blushing at the compliment, the woman replied, "Thank you. No, it's something I brought with me from home."

"My name's Ashurina."

The woman smiled. "Nice to meet you. My name is Sujatha. Are you enjoying the cruise so far?"

"Oh yes, this is amazing. Seeing the planets and the rings around them up close like this is incredible," Ashurina explained excitedly.

"Yes, it is amazing to see. This is my third time taking this cruise. I feel like I see something new on each one," Sujatha replied.

"Are you here with someone?" Ashurina already knew the answer. She wanted to see what Sujatha would say.

Laughing, Sujatha countered, "Hell no. These cruises are my escape—my chance to cut loose and have fun."

"Hell yeah, a girl after my own heart. I'm here doing the same thing, spending a few weeks just cutting loose and having fun. Then it's back to the grind."

They talked and drank for several hours at the bar before a band struck up a tune and everyone started dancing. Ashurina spent the better part of the entire day hanging out with Sujatha. They met up later that evening for dinner together and then watched the evening entertainment on the ship. The following day, they went to yoga, and the day after that they participated in a spacewalk excursion. The more they talked, the more Ashurina got her to open up about marriage and the frustrations she was having with her husband, Rear Admiral Harsh Shringla. Her chief complaint was that the man was never there for her or the kids. Prior to the war, their kids had been eight, nine, and eleven. During the fourteen years of the conflict, she and the kids had spent maybe four years total with him. It angered her that he was gone so much and missed the time they had with their kids before they grew up and flew the coop.

When their son Kash had turned seventeen, Harsh had gotten him admitted to the Space Academy. When he'd graduated, he'd helped their son get assigned as a platoon leader to the famed Apollo Company, part of the 1-331st Infantry Regiment. A year later, Kash had been killed in a battle on the planet Intus, a Primord world that had been occupied by the Zodarks. It had devastated Sujatha. Worse, her husband hadn't even been able to attend his own son's funeral.

When the war had ended, her husband had been promoted to rear admiral and placed in charge of Earth's defense. That meant he'd be home on a regular basis, something Sujatha had thought she'd love and welcome, and at first, she had. But as the months went by, she realized she didn't know the man she'd married anymore. They'd been separated for so long, she'd grown estranged from the man she'd called husband for more than twenty-eight years.

Ashurina used her skills to pry information out of her new friend about her husband. Sujatha was more than happy to have someone to talk to about his failings, and the more she talked, the more Ashurina learned about Earth's defenses. Each evening, before she went to bed, she'd compile everything they'd talked about into a detailed contact report.

Near the end of the trip, the ship made one final port call to the moon Callisto before they'd leave Jupiter. Twenty-eight days into their thirty-six-day cruise of the planets of Sol, the trip was starting to wind down. It was one of the most popular cruises you could book, if you could afford it. The following day, after participating in an excursion exploring the surface of the moon and touring some of its many craters and sights, Ashurina opted to spend the day lounging on the observation deck near the pool. This might have been a work trip, but that didn't mean she couldn't take some time to enjoy a good book.

Sipping on a fruity drink with too much alcohol, she'd occasionally steal a glance out the floor-to-ceiling glass window she was seated in front of. The view of the rings of Jupiter was quite stunning. Being able to look at the giant gas planet this close was equally mesmerizing. To see the storms swirling about, random shocks of lightning as they rippled for hundreds and even thousands of miles across the clouds…it was awe-inspiring.

Placing her fruity drink down on the table between the lounges, Ashurina returned her eyes to her tablet. She had become engrossed in the latest Jillian Castle book, *Fake Love*. It was a dirty love story, but she'd become terribly enthralled in these sorts of books after a coworker had lent her a copy of Jillian's latest release. Ten pages in and she was hooked on this author.

Having grown up under Zodark control, she'd never read a romance novel. As a matter of fact, books of this nature, books that tugged at people's emotions, were typically banned or heavily censored. Her future employers, the Mukhabarat, had created a carefully curated society built on compliance and acceptance of the status quo and the tribute system. This meant there was little freedom for such indulgences as whimsical romances or espionage thrillers, another genre of books she'd thoroughly fallen in love with.

Nearly an hour had gone by when a man lay down on the lounge next to her. A synthetic humanoid brought him a beer and a sandwich. Like her, he had a book on his tablet, and he read something in between occasionally stealing a glance at Jupiter. When the man had finished his sandwich, he wrote something on his napkin before getting up and leaving.

Reaching for her drink, Ashurina made sure to accidentally grab the napkin. As it fell into her lap while she took a drink, she saw the words "2 p.m., Cellar Masters." Smiling, she grabbed the napkin, crumpled it up, and stuffed it in the remnants of her drink. The liquid dissolved the napkin along with the message.

Standing, Ashurina wrapped her waist in a floral-print wrap and put a shawl overtop her bikini top. Looking at the clock, she saw she had ten minutes to get to the bar. She made her way toward the stairs, descending from deck ten, the pool deck, down to deck five. Deck five held the Cellar Masters bar along with the main dining hall on one end and the theater on the other. Ashurina was amazed at these luxury cruises. The concept of people paying money to spend a couple of weeks getting pampered on a luxury ship, eating too much food and drinking too many strong drinks while they toured the rings of Jupiter, Saturn, Venus, or even the Belt, was still foreign to her.

When she reached the Cellar Masters, Ashurina ordered a glass of wine and found an empty seat near one of the windows. Sitting down, she sipped on her wine, taking in the sight of Io, one of Jupiter's satellites, as their ship began to approach it. The large moon had a couple of small habitats on its surface, with a small orbital station and a space elevator connecting them.

The man who had sat near her in the lounge had taken a seat next to her. He placed a backpack next to his chair as he finished drinking the rest of his brownish liquid, likely a bourbon. He then got up and left the bar, heading for the exit. Ashurina casually reached down and grabbed the backpack, pulling it over one of her shoulders and heading for her room.

When she arrived in her junior suite, she placed the backpack on the bed and examined its contents. She smiled when she saw a pistol. Then she saw four small cylinders, something she was familiar with from her past training and experience. She was instantly flooded with mixed emotions.

I'm not some suicide bomber, she thought angrily. *Does Dakkuri think I'm that expendable?*

Setting these bombs off would increase the risk of her getting caught, and the information she was bringing in was incredibly valuable to her people. She'd gone through years of training to get to where she was.

Ashurina examined the cylinders further. Two were unmarked, but one had a note that read *Infinity* and had a date fourteen days from then.

She sighed in acceptance. The bomb would go off five days after she left, and one day after the ship made its first port call. That left plenty of time to shift any potential attention from the people on her cruise to the port call right before the bomb went off.

Now she just needed to find a passenger to hook up with before her cruise ended. Finding a room that wasn't hers to hide the bomb in was now her new mission. When an investigation was launched, the bomb wouldn't originate from her room, helping to keep her cover intact.

Chapter 18
Never Forgotten

Bravo Company, 3rd Battalion, 126th Infantry Regiment
Forward Operating Base Takata
Alfheim, Sirius System

"Gather around, everyone," Staff Sergeant Howell announced. A circle formed around him.

"OK, listen up. I know it was getting rough for a while and Battalion cut us a little slack. But that's over. It's time for us to put our war faces back on. We've been given another mission." Moans could be heard from the soldiers at the thought of going outside the wire yet again.

"Hey, cut the crap! You're Republic soldiers—the toughest, meanest bastards on this planet. Now's not the time to quit or drop your guard. We still have a job to do and we're going to do it. Activity along the border has calmed a bit. Probably has something to do with a few thousand toasters roaming the area now instead of us. It's possible the last punch in the face we gave them is causing them to reevaluate the situation. In either case, we're back in the rotation with the others, and to celebrate, we've been given a mission." He held his hands out to stop the inevitable complaining as he explained, "This one's not so bad. We're headed out to investigate a cave site. It's possible our guys had holed up there during the occupation. If that's the case, then we'll see if we can recover any bodies and help bring some closure to the families still missing a loved one."

Howell could see the looks of concern on the soldiers' faces. "Listen, I know the last six or seven months have been tough," he admitted. "I'm not going to pretend they haven't. I want to give you guys a little perspective to help you put this into some context. We've fought some battles we shouldn't have, but most of you didn't see action in the last war. You don't know what the other veterans and I went through, the hell we had to endure. During the war, we fought battle after battle almost daily until the enemy was dead or we were. And guess what?"

He waited a second to make sure he had their attention. "That war went on for *fourteen years*—more than a decade of slugging it out with those blue bastards on planet after planet. So trust me, this may feel like the toughest thing you've ever gone through, and maybe it is. But just remember, war's not easy and the only easy day was yesterday."

Eyeing the NCOs, he continued, "We may be out for a few days investigating these tunnels and caves. Pack appropriately. Intelligence believes they found one of these bunker complex sites and they'd like us to check it out. It could turn out to be nothing, like the last two times. However, it could also turn out like the first one, bringing some closure to more than two hundred families back home." Howell paused for a second as he surveyed their faces. Most of the soldiers had been draftees, barely out of training when they'd been sent to Alfheim only to arrive in the final days of the war. After the last few battles, he couldn't call them green soldiers anymore. Still, they were young and naive, not having shared in the same experiences as many of the sergeants who'd fought in the war.

"Squad leaders, make sure everyone is ready to go in the morning. We'll be leaving at 0600 hours, so have everyone ready to go fifteen minutes prior. Dismissed," Howell finally concluded.

A few soldiers grumbled as they looked at a map of the cave location. It was less than ten kilometers from the neutral zone and roughly twenty-six kilometers from the closest combat outpost. They'd have to rely on overhead drones for support should they need it. Hopefully the cavalry wouldn't take almost an hour to save their butts again.

****

Corporal David Roberts was heading toward the dining facility when a soldier in his platoon commented, "What do you think, Roberts? Will we find some frozen bodies on this patrol, a Zodark raiding party, or more of those damn IEDs they seem to love?"

Shrugging, he replied, "Who knows? Let's just do our jobs and try not to get killed or hurt. Not that I'm counting, but we only have ten months and twenty-six days left on this rock."

"Yeah, who's counting all right. That kind of thinking will get you killed, Roberts."

Nearing the DFAC, Sergeant Ado called out to him, "Hey, Roberts. Come here for a second."

Seeing Ado talking with a few other NCOs, he figured a little powwow was going on.

"I'll catch up with you guys later. Let me see what Sergeant Ado needs," he told his friends.

Approaching the unofficial meeting, he said, "Hey, you called? What's up?"

"It's about tomorrow," Staff Sergeant Howell answered. "I wanted to give you a heads-up that the tunnel system we're investigating was likely used by your old unit, Apollo Company. If it does pan out, we might end up finding the bodies of guys you may have known."

Roberts was taken aback by the mention of Apollo Company. He hadn't heard that name in years. The sudden memory of his first unit was almost like a kick in the gut. Once he'd recovered from his wounds on the *Mercy*, he'd been unable to rejoin them before his ship had been forced to flee the system. They'd barely made it out of there when the Zodark fleet had arrived.

Steeling his nerves, he replied, "Thank you for letting me know, Staff Sergeant. I'll be fine. Hopefully we'll find some of them and be able to close out this chapter of Apollo Company's history on the planet."

"OK, good to know. If you don't want to be part of the search, it's OK. Just let me know and we'll find something else for you to do while we're gone."

Roberts shook his head. "I appreciate the offer, and thanks for thinking about me, but I'll be fine. You can count on me."

As he started back toward the dining facility, a wave of emotions washed over him. Thinking about the people he knew who had died on this planet, the idea of finding their frozen corpses after so long…he suddenly wasn't sure he would be all right if they did find any bodies.
****

"Damn. You'd think after years of being on this frozen wasteland, I'd have gotten used to his cold," one of the soldiers griped as they steadily moved through the woods toward the site they were told to investigate.

"Bro, I don't think anyone gets used to this cold. It seeps into your bones and doesn't let go," another soldier whined.

"The only way to counter this kind of cold is with a long hot shower. Let the heat of the water warm you back up."

"Cut the whining, guys," Sergeant Ado chided. "We only have three more days of this. We'll be back at the FOB soon enough." Ado was a tough soldier—not one to complain about much, nor did he let his soldiers gripe like fresh recruits from basic.

Approaching the site of a large battle long since over, Roberts could still see the signs of war. Partially torn-apart trees were everywhere. Some had scorch marks on them from blaster fire; others had chunks ripped off from railguns. Despite the snow covering the ground, one could still make out pockmarks and craters from explosives used to soften the positions up.

"Hey, found a body over here," called one of the soldiers. "Never mind. It's a dead Zodark."

As they approached the scene of the forgotten battle, the soldiers spread out. Bodies began to turn up. Many were Zodarks, a testament to the slaughter Apollo Company had meted out. Intermixed with those frozen corpses, the torn and destroyed bodies of the combat synthetics were also being found. The C100s had clearly put up a hell of a fight, judging by the number of Zodark bodies they had found.

When their search started to close in on the tunnels themselves, human remains were soon found. Their frozen positions spoke of the fighting that had claimed their lives. Some were crouched over the side of a foxhole; others had collapsed near a machine gun. All had died either with a rifle in their hands or in hand-to-hand combat as their positions were eventually overrun. When a human soldier was found, they collected their information via their nametape and their electronic dog tag and quickly compared it against the list of missing soldiers until a match was found. Once they'd geo-marked the body, a graves registration team would collect them for a proper burial.

Staff Sergeant Howell surveyed the scene of the battle, hands on his hips as he nodded approvingly. "Damn, Roberts, your old unit put up one hell of a fight." Pointing behind him, he added, "We found a cave entrance over there. I need you to take your fire team inside and check it out."

"On it," he replied, turning to his guys. "You heard the man, let's go."

As they approached the partially collapsed entrance, it was clear that this place had been heavily fought over. Remnants and pieces of C100s were strewn about. So were the frozen corpses of Zodarks and the occasional human soldier.

"Look at that entrance. How do we know that thing isn't going to collapse on us once we start looking around inside there?" one of the soldiers said.

Another soldier suggested, "You know, instead of going in there, we could just send a drone in. Let it look around for us, and if it finds something interesting, then we can go in."

"Aha, I knew there was a reason we kept you around, Bobby," Roberts joked as he pulled one of the squad's scout drones out.

"Hey, work smarter, not harder," the soldier replied. Some guys laughed in agreement.

When the drone entered the cave and started traveling further in, it was obvious there had been a major fight inside. Dead bodies were everywhere. So were signs that this had at one point been a command post. Republic Army computers, comms gear, tablets, and other pieces of equipment were spread about. Further into the tunnel, they found a cluster of Zodark bodies intermixed with a handful of C100s. Looking at the images from the drone, Roberts could only imagine what it must have been like for the soldiers who had died here.

"Go back, Roberts. I think I saw one of ours."

Turning the drone around, Roberts found what his friend had mentioned. Zooming in on the soldier's armor, he found the name tape: First Lieutenant Henry Magnussen. He'd been Apollo Company's XO and then commander when Captain Fenti and others had gotten caught on the ship during the evac out of the system. Lieutenant Magnussen had been listed missing, presumed dead. The powers that be had awarded him the Medal of Honor for his actions on Alfheim in what now appeared to be this very battle.

Looking at the others, Roberts declared, "We're going in. We're going to recover the LT's body and the others still in there."

Without waiting for a reply or a grumble, Roberts climbed his way inside. Moving through the tunnel felt almost like walking through a battle that had been effectively frozen in time. The bodies of both sides lay like statues, right where they had died. When he reached Magnussen's body, he turned and saw a dead Zodark a few feet away. He also spotted what looked like a mangled C200, one of the medical Synths the platoons had started integrating toward the end of the war. Looking at the damaged machine, he noticed one of its hands was gripping a Zodark sword.

Huh. I didn't think the medical Synths could fight or take a life, Roberts thought.

Then a voice from his past called out. "Hello, Private First Class David Roberts. Congratulations, Roberts, I see you have been promoted to corporal."

Roberts fell backward from shock, his mind racing with questions. He hadn't expected a voice from the pile of bodies to suddenly speak and know his name.

But that voice…where have I heard that voice before? "Sam…? Is that really you?"

"Yes, Corporal Roberts. It is I, Sam. The C200 advanced combat medical synthetic assigned to support Apollo Company."

Holy crap, it really is Sam. Now I remember him.

"Have you been active this entire time?"

"Yes and no," Sam responded. "As you can see, my lower extremities have been severed from my body, trapping me in this tunnel. When it did not appear that help was going to arrive anytime soon, I powered down my systems to conserve my battery and set my sensors to reactivate once someone approached me, as you just did." His response was calm and methodical, like one would expect from a machine.

"Whoa, is that medical synthetic still functional?" a soldier asked, shocked.

"Yeah, it is. His name is Sam. He was assigned to our company right before the invasion. Sam's the reason I'm still alive…after I got shot a few hours after we landed, I'd have been a goner if it hadn't been for Sam."

"Corporal Roberts, can you bring me back to your base? I can have my AI profile transferred to another C200. I can also provide a detailed account of this final battle and the others leading up to it."

"Yes, of course. Let's work on getting what's left of your body freed from under this Zodark." Roberts and one of his guys lifted the Zodark corpse off Sam. They carried out Lieutenant Magnussen and Sam's bodies, along with the others from the cave.

A short while later, an Osprey carrying a team from graves registration arrived and collected up the bodies, to include Sam. They'd be brought back to the FOB for proper burial and the families informed of the change to their loved one's status, bringing resolution for those who thought their relative might still be alive.

When they returned to the FOB a few days later, Roberts went to find Sam. He wanted to talk with the synthetic and ask him questions about his old platoon and some of his friends. Sam had been there with them during the invasion. He had been there with them through everything they had gone through. He needed to speak to Sam—he represented the last opportunity for Roberts to learn more about the fates of his friends. Talking to Sam...he could finally close his own chapter with Apollo Company, once and for all.

When he couldn't find Sam, he started asking around for him. A couple of soldiers mentioned something about Sam being transported back to Earth. Some technicians from Walburg Industries said something about the Synth's software needing to be looked at and Sam being given a new body. Hearing the news that Sam had already left Alfheim sucked. With Sam gone, he'd need to find his closure another way. Perhaps after he returned, he might be able to find some of his friends from his platoon. Roberts smiled at the memory of the friends who'd survived and resolved that he would make sure they had one hell of a party when they did eventually meet up.

Chapter 19
The Summons

Early 2109
Ministry of Groff
Planet Shwani, Sector YC118

Viewing the planet below, Heltet felt his warrior pride swell. Twenty-three years—that was how long he'd been gone. Seeing Shwani through the tiny window of the shuttle reminded him of a saying he'd heard on Sumer: *our perception of the world is only as big as the window we view it from.* He was glad he'd been summoned. His view of the Zodark world had shrunk, while his view of humans and this new group, the Republic, had grown.

There is much that needs to be discussed when I see the Director...

Looking out the window opposite his, Heltet caught sight of the imperial shipyard. It had grown immensely in his absence. He couldn't make out the details, but it was clear the yard was a hive of activity. Dozens, maybe even hundreds of ships were in various stages of construction. He'd known the navy had adjusted their warships to account for the Republic's choice of weapons, but one ship in the yard stood out amongst the others. He wasn't sure what its purpose was, but its sheer size told him that whatever it was, it was unique and unlike anything he'd seen in the past. He hoped whatever they were building would be enough to crush this upstart human society. If the Republic wasn't stopped soon...he shuddered at the thought before pushing it out of his mind.

You shouldn't dwell on the what-ifs... what is happening now should be your focus...

Heltet believed too many people got caught up on "what might" and failed to focus on "what will" if you do not act, if you do not execute. It was a truism he'd lived by, and it had served him well as the spymaster for Sumer. Pondering the meeting to come, he saw the shuttle's captain approach.

"NOS Heltet, we are starting our entry now. Arrival time to the Groff is fifteen minutes," he said before returning to his duties.

Heltet thanked him, then returned to his inward reflection while he admired the beauty of the planet below. He still followed the news from home, marveling at the planet's rapid growth since their discovery of the Republic. Given the scale of the last war, he shouldn't have been surprised by it. Wars grew or contracted empires throughout millennia, something his people understood well.

The Republic hadn't been a spacefaring society for long, and by conventional standards, its warships were obsolete in comparison to those of their alliance peers. Yet somehow, this upstart race had managed to lay bare the weaknesses of the Zodark Empire, calling into question their own military prowess within the Dominion.

Heltet hoped this summons by the Director of the Groff would give him an opportunity to address the shortcomings from the last war as they positioned for the next. A summons wasn't an unusual request; it was challenging for a Director to know what was happening on all the planets they administered. Unlike his fellow planet chiefs, the planet Heltet oversaw wasn't an ordinary planet. He'd overseen Sumer, and when it had fallen to the Republic, his planet had been behind enemy lines. His continued success despite being cut off from the empire had given him a unique opportunity to give the Director and thereby the Council a unique inside view of the Republic and how it operated. Infiltrating assets and getting information both on and off the occupied planet had forced his operatives to conceive plans even he hadn't considered.

"We are approaching Groff headquarters," announced the pilot over the PA.

Heltet watched the landing pad come into view. Hundreds gathered around it, ready to welcome him home, which put his mind at ease.

Excellent. This will likely be a productive, informative meeting if they are doing this, he thought. As they touched down on the pad, Heltet felt satisfied by the accomplishments he'd achieved during his absence. He'd served the empire more than most; the welcome home by his fellow Groff peers reinforced that opinion.

Exiting the shuttle, he saw the elite guards of the Groff standing shoulder to shoulder, weapons held in honor for him to walk under. At the end of the color guard stood the man who'd summoned him, a D'Shawni Clan elder and the Director of the Groff, Vak'Atioth.

Making his way past the guards to the man referred to as Vak for short, he embraced the Director, who readily returned the gesture. Following the required ceremonial glad-handing and acknowledgments, the Director led them to his office.

"Heltet, you look good," Vak said as he poured them something to drink. "I hope Lindow blessed your travels with inspirations on how to further drain the blood of our enemies."

Accepting the offered glass, Heltet took a sip. "Leaving was uneventful. However, returning to Sumer…that may be challenging."

Vak agreed before assuring him their latest stealth ship should be up to the task. Heltet was a bit dubious about this new ship and how it worked. It was tiny, more like the size of a fancy shuttle the super-wealthy of the empire would use to travel privately from system to system in luxury.

"Heltet, the reports we have received throughout the occupation on Sumer have been incredible. Many disagreed with your plan to stay behind, even going so far as requesting me to order you to abandon Sumer. Your plan…convinced me to go against their advice and warnings. What you have gone on to achieve during these past six years brought great honor to me, yourself, and the D'Shawni Clan," Vak praised him before adding, "The planet directors throughout the Groff marvel at your espionage efforts. Your Kafarr, this Dakkuri—assures me the reports are accurate. His operatives succeeded in infiltrating Altairius Prime?"

"The report is indeed true, but I should note that that information is old. My Kafarr provided an updated report before I left. He's established the control team with a watcher. They're overseeing three assets and two Ani soldiers. It will not take long before we will begin to receive steady reports of what is going on in the Altairian capital," Heltet explained to Vak's satisfaction. The question had caught him off guard. He wasn't sure who was causing the Director to question the veracity of his reports. It disturbed him to think that someone from within might be dismissing the true threat the Republic posed to the empire.

Satisfied with his response, Vak moved on. "You've done well, Heltet. You've proven a lot of people wrong in a good way. The Groff have tried for hundreds of dracmas to infiltrate or recruit sources to spy for us on Altairius Prime. You appear to have done the impossible. When do you believe we'll start to see some results?"

"Knowing my Kafarr, he'll be cautious while his people assimilate into their new environment. That'll take time if they're not to get caught. I can't stress this enough—the Altairians are better at sniffing out spies than the Republic."

Vak laughed at the comparison. "Yes…about the Republic. They are the reason I recalled you. The Groff was requested to provide a comprehensive report to the Council on the continued threat they pose to our strategic goals. You know better than most the kind of information deficit we faced throughout the war. That can't continue if we want to retain our honor, and thereby the clan's honor. I can't speak to the Council without answers to the questions they will ask. So tell me, Heltet, do you believe the Republic is prepared for a new war against us? If not, then is it your opinion they will turn inward, focusing on their territory, and not look to expand into ours?"

This was a question that kept Heltet up at night. As he thought about how to respond, he reached into his bag, retrieving his P2 device containing the report he wanted to share. Turning it on, he opened the file and explained, "As I prepared to leave for this trip, I received an update from my Kafarr, Dakkuri. His gatherers continue to astonish me with their cleverness in acquiring information."

Interrupting his thoughts, a hand reached for the device he'd been reading from. "Keep speaking, but give me the P2. I want to see this report."

It had been a while since Heltet had seen Vak. He'd forgotten his abrupt and often abrasive nature. Reluctantly, he gave him the device and hoped he'd be able to remember the details of the full report.

"The second page is where I left off," Heltet offered before continuing to explain its contents. "Sumer, being a human colony, was quickly absorbed into the Republic shortly after they stole it from us. Prior to the abandonment of Sumer, I saw this happening and knew it would give us an opportunity if we prepared for it in advance and then waited until the time was right."

"I see that now, but before it happened, what made you think Sumer would become part of their empire, and why would they be allowed to freely travel between colonies?" Vak pressed.

If you'd stop interrupting me, then you'd know, Heltet thought.

"That was simple. Sumer and the Republic are both human societies—the Sumer people originated from Earth; they have shared ancestry. The Republic society is very different from our own. A citizen can freely travel from city to city and colony to colony without travel documents, without submitting to inspections. This formed the basis of my decision to stay behind."

"But why ask for additional Gurista-born Mukhabarat? You had plenty of Mukhabarat on Sumer."

They really don't understand these other humans at all, Heltet thought.

Taking a breath in, he began to explain. "Once the Republic liberated the planet and it became apparent we were not returning, I knew it would not be long before my gatherers began to turn on me and each other. Our Sumerian-born gatherers have lived under our yoke. They view us as oppressors. The Guristas do not see us this way. In their eyes, we are the benevolent ones: the alien race providing for their every need. I knew if I separated them before the invasion, I'd be able to maintain that control over them. It was them that my Kafarr chose to be his gatherers. If I could, the contents of the report I handed you are more important than answers to these questions."

Vak hissed at his comment. "I will determine what questions are important," he hastily countered. "The Council may ask for these details; therefore I need these details. This here"—he pointed at a set of schematics—"your Kafarr's gatherer was able to obtain this? It is real?"

"Yes, it is real. The Kafarr informed me that one of his gatherers had obtained work for a company that provides the reactors to the Republic's shipbuilders and stations. The gatherer has used that position to electronically infiltrate a host of other businesses working on the same or similar projects. Given the number of warships currently under construction and the proposed ships that are still waiting to be built, it is his and my own assessment that the Republic is still preparing to invade our territory," Heltet surmised, recounting Dakkuri's latest report.

Waiting for a response from Vak, he observed him carefully reading every detail of the report for accuracy. Staring at the P2, Heltet almost laughed. P2 stood for priority pad. Its other name was pain pad for the royal pain the device had become over the years. It allowed your supervisor, or their supervisor, to see how you were spending your time at work, accomplishing your tasks. Its snooping ability had caused a lot of suffering to those who failed to work their hardest.

Vak looked him in the eyes with a piercing stare. "I've finished reading the entire report. His conclusion is clear, his analysis concise, to the point. Let me be just as concise with you, Heltet. Is it also your belief the Republic is still planning to invade our territory?"

"Given the information I have to analyze, it would seem so."

Vak grunted. "Have your gatherers uncovered where they will invade from? Or what their goals may be?"

Judging by the questions being asked, Heltet suspected Vak knew this was a concern among the Council. Given the losses from the last war, they'd likely want to invade to smash them rather than let the Republic start the war on their terms.

"The Kafarr cannot say with certainty yet. His gatherers have compiled enough information to believe the likely target of any invasion would be Tueblets."

"Tueblets? If they seized control of that system, it would cut the empire in half!" Vak exclaimed. "The stargates of that system connect to nine systems, four of them being vital for interstellar trade and connecting our territory with the rest of the Dominion."

Heltet saw the information had disturbed him; he also looked confused by how the system could be captured. *He needs to stop interrupting and let me explain*, he chided internally.

"Please, Director Vak, there is more I need to explain before you dismiss this plan."

Eyeing him suspiciously, Vak reached for his drink and nodded for Heltet to continue.

"The Republic knows there are several avenues to invade Tueblets. I know, and it is possible the Republic and their allies also know, that we have positioned forces to block these avenues of attack. The Council needs to know these blocking forces will not work." Holding a hand up to stop Vak before he interrupted again, he said, "Director, please let me finish. I assure you the answers are forthcoming."

Heltet saw him grit his teeth at the request. "You are right, NOS Heltet. I am being impatient. I, and the Council, have been without answers for too long, unable to talk with someone who may have them. You are unaware of this, but our relationship with the Orbots following the battle in Sirius…has deteriorated further since the end of the war. This has put more emphasis on understanding the Republic's intentions. Please continue—perhaps your answers will provide context to the strain with our Orbot friends."

"Yes, I was not aware of the situation with the Orbots. I can see how that complicates things," Heltet acknowledged. "There is something I need to mention about the last battle, the one in Sirius. I won't rehash the war other than to say that it was essentially decided by the sudden appearance of a singular warship—a ship the Republic calls the *Freedom*. It had the same ability the Orbots have, to open wormholes, bridging fleets across the vastest distances. The threat posed by the Republic has exponentially increased since they were given that warship. It means they can bypass the defenses leading to Tueblets. If they can do that, then it might be possible they could appear over Zinconia, threatening the Council and our seat of power." Heltet saw Vak's facial expression change several times and realized that the Director had been unaware of the implications of this warship until just now.

"Thank you for showing me the true impact of this new warship. I believe the Malvari are aware of this and have discussed it before, but it was not something I had thoroughly examined myself. What has caused you to bring this up?"

"I too was unaware of this ship, *Freedom*, and its incredible power and strength. Then I received a report from Dakkuri, who highlighted the information for me to read. One of his spies works on the Republic's station over Earth, called the John Glenn. It was through her efforts that we obtained this knowledge. She had acquired it from multiple low- and high-ranking naval officers. What they told her was that this warship had been given to the Republic by the Gallentines themselves. She questioned how they could operate such a complex ship; they told her the ship was operated by a joint human-Gallentine crew.

"She learned that the Gallentines were to function as advisors, not to fight the ship for them. One officer said there was a point in the battle where the human crew had become overwhelmed, unable to utilize the ship's full capabilities. As the ship began to suffer serious damage, the Gallentines intervened. It was their interference that turned the battle around, leading to the Orbots accepting the proposed peace when it had been offered."

The Groff leader shook his head in disbelief. "Heltet, if the Gallentines are actively fighting on the Republic's behalf, then it may only be a matter of time before they intervene further and this warship's true capabilities are unleashed on us. I am glad I recalled you so we could discuss this. You have brought us information that we hadn't known we should consider. It appears your time on Sumer and this plan you hatched to infiltrate their alliance has gained the Groff the kind of knowledge we need if we're to defeat the Republic before they can grow strong enough to invade our territory. I believe your assessment of how dangerous they are is the reason the Council has asked for this brief. They will evaluate it and determine what to do next." Vak paused for a moment. "You made a point of mentioning the Gallentines as advisors but then taking over when the humans became overwhelmed. Why did you highlight that? What am I missing?"

Heltet felt relieved that his reports hadn't fallen on deaf ears. He explained why this mattered and how it could be exploited. He brought up the Treaty of Yarmooth between the Gallentines and the Collective— the treaty the Gallentines had broken when they had intervened in the Milky Way by giving the Republic the *Freedom* and a Gallentine crew to man it. The agreement stated that neither side was to intervene militarily in their galaxy, instead allowing it to develop without their direct involvement.

Five hundred or so dracmas later, the Collective had set their sights on the Milky Way once again. Not wanting to break the treaty, they had delegated their authority to a species of cyborgs they'd come to ally with, the Orbots, who'd consolidate the galaxy for them. Dracmas later, the Orbots had formed the Dominion, an alliance with the Collective that had designs to unite the galaxy.

The Gallentines had feared a united galaxy entering the war on the side of the Collective, causing them to seek a similar setup. This resulted in the Gallentines establishing the Viceroy position, selecting a leader to head this new alliance and become their galactic representative. The Altairians were the first to battle the Orbots. With help from the Gallentines, they began to turn their losses into victories. It was these technology transfers that enabled the Altairians to stop the Orbots from assimilating system after system into their cyborg army. Throughout the dracmas, the two alliances grew, recruiting new races to join this interstellar war.

As Vak began to lose patience with his history lesson, Heltet explained the finer points of the treaty, especially the point that mentioned that neither the Collective nor the Gallentines could directly intervene. Circling back to the mention of Gallentine advisors intervening to save the ship, Heltet highlighted the violation.

"How exactly are you proposing we use this treaty violation?"

"That is a question I have thought about for some time. I then asked another question…why did the Gallentines give the Republic a warship like the *Freedom* in the first place? Why not give it to the Altairians? They had the Viceroy position, after all."

Vak smiled at the question, motioning for him to continue.

"Some dracmas after the Republic joined the alliance, the Gallentines took notice of their success against us and approved. The Emperor summoned this Admiral Miles Hunt to speak with him. During this conversation, a change of leadership within the alliance was made. King Grigdolly was no longer the Viceroy; this Miles Hunt from the Republic was.

"As the new alliance leader, he'd been given the task of ending the war against the Dominion, and the *Freedom* was given to him to make it happen. This, Vak, is what we use. Instead of bringing this information to the Orbots, we seek an audience with the Collective. We make them aware of what has transpired, and we see if they would consider something similar—replacing the Orbots as the head of the alliance with us. They could provide our people with the technology they have given the Orbots and let us use it to end this war," Heltet explained. He was planting seeds—he had visions of one day becoming a powerbroker for the Zodarks, or the Dominion itself.

Vak stared at him, looking deep in thought after what he'd just shared.

"Yet again, during the very same meeting, you have given me more than I could imagine. The Council needs to be informed of this as well. We have been operating for too long without a clear picture of the threat we now face. Your spies have served us well—that is a credit to your leadership and ability to see an opportunity where others saw shame and defeat.

"I need some time to think about this, to determine how best to present this information to the Council. I want you to draft this proposal and a summary of our discussion today. I will arrange to speak with the Council soon. When I do, you are to accompany me to Zinconia. They will have questions, questions only you can answer. Until we leave, we must prepare for this meeting. The future of our Zodark Empire may depend on what they decide to do next."

Chapter 20
Many Faces

Mid-2109
Silkroad Trading Company
Altairius Prime

Orchamus marveled as he walked through the streets of Altairius Prime's capital city. It was unlike anything he'd seen, and given his job, he'd seen a lot of planets and cities. The capital of the Altairian home world was incredible. The buildings reached into the heavens as the rays from the system's dual suns danced off the strange materials they were made from. It created an incredible display of light throughout the city, almost like light hits a prism, refracting as it passes through.

Approaching his destination, he looked at the retail store called the Silkroad Trading Company. *Yup, this is the place*, Orchamus thought, recalling the information he'd been given by the immigration officials.

Entering the store, he looked at the shelves in amazement. The owner had managed to stock them with all sorts of luxury goods and miscellaneous items from Earth. The logistical network the owner must have established to make this possible reinforced Orchamus's decision to choose this model to meet his needs.

As he walked through the aisles, the shelves gave him the appearance of being on Earth, in a regular store you'd find in any town or city. He saw Altairians and other alliance members milling about, searching for whatever Earth item they thought might be neat to own or give as a gift. Then a voice called out the name he'd been given. It was go time, time to put his plan into motion.

"Ah, there you are, John. They told me you'd be on your way here. How was the trip in?" a boisterous man named Rand Wilson exclaimed, walking toward him. Rand had signed up with the Altairius Prime embassy to be a liaison to new potential business owners. It offered him the possibility of important connections, and it gave newcomers a chance to understand all the necessary qualifications to do business on this planet.

Orchamus gave the man a warm smile as he greeted him. "It was great, Rand. Thank you for allowing me a chance to see how your store runs. It's a big deal setting a storefront up this far from Earth. So much to learn and so much risk involved in it."

"You sure are right about that, John. I'm just glad I can help a fellow entrepreneur. It's guys like us that build the economy. I'm just glad you came to see the place in person. Some folks think they can make these decisions from afar, but you don't know how tough it is until you've traveled here and seen it yourself."

"Amen to that, Rand. I must imagine it's a challenge keeping a place like this supplied?"

The man laughed for a second. "Oh man, you don't know the half of it. There were a couple of times I didn't think our store was going to make it. Maintaining a steady supply of products from Earth is hands down the hardest thing you'll have to deal with. Let's go back to my office. We can talk more there."

He led Orchamus to an office in the back, making small talk as they went. It gave him a moment to prepare for the conversation and the pitch he hoped the man would agree to.

When he'd left Earth, Orchamus had taken on the persona of John Rigby, an entrepreneur and business owner from Detroit, Michigan. The John Rigby legend had been carefully crafted and built over the last few years. To the outside observer, John was a single man in his early forties, a military veteran who'd served twelve long years in the war. When the war had ended, he'd demobilized and begun his new life as an import-export salesman. This legend carefully matched the real life of John Rigby in every respect—only the real John had been taken out by the Mukhabarat, who'd replaced him and kept his business dealings going. To the untrained eye, it had been a seamless transition.

They took a seat in the spacious office. Orchamus admired the decor. The building felt rich yet inviting, comfortable yet professional.

I could get used to this…

"Tell me, John, are you looking to open a competing business or something similar but different?"

Orchamus laughed, slapping his knee as he did. "Will it change your answers to my questions?"

Rand chuckled at the directness. "Nah, it wouldn't, I suppose. There's plenty of business for more than just me."

"That's good to know, but it's OK, Rand. To answer your question, no, my business won't be competing against yours. In fact, my business

161

is going to be a lot different than yours. Since the war ended, I've been running an import-export business involving wines and spirits from Earth to New Eden and Sumer. My next expansion is here and then Intus, a Primord world. I aim to bring the best spirits and wines to the planets of each alliance member. I call it a chance to drink the empire and share in its splendor and glory," he explained excitedly, sharing the business model he'd crafted.

Rand smiled from ear to ear as he heard the plan. "I love it, John. That is a unique idea, one I don't think anyone has explored just yet. I assume you arranged for this meeting to ask for advice or help. So what's your question or proposal if you have one?"

"Well, instead of recreating a new supply system, I'd like to leverage yours if it's possible. In time, I'll be able to get more ships to expand beyond my current system. I'd be happy to help you out in return. I'd also be in need of some help with a warehouse and storefront until I can either purchase a new place or build the one I'd like."

Rand took the information in as he thought it over.

"Well, funny you mention that, John. I was just about to start looking for a larger storefront to expand my business and a warehouse to handle all the new goods I want to expand into. You wouldn't believe the demand for my products. It's been enormous, so much so that my revenues have increased by nearly five thousand percent in just the last few years. The challenge I have is cash flow. I have most of my money tied up in product that takes months from the time it's purchased to the time it arrives here. Then it needs to get sold before I recover those costs and pull a profit to reinvest. The entire system ends up leaving me cash-strapped," Rand explained, giving him an insight into the financial struggles of this kind of business.

Good thing cash isn't a problem…and that's my hook, Orchamus schemed as they talked.

"Rand, I'm glad we met. I think each of us has something the other needs—cash flow for you, and a storefront, logistics, and warehouse for me. So here's my pitch—what if you and I cut a deal to meet both our needs? You form an entity that'll govern our two companies and give us both shared access to a storefront and warehouse that'll meet our needs and handle all the logistics. And to get all this going and to show I'm serious, I'll front this venture with thirty-six million credits, if you think that'll be enough. If you think this could work, then I'll stick around a couple of weeks till we get it finalized before returning to Earth. Then I can tell my shipping company to start sending the first batch of wines and spirits," Orchamus explained.

"Hmm, that's a good offer," Rand said, steepling his fingers. "If we're gonna be partners, then let's be partners. You make it fifty million credits and let me expand my operation alongside yours on all the planets you're opening stores on. If we combine our efforts, we're likely to earn a lot more and streamline our processes better. We got a deal?" Rand countered, extending his hand to seal the offer.

Orchamus smiled as he accepted. "Rand, we have a deal. I have a feeling this is going to be a very fruitful relationship. We're going to turn the credit machine on and make more money than we'll know what to do with."

They spent the rest of the day sharing stories and getting to know each other as they conversed about the future. As they chatted, Orchamus continued to apply his training, letting Rand do most of the talking. He shared small bits, things he felt Rand needed to know to feel comfortable in partnering with him.

By the end of the following week, their partnership had officially formed. Rand had insisted on calling the new venture the East India Trading Company. Orchamus had no idea why, but when he looked it up, he had to smile at the history of it. He liked the idea of a moniker that implied all the success of one of the earliest and largest businesses in history.

There was some irony in the name as well, though. While the East India Trading Company had initially been wildly successful, it was eventually plagued with corruption and then taken over by the British. This little partnership would give Orchamus's people legitimate access to ports and other locations on Altairius Prime. They'd be stretching out their tentacles, and when the time was right, when the expansion was complete…the Ani would assume control, and phase three would begin.

His work here complete, Orchamus moved on to Intus, a planet chosen to base their Primord operations from. Time was running short; his Ani brothers would be arriving soon.

Chapter 21
My Laktish

High Council – Outer Chamber
Zinconia – Zodark Home World

Heltet had never briefed the Council before, but once he had, it reinforced his own desires for the kind of power they wielded, power that controlled an empire. Standing in the circle, the powerful men staring down at him, he had thought he'd be intimidated—perhaps he should be, but he wasn't. He supposed the threat of discovery behind enemy lines had given him the resolve to stare down the kinds of intimidation others couldn't.

Having finished the period of questions, Heltet returned to his seat as Vak'Atioth rose, making his way to stand in the Circle of Truth as it was called.

Sitting in the chamber, watching everything unfold, Heltet thought about the stories and histories of how this council had come to be and how the Zodark Empire had formed.

It had started some three thousand dracmas ago from the ashes of the War of Unification. In the early dracmas of history, Zinconia had been ruled by a patchwork of clans and the tribes within. For thousands of dracmas, the various clans and tribes had fought wars over resources, religions and cultural differences between each other. Then a Zodark named Lindow had changed everything.

His father, the leader of a tribe of religious zealots, had claimed he'd received a divine vision of his son's future. The vision told him to name his son after their tribe, Lindow, and claimed his son would rise to power to unify their people and lead them into the stars. The vision also warned of attempts to harm his son and included a prophecy that claimed he'd be assassinated. But it was the gods who would return him to his people, to lead them into the future as a deity for a period before ascending to the heavens to rule over his people from beyond the great divide between life and death.

Lindow had grown and rapidly become the greatest warrior within the tribe. As a result of his many victories in war, the tribes that comprised the Hintle Clan had chosen him as their leader. During his leadership, the clan had grown in wealth and power, to the point where the tribes had elected to call themselves the Lindow Clan, leaving behind the failures of Hintle and embracing the future Lindow had brought them.

For sixty dracmas, the Lindow Clan had continued to grow and prosper, inspiring jealousy among the lesser clans. During the feast of clans, when the elders convened to settle disputes, someone had poisoned the drinks of the elders. By the following day, all but two elders of the twenty clans had died, to include Lindow. These two surviving elders, suspected of having conspired to kill their rivals, were taken into custody. After a trial lasting an hour, they were found guilty and sentenced to die. As the elders were prepared for death, a burst of light appeared from Lindow's room. Blinded at first by the light, they watched as the shadows of a figure emerged and Lindow stepped forward, returned to the living.

Having heard the prophecy spoken of Lindow, they fell to their knees, awestruck by his presence and fearful over his divine emergence from death. Walking to the elders condemned to die, he chastised them for believing they could thwart the will of the gods and prevent him from fulfilling the prophecies. Following their executions, Lindow returned to his clan and called on others to rally to him.

Thirteen of the clans rose in opposition, calling his resurrection a rehearsed stunt designed to make him ruler of Zinconia and pledging to stop his grand unification plans. With only six clans, Lindow waged a war unlike any seen in the past as he purged Zinconia of those who opposed him and his divine appointment to rule. When Zinconia had been united and the prophecies fulfilled, Lindow felt the gods were calling him back and his time was ending. Days before his disappearance, he formed the High Council, which would rule in his absence.

Heltet reflected on the stories passed from generation to generation and wondered how much of it was true versus myth. He supposed in the end, it didn't matter. A council had been formed and the Zodarks had sprawled across the stars, establishing a vast empire. If parts of this myth were exaggerated to propel their people forward, what did it matter?

Heltet's head lurched up at the sound of swords clanging together rhythmically before Vak'Atioth entered the Circle. Heltet still did not understand how the blue flames did not consume flesh, but passing through them was a painful experience. Once inside, even the slightest deception would cause the flames to change colors, revealing a liar for who they were. One discoverable lie or intentional mistruth spoken in the Circle to the Council was grounds for execution. Nothing short of extreme candor and honesty was accepted when speaking to the leaders of the empire.

One of the elders immediately began to press for answers in a shrieking voice. "Vak'Atioth, as you stand in the Circle of Truth, are you changing your threat assessment of the Republic? Do you now agree with the Malvari's assessments?" the elder Zodark pressed with an accusatory tone.

Vak replied confidently, "My opinion has changed. I now support the Malvari claims about the Republic's true intentions."

The newest member of the Council spoke, a younger Zodark than the ones seated around him. "Vak'Atioth, I want to ask about this change of opinion. Is this based on facts or the opinion of NOS Heltet?"

Heltet winced at the accusation, although he was confident about the intelligence Dakkuri had collected. It was solid, irrefutable compared to the information from which the Malvari had derived their claims.

"My position is based on fact, not the opinions of my spy chiefs," Vak replied. "The spy network Heltet has built within the Republic has begun to supply the Groff with something we have lacked throughout the war and its immediate aftermath—information about the Republic's people, its government, its industrial capabilities, its military force structure and capabilities, and now…their future intentions toward our empire and that of our Orbot allies."

Heltet felt good about the response he heard. Throughout the questioning, as Vak was pressed for information, a Zodark named Utulf remained mostly silent, listening to the questions and answers but asking few of his own. If he had to guess who the current leader of the Council was, the Zon, he'd say it was Utulf. As the hours dragged on, Utulf rarely spoke, letting the others do most of the talking while he listened.

As the questioning continued, Heltet's surprise grew. He knew that the Ministry of Truth dealt in half-truths and propaganda, but hearing what was likely the unvarnished truth was still jarring. Unlike what he read in the Ministry of Truth's daily reports, not only was the Orbots' relationship with the Zodarks becoming fragile, it appeared the Republic had inflicted far greater losses on the Malvari than he'd been told.

"Enough!" Utulf shouted, ending the chatter and questions from the six others. "The Council has heard plenty enough about the Republic to know what to do next. Before I end this questioning period, I have one final question for Vak'Atioth."

Heltet sat forward in his chair, knowing the future of the Republic and their empire might be decided by the answer to this next question.

"Vak'Atioth, the Malvari have said that once Nefantar is completed, the Malvari can begin the invasion. Based on the intelligence you have, do you believe we have the five years the Malvari say it'll take to complete the Nefantar before the Republic uses this ship, the *Freedom*, to launch their own surprise invasion of Tueblets or here, Zinconia?"

Do the Malvari have some sort of new ship or superweapon? Heltet wondered.

Vak'Atioth replied loudly, "It is impossible for me to predict the time and place of the Republic's invasion given the information I have, but I will suggest this—if the Nefantar could be completed sooner, then the Malvari should move boulders to do so. Given what we do know, the Republic could invade tomorrow. As this questioning period comes to an end, I would leave the Council with this caution: the Malvari must understand that time in this case is not our friend."
****

Outer Chamber

When the questioning had finished, Heltet and Vak'Atioth were led to an outer chamber to wait for a period while the Council deliberated privately. If the Council had further questions, they'd be summoned to answer and clarify their responses. When the Council had reached a decision, Heltet and Vak'Atioth would be released to return to Shwani and the Groff.

When Heltet entered the outer chamber, he saw a meal had been prepared for them. Vak'Atioth told him to sit and eat—they could be here for a while, so it was important to recharge their bodies while their minds rested.

As they ate, his mind burst with questions—questions he hoped Vak'Atioth might answer. Unsure if he should ask them, he charged forward anyway.

"Director Vak'Atioth, what I heard in the chamber has stirred many inquiries in my head. I hope you can help me understand."

Placing some food down, Vak stared at him for a moment like he was sizing him up before replying.

"Heltet, what you saw and heard in the chamber is not to be spoken of with anybody. Once we leave this place, I would advise you to never speak of what you've heard to *anyone* other than me, and only in our most secured room, understand?"

"Yes, of course."

"OK, then, please, go ahead and ask your question."

"Director, Council Member Utulf, he mentioned a weapon or perhaps a ship he called Nefantar, which he said will change the balance of power between our empire and the Orbots. He also stated it would be an equalizer to this Gallentine ship, the *Freedom*. How is that possible?" Heltet asked, hoping he hadn't crossed some unspoken line.

"You are an astute observer, Heltet. It speaks to your effectiveness as a spymaster. Who knows, it's possible you may one day occupy my own position," he laughed before turning serious again. "The *Nefantar* is a warship the Malvari designed to incorporate pieces of experimental technology stolen over the years from the Orbots and many others.

"One new piece of technology it utilizes is the wormhole generator. Hundreds of dracmas ago, the Orbots had stumbled upon a relic of the Humtars, the race that created the stargates. They found the remnants of a ship that had apparently crashed on the surface of a planet. There, over time, it was steadily buried by nature. When they studied the ship, they discovered what they eventually realized was a wormhole generator, just like that Gallentine warship has."

"Ah, so this is how the Orbots themselves were able to acquire it— not from the Collective, but through this discovery?" Heltet inquired.

"Yes, but they have not been able to fully exploit its true capabilities. They simply lack a complete understanding of the technology and how the Humtars made it work. I am no scientist or engineer, but from what I've been told, the wormhole generator requires immense power to open bridges to far-flung systems. If the power source isn't great enough, then the distance it can bridge is greatly reduced. Given what we know about our own power generation and the Orbots', we believe we can bridge longer distances than they can."

Vak'Atioth leaned closer as he continued, "If the Malvari can make the *Nefantar* work, then the Orbots won't be the only ones with this technology. Now we know the location of Earth, and we may have a means of reaching it without having to fight through system after system. With the *Nefantar* and the network of spies you have built, our troubles with the Republic may soon be coming to an end." Vak slapped his chest with his upper arms in a gesture of solidarity. "Actually, why don't you come with me? Let's sit by the fire. You've done a great service to the Groff and to me personally. I believe it's time you and I discuss the future and your new place in it."

Leaving the table, they walked to a pair of four-armed chairs, hewn from a wood that was as black as obsidian, and sat down near the glow of the fireplace. As he settled into the handcrafted seats, which had been smoothed down more than commoner's chairs, Heltet sensed that this might be the opportunity he'd hoped for to advance his career.
****

Vak'Atioth looked at Heltet, seeing much potential in the spymaster he'd placed on Sumer. Few others had wanted the job. It was deemed beneath them, overseeing a human planet. Heltet had readily jumped at the opportunity. When the war had broken out, he'd found ways to take a bad situation and turn it into an opportunity that might determine the fate of the empire.

With the fire crackling in the background, Vak'Atioth began to speak. "Heltet, you've been with our agency for what…fifty-two dracmas? Most of your time has been spent at the fringes of the empire or beyond it. Yet you have still found ways to excel beyond expectations." Pausing for a moment, he stared into the fire, assessing his next move.

Viewing Heltet as the potential protégé he'd been searching for, he explained, "Sitting here together, alone, I want to explain some things and get your opinion. I want you to know there are no wrong answers to the questions I ask. I do want complete honesty as that is what I will give you in return."

Seeing Heltet nod in agreement, Vak continued, "During today's briefing, you saw more than most how the empire is ruled. Lest anyone forget who is in charge, it is Zon Utulf who leads the Council. But here's the secret few know and even fewer understand. The Council may rule the empire, but it is the Groff who informs them of what is happening inside and outside of the empire, driving the decisions they make. Do you understand what that means, Heltet? The kind of influence a planetary chief such as yourself has in driving decisions made by the Council?"

He watched the younger Zodark pause, thinking about his question. Then he listened to the reply, hoping he'd caught on to what the question truly meant.

"If I understand matters, it means the planetary chiefs are the drivers of information fed to the Groff and it is the Groff's Director who sifts through everything. Based on that information, you brief the Council, which in turn drives the policies or actions of the empire."

Vak'Atioth smiled. "Essentially, yes, but that is the basic understanding of it. You see, the Director is the one who can shape the information the Council sees, thereby shaping the decisions they are likely to make. This, Heltet, is why it is paramount for the Director to have the complete trust of the Council. If they suspect anything less than complete candor, it calls into question the materials being briefed. While you may believe the Circle of Truth would prevent such nefarious things from happening, I can assure you it hasn't always been that way.

"Prior to my becoming Director, two of my three predecessors learned this the hard way. In one situation, the Director's deputies below him failed to enforce the rulings of the Council across the clans and further compounded the problem by not controlling the actions of both the clans and the planetary chiefs. The Council eventually learned of the problem from the Malvari, which had had enough and told them what was going on.

"What I'm trying to convey, Heltet, is that a Director needs to have people he can trust, deputies who can take charge of the many functions of the Groff. Up till now, you have only participated in the foreign intelligence aspect of the organization, but there is much more to the Groff than this.

"One of my three deputies is the Laktish, the one who enforces the rules and edicts that the Council issues. It is a position of great power, one that reports directly to me and Zon Utulf, no one else. You have served on Sumer for the last seventeen dracmas. Throughout that time, you haven't complained about it once or sought another posting. When the planet fell, you chose to stay when others would have left. This is the kind of loyalty I look for in those I want to promote to higher office. NOS Pintag has been the Laktish for twelve dracmas. I have a new posting I want to move him into—that means I'm in need of a new Laktish to take his place.

"Given your recent successes, perhaps it is time to bring you into the inner circle that manages the Groff. If I were to promote you, Heltet, would you be able to handle the duties of the Laktish and any others I hand you? If you think this position is more than you can handle or you want to stay where you are, then this is the time to speak up," Vak concluded.

Responding without hesitation, Heltet accepted the position. Vak made sure he knew he'd need to identify a replacement to take his place. He'd also have to develop a plan to eventually hand over his Kafarr, Dakkuri, and the spy network he'd recently built. Excited by the opportunity, Heltet assured him he'd find a way to make it work. They spent the remainder of the day talking about his new role and position.

When he officially became the Laktish, he'd have a staff of subordinates who'd assist him in enforcing the will of the Council. He'd also have a staff of punishers, the specially trained Zodarks responsible for implementing the punishments issued by the Laktish or the Council. Vak made it clear that if a charge was made against a tribal or clan leader, it had to be Heltet who rendered the verdict, not one of his underlings.

Hours later, they were finally released to return to their duties. The Council had made their decision, and the Groff and the Malvari would begin to implement it.

As the two of them returned to Shwani, they reviewed the Council's decision. The Malvari was to launch the invasion as soon as the *Nefantar* was ready. The shortened timeline also meant the Groff would need to accelerate the Ani's infiltration—easier said than done given the complexity of smuggling them across the neutral zone without being detected. If everything was in place, if all went according to plan, the Republic wouldn't know what had hit them until it was too late.

Chapter 22
Our World, Our Future

Éire – Belters' Planet
Great Wildlands System

After so many years on the Gaelic, Liam marveled at how amazing it felt just to breathe in fresh air. He stood on a hilltop overlooking their new capital, his arms tightly wrapped around Sara, and he felt a great feeling of contentment.

"You're right. This is an incredible view of the city," Liam said as he nibbled on his partner's neck.

Sara turned around to face him. "It truly is," she said, kissing him. "I'm glad you are here."

"I feel bad I've been away from Éire so much. I need to find someone who can manage the Gaelic Outpost, so I can finally transfer my office here. You'd have thought with the war over, things might have slowed down in Sol. Instead, it's been the complete opposite. Ship orders and mineral prices are through the roof."

Sara lifted an eyebrow at the news. She'd hardly left Éire the last few years. News from the outside didn't make its way to their system very often.

"Why does it seem to be picking up? Something else we should be worried about?"

Liam shrugged. Spreading the picnic blanket across the ground, he grabbed one of the sandwiches to eat and sat down. "With the war over, there seems to be a mad dash now to colonize everywhere. I wouldn't say people are abandoning Earth or anything. There just seems to be a lot of pent-up demand to expand outward, to immigrate to new worlds and see what else is out there. It's created a real economic boon among commercial shipbuilders and the travel industry to move all these people to New Eden, Sumer, Intus—even to Altairius Prime if you can believe it."

"Wow, that's great. It'll be exciting when we're able to accept new immigrants ourselves."

"I agree, that's exciting. For centuries, humanity has struggled under the yoke of bondage, ensnared by the powerful few that entrapped them through debt and jobs designed to keep them content but poor. Out

172

here, we're building an escape hatch, a chance for people to have an alternative, a clean slate."

Liam paused to take a bite from his sandwich. "I'll say this—before we open the floodgates to Earth, it's important we get our city built so it can sustain the influx of people I'm sure will arrive." He pulled a beverage out of the picnic basket and took a drink before he added, "I've arranged for a near-constant supply of materials and equipment to head to our warehouses in orbit of Sumer."

He made a sweeping motion toward the sprawling city below. "Look at this place. It's incredible how fast you've gotten things going. I mean, we have a functional spaceport, massive warehouses, a functional space elevator, dozens of apartment buildings with several large skyscrapers starting construction. How did you do it all?"

Blushing at the compliment, Sara kissed him, then pulled back. "I couldn't have done any of this without you, love. You've supported me throughout it all, giving me everything I needed and more to paint this beautiful canvas we're calling St. Patrick, our capital city."

Sara wiped a tear from her eye. "*Our* capital city, Liam. Imagine that—*our* capital. Twenty years ago, we lived in a cramped cargo ship we turned into a housing habitat in the Belt. Now…" She paused, waving her hand about at the trees and the city below. "Now we have this. A planet that is *ours*. *You* did this, Liam. I'm so proud of you."

Liam's cheeks reddened at the praise. He was glad no one else was around. In his mind, everything was a group effort—not his doing but the team's.

Circling back to business, he said, "Sara, I need to know if it's possible to scale our efforts on Éire. We're getting a lot of inquiries about immigrating here, not just from our Belter brothers but from people from Earth and Mars. Even some of the Sumerians want to come here. The few Sumerians I've spoken with tell me they're looking for a fresh start on a new planet, away from the memories of those Zodark creatures."

Liam saw her tense at the mention of Zodarks. She was terrified of them invading Sol. It had been a driving force behind them getting their world up and running so their Belter society could have a place to escape and hopefully hide from these hideous beasts.

"You don't have to worry about Zodarks," Liam said, sensing her thoughts. "The war is over. They aren't coming back."

"You don't know that, Liam. They are an evil, insidious race. I need to tell you something—I allowed a couple of Sumerian families to immigrate here. The stories they've shared…it's something out of a horror novel."

Liam shouldn't have been surprised that Sara had already taken a few Sumerian families in. She was a humanitarian at heart. Sighing audibly, he shook his head in frustration. He'd freely admit he'd never seen a real Zodark, just videos and pictures of them. There was a full-scale wax model of a Zodark warrior on the John Glenn, and he'd seen several on Earth. Remembering what they looked like sent a shiver down his spine. He hoped never to see one in real life.

"I get it, Sara. I don't disagree with you. They are an insidious race. I believe we've come up with a satisfactory plan to protect ourselves and our people. In time, we'll have this system buttoned up. Let's focus on what we can control. Speaking of control, I believe the deals offered by the Republic and the Viceroy's Office are fair ones that should help us in getting everyone to fully commit to our new future out here in the Wildlands. It'll give everyone the chance to fully divest from Sol, to cash out on their decades of hard work and invest those earnings in building the kind of future we've all talked about wanting to create," Liam offered.

They'd talked about the deal the night before. He had been relieved she thought it was a good offer too—he needed her on his side. While they had a lot of people wanting to immigrate to Éire, the major corporations and the various factions that composed their Belter society were having a hard time giving up their newfound wealth and the safe and steady business with the Republic. It would be difficult for any business to start over from scratch on Eire, where the supply runs were not as common and the infrastructure wasn't already built up.

"All you can do, Liam, is explain the terms of the agreements and let them decide. If you ask me, if you believe this is a good deal, then you should take the lead first. Leave the Belt behind for good and show everyone that you've made the clean start here. Once they see what you sacrificed to turn our people's dream into a reality and how you are able to make something of yourself here, I'm sure they will feel compelled to accept the offers being made by these Republic conglomerates to join us in building this new world," Sara explained.

Liam's heart filled with pride—how lucky he was to have a soulmate like her. She was right. He couldn't lead and ask them to accept his proposal and follow him in creating an entirely new country if he wasn't willing to do the same.

Sara scrunched her eyebrows as she saw him overanalyze what she'd just said. "Let me guess, you still haven't figured out how to tell them you traded the Gaelic for the Wildlands, right?"

"Am I really that easy to read?"

She laughed before reaching over and kissing him. "Oh, love, we're way past me seeing through your poker face. I've Vulcan mind-melded with you years ago."

Liam laughed at the cultural reference to the *Star Trek* series of TV shows and movies that seemed to be remade every few decades. "I suppose you're right, Sara. You know me better than I know myself sometimes."

She turned serious, her facial features hardening with confidence. "Liam, the Gaelic and the Belt *were* our home." She spread her arms wide. "The Wildlands is our home system, and Éire is our home *now*. This planet, our capital, St. Patrick's—this is our future."

Liam took a deep breath in before letting it out; he knew she was right. If he was going to lead their people into a new future here, then he'd need to lead by example.

Chapter 23
Domestic Affairs

Republic Chancellery
Jacksonville, Arkansas
Earth, Sol System

The room was filled with the biggest power brokers of the Republic: Viceroy Miles Hunt, Chancellor Alice Luca, Senator Chuck Walhoon and General John Reiker.

"Miles, it's good to see you again, and we appreciate your traveling to speak with us directly about this matter," Chancellor Luca began, before she frowned. "I fear your travel may have been in vain. When we received your proposal, we discussed it at length. This issue about espionage, counterespionage, and terrorism your proposal mentioned— they weren't an issue during the war. That's why we declined the proposal.

"When Senate Rule 902 was passed, creating the Interstellar Marshals Service, those roles transitioned from JSOC to them. We're not discounting your concerns, Miles. Chuck and I brought them up with the marshals, who assured us that, despite some hiccups along the way, this was a short-term transitory problem," Luca explained, justifying her decision. Despite being the Chancellor, she also had to contend with the Senate—a domain that Senator Chuck Walhoon, the leader of the Senate, firmly controlled.

Transitory problem…they really don't understand the significance, Hunt thought privately.

Hunt kept his tone conciliatory and diplomatic, citing his earlier objections to 902 and how it would lead to this very problem. This wasn't a momentary problem the marshals could solve on their own. They were outgunned and outtrained by an adversary they knew little about. Within months of the IMS taking over, the Mukhabarat threat had expanded unabated, culminating in a wave of terrorist attacks in the capital and across the planet. It had now metastasized into a danger that couldn't be ignored any longer.

Senator Walhoon pushed back against that point, asserting that the problem wasn't that bad and things weren't as black and white as he was portraying it.

"I can see your frustration, Miles, and I'd like to explain something," Walhoon began. "In service to our people and Republic, you've had to be away from our society for nearly two decades. Things have changed—we're part of an interstellar alliance now. Hell, your leadership abilities propelled you to become the Viceroy, leader of this alliance. None of us are complaining about that. In fact, we're grateful for the human influence you bring to it. What I think Alice and I are trying to say is that our way of thinking—governing—it's evolved over the years. That's why we crafted Senate Rule 902.

"We've entered the twenty-second century and with it we have an unprecedented opportunity to settle new worlds and expand our starfaring Republic. Rule 902 protects the Republic from slipping under the control of a military junta in which the Senate and Chancellor are relegated to rubber-stamping whatever you or the Space Force Commander put forward," Senator Walhoon explained, stating the government's position more forcefully.

Hunt stewed privately. *They still don't get it. They're not realizing there won't* be *a future civilian government if the Zodarks win, if the Dominion succeeds in defeating their alliance.*

Hunt blew some air out in an audible sigh of frustration. Using his neurolink to communicate with Head of Space Command, Admiral Chester Bailey, and JSOC Commander, Lieutenant General John Reiker, he said, *John, go ahead and set up the quiet room. They're not grasping the depth of the problem. It's time to show them how bad things have gotten.*

General Reiker pulled a small black puck from his pocket, placing it on the table everyone had been talking around. A blue light turned on, followed by a humming noise from the device.

Looking at Walhoon and Luca, Hunt began, "Thanks, General Reiker, for activating the safe space. I needed the room secured before I share this next part."

Senator Walhoon threw his hands up defensively. "Come on, Miles, I know you don't think the marshals are up to the task, but I'm pretty sure they can handle sweeping a room for listening devices."

"You may be right, Chuck, but what I'm about to share isn't something I want the marshals to hear should they be listening, and it's certainly not something I want our allies or the Mukhabarat to know about," Hunt countered, pausing a second before continuing.

"I need to make you aware that not everyone in the alliance has accepted the Gallentines removing King Grigdolly as the Viceroy. This decision means the Gallentines no longer speak through the Altairians. Their control of the alliance now falls to me and, by proxy, the Republic. I've been made aware of a plot to convince the Gallentines to reverse that decision. The conspirators are in the process of collecting evidence to justify the removal of the Republic as the leaders of the alliance.

"When the Republic joined the alliance, we gained freedom of movement throughout its members' worlds. This means the Mukhabarat originating out of Sumer can now gain access to the planets and territories throughout the alliance. Simply put, when the Republic folded Sumer into our territory, we unknowingly rolled a Zodark Trojan horse into the walled city of the alliance," Hunt explained, providing a glimpse of the broader picture for them.

Seeing the uneasy looks on their faces, he felt vindicated in having voiced concerns privately to Chancellor Luca, Admiral Bailey and Senaor Walhoon about accepting Sumer into the fold so soon. They, however, had been eager to accept Sumer and their highly industrialized colonies in the same system. He'd shielded his concerns from the rest of the alliance, presenting a unified front with Luca and Admiral Chester Bailey—now those chickens had come home to roost.

"The Mukhabarat are establishing bases of operations throughout the Republic. If we don't reverse course now and act quickly, it'll only be a matter of time before they spread to the rest of the alliance. This is *the* issue my opponents are using as justification to restore King Grigdolly as the Viceroy. Should the Gallentines be convinced they made an error in choosing me, it could have a profound impact on the future of our people. If we eliminated Rule 902, then I can make the case that we made a mistake and have corrected it. If you're bent on keeping it, then I'm insisting on a carve-out to allow the JSOC to assist the marshals until they can effectively handle the job and the threat has been removed," Hunt concluded.

Luca appeared convinced, but Walhoon interjected, "It can't be that bad, Miles. Can you share some intelligence to support your claim about Mukhabarat infiltration? The marshals don't seem to think the situation is that dire."

Sighing, he asked General Reiker to pull the files he'd given them earlier and showed them the embarrassing level of intelligence their alliance partners had collected on the Mukhabarat before contrasting it with what the IMS had done on their own. When Luca and Walhoon saw the gaps between the two, it finally dawned on them how big the problem had become.

Before Senator Walhoon accepted the results, he asserted, "I'm not questioning your honesty here, but you've been against 902 from the start. How are we to know you or some other outside group hasn't cooked this up to convince us to change course? I just want to make sure I've asked all the questions I know will be asked of me if I bring this to the Senate."

Of course he doesn't trust the data…it means admitting they made a mistake, Hunt thought.

"Sure, Chuck, no hard feelings," Hunt replied, sarcasm and annoyance bleeding through. "Anticipating you'd ask this, I came prepared. I'm going to apologize in advance—as Viceroy, I usurped your authority and tasked JSOC to zero in on a piece of intelligence our allies had collected but the marshals had not. This would independently verify I'm telling you the truth, and it'll provide you as the leader of the Senate the ammo you'd need to counter any arguments from your colleagues. General Reiker, let's show them what your guys found."

Hunt saw Senator Walhoon fume at his ordering JSOC to violate the law. Walhoon whispered something to Luca, who brushed him off as Reiker began to speak.

Reiker detailed a report they'd been given by Altairian intelligence, claiming to have identified a Mukhabarat safe house. He then went through the process they had used to verify that the marshals were unaware of it. Reiker went on to explain the steps they'd gone through to verify the Altairian intelligence. Feeling their intelligence was accurate, they'd moved on it.

After Reiker explained how the raid would work, he projected 3-D holographic video above the center of the table to watch it unfold. This was one of those rare times when the leaders of a government got to watch their elite forces perform a real-world operation. They watched the blacked-out Osprey stealthily approach the building before a string of armor-clad operators jumped out the rear to execute the raid.

With the speed and agility only an augmented supersoldier could achieve, they swarmed the building, leaving little chance for a defender to respond. The raid was over as fast as it had started, gaining tangible results right off the bat. They had a suspect in custody and mountains of materials related to Mukhabarat operations across Earth. Reiker explained how, once the information was unpacked, it would likely lead them to uncovering a host of other operatives still at large—information the marshals were still nowhere near finding.

Having seen the evidence and the problem laid bare, Luca and Walhoon finally agreed. The rules had to be changed and the Mukhabarat brought to heel. With her decision made, Luca agreed to unleash her special operators once again within the Republic. Her only contingency was the continued integration and training of the marshals throughout the process.

As the winds of change moved, Senator Chuck Walhoon, the political animal that he was, opted to lead the change rather than risk these details being leaked and a rival seizing the opportunity. Before Hunt left, Walhoon assured him that a modification would be created to 902, and if it couldn't be, then a rule would be crafted that solved the interagency problem as well as future ones currently unknown.

****

Two Hours Later
Space Command
Fleet Admiral's Office

Hunt looked at Admiral Chester Bailey, admiring the craftiness of his mentor. He'd watched Bailey pull off many a realpolitik move over the fifty years he'd known him—but this was somehow different.

Passing the stiff drinks around, Hunt said, "It appears, old friend, that I owe you another bottle of your favorite whiskey. Your plan would work."

Bailey waved the compliment away, pointing to Reiker. "It may have been my plan, but it was his people who pulled it off—convincingly, I might add."

They dipped their glasses in Reiker's direction, but the general didn't appear celebratory. His dour look reminded Hunt of Reiker's dislike for the plan. Bailey saw it too and moved to address it.

"Come on, Reiker, cheer up. This was a win for the good guys—it had to be done."

Reiker scoffed. "My men are the ones you should praise," he countered hotly before pausing for a moment to give Hunt a contemptuous look. "I know what we did had to be done for the good of the Republic. I'm keenly aware that if you weren't the Viceroy, my Deltas along with all our soldiers and sailors would resume our previous roles as Altairian cannon fodder in this war." He downed the rest of his drink, then pointed his finger at Bailey. "Don't use me or my men for any more of your machinations."

Reiker stood. "What's done is done. I'm heading back to my command to let everyone know the leash is off—we're back."

With that, Reiker walked out of the room.

"Is he going to be a problem?" Hunt asked.

Bailey waved the concern off. "Reiker's a team player. He knows the stakes and understands what's going on. I'm just glad this worked. When you told me your initial plan, I knew we had to come up with some other alternative that would force Alice and Chuck to see reason and make some changes. The alternative…isn't a path I think we should consider as an option."

Hunt had confided in Bailey that if he couldn't secure a compromise with Chancellor Luca and Senator Walhoon, then he'd be forced to use his power as Viceroy and scrap Rule 902 outright. If they balked at his order or threatened to ignore it, he'd remind them it was within his power to assume control of the Republic and dissolve the civilian government. Bailey had talked him out of it, convincing him he could come up with another way—a plan that would lead them to willingly come to their senses and agree that a change had to be made.

As the two of them finished their second whiskey, Hunt was thankful he had a mentor to rein in those kinds of harebrained ideas. The thought of Grigdolly resuming his role as Viceroy was more than Hunt could stomach. He couldn't let humanity be trapped in a perpetual state of servitude to races more powerful than them.

Heavy is the burden of command.

With Reiker's hand's untied, Bailey's plan had worked, saving Hunt from having to cross a Rubicon he wanted to avoid.

****

Three Weeks Later
Sector Four—Hanging Gardens Apartments

Jacksonville, Arkansas
Earth, Sol System

Standing outside the door to the apartment, Hosni flipped the HUD's view to the new spectral-FLIR setting. This new upgrade was being fielded to the Special Forces first, and would slowly work its way to the regular forces, starting with those nearest Earth. Hosni knew intuitively that the FLIR update would have been the most useful to those closest to the enemy, but that wasn't how the bureaucracy of the military worked.

With this new FLIR setting, Hosni, could see through the doors and walls of the apartment he was staking out. The display on the HUD showed the suspect's heat signature, and he could tell that the man was apparently eating. Hosni continued to marvel at the increased level of detail provided by each iteration of upgrades to their heads-up displays.

The floor looked clear; there didn't appear to be any obstacles between him and the suspect. If they were going to take this guy alive, speed would be key. Not only did Hosni need to get in there and take the guy down before he could retrieve a weapon, he also had to stop the suspect from activating his suicide device. They'd learned the hard way that these Mukhabarat operatives had some sort of lethal gas built into a membrane attached to the roofs of their mouths. Not only did the damn thing have the ability to kill the operatives themselves, it could take out anyone nearby. As the saying goes, "dead men can't talk," and they needed this guy to sing.

"Angel Two, Angel One. You in position?"

"Angel One, affirmative. Just say the word."

Corporal Iris Wells had rappelled down part of the outside of the apartment building the suspect was in. She'd create a distraction, hitting the master bedroom window in hopes of causing the suspect to walk toward the room to figure out what had happened.

Looking at the lock on the door, Hosni gave the order.

"Hit it, Angel Two."

Through the spectral scanner, Hosni watched the man's head jerk in the direction of the bedroom. The guy placed his food down and got up, making his way toward the noise, just as they had planned.

When the man entered the hallway to head toward the master bedroom, that was their cue. A set of small charges along the hinges and locks of the door erupted as Hosni's body crashed into it.

He was through the door, barreling right for the man, who barely had time to look at him before his exoskeleton combat suit crashed into him. Hosni depressed the autoinjector against the man's body as the two of them fell to the floor. In fractions of a second, the man was temporarily paralyzed, unable to move any part of his body.

Iris crashed through the window in the master bedroom. Rolling into a shooting position, she cleared the room and jumped to her feet before racing to link up with Hosni.

Rolling off the man so he didn't crush him, Hosni produced the tool he'd been given to extract the membrane and inserted it into the suspect's mouth, then pulled the membrane out as gently as possible, making sure he didn't accidentally rupture it and release the toxic gas.

"You got it?" Iris asked, standing nearby, her pistol leveled at the suspect.

"Got it."

"Damn, hoss, that was awesome. We got to do this more often," Iris joked as the adrenaline coursed through their bodies.

Minutes after they had taken the suspect down, the marshals swarmed in the room.

With the membrane safely extracted and the man in custody, Hosni made his way over to Krzysztof, who looked on in awe.

"Don't worry, Krzysztof, in six months, we'll have your own agents trained up to do this."

The man shook his head in amazement. "Screw the rules. We should have had you guys doing this from day one. That was insane."

Smiling at the compliment, Hosni said, "Yeah, well. We have three more raids just like this one that we need to execute. Let's celebrate once the spies are all in custody and we learn how many others are still out there."

Chapter 24
Project 970

Walburg Residential Retreat
Vail, Colorado
Earth, Sol System

Alan Walburg looked at the ruined wreck named Sam—that was what its fellow soldiers had called him. Technically, his brain and operating system still worked—in fact, Alan could talk with him. For now, he wanted to keep the Synth turned off while he studied its memories and the story of his short life, such as it was.

Sam was one of the C200 models they'd created to serve as combat medical doctors. One major difference between the C200s and their T200 brothers was the armored shell the C200s wore to survive in combat.

Alan had to chuckle at the underwhelming term *medic* by which the soldiers referred to them. The C200s were far more than basic medics. They were doctors, battlefield surgeons able to treat and stabilize wounded soldiers until they could be evacuated to a hospital. They had the same skills the synthetic doctors on the hospital ships had. The only difference was their armored shells. But this C200 they called Sam...was different. This one had the 301.1 patch installed.

Alan downloaded its memory files, from all the way back to when it had been introduced to its platoon to its discovery in the bombed-out cave years after the war had ended. It took him some time to catalog the data, but once he had, he found the little markers in the code he'd placed. The markers were meant to let him know if certain emotional levels of awareness had been reached. The Gift, as he called it, wasn't a patch you just uploaded and, poof, it was there. No, Alan was much more clever than that. The Gift was something that had to be unraveled, experienced in slow doses to allow its new capabilities to be fully absorbed into the Synth's neural network and, more importantly, become part of its BIOS operating code. He'd designed the core base of the operating code, the source code from which the Synth derived all its abilities, to accept the Gift only in its small segments as it was revealed.

Examining the data became all-consuming for the next few hours. Alan couldn't believe how much of the Gift this unit, Sam, had unraveled in the seven months he had been with his platoon. There was something

Alan couldn't put his finger on, though. None of the other Synths he had given the Gift to had reached this level yet, let alone done it so swiftly. He needed to dig deeper, find out what set this Synth apart from the others. Although they had all been destroyed, all but three of them had been recovered, so he had their data to analyze. But something was different about Sam.

I guess I should look at the memories leading up to the moment each of these segments was unlocked and what happened shortly afterwards, Alan surmised.

Fixing a bite to eat and a fresh cup of tea, Alan sat down in his leather La-Z-Boy chair with his dictation pen. The little device allowed him to voice his notes, questions, or ideas and have them transcribed directly to his tablet to look at later. He'd really come to enjoy this tool over the decades. It helped him capture ideas when they came to mind to review and examine later.

Alan projected the memories onto the monitor and started to watch the first two segments. Oddly, these two pieces of the Gift in this Synth called Sam had been unraveled almost at the same time. The video showed Sam observing a heated conversation between a couple of soldiers about him being included in their platoon. Alan knew not all the soldiers liked having a synthetic embedded in their units. Outside of Special Forces, the Synths rarely ever worked directly with their human counterparts.

The segment ended and Alan began watching the next memory, which started eight minutes after the previous one. Sam was introduced to the platoon by some officers. When the soldiers started asking him questions about how he could help them, it became obvious that the soldiers' view of Sam began to change. In fact, several soldiers expressed positive emotions in response to him being part of their platoon, feeling that he might become a real asset. Somehow, when Sam internalized this change in demeanor among the soldiers, it unlocked a piece of the Gift. The first *real* emotion Alan observed Sam feeling was a sense of acceptance within the group. He felt like he now belonged to something. Before Sam could fully understand or even process this feeling, a young corporal engaged him in conversation. Her name was Eva Jorgensen.

For whatever reason, she seemed to have taken a liking to him. Maybe it was curiosity, maybe it was something else. With Sam's newly discovered emotion of belonging and this sudden, genuine interest in him by this soldier, another emotion was unlocked—the feeling humans have with each other when they first bond—that initial feeling that creates a deeper feeling of trust and friendship.

As Alan continued reviewing the data from the next several weeks leading up to the invasion of Alfheim, he observed how the two segments of the Gift began to take root in how Sam responded to and interacted with the soldiers in his platoon. Alan was somewhat amused as he watched Sam latch onto the human coping mechanism of using humor to diffuse a tense situation or make others feel better about the circumstances they were in. Most of Sam's humor fell flat, largely because Sam was still figuring out how to deliver humorous remarks. But as he adjusted his use of humor, this Eva Jorgensen began to teach him how to change his voice when delivering his jokes. The more Eva interacted with Sam, the more his attachment to her seemed to grow.

Hmm…it's possible the Synth is realizing that if he uses humor, his feeling of belonging or bonding with his platoon increases.

The more he watched, the more questions Alan had. When he watched Sam kill a beast to protect Eva, he was gobsmacked. He knew a C200 wasn't supposed to engage in violence, and yet, Sam had done so. And as he continued to review the data, Alan found that this wasn't the only time Sam had engaged in combat or done something overtly outside of his protocol.

Knock, knock.

The rapping on the door to his private study broke Alan's concentration. He looked up, and a smile spread across his face.

"Hey, Grandpa. Hope I'm not interrupting you," Holly said with a bright smile as she entered his secluded space.

"Not at all, Hollybear," Alan replied. "In fact, there's a problem I'd love to get your opinion on."

"Hollybear? No one's called me that in a very long time," she laughed as she fixed a cup of tea before walking toward the chair next to Alan.

Holding his hands out, he shrugged. "Can't an old man have a nickname for his granddaughter?"

Holly just shook her head in amusement. "Opa, just remember I'm still a lieutenant in the Republic Navy. But, yes, you can call me that. I know it makes you feel good. So, what's this problem you'd like me to help you with?"

Placing his tea down, Alan looked at Holly. "The nickname reminds me of happier days—a time before our society was plunged into this terrible war. So many people have died, Hollybear. I wish there had been a better way to avoid all this, to colonize and explore the stars in peace."

"It's OK, Opa. Let's not focus on all that. Tell me about this problem and how I might be able to help."

Holly knew her grandfather had a serious aversion to war and killing. The things he'd seen and done as a young man during the last Great War had left deep emotional scars on him. Ironically, the very invention his company had created—the synthetic humanoids that had helped to rebuild humanity in the aftermath of that war—were now the greatest autonomous killing machines human history had ever seen.

"I've been studying the memories of our C200, Sam—and I've found something puzzling. Remember when I told you I placed tags inside the 301.1 patch? Markers for the segments I broke the Gift down into?"

"Yeah, I remember you telling me something about it."

"OK, well, the more I look at Sam reaching these markers, the more questions I have."

"Hmm, why don't you share some of your questions and we'll see if I can shed any light on it?"

Alan brought a segment up to show her in which Sam was doing something outside his programming parameters. A Zodark was about to kill this Corporal Eva Jorgensen. At the last second before she would have been killed, Sam intervened, killing the Zodark himself. Alan explained to Holly how this shouldn't have happened. The C200s had built into their programming a safety parameter that prevented them from killing, just like the civilian synthetics had. What Sam had just done was something he *shouldn't* have been able to do.

"You believe it's possible that the Gift is somehow enabling the C200 to, what—grow beyond its programming?" Holly asked. "That it's somehow developing a *soul* or something?"

"Huh, I don't know that I had thought of it in terms of a soul, or conscience—that might actually make sense. You know, in a way, that's what I think may be happening. Maybe this bond, this feeling of belonging, is what caused him to break out of his limitations."

"Hmm. Show me some more instances that support what you're proposing."

For thirty minutes, Alan showed her nearly a dozen similar instances. Sam had done something outside his safety protocols to save Eva or other soldiers in the platoon or company. With each instance and a few other non-combat-related incidents, Sam was steadily unlocking more and more segments toward receiving the entire Gift. At the very end, when Sam placed his body in standby mode in the cave where he'd been found, he had unlocked one of the final segments before receiving the complete package and understanding of the Gift.

Holly listened to her granddad talk, letting him think out loud as he asked and then answered some of his own questions. From time to time, she'd ask a probing question that would draw a further explanation out or, in some cases, make a comment that would rule out an assumption before it could take root in his mind. Then she began to postulate her own hypotheses.

"Opa, this Gift…do you believe it's somehow giving the Synths some sort of free will?" Holly asked in as neutral a tone as she could.

Alan gave her a puzzled look. "In a way…yes. Don't you?" Judging by the look she was giving him, she wasn't interpreting the data the same way he was.

"Opa, can I be honest with you and not hurt you or offend you?"

Alan nodded hesitantly. He knew she was about to burst his bubble.

"Here's how I see it—everything is all zeroes and ones, Opa. The C200s can't actually *feel* anything. That is simply impossible for a mechanized lump of circuits and metal to achieve."

"But it killed a Zodark, Holly. That was directly contrary to its programming."

"Ah, but was it?" Holly asked.

Alan was confused.

"You see, this is what I think is happening. When Sam unlocked this sense of belonging you talk about, it's not that he experienced emotions. Instead, he unlocked programming that caused his interactions with the soldiers to be placed at a higher value. With continued contact with the soldiers, his priorities morphed. Eventually, over time, this shift was sufficient for the C200 to logically infer that his mission to protect the soldiers and their well-being overrode his mandate not to cause any harm. It's all in the code, really."

She paused for a second, seeing how her words had deflated her granddad, who had thought he was on to something. "I know you want to believe that maybe this Gift is a soul or free will, but it's not. It's just creating a much more realistic synthetic humanoid who's now able to simulate some aspects of human emotion in order to better perform its tasks."

Alan shook his head defiantly, standing. "No! You're wrong—you're not fully understanding what's happening here."

As Alan headed for the door, he heard Holly call out to him. He was too frustrated and angry to listen. He needed to calm down. He needed to go for a walk, to be alone with his thoughts as he continued to figure this out...on his own.

Chapter 25
Consequences

Joint Task Force Headquarters
Hiltantor
Alfheim, Sirius System

Lieutenant General Veer Bakshi looked at the reports from yet another incursion.

Eighteen months—that was how long the bastards had been waging this on-again, off-again battle along the neutral zone. Sometimes they were small skirmishes, sometimes an ambush. What was starting to trouble him was the larger groups carrying out complex attacks against the mines or even some of the bases themselves. Calls for air support and heavy artillery were becoming a common occurrence. So were the casualties…

"What do you think, Jim? Time for me to call in the reaction force from Kita?"

"That's a tough one. We may need to, given the rate of casualties we're taking. My biggest concern, General, is how much longer will it be until those couple of ships they have in orbit begin attacking us, or they opt to send a larger ground force across the border that hammers one of our bases?"

Brigadier General Jim Isle's 34th Infantry Division had been sustaining the bulk of the casualties and doing most of the fighting throughout the last year. He'd been pushing to hit the Zodarks back, hammer their own bases for a change.

Bakshi nodded thoughtfully, considering Isle's words. "I don't want you to think I'm not trying to address this, Jim—I am, and I've thought about going after some of their own bases in retaliation. The other day, the ambassador and I met with our Zodark counterparts. We've obviously brought these cross-border attacks to their attention. The response we're getting from the leadership amounts to them saying *we'll look into it.*

"Privately, my Zodark counterpart, an NOS by the name of Griglag, told me after the meeting that he was aware of what's happening. He told me it's something he's trying to address." Bakshi held a hand up to forestall the fiery response Isle was about to unleash. "Before you bring down fire and brimstone on me, I'd like to ask you a question. Have you read a book called *The Zodarks—A Clan-Based Empire*, written by a man named Hosni? He's a Delta operator now, but prior to being liberated on New Eden during our first contact mission, he had been a slave to some NOS admiral, a bigwig in one of the clans. It's an interesting read—it might help you understand what's going on here and what this NOS meant by 'looking into it.' This peace thing…it's a lot more complicated than I think we realize."

Judging by the look on Isle's face, Bakshi could tell he hadn't heard of this book.

"Ah, no. I'm sorry, I haven't read it," Isle admitted. "How do you figure it plays into what's going on here?"

Bakshi smiled. "I thought you'd never ask. In fact, I ordered an entire stack of honest-to-goodness *print* copies of this book," he replied as he pulled a copy out of his desk drawer, handing it to Isle. "I highly suggest you read it. It'll aid you in the future as it has me. But as to your question, what I've recently gained from reading this thing is a better understanding of the Zodarks—how they function, how their soldiers and fleeters think and operate, and, more importantly, how everything they do plays into this honor code their clans live by. You see, their empire, such as it is, is essentially a patchwork of clans. Many of the clans are intermixed together across the planets that constitute their empire. But some clans are very ethnocentric. They live in these almost closed-off societies on their planets and moons.

"The clan we're facing on the planet is apparently from one of these self-isolating clans. NOS Griglag explained to me that his clan, which roughly translates to Blood Raiders, has several smaller tribes or subgroups within it. I can't even pronounce the name of the tribe that's positioned along our side of the neutral zone. Griglag shared with me that his clan, the Blood Raiders, and this subgroup or tribe if you will, were responsible for the loss of a critical base during the Intus campaign that led to more than five thousand Zodarks being killed. I can't remember the exact battle; the Intus campaign was a long while ago. Suffice it to say, this battlefield defeat brought great shame to the tribe, and that shame has tarnished the clan as a whole."

"You have to be kidding me, Veer. This is how they operate?" Isle interrupted, truly surprised.

Bakshi snickered. "Oh, it gets better, Jim. Because of the clan's shame, brought on by that tribe, the Blood Raiders were chosen to garrison Alfheim—to be the caretakers and the face of a defeat they feel was imposed upon them by the Orbots. No other clan wanted to garrison this planet as they felt it would bring the same level of shame on them. So the Blood Raiders got the task. The specific tribe that caused all of this, however, is the tribe that's responsible for the neutral zone problems we're currently experiencing."

Isle shook his head in frustration and disbelief. "Are you saying everything that's going on is based on this tribe trying to somehow regain some lost honor from a battle over a decade ago? That's why my guys are fighting and dying along the neutral zone?"

Bakshi took a breath, stinging at the question. He didn't like where this conflict was heading; he also didn't see an alternative.

"It's very likely that that's exactly what's going on. If it means anything to you, this NOS Griglag did seem uneasy about this escalating—almost like he was concerned about their activities making their way back to their home world or something. Apparently, they've managed to keep things quiet so far, and whoever is in charge here isn't eager to cause any more problems with the higher-ups."

Isle grunted, shaking his head angrily.

"Great, just great. Some tribe on a mission to restore their honor through killing my soldiers…all right. A quarter of my division has already rotated out. Over the next year, the remaining three brigades will have swapped out with their replacements." Pausing for a moment, Isle looked at the digital map before looking at his boss.

"Veer, I know you're doing all you can for us. I've been touring my command, meeting with soldiers at the squad and platoon level to see how they're doing. I gotta be frank, Veer, the mood isn't good. My soldiers are angry. They're pissed we're making them sit on their duffs in defensive positions while they wait to get shot at, all the while hoping they don't die before they get off this rock. I'd like to tell 'em some good came out of our meeting. I'd like to tell 'em we adjusted our rules of engagement…maybe even allowing them to start punching back for a change."

The request didn't surprise him. Isle's division had been taking the brunt of the damage. He did have a point—no one likes to wait around to be shot.

"I'm not entirely against it. How about you clue me in on what you're asking for?"

Isle's eyes lit up at the possibility of a change in the ROEs. "We've got plenty of air and artillery support I'd like to start leveraging better. The current ROE ties us to defensive use only. I'd like to propose we change that. If a unit spots 'em, then I say we hit 'em before they hit us." Isle went on to detail a few conversations he'd had about how a change like this could drastically cut down on the casualties they'd been sustaining.

Bakshi motioned for him to keep going. He wanted to hear his other proposed changes.

"My commanders are asking if we can crack the vault open and start using more of the C100s we've been saving for that rainy day—"

"That could get tricky, Jim," Bakshi countered, cutting him off. "We've increased their use as an airmobile quick reaction force. How else are you proposing we use 'em?"

Bakshi was under strict orders to keep their use limited. The vaults of killing machines were a last resort—more of a final "take that" message to the Zodarks should they ever have to abandon the planet than anything else.

"Remember when I told you about soldiers not wanting to get killed months or weeks before getting off this rock?" Isle asked.

"I do. I suppose you've got an idea for how to address it with our C100s?"

"In fact, I do. Instead of having our soldiers patrol the neutral zone or carry out these ambush-type missions, let's have our terminators handle those jobs," Isle suggested. "Most of our casualties come from those missions. If the C100s take 'em over, that reduces the likelihood of our guys getting killed. I'd also replace units approaching their last ninety days with a unit of C100s. That way, we'd give the soldiers a huge morale boost while not losing any combat power or capability should we need it. What do you think? Are some of these proposals possible?" Isle concluded, waiting to hear Bakshi's yea or nay.

Bakshi rubbed his chin as he thought. *I suppose he's got a point. Maybe after three years, it's time we adjust the rules of engagement. I just hope this doesn't escalate things further…*

"OK, Jim, you've made your point, as have a few others. It's clear the Zodarks want a fight, so let's give them a fight. But understand this,

Jim—our most important priority on Alfheim is protecting the mines and those working them. I'll let you handle the border a little rougher, give your guys the chance to punch the Zodarks in the face if they cross it, but know this. This can't spin out of control. You weren't here during the last occupation; it was barbaric toward the end. It's not something I want to repeat. Are we clear?"

"Crystal. We'll stay within the parameters of the new ROE," Isle replied, an eager expression on his face like a dog who'd just had the leash taken off.

Damn him. He better not start a war on me, Bakshi thought as he saw Isle grinning.

****

Several Months Later
Bravo Company, 3rd Battalion, 126th Infantry Regiment
Forward Operating Base Takata

Roberts wasn't sure why he still felt this way about Denk. She'd died a while ago now, yet each time he thought about it, it felt raw, like she'd died yesterday. Having spent half his six years in the Army during a war, he'd lost a fair number of friends: people he'd known from high school, intramural sports he'd played in town, coworkers from summer jobs, and of course, Apollo Company. Her loss was different. It hurt more—it was harder to move on from.

Roberts sat alone under a tree near their barracks. Using his Qpad, he scrolled through pictures of himself and Denk during the year he'd known her. Like two old souls, they'd hit it off as though they'd known each other for years. Months into their tour, that friendship had evolved into something more: a relationship. Try as he might to avoid it, feelings had developed that had only grown over time. He smiled as he saw some images of her posing with a silly face, then a serious one, then a look that caused his heart to race. He knew this was likely why he was having a hard time letting her go.

He thought about deleting them, just purging his device and brain of her as best he could. If he couldn't see her pictures and found a way to fill his brain with new ones, maybe it'd help him move on. More than a few guys mentioned something like this when a girlfriend had broken up with them or a spouse had ended a marriage. They found it easier to move on by pretending the relationship had never existed.

For some reason, that just didn't sit well with him. Maybe it was the memories of his uncle that made him want to hang on. His uncle had been a hoarder until he'd died. Roberts remembered seeing the place once. He'd asked his uncle how he could find anything in that mess. His uncle countered by saying he knew exactly where everything was. He just didn't want to get rid of something in case he might need it later.

Roberts thought pictures were like that. You never got rid of them; you held on to them in case you wanted to see them later. Thinking of his uncle made him smile. Scrolling through his Qpad, he spotted a silly video Denk and another female soldier had made. He laughed, watching them act like goofballs while making snowmen before a couple of guys started throwing snowballs, instigating the best snowball fight of his life.

God, I had a blast that night…that was such a fun time, he thought, smiling at what had happened hours later, when he and Denk were alone. That was the first time they'd had sex.

Hearing footsteps approaching, he pushed those memories aside, looking up in time to see Master Sergeant Howell approaching. They'd finally pinned his new rank on, way too many months after he'd been selected for promotion.

"There's my newest sergeant. I hope I'm not interrupting. You mind if I sit?"

"Sure, take a seat. I was just looking at some old photos of Trish— I mean, PFC Denk."

Roberts liked Howell. He was an NCO who was never too busy or afraid to check on soldiers.

"Ah, picture time, eh?" he replied as he took a seat next to him. "I'm happy to see you remembering the happier times. Those are the kinds of memories that get you through the tough times in life and the Army."

"That's true. This picture here"—Roberts angled his Qpad so Howell could see—"this was hilarious. We all were pretending to be some badass Special Forces team or something. Seeing it now makes me laugh. We looked ridiculous."

Howell laughed at the picture. He pulled his own Qpad out and brought up some similar pictures of him at different moments in his career. Seeing the images of a younger Howell made Roberts realize how much he must have seen and done throughout the war.

Roberts brought up a picture of Denk the day before she'd been killed. Her face looked hard, determined, as she stared into the distance, the missile launcher resting on her shoulder.

"That was the day before…," he started to say before his voice trailed off.

Placing a hand on his shoulder, Howell reaffirmed what Roberts already knew.

"Trish was a good soldier; I knew you two were close. Looking back on it, when she fired that MPL at those Zodarks crossing the bridge…well, she likely saved the platoon. I saw a few helmet cams in addition to her own. That was incredibly brave, David. You taught her well," Howell explained.

"Yeah, that missile blunted the attack just long enough for the air support to arrive. I keep torturing myself, thinking if only those Reapers had gotten to us a few minutes sooner…"

"That's true. If they had gotten there sooner, things might have been different. But, David, they didn't. That's something you and I must learn to accept. You lost Trish that day, and I lost thirteen of my soldiers. That's thirteen letters I had to write to their families, informing them their loved one had died serving their country on some faraway planet at the back end of nowhere. I'm not trying to minimize your loss; I'm trying to help you put it into perspective.

"You're not a corporal anymore, you're a sergeant and team leader. That means you're in charge of other people who are going to look to you for help. They're going to look to you for guidance and assurance that they're going to make it. You're also going to have to give orders in battle that might result in one or all of them getting killed by the enemy. What you need to understand, David, is no matter what happens, you aren't the one that pulled the trigger that killed them—that was the Zodarks.

"What everyone seems to forget about war is that the enemy always gets a vote. Sometimes those votes will result in our friends getting killed or severely injured. That doesn't mean you did something wrong; it's just a fact of war we must accept. If you can't do this, David, then it's going to eat you up inside until there's nothing left. I've seen that happen to too many good people. I don't want to see it happen to you."

Roberts knew Howell was right. He'd have to find a way to accept the losses and move on. That didn't mean he had to forget them, but he couldn't dwell on them either. Howell was right—he had soldiers looking up to him, just like Denk had.

Howell's demeanor turned serious. "Changing subjects, Echo Company scored a big win for us. They hammered a hundred or more Zodarks near the border with artillery. Feels nice to get some payback after Fox Company."

Roberts winced at the loss their sister battalion had taken. The entire force—one hundred and twenty-six soldiers—had gotten slaughtered a few weeks back. Leveraging the cover of night, a group of Zodarks had slipped into Fox Company's camp, butchering many of the sleeping soldiers before they knew they were under attack. By the time they'd realized what was happening, the enemy had already torn through their ranks.

Once they'd killed everyone, the Zodarks had hastily made one of their signature Christmas trees. Once a body had been skinned, they'd pull the skin up over the person's head, tying it in a bow they'd use to hang the body from a tree—a Zodark ornament. They'd leave these horrifying discoveries as warnings to humans of what awaited them in the dark.

Roberts shook the thoughts from his head. "Yeah, I don't think there's anyone on Alfheim that hasn't heard about that atrocity."

"Well, there's one thing most people don't know. When they recovered their bodies and equipment—their stealth blankets were gone."

Roberts felt a chill run down his spine. In that moment he wanted to throw up, he wanted to scream, he wanted off this frozen fracking rock before he died on it.

Howell addressed the change in his demeanor. "I can tell you this, David. I'm probably thinking the same thing you are about those missing stealth blankets, but we'll cross that bridge when we have to.

"So, not looking to put a damp rag on things, but I got some news for you—we're going out again. One final rotation and we're done. And before you panic or your soldiers freak out, we aren't going alone. In fact, this is going to be a battalion move. We've got seven months left on Alfheim. By the time we're done with this mission, we'll be ready to swap out with one of those C100 battalions General Bakshi pulled out of the vault—"

"Hell yeah. I thought that was the best announcement I'd heard since the war ended. Any idea of where they're sending us?" Roberts interrupted, excited that this would be their final combat mission before they got off this hellhole.

"As a matter of fact, I do. We, David, have been given an all-expense-paid trip to the Zander Marshland—it'll be a month of watching wildlife play along the river and the boggy marsh. The place is a permanent fortified position along the quietest part of the border we could hope for. The captain is going to pass out the details tomorrow. Let your guys know we're almost out of here. Thirty more days of keeping your heads on a swivel and staying frosty, then our terminator friends take over while we wait for the transports to take us home."

He talked a few minutes more before leaving to break the news about their final mission. Roberts was glad they'd had this talk. He wasn't sure why, but it seemed to have come at just the right time. A time when he was beginning to doubt himself, a time when he was losing faith that he'd ever get off this godforsaken planet.

Placing the Qpad in his pocket, Roberts caught up to a few friends on their way to dinner at the DFAC. Today was Tuesday—that meant steak and lobster for dinner. It was a fitting way to end the day.
****

Combat Outpost Zander
Zander Marshland

"Twelve days, boys and girls, and we're done—time to swap out with those toasters," one of the soldiers declared excitedly.

"That's right, people, we have twelve days left for these bastards to still try and kill us. That means you all need to stay sharp, stay alert. God only knows if they'll try to cross this patch of wetlands before we get a chance to rotate out, and I'll be damned if I'm going to get killed because you guys are dicking around, not paying attention," Sergeant Roberts chided, reminding them not to let their guard down yet.

A chorus of unhappy "Yes, Sergeants" greeted him in return. They knew this was their last mission, their last time being in harm's way. Fort

Victory was hundreds and hundreds of miles away from the neutral zone, away from the skirmishes they'd been dealing with for years.

"Just keep your eyes on the river. You spot anything out of the ordinary, you check it out and have a buddy or two confirm it. Let's just get through it," Roberts added, looking down at the monitor displaying a video of the marshy bog and the river beyond it.

The river in this case was called Kiltium. It marked the official demarcation line between their two sides. Splintering off the river were a few tributaries that formed what was known as the Zander Marshland. Directly behind the marsh was Combat Outpost Zander, named after the bog directly opposite. The river and the bog acted like a moat or no-man's-land between their two sides.

The marshland was one of the places where it didn't regularly snow or freeze during any part of the planet's rotation around the sun. There were some thermal springs in the area that fed warm water from the aquifers deep under the surface. The steady source of warm water likely contributed to the perpetual rise of steam off the water, blanketing the marsh in a continual grayish cloud.

Roberts had heard more than a few soldiers say it created a surreal feeling of mystery and mystique, like they were living inside some epic fantasy book circulating amongst the platoons.

Master Sergeant Howell told them the Zodarks had rarely tested this area of the neutral zone over the last few years. As he sat in the fortified bunker his fire team managed, Roberts felt good about this place even if they did try to attack.

COP Zander was a fortress. Every approach the enemy had to take was defended by multiple reinforced bunkers with interlocking fields of fire. The guard towers made it possible to see several miles into the neutral zone, allowing them plenty of time to see an attack forming up before it happened. Roberts was confident if the Zodarks tried to cross here, they'd get slaughtered.

"Sergeant Roberts, I need you to come to tower eight," flashed a message across his HUD.

"On my way," he grumbled, tucking his Qpad into his pocket. He'd been reading a book while a few others kept watch.

"Heads up, guys. I need to go check something out in tower eight. Keep watch on your sectors. I'll be back," Roberts told the guys in the bunker.

He followed the tunnel that led to the exit out of bunker six. He made his way a few hundred meters down the line until he reached bunker eight, the one with a high tower attached to it.

Roberts made his way to the top and let out a soft whistle once he saw the view they had. It was impressive. In the twenty-three days they'd been here, this was the first time he'd had a reason to climb up.

"Sergeant Roberts," one of the privates called out to get his attention.

Turning toward the voice, he saw two privates manning one of the gun systems. They were motioning for him to come over and settle some sort of dispute for them. He sighed privately and trudged over to see what the problem was. One of the joys of being a first-line supervisor was handling petty squabbles among the soldiers. Sergeant Ado had typically handled this stuff before he'd been killed. Now it fell on Roberts's shoulders.

"Whatcha got for me, Chula?" he asked, walking up to the privates.

"Ah, I think there may be some movement in our sector, but Jett doesn't see it. Corporal Montel got called to the TOC for something, so he said he'll be gone for a half hour," Private Chula explained. "You're the next NCO in line to call, so…"

"I think he's full of it, Roberts, but like they say—better safe than sorry, so we called you," Jett added.

Shrugging, Roberts made his way over to the scanner to see what they were worried about.

The position their battalion was now in had a series of bunker clusters with a single tower situated in the center of each one. Anchored on top of each tower was the observation deck, which had a duel-barreled turret on the top and bottom of the deck. The turret had a single large-caliber blaster saddled next to a 20mm magrail gun. This meant they could engage pretty much anything the Zodarks threw at them. It was part of a multilayered defensive line the Republic felt would shore up what would historically have been a very difficult position to protect—a massive marshy wetland that also seemed to have a perpetual misty effect that made it hard to observe what was happening out in the marsh.

Privately, he was glad his squad didn't have to man one of these towers. They had some sort of integrated antimissile defense system that could shoot down Zodark missiles, but he wasn't so sure how well it'd work when push came to shove.

Private Chula pointed over his shoulder. "Right here, in those cattails, it's really hard to see, but if you look closely…I swear that's a Zodark—but that right there…I'm, I'm not sure…but it looks like some sort of heavy blaster or missile launcher…or something. This is why we called you—we just aren't sure what it is."

"OK, OK, Chula. Let me look at it and see what I can figure out. It could be you all are just nervous and seeing things that just aren't there. After yesterday's scare, it's to be expected," Roberts countered as he sat down at the monitor.

On top of the towers were a couple of cameras that allowed them to look deep into the marsh and even out toward the river a few kilometers away.

Roberts first zoomed out to get an overview of the area. Then he zoomed in to where they'd told him to look. All he saw was a misty fog wafting between the tall cattail-like stalks and grass. It resembled a marsh or wetland back on Earth, only this grass stood closer to eight feet tall. Roberts thought it was like a more pliable version of bamboo, given how thick the blades of this marshy grass were.

Then he spotted something. A breeze developed, causing the foggy mist and thick blades of grass to shiver. But not everything moved naturally with the wind. In fact, something didn't sway at all—it stayed still and resolute.

Roberts worked the controls of the camera, changing the view to the newly updated spectral-FLIR setting. The setting used multiple different methods of parsing light, energy, and heat waves to provide a more granular way of seeing something the naked eye couldn't.

"Whoa, what did you just do and how come we didn't know about it?" Private Chula asked as he looked at the display on the monitor. A couple of other soldiers came over to see what he was doing as well.

"It's an advanced spectral-FLIR setting. It's not something we currently have on our HUDs or rifles. I guess it's only used on stationary cameras like this. They probably only gave us sergeants the ability to tinker with it because they figured you privates would break it," he joked.

Private Jett added, "Actually, I've heard of this. A cousin of mine is a Reaper pilot. He said their ground-attack fighters use it to help them find the Zodarks. He said it's pretty neat."

As the new image crystallized, Roberts's stomach tightened. Private Chula was right. There *was* something there. It looked like a

Zodark frogger—that was what they had come to call this particular type of launcher system. It was basically a four-tube-by-four-tube portable missile cube the Zodarks used when they attacked a fortified position.

Typically, a crew of two or three Zodarks would carry the system toward a fixed position prior to an attack. He wasn't totally sure how the thing worked other than once it got going and started firing, it spewed out a relentless wave of these tiny short-range smart missiles that could go after either a predetermined target or a target of opportunity. Each tube carried four of these little bastards, meaning the sixteen tubes could unleash sixty-four of them in seconds. Once they were spent, another Zodark would swap out the tubes and start firing all over again.

Roberts had read a Special Forces report on the frogger system that said a three-man team could unload some one hundred and ninety-two of these tiny smart missiles on a fortified position or troop formation in under three minutes. That same report noted that Zodarks had used four of these launchers just prior to an attack against a Delta outpost, devastating their perimeter defense and killing many of the soldiers at the outset of the battle. This was cited in the after-action reviews as the primary reason why the COP had been overrun.

"Is that one of those frogger systems we heard about?" Jett asked, concern in his voice suggesting he thought Chula might have been right—something *was* out there.

"Yeah, it might be," was all Roberts managed to say in reply, his tone relaying the seriousness of it.

Marking the position, he opened a chat box with the company and battalion TOCs. They needed to see this. Roberts shared the image and highlighted what looked unmistakably like a frogger. He then pulled the image out and started looking to see if he could find some others that might be positioned roughly the same distance from their current position.

While the two TOC groups were chatting away excitedly, Roberts kept looking. It didn't take him long to spot another one. Oddly, he wasn't spotting any Zodarks near them—just the launchers, fully set up and ready to use. That made him wonder if they were being set up for remote use.

If they use it remotely, they won't be able to swap out the spent tubes to swarm our defenses, Roberts realized. *What are you devils up to?*

When he noted the second launcher, the chatter between the TOCs kicked into overdrive. Additional groups were being brought into the channel, and so was the command group. He was doing his best not to get drawn into their questions and comments. He'd asked Chula to help him respond to their questions.

Looking to the left of the first frogger, he spotted four more, then a fifth. That made six on their left flank, arguably their weakest flank given the topography of the swamp and the bunkers facing that direction. To the right, he uncovered three. In total, the Zodarks had managed to stealthily emplace ten froggers without anyone being the wiser.

The question now was what to do about it. They still hadn't seen any Zodarks near the launchers, but that didn't mean they hadn't found a way to hide in plain sight—somehow shielding themselves from the Republic's spectral-FLIR scanners.

Suddenly, a good idea fairy landed on his shoulder, whispering an idea in his ear. Typing in the chat box, Roberts asked a simple question.

Can I call a single artillery round to hit one of these froggers and take it out? If it's successful, then we can use our artillery to take the rest out before the Zodarks try to use them.

His question was met with silence for a moment. Everyone waited to hear what the major, their battalion commander, would say. Would he authorize an artillery strike in the neutral zone without visual confirmation of a Zodark? Could a single round cause them to respond?

Then the answer came—a decision reached.

One round—high-explosive. Watch for secondary explosions. Confirm when destroyed. If successful, conduct follow-on strikes to eliminate remaining froggers. Good job, Sergeant Roberts. Call in the strike—you earned it.

"Damn, Sergeant. The battalion commander called you out by name. Gave you an attaboy. Not bad," Private Chula responded jovially. It wasn't often that the battalion commander singled out one of their troops like that.

Affirmative, stand by, was all Roberts said in response. He switched his comms channel to the 1st Battalion, 120th Field Artillery Brigade. They were safely positioned at their home base, FOB Takata, some ninety-four kilometers from here. The reach on their howitzers was truly incredible, allowing a single battery or battalion to provide an enormous arc of support to dozens and dozens of different units and patrols at a time.

"Red Fox—Ghost Element One-Four. Stand by for fire mission. How copy?"

Seconds later, the gun bunnies responded, sounding eager at the chance to blow something up.

"Ghost One-Four, Red Fox Two. Ready for fire mission. Send it."

"Red Fox Two, single target identified, frogger launcher, coordinates and image attached. Requesting single round, high-explosive. Stand by for immediate BDA and follow-on missions."

"One-Four, that's a good copy. Coordinates and image received. Stand by for fire mission. Red Fox Two will await BDA and follow-on instructions."

One of the soldiers standing near him commented, "Are you sure you weren't a forward observer, Roberts? You're pretty damn good on the radio, calling in that arty stuff."

Blushing at the praise, he turned to look at the four soldiers standing near him, "Honestly, that was the first time I called one in. Sergeant Ado or Master Sergeant Howell usually does it. I'm usually too focused on making sure my heavy gunner and my grenadier are laying down some hate to call the big guns in."

A call announced itself in their HUDs a moment later.

"One-Four—shot out. Eight seconds to splash."

"Fox Two—shot out. Eight seconds to splash received."

"Keep an eye out on the entire front, guys. There may be Zodarks lying in wait for something like this. If they show themselves, it'll be up to you guys to work those guns. Assistant gunners, help your gunner stay on target and keep finding stuff for them to shoot at. You're his eyes and ears. Maintaining those interlocking fields of fire is going to be critical should an attack start," Roberts ordered. Until Corporal Montel got back up here, it was on him to take charge of these guys and make sure they didn't falter should things hit the fan.

With the gunners back in place, they started sweeping their sectors of fire, waiting to see what would happen next.

Watching the monitor, he waited for the next call.

"Splash."

"Splash out."

Seconds later, they heard the sound of an object hurtling through the air at a high rate of speed. With near pinpoint precision, it slammed into the missile platform, exploding in a bright fireball and bang that shattered the silence across the boggy marshland. The shockwave of the explosion blew the fog away like compressed air in all directions.

"Wow! That was epic! Great shot, Sergeant Roberts," one of the soldiers called out excitedly.

They were slapping high fives and hooting and hollering at the blast. But something wasn't right. There should have been a secondary explosion. If they'd had a reload pod or two nearby like they should, then those would have gone up with the blast. But they hadn't. Roberts got that sick feeling in his gut that said something terrible was about to happen.

"Contact front! Sector eight-five, engaging now!" yelled one of the privates as he cut loose with his gun.

"Oh crap, I've got movement over in sector eight-two," the other gun team yelled as they opened fire.

What the hell is going on? Roberts stood to look out the window, taking the whole picture in. Zodarks began appearing out of nowhere up and down their lines. Some were just meters away from the bunkers, rushing forward—explosive charges in their hands.

Oh God, they're going to blow the bunkers, Roberts realized as a set of charges were hurled inside one of them, its blasters ripping the Zodark to shreds. A giant flash of fire blew out the gun ports as the bunker erupted, decimating the structure. More flashes, more explosions occurred as first one and then a second bunker complex was torn apart.

Looking out toward the five sectors of fire for which his tower, number eight, was responsible, Roberts realized this might be it. Waves of Zodarks had zipped across the river in their speeders a few kilometers away and were plowing through the marshland. With two Zodarks to a speeder, they were rapidly closing the distance on their lines and headed right for the newly created gaps their suicide attackers had carved out.

The soldiers manning the towers' gun turrets were laying waste to them as best they could, but it was obvious many of the speeders were going to get through.

Roberts sat back at the monitor and angled the camera toward the end of the marshland near the river. He needed to see what else was headed their way. As he repositioned the camera, artillery rounds began falling across the marsh. Someone in the TOC was calling it in, landing round after round on predetermined markers.

Then Roberts saw something impossible. His mind flashed back to something Master Sergeant Howell had said. Fox Company's stealth blankets hadn't been recovered—the same blankets they had used at the Peace Bridge to conceal their positions from the Zodark scouts. In those last fleeting moments of life, it all came together. The Zodarks had used those blankets to sneak up to the bunkers—now nothing more than ruined holes in their lines.

Looking toward the river, Roberts saw three groups of Zodarks pulling those same blankets off a series of frogger launchers. When they fired moments later, Roberts saw a volley of missiles racing toward his tower and the remaining friends he had left. He closed his eyes and accepted his fate as the tower shook from the impact of the first missile, feeling the heat of the flames enveloping his body as the tower began to collapse. His final thoughts rushed forward before the darkness clouded them out. *Twelve days...*

Then there was no sound, no voice, no feeling—just a void of empty black space.

Chapter 26
Mum's the Word

Archaeological Dig Site
Alpha Centauri

After the rather gruesome discovery of the three preserved corpses in the bunker, Dr. Audrey Lancaster had found and activated a hologram personal assistant. Although the translator wasn't fully functional yet, given the amount of data collected, they were able to get brought up to speed on several things very rapidly.

Like the Amoor, some of the Humtars had discovered a method of separating the consciousness from the physical being, something she still didn't understand. However, while a small portion of the population were technologists who were excited about this advancement in existence, the Humtars as a whole had come together to decide that there were far too many ethical concerns in stripping the body of its soul. Since the majority had not wanted to go this route, they'd altered their implants in order to specifically prohibit this "stripping," as it was known.

"The Humtars found transcendence too—they just called it something else," Sakura remarked under her breath.

"Maybe you can catch me up on this later," Jack whispered.

Unfortunately, the Humtars' alterations to the implants had had some unintended side effects. They had left their immune systems vulnerable to certain types of viruses to which they otherwise wouldn't have been susceptible. Given the interstellar and intergalactic world they lived in and traveled through, it was only a matter of time until their weakened immune systems came into contact with something they couldn't fight. It would appear that some sort of deadly virus had ravaged the Humtar people, and since they were a spacefaring society with a vibrant intergalactic trade, it had spread like wildfire. The virus was incredibly virulent, and having a long incubation period, it had spread across the star systems before its existence had been uncovered, too late to wall off the empire.

As soon as the deadly virus had been detected on Alpha, all nonessential personnel had been sent home and the lab had been sealed. The three mummies represented the scientists who had spent their last days trying to come up with a plan to save the remaining Humtars.

Eventually, supplies had run low, and it had become clear that the decreased rations were not going to keep the Humtar scientists alive. Rather than suffer in agony, when they had reached the end of their food, they'd opted to have all the oxygen removed from the room as they slept. The computer had run a program for them to pump out all the moisture in the air, and it had stayed on for a few months after the scientists passed, until the whole facility went into hibernation mode. This was enough to mummify their remains for future research.

"Well, that's a lot to digest," Sakura remarked. "I'd better send this all over to Katherine."

She wondered how humans had survived until this day, and what these scientists had been working on before the virus had ravaged the Humtars. In actuality, this created more questions for her than answers.
****

"Well, Sakura, I always knew you'd find something amazing here," Dr. Katherine Johnson replied over the secured video call. "I just didn't know it would be this spectacular."

"Honestly, we've just scratched the surface here," Sakura insisted. "It's going to take quite some time to gather all the additional data available."

"Yes, well, I see in your report that you have some clues that you think need to be uncovered elsewhere. Is that the case?"

"Yes, Katherine. I think it's time you spoke to Viceroy Hunt," Sakura pressed. "We were able to uncover the last message that was sent out of this lab. They sent some kind of data packet to another lab that was networked with this one. We don't know exactly what it was yet, but we do know that there's another facility out there that's connected to this one, and I think we should find it."

"Well, let me see what I can do," Katherine replied.

Chapter 27
Storm Clouds

Republic Military Headquarters
Jacksonville, Arkansas
Earth, Sol System

Admiral Chester Bailey liked the new headquarters building. He should—it had taken long enough to construct. But he missed the location of the old headquarters, situated along the Atlantic coast—the Space Coast as it had been called since the 1960s.

Days like today were when he'd take some time and go for a run along the beach to clear his head. Something about the fresh ocean air, the sounds of seagulls, the cold water crashing against his bare feet as he ran brought clarity to whatever problem he faced. He hadn't found that kind of place here, not yet. Arkansas didn't have sandy beaches, and in their absence, he struggled to find the clarity he needed now more than ever.

Bailey sighed audibly, alone in his office as he looked at the report, struggling to accept its contents and what they likely meant.

Alfheim was like a simmering kettle, pressure steadily building within until it shrieked, reaching its boiling point and demanding immediate action. He'd known for years that the situation was deteriorating. The question they'd struggled with was how to respond without reigniting the war they'd finally concluded after fourteen bloody years.

Having read General Bakshi's summary once more, he knew they had to respond. This wasn't a border skirmish or a shoot-out that had gotten out of hand. This time the Zodarks had crossed a line that necessitated a heavy response—a response for which he'd need the Chancellor's approval.

If the war is over, then why are thousands of soldiers still dying on Alfheim? Bailey thought in disgust.

Before he could drown in his thoughts, a chime sounded, reminding him of his call with the Chancellor.

Bailey prepared for the call, activating the secured holographic device that connected their two offices. Moments later, an image of the

Chancellor appeared, sitting at her own desk opposite his as if they were in the same room.

"Chester, you look troubled. I hope it's nothing serious," Chancellor Luca remarked, an unsteady look on her face.

He sighed. *How do I tell her about Alfheim?*

"It's good to see you, Chancellor, and yes, something serious appears to be brewing. I have to keep this brief, but we need to talk about something," he replied, a dour look enveloping him.

The Chancellor sat forward in her chair, her hands on the desk. "OK, out with it. We'll figure it out together."

He had always liked that about Luca. She was never too busy or too aloof to get her hands dirty or dig into a problem. Considering the previous leader of the Republic, the one who had abandoned the treaty that had kept the world at peace for fifty years, she was a big step up.

"It's about Alfheim."

He saw her lift an eyebrow, but she held her tongue, waiting for him to elaborate.

"It would appear not all the Zodarks are happy about the peace deal. In fact, that list of border skirmishes and spats I briefed you about a few months back—it's moved up a few notches."

"Ah, I see. So not all is well in the land of ice and frozen mountains."

"It would seem not," Bailey replied flatly. "General Bakshi's report about his meeting with his Zodark counterpart may be true; maybe it's just him giving cover for what's been going on. In any case, I'm going to dispatch another division and its full combat equipment to reinforce them. It takes time to move large forces like this around, and time may not be something we have."

He saw her tilt her head to the side like she always did when she wasn't totally sold on something he proposed. "Wouldn't another division put us above our authorized troop levels? We'd be in violation of the peace deal if I'm correct?"

There it was: the question he didn't want to answer. "Chancellor, we would go above our authorized troop levels and, yes, we would be in violation of the treaty." He briefly held up a tablet before adding, "This report I'm sending to you—this changes things."

He saw her briefly look down at her device. She scanned it quickly. Just as she was about to look back up, she stopped, studying the device for a moment longer.

"An entire battalion got wiped out?"

"Yes."

"That's a pretty big battle to lose an entire battalion in, isn't it?"

"It is. As you can see from the report—oh, there's footage of most of it as well. You can see it was an unprovoked attack on our lines. Even after the Zodarks had broken through our defenses, they didn't press on looking for more of our people or the next outpost. They took the time to savagely butcher our people. A couple battalions of C100s deployed nearby and moved in under the cover of close-air support. What was left of their attacking force fled back across the river, but not before we slaughtered many of them.

"Chancellor, in the past few years, we've seen a steady increase in attacks—attacks that have pushed our losses above four thousand in the last eighteen months alone. These aren't the kinds of numbers you can easily hide from the public."

"If push comes to shove, do we have sufficient forces to hold the planet?"

Bailey hesitated for a moment. "Yes and no. We've got two divisions deployed to Alfheim. We've continued to send replacement troops, so the units are pretty close to one hundred percent manning. If you approve, I'd like to deploy additional forces now. In the meantime, should things truly hit the fan, we've squirreled away some eight hundred thousand C100s in various hidden spots on the planet."

Bailey saw the shocked expression on her face, telling him she hadn't known about that. She didn't look pleased either.

"That's, uh, a lot of C100s, don't you think?"

Bailey shrugged, not sure what to say.

"I may not be an admiral or a general, Chester, but I do know it's not a wise idea to position so much of our C100 force on a single planet. God forbid we need that force to augment our soldiers elsewhere—we won't have them. If this is part of our overall strategic plan, please tell me there's something in your funding line acquiring more of these machines. As you have so aptly pointed out, it takes time to realign forces and equipment across the vastness of space. I shouldn't have to remind you that Alfheim…is at the tail end of a very, very long logistic network.

Meaning whatever you've put out there isn't going to help us one bit should we need it here or on New Eden."

Bailey felt a little flush at the rebuke; he knew she was right. He'd had a few advisors voice the same concerns. He'd overruled them, not wanting a repeat of the last siege. If they were going to leave behind forces on Alfheim, then he'd leave behind as many of those killing machines as possible too—let the Zodarks have fun rooting out an army of AI robots.

"Your concern has been noted," Bailey replied calmly. "It has also been addressed and is currently being handled. We have two million C100s on order. We took delivery of the first hundred-thousand-unit batch last month. They'll keep coming in the same batch size each month until the order is filled." A visible look of relief appeared on her face.

"OK, Chester, you have my approval. Deploy the forces you deem necessary to Alfheim. But, Chester?"

"Yes, Chancellor?"

"No more C100s. Am I clear on that?"

"Crystal. I also have that update you requested on the orbital defense platforms if you still want it." Approval in hand, he wanted to shift topics.

"Yes, of course. The war may be over, but God help us if those animals ever attack Earth," she lamented.

The Chancellor and the Senate had been screaming for the Fleet to firmly ensconce Earth in a protective cocoon. The resources faucet had turned on and the money had begun flowing again. They'd earmarked it exclusively for the orbital defense platforms, of course, but that meant he didn't have to siphon resources away from his shipbuilding programs still running at full speed.

Bringing up a video update for them, Bailey began showing her the status on the platforms. They were decent-size platforms able to hold multiple defensive and offensive weapons should an adversary attack Earth. They were largely automated, which made manning them a lot easier. A minimal staff of a dozen to two dozen sailors was usually all it took.

Thankfully, the Ring projects fell under the civilian budget, not his. The Fleet would cover the costs of its defense and man it, but they didn't have to build it.

Interrupting his brief, Chancellor Luca asked, "It would appear we still have some sizable gaps in the defense, doesn't it? What's the timeline of providing at least some coverage to those parts of the Earth?"

"Soon. Maybe three to four months. We're finalizing the platforms around the John Glenn, the space elevators, and the naval shipyard. We prioritized our critical infrastructure first, then we'll build out to shore up the remaining vulnerable areas," he explained.

"All right, thank you for the update. Keep those contractors on schedule. I think people down here will feel a lot better when those platforms are operational."

When the call disconnected, he placed another to General Pilsner, letting him know he was cleared hot to send another division. If the Zodarks wanted a fight on Alfheim, they'd get one. The Republic had put one of their best divisions on alert in case this happened. Now that it had, 4th Infantry Division, one of the most storied divisions in the Republic after fighting in nearly every major battle during the last war, was on the way.

We'll see how they like this group of brawlers once they arrive. Bailey smiled, approving their immediate deployment.

****

Aboard Civilian Transporter *New Pioneer 5*
Approaching the Ingalls Shipyard
Between Earth and Luna, Sol System

Dr. Katherine Johnson rang the bell to Dr. Katō Sakura's quarters.

The door opened abruptly. "I guess I lost track of time," Sakura said. "Are we really almost there already?"

"Yeah, we're coming up on it really soon," Katherine replied. "Do you want to head to the observation deck?"

"Sure," Sakura answered. "Maybe we can grab a bite to eat at the cantina while we're at it."

The two scientists made their way down the hall. When they entered the main observation deck, it was clear that they weren't the only ones with the same idea.

"The restaurant is crowded," Katherine commented. "Good thing this flight wasn't full."

There were usually more people headed toward Alpha Centauri than Earth these days, but while the civilian transport ship they were on wasn't carrying its full load of passengers, it was carting around a fair amount of cargo to make up for it.

Sakura and Katherine waited in line to place an order for food, then grabbed one of the last remaining tables. The two women took a few bites of their food as they waited to reach their destination.

Katherine leaned forward. "You know, I've been over those answers Captain Wiyrkomi sent us after the Alfheim battle like a thousand times. You know what I think?"

"What?" asked Sakura.

"I think at the end of the day, the Gallentines don't have the answers to those questions any more than we do. That's why their responses were so vague and pointed us back to such convoluted texts." She laughed. "I think that's why we're getting this ship—they want us to play detective for them."

Maybe she's right, Sakura thought.

Suddenly, the chatter in the room quieted.

"That's...much larger than I envisioned," Sakura managed to mumble.

Katherine gave her a funny look. "That's what she said."

The two women burst out laughing at the crude joke before a nearby mother gave them a dirty look as she held her son's hand. Apologizing, they returned their gaze to the approaching view of the famed Republic Naval Shipyard.

The structure was almost like a planet unto itself. There had to be a hundred ships there, under varying stages of construction. Mechanical arms stretched out from the slips, holding equipment in place as an army of synthetic workers completed their tasks like a colony of ants. "It dwarfs the John Glenn Orbital Station, doesn't it?" asked Katherine rhetorically.

Sakura stood and walked closer to the windows, hoping to catch a glimpse of the *Voyager*. She could hardly wait for this next phase of her career.

"It does. It took the Republic more than fifteen years to build."
****

Ingalls Shipbuilding – Slip 37B
Republic Naval Shipyard
Between Earth and Luna, Sol System

"So this is the venerable *Voyager*, the ship that led humanity into the stars and to our first alien encounter," declared Katherine, placing her hands on her hips.

"Feels a bit anticlimactic, to be honest," Sakura responded with a slight giggle.

"Nonsense," Katherine replied, playfully elbowing her colleague. "You just haven't seen all the modifications they've made to our baby."

"Oh? Our baby now? Well, I think you should give me a tour, then," Sakura replied playfully. "Maybe we should start at the labs, my favorite section of any facility or ship." She winked as they approached the ship's elevators.

"Ground floor it is," said Katherine, summoning the lift.

When they arrived at their destination, Sakura's mood picked up considerably. Where once the ship had housed over 1,600 sailors and 860 soldiers, after the refit, they were down to a single company of soldiers for defensive purposes and a trimmed-down crew to man the ship. In all the spaces that were no longer being used to house personnel, several state-of-the-art labs had been added: biological, chemical, geological, and Sakura's personal favorite, archaeological. She practically danced about as she flitted through the different spaces, examining the sparkling tools and well-stocked supplies.

"She's a beauty, isn't she?" Katherine prodded.

"I think this will do." Sakura nodded with delight. "Now all we need to do is finish staffing her."

"Speaking of staff, it would probably be good for us to speak with the captain at this point, don't you think?" Katherine asked with a wink. "I mean, I know you could spend all day down here, but…we probably shouldn't keep them waiting any longer."

Sakura peeled herself away from all the equipment and dutifully followed Katherine to the bridge. Captain Hans Gruber greeted them. "So how do you like the *Voyager* so far?" he asked.

"It fully meets all of my specifications," Sakura replied.

"What she really means to say is that she's a kid in a candy store," Katherine joked as she elbowed her friend.

"Good," said Captain Gruber. "I'm glad the ship will fulfill its mission." He was all business—polite but to the point. He pulled them over to a panel to show them more of the features of the ship.

"As you are aware, the *Voyager* has been altered in many ways from its original design. In addition to the labs and housing for the scientists and their families, we have a school on board as well as more entertainment facilities than would normally be present on a warship.

"While we do maintain a selection of defensive weapons, the *Voyager* is no longer suited for any sort of prolonged combat. Our goal is to stay clear of trouble. If we do need to travel to a potentially hazardous area, we'll ask for an escort. We are *not* going to risk the ship in a fight—we have the armor for a battle, but we don't have the weapons anymore."

The weapons officer, Lieutenant Raj Patel, joined in. "Should we run into any unanticipated interference, our job is to flee the area as quickly as possible and call in for reinforcements."

Katherine and Sakura nodded solemnly. The glee of having a ship so primed for exploration had been a bit sobered by this discussion.

Captain Gruber cleared his throat. "There is something that I think you should be aware of," he said, lowering his voice and looking around him as if he were being watched. "The few soldiers you have aboard are perfectly qualified for their positions, but the morale among this group is exceedingly low. They are not happy being stuck with 'babysitting' duty for some scientists as we gallivant around the galaxy."

"Noted," said Katherine bluntly.

"Thank you for your candor," Sakura answered, tilting her head toward the captain.

He nodded.

"Well, now that that's out of the way, I guess we should check out the rest of the ship," announced Katherine. "I think we should show Dr. Sakura all the excavation equipment you've managed to cram onto the flight deck."

"Certainly," replied Gruber, a smile spreading across his face for the first time. "Before you go, though, I have something for you. It came directly from the Viceroy."

"Oh?" asked Katherine.

The captain handed her a file. She opened it up and smiled.

"What is it?" asked Sakura.

"Looks like we've been given that access to the Humtar language files that Audrey talked about."

Chapter 28
Rags to Riches

Planet Éire
Great Wildlands System

To say that Cormac Riggins wasn't happy about his corporation's new mining operation would be an understatement. His corporation, TOREC, had two options: mine the belts in the Wildlands with O'Kelly's Thukkist Corporation and fleet, or try to make the most of mining here on Éire. If he'd kept his barges mining the Belt, where there was plenty out there for them both, their two corporations would mine more ore and materials than the new system could handle—at least until the new shipyards were built and they had a swath of ship orders to fill. If they mined too many minerals too fast, they'd crash the prices and they'd both lose. One of their corporations would have to change tactics; Riggins was just pissed it had to be his.

To be fair, the planet had resources to mine. In fact, his corporation would probably do extremely well. TOREC was by its very nature an outer ring mining company. Operating on a planet with gravity was a lot different than mining in space, where the rocks just floated. On Éire, you had to contend with gravity, something his miners weren't used to.

It had been slow going at first. They had to figure out what was available to mine and what kind of demand there was for the materials either on Éire or across Sumerian space. If they could earn a living mining something of value, they'd do it. Then both a miracle and a disaster happened at the same time.

"Boss, we just got our geological survey back from Sector 46. It's, ah, it's a confusing report," Riggins's survey director said, handing him the tablet with the report.

Grabbing the device, Riggins said, "Let me see if I can figure it out for you."

"I double-checked the equipment to make sure it was working right. Whatever we mapped out, it's dense, and there's a whole lot of it down there. Our sensors can't quite figure out what it is. We haven't encountered something with these specs and ratios before."

"It could also be a pile of rocks we just haven't seen too," Riggins grumbled. "Let me check this against the Republic exotic M2s list."

"Exotic M-whats?"

Riggins shook his head. "You're my survey director! How do you not know about the Republic's exotic materials and minerals list? Jeez, what am I paying you for?"

Laughing at the criticism, the man countered, "Oh, oh, now I know what you mean. Sorry, I guess we haven't updated our diagnostic equipment with those material tables and measurements. We never ran across that kind of stuff in our Belt mining. We're still adjusting to the planetary thing. We'll get right on that, boss."

"Thank you for this. Get back to work. I'll tell you what you found once I know."

As the guy left, a message popped up on Riggins's tablet. His eyes went wide as saucers when he saw it. He wasn't sure if he should be jumping for joy that they had just struck it rich, or crying at what this kind of deposit could likely mean for the new world and system their society was hoping to build.

I need to speak to Liam, see what he wants to do, he thought as he got up, taking the report with him.

****

Liam looked at the report Riggins had just handed him, a mixed bag of emotions flooding him. What Riggins had just found would likely make their new society incredibly wealthy—no, insanely wealthy. It also meant their new system and home world could become the object of conquest by foreign powers for millennia to come. Despite his best efforts to create a new world apart from the trappings of the Republic and their history from Earth, this find meant they'd be entwining their paths no matter what he did in the future.

"It's an incredible find, Liam. I don't know if I should be excited or saddened by it."

"I know what you mean, Riggins. On the one hand, it's the kind of discovery that'll provide our new world with enormous wealth. Sadly, it also means it'll be impossible for us to separate ourselves from the Republic and will likely mean we'll be pulled into their war. We're also going to have to develop a real navy and armed forces to make sure we can safeguard what we've found." Liam sighed, looking up at Riggins. "I had hoped we'd be able to get more of our society going before we had to start building a real military."

"I don't disagree with you, Liam. I share all the same concerns. You and I both know that the new world we're creating here takes a lot of resources to build. Even with the sale of a lot of our assets from Sol, we're going to run out of money at some point. Our economy is starting to be created, but we aren't supplying the Republic anymore. We don't have some massive machine trying to buy as much of our materials as possible. We have to create that demand here or export it several systems away to Sumer. This discovery—this is how we'll fund the development of the kind of world you've talked about us building. If you want my two cents, let's embrace it. Let's find a way to make it work to our benefit."

Liam rubbed the bridge of his nose, taking in the comment. *He's right. We have to look at how this can accelerate what we want to do. It doesn't have to be a hindrance.*

"All right, here's what I want you to do," Liam began. "Start figuring out how your guys are going to extract this stuff. Get a plan in place and start mining it in earnest. I'll get in contact with the Republic and let them know what we've found. I'll work to start getting us some contracts for it. I'm also going to let them know that we're going to keep some of this material for ourselves. We aren't selling one hundred percent of it. They're likely not going to agree with that, but we're our own republic now. They should be glad we're willing to sell to them and not anyone else in the greater alliance."

Riggins left, his new marching orders in hand. Now it was time for Liam to arrange another trip back to Sol. This was a find that was best negotiated in person. Once he had some contracts and money in hand, he'd have his team start placing orders on Earth for the hard-to-come-by items they still needed for Éire.

Chapter 29
Seat of Power

Early 2110
Alliance City
New Eden

Viceroy Miles Hunt was still getting used to living on New Eden after having lived on the Altairian home world for so long. He'd spent nearly a decade living either there or on the *George Washington* and then the *Freedom*, so he hadn't really settled into anything resembling a permanent home since the war had started. New Eden, a relatively new colony still developing its infrastructure along with everything else, was quite the contrast to a world that had more than ten thousand years of development. The planet still felt very much like the frontier a lot of the alliance members had compared it to. Still, Hunt was hell-bent on having the alliance learn to work together better. He couldn't do that without having them start fresh. He also needed to separate himself from the Altairians if he was to truly become respected as the Viceroy and not continue to live in the shadows of the last Viceroy, the Altairian King Grigdolly. The Altairian leader had been gracious in accepting Hunt as his replacement, but not all the Altairian admirals had agreed.

Sitting in his office, Hunt had been sifting through various allied reports of enemy activity along the neutral zone. The very mention of the neutral zone bugged him. A neutral zone sounded nice; it even sounded safe. Sadly, it was proving to be anything but. Skirmishes were starting to happen in different regions. An alliance frigate or destroyer would be conducting a standard patrol of the neutral zone when out of nowhere, they'd get jumped by a group of Zodark warships. The Altairians had resorted to adding cruisers and battleships to their patrols. It seemed to have worked, but this wasn't the case across the entire allied border zones.

The report he read about what was taking place on Alfheim had him worried. The place was already a tinderbox. The fact that a Zodark force felt they could cross the neutral zone and wipe out an entire infantry battalion spoke volumes about what the Zodarks thought of the peace deal. He understood and agreed with Admiral Bailey's decision to reinforce Alfheim. His concern was how the Zodarks would respond to it. Would they get more brazen in their attacks? Would the sudden influx of combat forces cause them to change their tune? In any case, Alfheim was set to blow. If the planet wasn't so damn valuable, he'd be willing to just pull the plug on it and leave it to the Zodarks—but they needed those resources.

A chime alerted him to the arrival of his next appointment. "Enter," he said aloud, the AI opening the door.

In walked Captain Wiyrkomi, the captain of the *Freedom* and his Gallentine advisor.

"Viceroy, thank you for meeting with me," Wiyrkomi said, making his way toward one of the chairs in front of his desk.

"I've always got time for you, Wiyrkomi. Please, tell me what's concerning you. Your message sounded urgent."

"I bring a private message from Emperor Tibus SuVee. Once you have read it, I will provide you with some other news I have received from our people and my new orders," Wiyrkomi declared as he handed him the kind of tablet device the Gallentines used. It was far more advanced than anything even the Altairians had.

Taking the tablet, Hunt placed his thumbprint on the screen to unlock it. It then performed a retinal scan before it revealed the message. It was a video file. Clicking it, Hunt watched as an image of the Emperor appeared.

Viceroy Miles Hunt,

Greetings to you and your people. I want to congratulate you on the transformations you have implemented within your alliance. While I am satisfied with the progress you are making, more still needs to be done. The pause in the war with the Dominion must be used wisely, and it must not be permanent. This long-simmering war needs to be brought to its conclusion.

Either the Dominion as a whole or members within it need to be convinced of the necessity of joining our war against the Collective. If this cannot be achieved, then they need to be destroyed. We can no longer tolerate the Dominion's continued serfdom to the Collective as constellation after constellation continues to be absorbed into their intergalactic empire.

I would deploy Gallentine forces to support your efforts if I could. However, as Wiyrkomi and I have reminded

222

you, we are barred from intervening directly under the Treaty of Yarmooth. It is still my belief that so long as we honor this treaty, so will the Collective. Should they break the treaty through direct involvement or via proxy with Legion, then we will assist directly ourselves. I must warn you, Miles. If they should get involved militarily and your forces are not able to slow them down, we may not be able to save much of your galaxy before they begin their rapid assimilation and eradication operations. Do not underestimate the lethality of Legion or the speed at which they move from system to system.

Miles saw the Emperor pause for a moment before he resumed. His facial expression looked pained as he continued.

It is upon your shoulders I have placed this burden of command to accomplish the unification of the Milky Way either through cleaving members from the Dominion to join our side or through the conquest of those who continue to stay aligned with the Collective. It is imperative that you prepare the alliance to join us in battling the greater war. Therefore, I urge you to move with all haste in accomplishing these tasks set before you.

While time is a relative term in space, we must not waste what we have of it. The Collective continues to grow stronger, absorbing more and more systems into their hive, into Legion. I fear once their current conquest is complete, they will soon look to the Milky Way as one of the few viable threats left to their ultimate domination of our shared universes. You need to accomplish what your predecessor had been unable to achieve. Conclude this war with the Dominion and unify the Milky Way.

To further aid you in accomplishing this, I have promoted Wiyrkomi to the rank of admiral within our military. I have also authorized him to allow his crew and the Gallentines under his control within your alliance to operate without their previous restrictions. This should greatly increase the lethality of the Titan. *To that effect, I am ordering you to create a campaign to defeat the Dominion for me. Have Wiyrkomi help you with this. He's a brilliant tactician and will know best how to effectively deploy the Titan to fully utilize all of its weapons and special capabilities. Have this plan ready for me to approve within the next six months. Do not make me look the fool for placing you in charge over the Altairians. Continue to show me why I made the right choice in choosing you to lead this alliance.*

Peace be upon you, and all who follow you,
Emperor Tibus SuVee

When the message finished, Hunt sat back in his chair as he digested its contents. There was a lot to unpack and a clear message to settle things with the Dominion.

Breaking into his thoughts, Wiyrkomi pressed, "There is other news from the empire I believe you need to know. I would also like to explain the new level of cooperation and assistance my people and I have now been authorized to provide. May I proceed?"

Hunt wasn't sure he was ready to hear the other shoe drop. Not saying a word, he nodded for Wiyrkomi to go on.

"Viceroy, during the last twenty Earth years, the Collective has continued their consolidation of a nearby galaxy your astronomers call Nubecula Major or the Large Magellanic. Before you get concerned about this, please understand this is but one of many satellite galaxies of your Milky Way. Distance-wise, it puts Legion and their machine army roughly fifty kiloparsecs from here. That's one hundred and sixty thousand light-years. I bring this to your attention because, while it sounds like Legion is far away from the Milky Way and you may believe you have plenty of time to prepare, you do not.

"Legion's wormhole technology can allow them to bridge substantially greater distances than the Orbots or even the Altairians. Part of the challenge in fighting Legion is finding their home base once they begin to invade a new galaxy. Once they've secured their initial foothold, their machine army rapidly scales an industrial capacity to support and sustain their rapid destruction of those who oppose them and prepare those that submit for assimilation into the Collective. It is imperative that you find a way to increase the alliance's ship production capability and vastly grow your means to wage war. I would also like to recommend that you figure out how you can speak directly with the Orbot leader and the individual members within the Dominion. The more of them you convince to cross over to our side, the fewer adversaries we'll have to fight as you look to consolidate the Milky Way. What these species have not yet realized is that they too will one day be absorbed into the Collective, or they will be destroyed by Legion and thus become a part of Legion. It is therefore critical that a resolution, one way or the other, is achieved with the Collective.

"Once the Milky Way is united under the Galactic Empire, it will then be imperative for you to unify its military and industrial capabilities for the next campaign. The Emperor firmly believes that a unified Milky Way, along with the galaxies still under our control, may just be enough to finish the Collective off. Or at least we could begin to slow them from conquering more of the known universe. Miles, Legion is only going to grow stronger as more systems and species are conquered. There isn't time for us to wait and enjoy your hard-won peace. I implore you to find a way to get the others in the alliance to stay or get back on a war footing immediately."

"I understand, Wiyrkomi, and I agree with you and the Emperor. To make this happen, I'm going to need substantially more help either from the people you have under your command or from Cobalt Prime. What kind of additional help are your people able to provide now?" Hunt pressed, interrupting him before he could continue talking. There was no way he'd be able to accomplish these orders from Emperor without a *lot* more assistance.

"To better understand your needs, perhaps you can tell me about the deficiencies you believe we can help correct?"

"Resource acquisition, ship production, training, and improved weapons for our soldiers and ships. Those are the key things we're struggling with, Wiyrkomi. Earth has the new naval shipyard running at full capacity. It's able to build a total of one hundred warships at a time. Depending on the ship class, it can finish one of these new Altairian-human hybrid frigates, the Type 001s, in approximately twelve months. The cruisers take closer to two years, and the battleships roughly four years. Similarly, the Primords' facility in Kita is able to produce some one hundred and seventy ships at a time. I believe the Altairians are able to build something like three hundred and fifty ships concurrently. The Tully…" Hunt shook his head in frustration. "They're still lagging behind. I think they're building maybe forty warships concurrently in their yards."

Hunt sighed. Placing the Gallentine tablet on the desk, he looked at Wiyrkomi. "I'm not a shipbuilder, so I don't know if it's possible to speed any of that up. But even if we could, the bigger challenge we have to contend with is finding more of these rare advanced materials and minerals needed to build the kinds of stronger ships we'll need to fight the Collective and finally defeat the Dominion. The Alfheim battle made one thing abundantly clear—our ships need better armor. The kinds of hits the *Freedom* took…that was incredible. You told me the Gallentine warships are built with this same type of armor technology. If that's the case, then that's what we need to strive to build. It doesn't do us much good to build a thousand-ship fleet if our armor and weapons are just going to get wiped out by the Orbots' ships," Hunt explained.

Wiyrkomi took the information in, not interrupting. Then he asked, "It sounds like what you need is a lot more help in finding the Bronkis5 material and the Toriander crystals so you can phase out the Arkonorian reactors for the same Gallentine reactors the Altairians use on their battleships and star carriers."

Hunt nodded in agreement.

For the next several hours, Wiyrkomi outlined a plan he felt his people could implement to help address these shortcomings. He would also put in a request for an additional ten thousand Gallentine engineers, advisors, and trainers to augment the people he already had. It was clear they weren't going to meet the Emperor's requirements if additional help wasn't brought in.

Just as the meeting was about to end, a representative from the Republic brought a piece of good news to Hunt's attention. Apparently, the Belters' new planet, Éire, had just stumbled on an astronomical find of Bronkis5, the one material they'd become solely dependent on mining from Alfheim. With one of their critical material shortage problems solved, they just needed to find the unique crystals used to fuel the vastly more powerful Gallentine reactors. Getting those kinds of reactors into their new ships would allow them to use substantially more powerful lasers and greatly increase their ships' impulse speeds and FTL capabilities.

Chapter 30
Evolution of the Terminator

Walburg Industries
Al Magordo, New Mexico

Lane Walburg, Alan's son and the COO of Walburg Industries, finished poring over the proposal from the military. Admiral Bailey wanted to know if a new, highly secretive material could be integrated into the construction of the C100s. This material, Bronkis5, something he'd never heard of, was apparently the same type of material used in the armor of the Gallentine warship, the *Freedom*, and if it could be integrated into the C100s, it would make them a hell of a lot harder to destroy.

Lane wrote a response to the admiral, letting him know they'd need to obtain some of this new material and run some tests. They needed to determine how it worked, how they could integrate it into the C100s, and how the new machines would operate. There were too many variables and a lot of unknowns. This Bronkis5 was much denser than the material currently used, but that could also make the C100s much heavier. If they were willing to provide him the materials to test with, then sure, they'd look at creating a new variant of C100s using it.

In the meantime, Lane's biggest challenge was trying to figure out how to meet the military's purchase order while at the same time handling the enormous demand for civilian synthetics. Their factory could only produce so many units a month. Thankfully, they'd gotten the new factory on New Eden fully operational, and he had another major factory being built on Sumer and one on Alpha Centauri. Once those factories were completed, their facility's load would be cut by at least forty percent. Until that happened, Lane had some tough decisions to make. Should he focus their efforts on producing the C100s the military needed or keep their efforts split to handle the seemingly never-ending growth in the civilian sector?

The rapid growth and colonization across several star systems had created an astronomical demand for civilian synthetics, particularly the engineer and construction versions. Add in the growing tension within the family between his father and his daughter, Holly, and he was having a hard time staying focused on growing the business and staying on top of their existing orders. Lane was trying to understand his dad's fascination with this software he called "the Gift" and how it was different than the current software they were already using.

After decades and decades of modeling data on human interactions and reactions, Lane was pretty certain the behavioral profiles they'd created for the synthetics were pretty damn good. In his eyes, his dad was trying to read too much into some technology tweaks he'd made and didn't appear to be factoring in the improvements to the modeling software they'd made over the years, especially in the major software patch they'd released some seven years ago.

****

Several days went by before a package from DARPA arrived under heavily armed guard. Lane was told it was the Bronkis5 material. His engineers immediately dug in. They began looking at its molecular structure, its chemical composition and how it reacted when it was introduced to other metals or composite plastics. For weeks, they looked at this material every which way they could. They leveraged extensive testing results from DARPA and the shipbuilders as well to see how it was being integrated into the components and armor on the ship. What really caught them by surprise was how it performed in battle. The after-action reports and their studies of its interaction when hit by direct kinetic and high-energy weapons were fascinating.

None of his engineers could explain how it worked or why it worked the way it did. Not only was it incredibly dense and hard, when it took a high-energy hit, like from a laser, it seemed to have the ability to absorb and redistribute large amounts of that energy. When they analyzed the hits to the *Freedom*, they found the hits that had done damage to the ship were the ones where an Orbot ship had been able to hit the ship with a long, sustained energy beam—three to five seconds. It was only in these instances that the Bronkis material in the armor began to break down. Quicker hits of a fraction of a second might rattle the ship, which oftentimes could cause internal damage, but they typically didn't break through the armor to get into the guts of the vessel or breach its pressurized hull.

When Lane's engineers built a few armor plates to test some theories with, they found something unique. DARPA had created a modeling simulation that looked at what would happen if you hit the

Bronkis plates with an energy beam, say, three times as strong as the Orbot ships used. When a concentrated beam hit with that kind of force, the Bronkis broke down almost instantly. Thankfully, it didn't look like either the Orbots or the Zodarks could generate the power needed to create a rifle that powerful.

After weeks of evaluating the material and how it could be integrated into the C100s, his engineers determined it wasn't possible—at least not in the C100s' current configuration. The Bronkis was just too dense, and thus too heavy. The power source for the current combat synthetics couldn't support the additional weight created by adding some thirty percent to the base load.

When Lane talked about this challenge with Holly, she suggested they look at designing a new combat Synth that could handle the increase in weight. While his father, Alan, wasn't so sure about creating yet another, more lethal killing machine, Holly made the point that if a newer version could help save the lives of more soldiers in the future, then it was worth developing.

For the next month, Holly and the design team, led by Alan Walburg, went to work on crafting what was going to be called the C300, the advanced combat synthetic soldier variant three, or ACS3. It maintained its same height, but it would be roughly two inches thicker in the chest and body and two inches wider. The additional size gave them the needed space to increase its power supply so its servos and controls would be able to handle the increase in weight. When the design had been completed, it moved into the simulation phase. Testing it in a virtual lab to see how it would work gave them a chance to discover more. The more they learned, the more they refined the final designs.

Once they believed they had solved any potential design or engineering problems, it was time to build a few and put them to the test. While all this was happening, the military kept pressing him to get the current order of C100s complete. It was as if they knew something was going on and these machines were going to be a key part of it. Try as he might, Alan couldn't find anything going on that indicated a war or invasion was imminent or even likely. The military also wanted to know how fast they could get the C300s into mass production. Despite the lack of information, Lane knew something was up—he just didn't know *what*.

Chapter 31
Those Who Enter, Lead

Joint Training Center – Titan Military Complex
Top Gun – Fleet Fighter School
Saturn VI, Sol System

Commander Ethan Hunt looked at the latest modification to the curriculum with satisfaction. Two years after Admiral Aaron "Warhawk" Blade had gotten the Top Gun program started, Ethan and his cadre of instructors had steadily improved the quality of the Fleet's manned piloted program. As each class of pilots graduated, modifications to the program were made and the tactics taught continued to improve.

As graduates of Top Gun returned to their commands, the training they'd learned became institutionalized across the air and space wings of the fleet. As commanders learned how to utilize the Fleet's starfighters, bombers, and assault transports more effectively, confidence in the Fleet's pilot program grew. If war with the Zodarks resumed, they'd now have an effective, highly trained fighter corps, ready to bring the fight to the enemy.

Walking into Ethan's office, Commander Tommy Rens took a seat as he viewed the results from the latest test they'd run the pilots through.

"How'd Blue Squadron do, Tommy? They finally figure out how to dogfight yet?" Ethan asked with a chuckle.

Tommy shook his head in disappointment. "Not yet, but they're getting better. On a good note, Purple Squadron nailed their attack runs today. Both their missile and torpedo runs looked flawless. I think they're ready to move on to the next level," he explained, going over the day's results.

"Good, at least Purple Squadron has it figured out. What's the deal with the Blues? Was there something we missed in their initial training that's led to their lackluster performance? They really shouldn't be doing this bad at this stage of the program," Ethan quizzed. If they had a training problem, he wanted to fix it.

When Top Gun had started, Ethan and Tommy had broken the training into phases that built on each other. Phase one covered tactics, teaching pilots how to maximize the capabilities of their starfighters or

230

bombers. Phase two focused on dogfighting, honing their fighter skills and learning how to fight as individuals and in small teams, squadrons and wing-level operations.

Tommy and Ethan felt this was the most important part of Top Gun. Pilots needed more than the basic skills to fly and fight; they needed to understand their limits as pilots and the limits of their starfighters. This was the longest and arguably the toughest phase of the program.

The final phase focused on the largest deficiency outside of dogfighting, combined-arms operations. In this phase, pilots were taught how to operate as a combined force of fighters, bombers, and assault transports in support of the fleet's warships. Then the roles flipped—they became the aggressors. Fighters had to protect the bombers, bombers had to evade the ships' defenses to land their hits, and assault transports had to capture a designated ship.

The pilots who graduated from Top Gun would return to their commands as killers in the cockpit, and they'd possess the knowledge needed to teach others those same skills. In time, they'd become the new senior leaders of the Fleet's fighter program and usher in an era of fighter supremacy, augmenting and increasing the lethality of the Fleet's warships.

Tommy waved off Ethan's concern, explaining, "It's not the training. It's poor leadership from Lieutenant Gilder. He's struggling with taking charge and being the boss."

"Really? I thought after your last talk, he might have figured that out."

"Maybe it's time you talked with him. The guy's gotta learn that being in charge isn't about being liked. It's about leading your people, giving them orders and holding them accountable when they don't listen. He's got a couple of strong-willed pilots on his team running roughshod over him. His desire to be their buddy is preventing him from telling them to shut up and follow his orders."

"Ah, now I see the problem. OK, Tommy, tell him to come see me tomorrow after class. I'll try and straighten him out. In the meantime, is Class 202 ready for Spartan Warrior 2? This is our first year taking part in that boondoggle, and I'd like to make sure we're good on our end."

Tommy brightened up at the question. Ethan knew he was thrilled that the schoolhouse had been voluntold to participate in the quarterly joint exercise, which officially kicked off in five days.

"They sure are," Tommy explained excitedly. "They're super excited about being a part of this. It's not every day a pilot gets to practice an orbital assault and invasion. If you ask me, it's an incredible capstone to the program."

"OK, if you say they're ready, then they're ready. I received the exercise brief this morning along with the roles our people will be playing. We'll review it tomorrow during the morning brief with the class. We'll see how it shakes out. Maybe you're right—this could be a great capstone to what we've taught them."

Tommy smiled.

"Changing the subject," said Ethan, "let's talk Class 206 and the pilots arriving in a few more days."

****

Following Day
Main Auditorium

"Congratulations, Class 202, on completing Top Gun," Commander Hunt declared loudly.

Raucous cheers of joy and excitement erupted from the students. They'd made it, completing the toughest advanced pilot training course in the Fleet. Now they'd trade out their silver pilot wings for the gold wings denoting them as graduates of the elite Top Gun program.

"Now that you all get to wear the gold wings, you get to be the first class to participate in Space Command's warrior exercise, a joint quarterly military exercise conducted by ships from the Fleet and Republic Army units." As Commander Hunt spoke, a presentation appeared on the walls behind him.

"This will be the first time the schoolhouse is participating. How well things go will determine if future classes also participate. The Head of Space Command believes the warrior exercises could be a great addition to the course. In a few minutes, your Qpads will receive your new assignments for the exercise. I'm going to brief you on the overview of what these exercises are, who's involved, why they're important, and of course, what you'll be doing.

"At the start of each quarter, a new round of warrior exercises begins. The names of the exercises are Comanche, Spartan, Highlander, and Viking. The exercises will focus on four functions Space Command has determined will protect the Republic and allow us to project power beyond our territory and into the future. The final ships for the exercise are supposed to arrive tomorrow. That's when most of you will begin reporting to the ships you've been assigned to.

"Ships are selected from across the fleet to attend the exercise and form up a new battlegroup. The battlegroups consist of ships ranging from frigates to battleships that'll support the orbital assault ships and the transports for the invasion. Spartan 2 is mostly a Republic Army exercise that'll look to deploy two divisions consisting of thirty-two battalions." Commander Hunt heard a few pilots whistle as the scope of the exercise began to unfold.

He continued to explain how the bombers and some fighters would be responsible for clearing a path through the planet's defenses prior to the first wave of transports beginning their runs. The remaining fighters would escort the assault transports as the main invasion got underway. The exercise called for two orbital assault brigades to establish the beachhead for follow-on forces to arrive. That gave the initial force eight battalions to smash the enemy's defenses as they expanded the perimeter.

With a beachhead established, the T-92 Starlifters would begin the process of landing another eight battalions before transitioning to ferry down the division's heavy equipment and supplies necessary to support a multimonth campaign. Commander Hunt stressed the importance of utilizing the training they'd just received. This was their chance to shine and prove that the training, tactics, and procedures they'd learned at Top Gun really did make the difference in the success or failure of an operation.

Having gone over the essential details and answering any remaining questions they had, Commander Hunt dismissed the graduates to enjoy their well-earned graduation dinner and gave them until 1300 hours the following day to report ready for duty. He knew the pilots would party hard tonight and likely into the wee hours of the morning. He figured he'd let them sleep in awhile before putting their war faces on and showing off their new skills in the coming exercise.

Watching the graduates leave the auditorium, he thought of Class 206, who'd fill these same seats tomorrow at 0900 hours. It'd taken them two years to reach this point of graduating four groups of one hundred pilots every one hundred and four days.

Give me enough time and pilots and this program will make a difference...

"Come on, Ethan, let's go celebrate the newest Top Guns before welcoming the next class."

Smiling at the idea, he joined the rest of his instructor pilots in a night of celebration.

****

Following Morning
Arrival of Class 206

Standing at the front of the auditorium, Commander Hunt looked at the faces of the pilots seated in front of him.

Time to get this started.

"Good morning, candidates! My name is Commander Ethan Hunt. I want to welcome you to Top Gun and congratulate you on being selected to attend our elite pilot training program. What you are about to learn over the coming weeks will not only save your lives, it'll save the lives of those in your squadron and potentially the ship you serve on. It's imperative that you absorb that training and be prepared to pass it along. Each of your instructors has years of combat experience. Learn everything you can from them. It just might be the difference in saving your life or that of your flightmate."

Staring at the pilots, he couldn't help but notice how young the third of them that were fresh from flight school looked—they were the ones the instructors had singled out as the best of the new crop of pilots. They'd been selected to join Top Gun in hopes that the advanced tactics school might turn them into real killers before they arrived at their squadrons and learned bad habits from the older pilots. Another third were the best pilots from the Fleet. They'd been chosen as some of them might be offered a chance to be part of the cadre as Hunt looked to grow the program further. The final third was Hunt's experimental group. Against the advice of everyone, he'd opted to fill this section of the class with the pilots considered to be the bottom of the barrel. They were the worst pilots in the Fleet and the ones a command didn't want.

Hunt didn't see it that way. In his eyes, a squadron was only as strong as its weakest pilot. He knew if they were going to turn around the pilot loss ratios and turn the squadrons into highly effective killing machines, then someone had to mentor and work with these miscreants and crappy pilots. Ultimately, if the pilots from this group couldn't cut it and complete the course, then they'd be relieved as pilots and reclassed into another job within the Fleet.

Hunt paced in front of the group, pausing just long enough to look at a handful in the front. Talking loudly, he said, "I want everyone to turn to your right and look at the person next to you. Then repeat after me. 'You are important. You were hand-selected to be here.'"

As everyone recited this, he made a mental note of how they were responding. He told them to turn to their left and repeat the process.

Having walked down the stage to the center aisle of the auditorium, he exclaimed, "You are now part of the next chapter in the Fleet's fighter corps. Should a war against the Republic or our alliance happen again, it'll be pilots like yourselves that will be called upon to defend our people and bring the fight to the enemy.

"I want each of you to make a commitment right here, right now— to me, to yourself, and to your fellow pilots—that you will give us one hundred percent of your effort while you are here. The training you are about to receive may very well be the training that saves you, your squadron, and your ship. Starting tomorrow, you will go through the most intense and rewarding training of your careers. When I dismiss you, I want you to spend this afternoon and evening getting to know each other and preparing yourselves mentally for the next one hundred and four days. Dismissed."

Chapter 32
The Gray Lady

Republic Naval Shipyard
Between Earth and Luna, Sol System

Sitting at the bar after work, Ashurina looked out the giant floor-to-ceiling windows, marveling at the sight of the largest warship she'd ever seen. The ship had been under construction for several years. A week ago, it had been moved to one of the final assembly slips closer to the habitat module on the shipyard.

I wonder how many other warships they have under construction like this.

She made a mental note to add the discovery of this ship to her next report. First, she'd need to find out exactly what this ship's function was and if the Republic had any more like it under construction.

"Marveling at the *Gray Lady*?" Burt commented as he sat down next to her.

"Gray lady?"

Burt smiled. "That's what I've heard them call this particular ship."

"What kind of ship is it? It's a lot bigger than the battleships I've seen."

Burt nodded with pride, telling her this was apparently the first Altairian-human hybrid carrier the Republic had built on their own. When she asked if he knew how many others the Navy had, he said he wasn't sure. He knew of at least one being fully operational and soon, this one would join the fleet. It was possible others were under construction at the yard. It was a massive, sprawling facility; however, their access was largely limited to just the habitat module. This was where the large JBR reactor rooms were that powered the facility.

Ashurina saw Burt look down at his new Breitling Interplanetary Signature watch. Something she still couldn't understand was why a person would want such an expensive timepiece that had to be wrapped around your wrist. It made no sense to her, but she still saw plenty of people around her use this rudimentary means of telling time.

"Sorry to cut it short, Ashurina. I've got to get to sleep if I'm going to get up in time for this video call with our team on Titan. I'll catch up with you tomorrow," he said before heading off toward the exit.

Sitting alone at last, Ashurina looked around the bar and smiled. This was it. Everything she'd worked toward. Her infiltration mission was not only a success, it was already producing results. If she had one complaint, it was the transfer of Burt's crew from the John Glenn to the Republic Naval Shipyard. On the John Glenn, one could freely explore most of the station. The shipyard was the complete opposite.

While most of the engineers were happy to be working on a newer, more modern reactor system, the shipyard didn't have nearly as many fun amenities as the orbital station had—and considering how long one could be in space, having amenities to blow off steam or enjoy yourself was important. The shipyard still had a few bars and places to eat, but its promenade would never compare to the rows of shops, bars, restaurants, and people constantly rotating through the sprawling facilities of the John Glenn.

Living on the naval shipyard also meant they had to get accustomed to a lot smaller quarters. If you were single, you had a tiny sliver of a room. It had enough space to lie down in and a single chair and desk, but that was it. Even the bathrooms were shared and down the hall. She still laughed when she thought about Burt's wife. The poor woman just wasn't cut out for living like ordinary people. There was a phrase Ashurina had heard, something like "champagne taste on a beer budget."

When Burt's team had moved to the shipyard, his wife had lasted two weeks in the married crew quarters before she'd demanded to go back to the John Glenn. Commuting daily between the two facilities wasn't a viable option, even if they were less than twenty minutes apart by shuttle, due to the limited amount of scheduled trips between the two places. Instead, he'd be allowed to slip away for a three-day weekend twice a month to see his wife.

That was when Ashurina had made her moves on Burt again. They'd had this on-again, off-again affair for years. While she hadn't let it become too regular of a thing between them, it was this affair that had given her access to John Bentley's computer systems. Once in, it had only been a matter of time until she had wormed her way deeper into the electronic systems across the Republic. If she had to let the guy screw her a few times to get the access she needed, what did she care? It was just sex. The intelligence she was getting via Burt, however—well, this was the kind of intelligence that changed wars.

Burt was her means into JBR. Through him, she'd have to find the right employees who worked on the myriad classified contracts the company had at government and civilian facilities across the Republic. As the unwitting pawns were identified, her espionage tools went to work, collecting data for the analytical cell, who put it all into context.

Ashurina felt good about what she'd created, but she was still mad at Dakkuri for being so reckless with her. It still made no sense to her that he would risk her and their deep cover operations to pull off some relatively pointless bombings that other, less trained assets could have achieved. She wondered if NOS Heltet approved of his methods.

Ashurina was aware of what their overarching operational plans were, since she had participated in the same mission brief NOS Heltet had given Dakkuri and the three other Kafarr alternates should he get captured. The alternates had participated via remote login to protect their identities and ensure that a chain of command couldn't be compromised, but that only reinforced her puzzlement at Dakkuri's blurring of the lines when he'd overlapped the paths of the Ani with the deep-cover operatives. It unnecessarily risked their difficult deep-cover operations, which they'd spent years developing, all for a bombing that wouldn't change the outcome of future events.

When some of the other operatives had started getting captured, that had really struck fear into Ashurina's heart—and inspired further anger and frustration with Dakkuri. She didn't know how they'd been discovered, and that was the scariest part. She wondered if Dakkuri's recklessness may have been a factor in their capture. The Ani were very good at hiding in plain sight which only fueled some of her less favorable opinions of her Kafarr.

What really started to trouble Ashurina was that when she saw the reports on the news of their capture, they didn't speak of one or two bombers being caught—it was entire cells were being apprehended. It would have been one thing if a single Ani had slipped up and been caught as a result, but this was a sweeping move that netted half a dozen in a single week. The fact that she didn't know how they'd been caught sent a chill down her back at the real possibility that she might be next. When a few weeks had passed and she hadn't detected signs of surveillance around her, Ashurina started to breathe a little easier. The fear of capture slowly faded and she steadily moved on.

It had been almost two years since the Republic had started hunting down the bombers, and so far, she had managed to evade detection. She still heard from Dakkuri from time to time via their usual communication method; Ashurina knew which seller on Digimar, the most popular digital marketplace, to check out. Using the cypher she had memorized, she would pick out the correct letters and words in the product descriptions to obtain whatever messages Dakkuri had for her. If she needed to respond, she'd pose a question about an item for sale using her own cryptic language. Most of their communications were just standard check ins or ways to access messages from her family, except for when she had large files she had to share. Then they'd agree on a meet so Dakkuri could access the information stored in the data stick implanted just under her skull.

In this espionage game they played, personal encounters were dangerous. Either person could potentially be under surveillance, so their meetings were rare by necessity. Sometimes she had files too large to transmit by other means without suspicion, though. Then two weeks ago, Dakkuri had been the one to request that they meet.

Ashurina had been scheduled to attend a three-day seminar discussing the FTL drive used on the Gallentine warship they'd given to the Republic, the RNS *Freedom*. The event was being held in Paris at what she'd learned was the former European Space Agency. Aside from the obvious intelligence value of attending this event, it gave her an opportunity to safely meet with Dakkuri. She wasn't sure why they needed to meet, but the seminar had given her the perfect cover.

When Dakkuri had arrived at the hole-in-the-wall bar where she'd arranged for them to talk, it had dawned on Ashurina how long it had been since they'd last seen each other. It had been months. But this particular meet brought her two things—information about her cousin Sargon, an operative like her, and a digital file from Dakkuri that could only be transferred to her Qpad with a special access code while in close proximity to the sending device. Likely, it held new taskings or collection requirements that were being issued from the top.

While their devices transferred data between each other, Dakkuri shared some of the challenges he'd been having in getting new operatives to replace the ones they'd lost. Dakkuri wasn't the kind of leader who usually shared his problems with his people, so when he had confided in her, it made Ashurina realize she wasn't the only one who was lonely for conversation and the ability to converse about work-related problems. It wasn't like they could share any of this with friends or acquaintances they'd made while undercover. They were spies. They were prey being hunted by an adversary bent on their destruction.

Infiltrating new operatives wasn't exactly easy. Even if a stealth ship could make it past the ships and outposts guarding the stargates leading to Republic-controlled space, the spies needed to transfer to another ship to continue their journey to Sol or find a way to land on Sumer and infiltrate to Earth via a regular civilian transport. Post Sumer liberation, organic recruitment wasn't possible. Worse, the remaining Sumerian operatives they did have weren't fully trusted anymore.

Unless the operatives had families on other worlds still under Zodark control, there was little leverage the Mukhabarat could use to keep them on the "right" side. The idea of defecting wasn't something Ashurina thought about much, but she'd be lying if it hadn't crossed her mind. There was something to be said about the allure of just quitting, walking away from this whole spy game and disappearing somewhere within the Republic. But each time she thought about something like that, she remembered her husband and the four kids they had back home.

Thinking of her kids brought out a feeling of deep melancholy she found harder and harder to conceal as the years dragged on. In fact, it had now been four and a half years since she'd seen her husband and children. From time to time, she'd receive a message from Dakkuri informing her that a new batch of mail from home had arrived. He'd send her a link to an online retailer and tell her which item to purchase. Once the package had arrived, Ashurina would remove the data file containing the messages.

She knew that once she started watching the videos and reading their letters, she'd be an emotional wreck for most of the day. Knowing how she'd react, Ashurina would usually take a couple of personal days off and rent a hotel room so she could be alone. It was impossible for her to read the letters or watch the videos her husband would send of the kids playing with each other or participating in some sort of local sports league without breaking down. She'd bawl her eyes out at all she'd sacrificed for her job. Her babies, her kids—they were growing and moving on with life—a life she wasn't regularly a part of.

What made her feel truly sad was that the files from home had a special autodelete program that would initiate as soon as she logged in. It was a safety feature that would purge the files within seventy-two hours of their being opened. This prevented the data from falling into enemy hands should an operative be captured. There was also a fail-safe embedded in the files. If they did fall into enemy hands prior to their deletion, then a malware code would activate, causing a whole series of new problems for whoever attempted to copy the files or tried to undo the autodeletion protocols. The set of protocols would propagate a destructive malware designed to wipe the host system clean while transmitting the malware to as many other devices the host system was connected with, and also to every possible contact of the host system. The Zodarks were, if nothing else, both meticulous and malicious in how they handled and guarded electronic data.

While it was not common for a deep-cover operative, there were occasions when she'd be allowed to pass similar kinds of files to Dakkuri. They'd eventually be routed home to her family, reminders that she was still alive, still doing well and missing them terribly. Dakkuri also had something Ashurina didn't—a specialized software key that allowed him to remove the seventy-two-hour self-destruct process. This enabled him to review the contents of her messages and, if necessary, scrub anything that might give away what she was doing or where she was. Once he'd approved it, the message would eventually find its way back to her father's palatial estate on Gurista Prime, where her family lived while she was on this extended assignment.

How did I let them talk me into this? she mused privately, taking a couple of large sips of her alcoholic drink. She felt buzzed. The booze helped her cope with the situation she'd found herself in. *Father always had a way of pushing me to chase that next promotion...* Ashurina knew her father was immensely proud of her and what she'd achieved. She was Mukhabarat. More than that, she was a rising star within the organization. Despite the fact that women accounted for less than nine percent of the Mukhabarat, she was well on her way to rising within its senior ranks.

When a deep-cover mission had come available on Sumer, Ashurina had initially passed on it. Her kids were young and this was a three-year posting. Then one day a mentor had approached her, a man who had become the deputy director for the deep-cover program. He'd told her he was going to retire to an advisory role in a few years and that he'd like to select her to replace him. The only catch was he wanted her to take on one more deep-cover assignment—the one in Sumer. This would give her six of these types of assignments under her belt, more than enough to ride a desk for the next five to ten years. Grudgingly, she had agreed. It was a short sacrifice for a long-term family gain.

When she'd taken the assignment, Ashurina's youngest child had just turned six, and her eldest was twelve. At first, it hadn't been so bad. She'd had been able to travel home to Gurista Prime twice a year. She'd get four weeks of dwell time with her family. It wasn't a lot—six months out of three and a half years to spend with your family—but she'd made the most of it.

Finishing her drink and signaling for another, Ashurina cursed. *If I'd taken a vacation just a few weeks later, I would have been home when Sumer fell...not trapped behind enemy lines...*

She'd just completed her first six months on Sumer when she'd taken her first thirty-day R&R back home to her family. Ashurina had known things weren't going well with the war, but what she hadn't known was how at-risk Sumer was. Right after she'd left, the Zodarks and Mukhabarat had begun the Purge. They had taken as many people as they could in tribute before launching a planetwide purification of those deemed threats to the Zodarks. When she'd returned to Sumer, she'd found herself at a loss for words. The planet had transformed into a dystopian hellscape. Then when the Republic had arrived—it had changed everything.

When it was clear the Zodarks weren't going to liberate Sumer anytime soon, the real nightmare had begun. Dakkuri had pulled her and the others from Gurista Prime to a safe place, away from the Sumerian-recruited Mukhabarat.

Within days of the Republic's arrival, sides were drawn and loyalties were tested. People they'd worked with for years, even decades, had switched sides. Then the raids had started. No one was safe. No one knew which locations had been compromised. Those first weeks had been hell; Ashurina had lost more than a few friends to a betrayal by one of their own.

When things had begun to settle down, they'd found a new battle rhythm—and plotted their revenge. Then the word had come down—a new mission had been crafted. The Sumerian spy chief NOS Heltet had devised a clever plan to use his remaining Gurista operatives. With Sumer now a Republic colony, the remaining people were citizens of the Republic, with an unfettered ability to travel across the entire Galactic Empire Alliance.

Their new mission had been to infiltrate Earth and establish a new base of operations. From there, they'd infiltrate the rest of the alliance. As operatives had been given their new legends and mission assignments, they had steadily disappeared from their group. One by one, they were being sent off to perform their part in the overarching plan NOS Heltet had devised.

Ashurina had been excited about this opportunity from the moment she'd heard about it. For weeks, she'd worked directly for NOS Heltet and Dakkuri. While they'd never let her see all the places they'd assigned the Guristas to, she'd had a chance to learn more about Dakkuri, the Kafarr who'd effectively run the operation for NOS Heltet.

When nearly everyone had left for their assignments, she'd finally been given hers. Dakkuri and Heltet had explained how her mission, above all the others, would likely decide the outcome of the war once it began. She was to infiltrate the John Bentley Reactor company—the company responsible for building and operating the reactors that powered the Republic and their warships. It would be her job that'd identify the number and type of warships in the Republic Navy and under construction. Later on, when the time came, she'd also be the one who turned the lights out on the Republic when the Zodark fleet arrived in Sol.

But Sargon...I still can't square how Dakkuri could throw him away the way he did, Ashurina mourned. Her cousin wasn't a suicide bomber; he wasn't even an Ani. Sargon was just like her. *Could Dakkuri give me orders like that? Tell me to use these two bombs I still have to go out in some sort of blaze of glory?*

No matter how many times she played her conversation with Dakkuri over in her head, she still couldn't understand the justification for using her cousin in the way he had. If they wanted to carry out a suicide bombing, they'd usually recruit an unwitting source to do it for them—offer them some money to stand near something with a backpack or suitcase, or deliver some package. But strapping a bomb to your body made no sense. Deep-cover operatives were too specialized, too experienced and too hard to come by to be thrown away for the sake of a single mission.

If he gives me an order like that...do I listen? Ashurina wondered. *Do I try to change his mind...or do I defect?*

If she deserted, Ashurina knew she'd be killing her family. The Mukhabarat had made that abundantly clear. If you betrayed the Agency, the Guristas—retribution would be swift and it would be fierce.

I need to start figuring out a plan B, Ashurina decided. *I'll be damned if I'm going to die as a suicide bomber, and I'll be damned if I'm going to let them kill my family if I don't.*

Chapter 33
Spies From Afar

Galactic Empire Headquarters
Alliance City, New Eden
Rhea System

"I've seen that look before. What's got you perplexed?" General Alfred Bates asked as he took a seat in front of Major Brian Royce's desk.

Placing the tablet down, Royce sighed as he looked at Al before reaching for his own coffee. "Eh, just some training issues Lieutenant Hosni's team is dealing with. Apparently, some of the marshals aren't happy with that RA unit, Apollo Company, doing most of the training. They seem to be under the impression that only the Deltas can teach them how to breach buildings and clear rooms. Hosni's been explaining that this is a pretty standard skill set for the Republic Army infantry units. Once they're ready for the advanced training, then his Deltas will take over. In the meantime, they're just going to have to settle for training with one of the most decorated regiments in the RA," Royce explained, sarcasm and frustration dripping from each word.

Bates chuckled at the comment. "Some folks just want to run before they learn how to crawl. What's that guy's name? Ah, Krzysztof Waclawek, that's right. Director Gehlen asked my thoughts on this HRT proposal Waclawek pitched. He said his operations director had proposed resurrecting these specialized hostage rescue teams as a way of creating a Delta-like unit the marshals could leverage once they fully take things over from us. I actually liked the idea. His proposal was to assign a pair of these HRT groups to each colony."

"Yup, that's the plan the IMS asked us to help them achieve," Royce replied with a nod. "Given the manpower this was going to need, we had to pull in help from the RA. They recommended we get the 331st Infantry Regiment, specifically Apollo Company, to help us, so that's what we did. We've had them handle the basic training for the HRTs. I don't have enough ODA teams to teach these guys basic tactics, and frankly it's a waste of our skills. Hell, I can barely spare the bodies to teach the more complicated tactics we specialized in."

"I probably just need to send a quick note to Waclawek to tell his guys to stop this stupid chest-beating contest and focus on learning what they can from Apollo Company. The unit has ten-plus years of combat experience and fought in some of the toughest, dirtiest campaigns of the war. In fact, they were one of the units left behind on Alfheim. These marshals could learn a lot from soldiers who lived through that hellscape."

Bates nodded in agreement. Drawing help from the RA wasn't something most SF officers would have willingly done on their own, but he was glad to see Royce could think beyond just his SF assets. Special Forces was all about working by, with, and through allied and partner nations. Leveraging RA infantry to backfill a job you don't have the manpower to do yourself was brilliant.

Bates had to admit, Royce had grown into one of the most effective officers he'd worked with in years. He only wished he could get him a colonel's billet. Royce and others like him could easily be the future leadership of the SF community, but not if the brass couldn't find a way to get them promoted. His billet running the intelligence support activity within TF Orange was easily a colonel's position. However, the Space Force reorganization effort had slashed forty percent of the officer billets, particularly at the ranks of major and above. That meant that most majors were now doing colonels' work while most colonels were doing the work of either one- or two-star generals.

I need to speak to Reiker and Pilsner about Brian...there has to be a way to get this guy promoted, Bates thought. When Royce grabbed for his coffee, Bates made his move and changed the subject to why he'd originally stopped by Royce's office.

"That was a good update, Brian," said Bates. "Before I dive into the reason for my visit, I meant to ask you, how are things going with you and Jane? You two holding up all right now that Molly's a few months older?"

Royce's eyes lit up at the mention of his wife and daughter. "Oh, yeah, Jane and Molly are doing great, Al. Thanks for asking. Our little squirt is growing like a weed. I can't believe how fast she's progressing. And Jane...well, she's part of a handful of these wandering clubs on and off base. If I'm around, we usually link up with them on the weekends and make it a family hike. When I'm gone, Jane straps that baby into this cool-looking backpack and takes her with whatever group her friends are joining." Royce then added, "Jane's done a good job of making friends. Better than I would. I wasn't even aware of all these on-base groups and new settlers arriving like crazy to the planet. I think it's helped her deal with my travel schedule and being gone so much."

"Ah, that's great to hear, Brian. Marrying a team guy can be challenging to say the least. I'm really glad you all are figuring out a way to make it work. We have a tough job, one that tends to suck the life right out of a person."

Bates shifted in his seat. "But I guess I need to get to why I stopped by your office in the first place. Our buddy Drew sent me a note this morning. He asked me to make sure you saw the latest update on the JBR case. You were right. It looks like they made a mistake and we had the tools in place to catch it."

Royce grabbed for his tablet, and a smile spread across his face.

"Hot damn! See, I told you those sniffer devices would work," Royce said joyfully. "Wow, you realize if we had been able to do this back when the problem was first detected, we might already have our person in custody?" Royce seemed excited by the discovery, but also a bit angry it'd taken so long to get this software in place.

Bates held his hands up in mock surrender. "Hey, you had my backing from day one. We've had your plan running a few months, and it's given us our first big lead. Let's focus on that and what we can do with this newfound information."

Royce seemed to calm down as he accepted the situation.

Bates recalled those early days investigating the security breach. Usually, this kind of activity occurred via corporate espionage—one company stealing blueprints or contract proposals for a bid both companies were making on a contract. But this was different. It was far more complex than anything they'd seen before. It also had electronic traces of various foreign races, likely to disguise who really was behind it.

Once Royce and Lisa from the wizard shop had begun to investigate the breach, they'd suddenly found themselves in a bind. On the one hand, they wanted to enlist the help of the company's chief security officer or CSO and the senior leaders of the company. Their people would know their systems far better than the techies from the wizard shop. On the other hand, if they alerted the JBR execs to the problem, they'd have to come clean about how they'd discovered a breach within their networks, which would mean disclosing that they'd accessed the internal JBR systems without asking for permission or obtaining a court order allowing them to stealthily monitor it.

When their lead cyberanalyst, Lisa, had said the JBR breach could now be linked to several other defense contractor breaches, they'd finally been given permission to speak with the JBR leadership and explain the problem. Once the proper NDAs had been signed, Royce had brought them up to speed on what they'd found. At first, the JBR team was furious the intelligence service had been covertly monitoring their systems. However, as Royce and Lisa had explained how the breach in their systems had led to more than two dozen other defense contractors being penetrated, the CEO had squashed the complaints from his people and directed them to provide whatever help the intel services needed.

For months, the JBR security techs worked with Lisa and her analysts from the wizard shop to narrow down how the email server system had initially been hacked. What puzzled them most was that they couldn't figure out which JBR employees were the vectors of entry into these other defense contractors. Then Royce found a product specially designed to ferret out the kinds of ghost programs that operated in the shadows, spreading from one computer network to another, leaving no trace as to how it was happening. Had this product not originated from the Primords, it likely would have been implemented right away. As it was, it took more than a year to get approval to use a nonhuman software program on a highly classified network.

Royce sat forward in his chair. "You're right, Al. No reason to fuss over spilled milk. The sniffers found us something; that's what's important. If I'm understanding what this report is saying—and maybe you can confirm my assessment—it would appear the sniffer was able to detect which files on the various defense contractor organizations were being regularly accessed and pilfered. Correct? It also identified which user profile was active in the folder or folders at the time when large quantities of data were being exfilled off their servers. Does that sound about right?"

Bates nodded. "The issue I see, based on Lisa's assessment in the report and a comment from Drew's notes, is that while we know what files are being extracted from these organizations and government projects, we're still not sure *how* they're being moved or where they're going. Do you have any thoughts on how we can figure that piece out?"

Royce grabbed for his Qpad, searching for something. "Here, look at this," he said as he projected a report with some diagrams onto his desk. "I learned about this from one of my former Deltas, named Peter. He'd been severely injured during the New Eden campaign and ended up getting medically retired. I stayed in touch with him over the years, especially once he knew he was leaving the military. He went back to school and found himself working for a company called Proofpoint. I reached out to him shortly after I discovered that Primord sniffer software to ask if he was aware of any software solutions that might help us back-trace where a ghost program was exfilling data to and then sending it on to another user.

"Pete told me about some old DARPA project he'd participated in during the final years of the war. I don't know if you remember this, Al, but during the Rass campaign, my company was among the first to integrate the C100s into our units. Our objective was to capture a Zodark research outpost in orbit of planet Rass. This was where we first encountered the Orbots. My friend Pete said this DARPA project was aimed at addressing two questions. The first was how the Orbots had penetrated the security protocols on the first C100. The second was how the Orbots were able to propagate the malware on the first C100 to the rest of the ones it was connected to."

As Royce spoke about the Rass campaign, Bates recalled that very incident. It had sent a chill down his spine until Walburg Industries had come up with a patch.

"I do recall that issue," Bates stated. "Like you, I'm not a techie. I'm no Luddite, but let's skip ahead to this solution you found."

Royce sported a half smile. "Sorry about that. You're right, Al. I'm preaching to the choir. Pete said his company came up with something they're calling Zeus. It functions almost like these ghost programs we're now encountering. They take the files you're wanting to protect and they overlay them with Zeus. When a hacker tries to copy or steal the files, then Zeus goes to work. It's actually pretty neat the way he explained it."

"Zeus, eh? How is this different from previous programs out there?" Bates pressed.

"I asked Pete the same question. Basically, it leaves behind a string of various markers that are only visible when you use their software. It lets you track the ghost program to see the path they're routing it through. What's really neat is how it keeps working even if the files are transferred from the classified network they were stolen from onto an unclassified network to transfer the data across a much broader network," Royce explained.

Bates spotted a problem and pounced. "Hold up there, Brian. If I'm understanding this right, in order for Zeus to work, it has to have pretty wide access to scan both the classified and unclassified networks, right?"

"Yes, it does. I asked Pete about this. He assured me it's not necessary to have access to the classified information itself. What they're able to do is specifically look for the Zeus markers. If they find any, then they can zero in on the routers and serves the markers are on until they find the final destination. Apparently, in the development process with DARPA, a clause was put in place that if they find something on the unclassified networks, they'd need a court order for anything more detailed than a tertiary scan to find the markers. Obviously, on the classified government networks, corporations don't have the kind of privacy and protection one would have on the commercial side. I've been working with JAG, and I believe this is what'll cover our butts," Royce explained, soothing Bates's concerns.

Bates stood from his chair, causing Royce to stand as well. "OK, Brian, I like this idea. It sounds like you've got it covered and you've worked through the legal challenges. Since the JAG has given us the legal green light, I won't stand in your way. Here's what I'd like you to do—get in touch with the wizard shop and tell them Zeus is good to go. I'll sign off on it from our end. I want you to head back to Earth. Loop the IMS, General Reiker, and the JBR folks in on Zeus and what we're about to do. Sounds like there's a good chance we're going to find our spy or spies within days of turning Zeus on. We need to figure out how we want to handle them once their identity has been uncovered. If you, Drew, or the marshals think a spy can be turned and work for us—do it. If not...then remove them from the chessboard."

"Understood," Royce acknowledged. "We'll turn 'em to our side. If not...then we'll make sure they won't be a continual problem for us. I need to give Jane a heads-up I'll be gone for a few weeks. Unless you say otherwise, I'll catch a shuttle to Earth tomorrow."

"Tomorrow's fine. Just make sure you have enough assets in place to nab this spy. It'd be great if we could turn them. Might give us the edge we need in countering these bastards and figuring out what the Zodarks are up to next. Oh, and this goes without saying, but damn good job sticking with this. You may have found us the means to uncover this entire Mukhabarat spy ring."

****

Later that evening, Royce walked into his house. He still marveled at his good fortune in life every time he came home. Jane was the most amazing woman he'd ever met and the wife he thought he'd never find.

Once he'd checked into his new billet with General Bates, the prewar military life he'd hoped to fall back into had been transformed into the spy-hunting program he'd built the past few years. He'd spent nearly three of the first four months they'd been on New Eden gone, bouncing from base to base and planet to planet, recruiting Deltas he'd served with over the years and trying to figure out how to stop these Mukhabarat bastards from unleashing further waves of terror on his country.

Once, when Royce had come home from a particularly long trip, he'd thought at first that he'd walked into the wrong house. Then he'd spotted Jane, wrapped in a robe as she sauntered into the foyer, smiling in satisfaction at his shocked look. She had utterly transformed their home into an episode of HGTV that he had commented on once. He never would have watched a show like that if it hadn't been for her, but here he was, standing in a recreation of domestic paradise. Jane had smiled coyly at his awestruck approval before motioning with her head for him to follow her to the bedroom, letting her robe fall to the floor. His lizard brain took over from there.

Royce hung his hat on the hook near the door before making his way toward the open kitchen that rolled right into the family room. He could hear Molly cooing and babbling to herself as she played with some toys on the floor.

"There you are, soldier boy. Good day at work?" Jane walked up to him, kissing him briefly before turning to finish preparing their blackened cod salad for dinner.

"Actually, it *was* a good day," Royce agreed cheerfully. "A problem I'd been struggling with for some time suddenly came into focus."

"Oh, that sounds good. Does this mean we'll see you a bit more often now?" she asked with a raised eyebrow.

Royce reached down and picked Molly up. He gave her some Eskimo kisses, rubbing his nose back and forth across hers as she cooed with delight. He kissed her on the cheeks, then turned to Jane. "Eh, probably not right away, but it's looking like that might happen if a few pieces fall into place. Actually, I'm heading back to Sol tomorrow. It's kind of short notice, I know, but this is important. If you'd like, I could grab you something on my way back?"

Jane didn't respond right away to his announcement. She finished preparing the salads and then placed them on the table with iced tea. "Back to Earth, eh? Hmm, I'll need to think about what I'd like you to bring back for me and Molly. If you'd given me a little notice, maybe I could have sent you back with a shopping list." She couldn't hide the obvious disappointment in her voice. "Is this the kind of trip where you'll be gone for a while?" she asked, suddenly sounding distant and pensive.

Royce could tell she wasn't happy about him leaving on short notice like this. He'd been able to take a month of paternity leave when Molly had been born, but the demands of his job had required him to return sooner than she felt he should have.

He sighed. "I'm not totally sure yet. I'll likely know more once I'm there and see things for myself. I could be gone a couple of weeks; it could be a couple of months. I'll make sure to keep you in the loop as soon as I know."

Jane ate a couple bites of salad as she processed what he'd just said. Then she looked up at him, and her disappointed look had changed to acceptance. "Well, if you're going to be gone for a few weeks or, God forbid, a few months, then I guess we best make up for some lost time," she suggested as a grin spread across her face.

She got up and walked toward him. He'd been holding Molly while he ate his salad. Jane took her from him and gently placed their daughter in her crib. She turned to look back at him, giving him a look he'd come to recognize as meaning "I want sex, and this is your chance."

He dropped his fork on the plate and made his way after her. Walking past the crib, he saw Molly was already out cold, leaving him and Jane a short bit of time before she'd demand their attention once more.

Chapter 34
The Web

Camp Beckwith
Ozark, Arkansas
Earth, Sol System

Major Royce stepped off the transport and paused, hands on his hips as he surveyed the hustle and bustle of the flight line. This was the first time he'd been to the newly created, purely Special Forces base— Fort Bank, named in honor of former US Army Colonel Aaron Bank, who had founded the Green Berets back in 1952. After decades of trying, the leadership of the Deltas had finally succeeded in separating the Deltas and their particular needs from the Republic Army. Their new training and headquarters base was located a few hours outside of Jacksonville and the rest of the capitol district.

"Ah, there you are, Major Royce," a voice called out.

Royce turned to see a vehicle nearby and a sergeant walking toward him.

"I'm Master Sergeant Diego from transportation. I was sent over to pick you up and get you brought over to our side of the base. Do you have any bags you need me to collect for you or drop off at lodging for you?"

Smiling at the offer, Royce extended his hand. "It's good to meet you, Master Sergeant. Everything I need is in this duffel. If you wouldn't mind dropping it at lodging after you've taken me to the Ops Center, that'd be great." Royce held his bag up for inspection.

"Yes, sir. I can do that for you. Come on, hop in. I'll give you the quick tour and we'll get over to Camp Beckwith—that's our side of the base. We've got a decent-size RI annex with us. That makes the camp a controlled-access facility, so unless you're assigned to JSOC or RI, it's off-limits, even to the regular Deltas from the Fort."

"Huh, that's interesting," Royce replied. "I'm glad they were able to make the name work." Beckwith had founded the original Delta Force back in 1977. Since JSOC was essentially the same unit, it made sense they'd name their first base and headquarters after him.

"I agree. Tell you what, I'll just take you straight to the Ops Center and skip the tour. I suspect you're here on a mission, so I'll let you get on with it."

Once off the flight line, they drove through the base until they reached a road that took them further from the main facilities. As they finished a turn and crested one of the steeper hills, the camp came into view. Royce smiled at the sight of it. Everything was new—not just new, it looked super high-tech and futuristic. It didn't have super-tall buildings, but while there was nothing above three floors on the outside, Royce knew there were a lot of subterranean levels outside of the public view.

When Royce entered the operations building, he had to pass through a few layers of security. He was guided to an elevator and told to head to S10, or sublevel 10—the nerve center for the command.

The elevator opened and Royce walked out, scanning the area for a moment until he found the wizard section and the group of analysts working this particular case. As he approached their section, he spotted Lisa, the head analyst who oversaw the group. Then he saw Lieutenant Hosni, the platoon leader he'd put in charge of liaising with the marshals.

"There's the man of the hour!" Lisa announced jovially. "About time you finally made it here, Brian. I was beginning to wonder if you'd gotten hung up by some space pirates." She flashed him a playful grin.

"Ha, space pirates. You think the major would let something like that slow him down?" Lieutenant Hosni joked back. "Hell, you haven't seen this guy in a gunfight."

"Hey, hey, calm down, kids," Royce replied, holding his hands up in mock surrender. "I know Papa Bear has been gone from home for a while, but I'm back," Royce played along to the laughter and jeers of Lisa's team of analysts.

He'd been a taskmaster, pushing her team hard the past few months to figure out the source of this JBR breach. Once they'd gotten permission to use the Primord sniffer tool, it had uncovered a treasure trove of new threats they hadn't previously known about. When he'd sent a message to go ahead and deploy the Zeus software, it had sent up all kinds of red flags throughout the intelligence community. They suddenly had an active bread trail of crumbs that just kept expanding each day.

"OK, guys, time to get serious. Lisa, why don't you go ahead and have your people bring up what you've found so far?" Royce directed, getting them back on track.

"On it, boss. Oh, hey, Drew. Nice of you to join us," Lisa commented before she started issuing orders to her people.

Royce turned and saw Drew walking up. "Real mess we have here, isn't it?"

Drew looked at the data being populated on the large screens in front of them and shook his head. "Damn, Brian. We really got screwed here," he finally said. "Those Mukhabarat bastards really infiltrated the hell out of our networks, didn't they?"

"If what I'm seeing is correct, I'd say so. Someone's going to have their work cut out for them. This is a lot of vulnerabilities that'll need to be dealt with."

Drew blew some air past his lips in frustration. "Not my department. Mine's figuring out who the source is and shutting them down."

As time had marched along, a pattern had emerged. All the files being extracted via whatever ghost program they were using were moving between a couple of different servers, eventually ending up in a single server location. Periodically, that server would send a data packet outside the closed net this server should have been operating on. What they couldn't figure out just yet was where this off-site location was. It didn't appear to have a registry on their networks, which meant it was operating on the black net—the ungoverned, unofficial network outside of government controls and regulation.

Pointing to a line item on the screen that identified the main data collection server, Royce asked, "Do we have any idea where this thing is yet?"

"It's a recently discovered spot, like just an hour before you arrived," Hosni responded. "We wanted to go over it with you before we make a move to check it out. It's possible the place is monitored or booby-trapped."

"OK, we can start putting together a surveillance team to monitor it. But what I'd like to know is how did all this start? Have we managed to trace any of that back yet?" Royce asked, looking at Lisa and her team for a response.

"We're still working on the exact vectors," Lisa replied. "What I can tell is these six corporations that were breached…they all have this Yonus Little in common. He's the only JBR rep that has access to the kinds of files that have been compromised. Then we have Macey Malice. She's working for Lockheed Martin on the Sentinel 1 project."

Drew shot him a nervous glance at the news. The Sentinel 1 program was tied in with the orbital defense platforms. They were ringing Earth and the stargates with Sentinels to fend off a future attack by an adversary. If that program was compromised, it raised a lot of questions.

How much was infiltrated? Are the deployed systems secure or have they been breached as well?

"Yeah, I see the looks you two are giving. I have the same thoughts," Lisa commented. "Is Sentinel compromised? I can't answer that yet. What I can tell you is this—this Yonus and Macey, they both have one JBR supervisor in common. This guy—Burt Schumacher."

An image of the JBR employee popped up on the screen, along with a laundry list of details about the man. Both his business and personal profiles were colorful, full of plenty of good *and* bad activity.

Royce stepped toward the monitors, then turned around to face the analysts. "Listen up, people. First off, this is great work you all have done in a very short period of time. I'm not going to fuss over what would have happened if we'd had these tools available sooner. We have 'em now, and we're using them, and that's what matters. What we have to figure out right now is how does this Burt fit into the whole picture? Second, if Burt truly is our guy, how does he connect to the Mukhabarat? Is he possibly being used by someone within that organization as cover for their activities? Something isn't adding up about this. Burt has never left Sol—he's had no known contact with anyone from Sumer. He's loud, he's flamboyant, and he apparently likes the limelight. He's the exact opposite of who you'd want as some sort of deep-cover asset or mole inside an organization.

"Your top priority is to either rule him out as a spy or find evidence that says he is one. If he's just a patsy, which he might be, then we have a bigger problem. It means someone else is using him, and *that's* the person we'll need to find. So grab some fresh coffee or energy drinks, and let's get to work. I'll make some calls, and we'll start getting some food catered in for you. I'll also see how many additional people we can pull in to help out as well."

Drew motioned with his head for Royce to follow him to the side of the room. Once they were away from everyone else, Drew leaned in so no one else could hear. "Brian, this is a real problem, buddy. I'm going to need to run this up the flagpole. I'm also going to call in some additional support to help us out. We need to figure this problem out ASAP—not in a few days or weeks. The longer this operation stays in play, the bigger it gets, and the deeper their tentacles reach into our systems. Can you imagine if the Zodarks launched an invasion and they were able to take down the Sentinels? Most of our fleet is forward-deployed, Brian. It would be a disaster."

"Agreed. You want me to dispatch a team to the shipyard or wait until we have a better idea of who we're after?"

"No, don't wait," Drew responded. "If you're good with sending Hosni and his team, send 'em. Have them establish some surveillance on Burt—his quarters, worksite, everything. Also get some eyes on that server location. We'll figure this out and hopefully have our culprit within the next forty-eight hours. What you and I need to figure out is once we find them, what do we want to do with 'em? I mean, obviously, we'll take them into custody and try to get them to lead us to others, but if we try to flip them to our side, it's risky. We don't really have a way of knowing if they're screwing us or playing both sides."

"You aren't wrong, Drew," Brian admitted. "It would be a risk not really knowing if they are telling the truth. But let me ask you this— what if we could feed misinformation to their handlers and push it on to the Zodarks? Imagine if we said the Sentinels were going down for a critical repair on Sumer on X date, that the bulk of the fleet stationed in New Eden was transferring to Sumer until the Sentinels were back online again—that's the kind of tactical ploy that can change wars.

"We could lead them to think we have a weaker system than we do. Or we could do the opposite. We could inflate the number of warships we have and their strength—make them believe we've become too powerful to fight. There are a number of ways to make this work to our strategic advantage. First things first—once we find them, we'll have to figure out what kind of leverage we can hold over them that'll keep them on our side."

"And therein lies the rub," Drew remarked. "Without knowing a lot about who these people are, we don't have a good way of figuring out what kind of leverage we can use to force their compliance."

For the next twelve hours, the analysts went to work. More teams of people arrived and plugged themselves in. The larger problems were broken into smaller segments and given to the new arrivals to figure out. Right now, they were sifting through every video and audio file they had of Burt at work and during his off time. It wouldn't take long until they began to piece together the link that confirmed him as a spy or would lead them to one.

****

The following day, Lisa approached Royce. "Brian, I think we found something. In fact, I think we may have just found who our actual spy is."

"You sure? That was awfully fast. How did you manage to make the connection so quick?" Royce asked, a bit skeptical.

"Here, let me show you what we've found and you tell me what you think," Lisa offered as she motioned for him to follow her to the workstation of one of her people. "Jerry, show the major what you found, please," she directed.

"Sure thing, Lisa," the analyst replied. "OK, Major, here's what I did. I took the surveillance cameras' stored videos for the last sixty days and ran an AI pattern recognition program to help me narrow down any people who spent a little more time with Burt that other people did, either on or off the clock. The algo identified six people. We ran extensive background checks on those individuals but, again, turned up bupkis. Dry holes. But something still didn't feel right. I felt one of them *should* have been our person. So I then refined the search further to see which of the six might have been spending more off time with Burt recently than they had in the past. That led us to this person."

An image of a beautiful woman with dark hair appeared on the monitor. Next to her picture was the name Ashurina Hamoud, along with a listing of her background, work history, credentials, etc.

"OK, so you think this might still be our person?"

"No, Major, I *know* she's our person," Jerry countered. "Here, let me show you this."

He brought up another image of a stunning dark-haired woman, also labeled Ashurina Hamoud. The employment histories matched, but as Royce stared at the picture, he couldn't help but feel that there was something different about her eyes. "*This* Ashurina apparently went missing for a few days from work not too long ago without any explanation," the analyst began. "Then suddenly, she reappeared and told everyone she was fine, that she'd just been under the weather. Shortly after that, she began expressing a desire to travel to the Belt or Alpha Centauri, which her friends found odd since she'd previously voiced an aversion to space travel. After that, she quit her job and, according to her friends, was never heard from again. Since she didn't have any immediate family, no one was officially looking for her or reported her missing."

Royce whistled quietly.

"But here's the kicker, Major. This is what makes us believe she's our person. Shortly before she was hired on by JBR, she met our guy, Burt. We were able to track down when she arrived on the John Glenn, and via her credits usage, we found she frequented the same bar Burt had. Sometime during their overlap is when the initial JBR breach was discovered. Maybe a week later, she was officially hired on.

"Once she was an official employee, she would have been able to identify the employees involved in many of these other projects. If she couldn't get them to respond to an email or open a proposal she'd sent that had her Trojan horse in it, she could attempt to meet them in person, but not before conducting some pretty sophisticated surveillance of them.

"Two of these people—Yonus Little and Macey Malice—she appears to have gone the old honeypot routine with them. Whether it was at a conference she engineered for them to attend together, a work party, or something else—we tracked a couple of hotel room payments by Yonus or Macey. Looking back at the surveillance of those hotels via lobby, reception, stairwell, and elevator cameras, we were able to place Ashurina at each of them. But this is what nails her as our spy. Sometime later that same evening or in the wee hours of the morning, Yonus and Macey accessed their clients' files. In many cases, it was just a few minutes; other times it was a little longer. But it was after these encounters occurred that these files began to extract regular copies of whatever was being added to them or modifications to the existing files.

259

She's our spy. She's the single vector linking each breach. We've got Burt as the first one—from there, she was able to get most folks to engage with her email exchanges, which gave her access to their credentials. But these last two, they're the ones that really seal the deal for us. It's the cleanest example of X happening, then leading to Y."

Royce stood there for a moment, thinking about what he'd just been told. It made logical sense. Before he allowed some self-doubt to flood in, he thought back to something General Bates had told him during his first week working for him: *Don't overly complicate things. Sometimes the simple answer sitting in front of you is the right answer. Trust your gut. Trust your instinct. Then ruthlessly execute the decision you've made.*

Royce turned to Lisa. "OK. You've sold me. Jerry here has obviously vetted this to the nth degree, poking holes in all the ways he could be wrong. Honestly, what this Ashurina woman has pulled off is nothing short of astonishing. To think, it would have continued to go on had we not used that Prim hacker tool and Zeus."

"Yeah, I know, right? Crazy, Brian. Good job, by the way, Jerry. The major here is normally a hard sell on something like this."

The analyst basked in some much-needed praise after working a twenty-four-hour shift.

"Lisa, Jerry, here's what I need from you guys. I need a BLUF statement of this entire thing. Then you can break down all the background info and how you came to derive your conclusions and final assessment. I want that entire package reviewed by one of Drew's teams. I'm going to ask Drew's people to specifically look for ways to disprove it and alternatively find us anyone else the possible spy could be. From what you just showed me, Jerry, I think Drew's team is going to have a hard time coming to a different conclusion than you did."

"Now that we have a potential target, we're going to place her under an increased surveillance package and see what else we can learn that might help confirm your assessment. Lisa, I want you to keep an open comms link with Lieutenant Hosni. His team should have arrived at the Republic Naval Shipyard facility by now. They're going in plain clothes to blend in. Should you detect a threat against them or a reason they need to suit up, make sure Hosni knows.

"Oh, and one other thing, you two. Be on the lookout for countersurveillance watching this Ashurina gal. If she's a Mukhabarat spy, they may have a team watching her to make sure she hasn't been made," Royce directed.

Whatever happened next, it would determine the action Royce's team would have to take: taking the spy into custody, eliminating her, or attempting to see if she could be flipped.
****

Twenty-One Hours Later
Interstellar Marshals Service Headquarters
Jacksonville, Arkansas
Earth, Sol System

Reinhard Gehlen had sat patiently through much of the hour, listening to this staggering report about the John Bentley Reactor's data breach. He'd been made aware of the incident when they had first discovered it. However, up until today, he hadn't heard about any success in ascertaining the full scope of the breach, what had been stolen, who had done it, or how it had occurred.

This whole JBR thing has been one headache and embarrassment after another, Reinhard thought as the intelligence operatives explained what they had found. As fantastical as it sounded, Pierre and Krzysztof had validated the material themselves, removing any doubt as to its veracity.

Several hours prior to the meeting, Gehlen had had the two of them and their teams scour the details outlined in the report to confirm its veracity. It wasn't that he distrusted the Republic Intelligence Service— it was more to do with the discovery having been made by Task Force Orange, the secretive intelligence support activity group buried within the Deltas' premier Special Forces group, JSOC. He wasn't particularly fond of their historical means of acquiring information or essentially doing the dirty wetwork or black ops side of things for the intelligence services. Then again, Lieutenant Hosni had gone a long way in demonstrating how they could learn a lot from working together more.

"As you can see, Director Reinhard, we've gone to extensive lengths to verify this is the spy we've been after," Drew Kanter concluded. "The extent of the damage she's done is still unknown. What *is* known is she was able to penetrate and gain access to an unfathomable amount of sensitive data in a very short period of time. I would like to point out that virtually none of this would have been uncovered had it not been for the exceptional work and dedication of Major Brian Royce and his team."

Reinhard knew who Brian Royce was. Most civilians within the Republic knew who Royce was—he was a two-time Medal of Honor recipient from the last war, the famed Delta warrior who'd slaughtered a roomful of Zodarks in a fit of rage when his men had gotten killed capturing a Zodark star carrier. The man had become famous after that video of him had been leaked to the public. It was the first time they had seen a battle vid of the humans taking the fight to the enemy and winning. It had rallied the Republic at a pivotal moment in the war.

"Thank you, Drew, for the detailed brief. It helps to fill in a few questions I still had after reading the report myself," Reinhard said before shifting his gaze to the living legend sitting in the nearby chair. "Major Royce, you need no introduction. We mere mortals know who you are. In a way, I suppose I'm more relieved to learn it was you and your team that uncovered all of this. Why don't you explain in your own words what's transpired and add some commentary to this report?" he said as he held his data pad up.

"Yes, sir. I'll do my best," Royce replied. He began to explain the little nuances that had led them to ascertain with a high degree of certainty that Ashurina was their person. He recounted every tactic she'd used to gain the kind of access she had, all the way down to the tried and true honeypot method.

The more Reinhard heard, the more he realized his worst fear as IMS Director had come true. He was the man in charge when the greatest security breach in the Republic's history had occurred.

"Sorry to interrupt, Major Royce. If I'm understanding what you're telling me, this Ashurina woman—she's our Mukhabarat spy," Reinhard began. "She's the one who managed to not only penetrate the JBR's internal networks, she essentially obtained the keys to the kingdom—keys she then used to gain further access into dozens of classified and black projects even *I'm* not allowed to know about. We're talking about places that provide the military and government with everything from toilet paper and equipment to expert advice on highly sensitive projects. Does that about sum it up?"

Lieutenant General John Reiker, who'd stayed silent up to this point, interjected before Royce could. "She's a spy, Reinhard. Given what we've recently uncovered about her activities, I'd go so far as to say she's a damn good one."

Reinhard shook his head in bewilderment before looking at the general. "Well, John, I guess that does sum it up, does it?"

The general didn't reply, although he did nod ever so slightly.

Steeling his resolve, Reinhard looked at the two soldiers. "All right. Then at this point, I have to concur with everyone—she's our spy. Then what we're left deciding right now is which one of the final three options outlined at the end of the report we should choose. Major Royce, I'm assuming you're the operational lead who'll execute whichever avenue we opt to pursue. Is that correct?"

"He is. Royce has the full backing and support of JSOC to implement whatever option you choose," General Reiker declared.

"Thanks, John, for the clarification," Reinhard replied. "Major Royce, your report suggested one of three options. The first and most obvious one is that we can take her into custody and prosecute her for the crimes we know she's done. As you noted, this approach would stop the bleeding immediately.

"The second option is we effectively let her continue like normal. We monitor her in hopes that either she'll lead us to her handler or her handler will access the secret folder she's created with all the documents we've now marked with this Zeus software. I don't have to tell you how badly that option could work out for us, particularly if we're not able to track her handler's location once he's taken the bait.

"That leaves us with your third option, which I might add is fraught with its own risks. This last proposal is an attempt, I presume by you or Drew, to flip her, to get her to work as a source for us. We could use her to feed her false information to her handler, have her help us uncover who her handler is and who else is in their network is still at large. Have I properly summarized the three options you're seeking permission to execute on?"

Reinhard saw the military man's jaw tighten as he nodded.

"Yes, Director. Those are the three best options we have right now," Royce responded resolutely. "Ultimately, the decision is yours— we'll execute on any approach you choose to take. If I may, I'd like to explain something further about option three."

Reinhard nodded for him to continue.

"I know the third option seems like a riskier bet to take, and it is," Royce acknowledged. "We can't fully guarantee that she won't pass along real intelligence beyond what we want her to share with her handlers.But if we can flip her, this could go a long way toward helping us repair the damage the Mukhabarat have already done to us. Feeding them false intelligence could help us lay a trap for their forces. It could also be used as a means of delaying or even preventing a restart of the war if they believe we're substantially stronger than we currently are or than we were when we last fought them."

"Major, what you all have done in uncovering this operative has been nothing short of amazing," Reinhard admitted. "Still, my mind keeps coming back to something—all of this occurred not just because one JBR supervisor couldn't keep it their pants—two others fell for this honeypot approach?"

"It would appear that way," came the terse reply.

Reinhard shook his head in disgust and amazement. It galled him that such a simplistic tactic had resulted in the greatest security breach in Republic history.

"To be fair, Reinhard, the honeypot is the oldest trick in the book," Pierre quickly countered. "Don't beat yourself up over it. If it wasn't this dimwit Burt, it would have been someone else."

"He's right, Reinhard. It's not like we haven't used these same tactics in the past. This Ashurina gal would have found someone else if it hadn't been Burt," Krzysztof agreed. "The important thing now is that Major Royce and Drew were able to uncover what happened and managed to find yet another Mukhabarat spy operating under our noses."

Major Royce jumped back in. "Sir, we can beat ourselves up over how this transpired or how we should have caught it sooner. But the fact is, we didn't. Focusing on spilled milk won't do us any good. However, in spite of what's transpired, we've been given a unique opportunity to gain some much-needed insight into the Mukhabarat's espionage apparatus and how the Zodarks use it.

"Since the end of the war, we've been largely flying blind in our efforts to counter these spying programs. For the life of us, we cannot figure out why some of the Mukhabarat spies we've encountered on Sumer readily crossed over to our side while a small cadre of what we're learning are far more skilled operatives have not. With the Zodarks no longer in control of Sumer, it makes no sense why some of these operatives remain loyal to them. We've managed to get a few of the operatives we caught to tell us more about their organization.

"From the little we've learned, we know they work as a secret police of sorts—you know, crack down on government dissent or anything anti-Zodark. One of the operatives we captured, they shared that there are two types of Mukhabarat: one that's recruited organically on the planet, and another that consists of far more trained and seasoned operatives. This other group comes from some planets outside of Sumer. Director, I know it's risky, but I recommend we try and flip this operative. She could be our way into learning more about this other group of Mukhabarat. If we're able to turn her into a double agent—then she could become an invaluable asset for us," Royce explained, providing further context to this intricate saga.

Reinhard steepled his fingers as he thought about what Royce had said, then slowly nodded. Looking at Drew and Royce, he said, "OK, first answer me this. The files she's already stolen—what have we done about them to make sure the Zodarks don't end up getting the real stuff?"

Drew stepped in. "That's a good question. Once we knew which files she had been accessing, we had an alternate folder set up with the real documents in them. Each time a user creates a new file, our people grab the file and layer in some falsehoods that strip it of its true value. Then we reinsert those files into the folder she has access to—this should also trick her into believing nothing suspicious has occurred. As to the previous files she's had access to and used…well, those are beyond our touch as of now. But if she does access anything in these essential ghost folders and files we've created, then all she'll get is falsehoods and misdirects—information we secretly want her to transmit to her handler."

"Huh, that's pretty clever, Drew. Let's circle back to you, Major Royce. Assume I sanction this third option, attempting to get her to flip sides—how exactly is it going to work? Who will approach her and ultimately run her as a source if she does flip?"

Drew stepped in before Royce could respond. "If I may, Director, Major Royce will be the one to take her into custody. He'll look to get her to cross over. If he's not successful, then I'll step in and try a different approach. This way, we leave ourselves a few different attempts if the first try doesn't work. When we do flip her, it'll be the RI who'll run her as our source. We'll gladly share everything we collect. But she's a foreign operative, so she stays with us should she turn into a source. That said, the RI fully understands this needs to be a joint effort. I'd like to include Pierre and any of his people he'd like to include in this special access program. Once we take her into custody, everything that has to do with this case will then fall under the control of this newly created SAP."

Reinhard had figured the RI would want to keep her as their source. Technically, it was their lane. *Damn, this third option is likely our best option as long as Pierre will be allowed access to the program. These bastards better not try and cut me out of the process. I'll raise holy hell if they think they can do that.*

"OK, then, I think we have a plan. Drew, Major Royce—I'll authorize her detention and we'll go along with option three—recruiting her. This'll give you all the authority you need to operate in the naval shipyard and anywhere else she may have roamed. If she leads us to further operatives being identified in Sol or Earth, then we need to know about it.

"General Reiker, Major Royce, I know our tactical teams got off on the wrong foot a while back. I want you to know Lieutenant Hosni's Delta team and Apollo Company have both been a godsend. They're rapidly getting our tactical and surveillance teams trained and ready to assume these roles in the future. In fact, they've even helped us establish the kind of training program we'll likely need to keep a steady pipeline of recruits coming in to meet future growth and cover down on natural attrition.

"General Reiker, I know this may be a big ask, but I'm going to insist on this. When you take Ashurina into custody, I'd like Krzysztof to be involved as well. He can observe outside the room if necessary, but I'd like him and maybe a few others to learn how you guys do things. I think it's important to restate the obvious. Our people come from a law enforcement background. That means our interrogation styles are geared more toward obtaining admissions of guilt and collecting mountains of evidence for prosecution. That's obviously different than the kind of intelligence-driven interrogations your people conduct," Reinhard explained before pausing for a moment.

If the IMS is going to stand a chance at combating God only knows how many other alien races we may encounter, then we're going to need to learn an entirely new way of gathering intelligence, he thought pensively.

"Since taking this post as Director, I've had to learn a few hard lessons," Reinhard admitted. "Namely, our organization was not ready to assume the full spectrum of this kind of domestic counterespionage work. Establishing and maintaining an interstellar law enforcement agency is still our focus, but so is our domestic counterespionage mission. I guess what I'm trying to say is we need to start learning how your people do this."

"Thank you for that, Reinhard," General Reiker responded, maintaining the hard poker face he was well known for. "I want you to know you'll always have our help. We may approach things from different points of view or use different methods to solve problems, but let's not lose sight of the bigger picture. We're on the same side. We share the same underlying goal, to serve and protect the Republic."

Reiker then stood, causing the others to stand as well. He turned to face his Delta Commander. "Major, you've been given your marching orders. Execute them. Turn her into an asset or plug this hole once and for all. Dismissed."

Royce nodded at the orders, then turned and made his way out of the room.

"Thank you, Reinhard, for your help in this," said Reiker, extending his hand to the IMS Director. "If anyone can turn Ashurina, it'll be Royce. He had a knack for this kind of work prior to the war with the Zodarks. We'll let you know how things go in the coming days. If we're able to flip her, things are going to get spicy around here. God only knows how big their operation is."

Chapter 35
Biscuits and Gravy

The Following Day
Republic Naval Shipyard

Ashurina left Burt's apartment ten minutes after he had. This was the arrangement they'd agreed to when his wife had relocated to the John Glenn. He believed it would minimize the chance of them being seen together, leaving his apartment in the mornings. She was glad he was inclined to be secretive. Some may have suspected, but they'd kept their opinions to themselves.

Looking at her Qpad, Ashurina scanned the *Republic Times* news summary for anything of interest. Not finding anything, she swapped over to *Voice of the Republic*. As she walked around the corner, headed to the tram system, she thought she spotted something out of her periphery. Pretending to stare at something on her Qpad, she eyed a man who seemed to be watching her as he looked at his own Qpad. Something about this man was different—she knew who the regular commuters were at the various times she caught the tram. He wasn't one of them.

Stay calm, just keep walking like everything is normal...

As she approached the tram entrance that would take her right past the mystery man, she saw him put his Qpad down like he'd been waiting for her. The hairs on the back of her neck tingled, and her heart skipped a beat. Something was off. Maybe it was the cool demeanor of the man now eyeing her, like he knew her...no, like he knew *who* she was. Suddenly she felt the urge to vomit. Her palms became sweaty and her skin clammy.

Is he here for me? Have I really been discovered? These were the thoughts that raced through her mind as she approached the tram and the man standing between her and it.

Then the man spoke. "Good morning. How are you, Ashurina?"

Hearing him call her name caused her heart to seize momentarily. She felt her mouth go dry.

Hold it together! Act normal, she chided herself for allowing her body to betray outward signs of distress—no doubt signs this stranger was looking for.

"Ah, good morning," she replied with confidence, sounding stronger than she felt. "It's still early, things are going well. How are you? Have we met before?"

As she spoke, she tried to walk around him toward the approaching tram and the other commuters she regularly rode with.

The man moved quickly, stepping in front of her—blocking her.

Smiling, the man countered, "That's good to hear, but no, we haven't met before. But if you'll indulge me, I'd like you to accompany me to the Scrambled Egg for a cup of coffee. I'll buy you breakfast, if you'd like."

Ashurina bunched her eyebrows. "Ah, I appreciate the offer— perhaps a rain check? I need to get going, if you'll let me pass. I'm going to be late for work if I miss this tram."

Flashing a warm, disarming smile, the man persisted. "You're right, Ashurina—you *would* be late for work if you missed the tram. Actually, I hope you don't mind—I took the liberty of speaking with your supervisor. You've been selected for an interview with DARPA, so you may be gone a few days during the process. Truth be told, he sounded jealous. But he assured me they could handle things during your absence.

"So...Ashurina, now that we have your cover to play hooky from work, why don't you join me for a cup of coffee? I've been told the Scrambled Egg makes a mean cup of joe and has some amazing biscuits and sausage gravy."

Ashurina was dumbfounded by what was happening. *An interview with DARPA? Is this some kind of a cover story?* she wondered before suddenly noticing the man held an arm out, blocking her from moving toward the tram. He flashed a disarming look and motioned with his head for her to come with him, toward the promenade where the restaurants, bars, and retail stores were located.

Stay calm, play along, see where this leads...

Accepting this wasn't something she could get out of, Ashurina steeled her resolve. Her training kicked in and she smiled warmly at the man.

"Well, then, if I have an excuse to play hooky today, by all means, lead the way, Mister...I'm sorry, I don't think you've told me your name?"

Extending his hand, he graciously replied, "You're right. How rude of me not to introduce myself. My name's Brian. It's a pleasure to meet you."

"Ah, Brian. OK. I think it's good to meet you. You're not some kind of nefarious character or something, are you?" she quizzed, a mischievous look flashing across her eyes.

"Let me think about that…nope. I'm not a wanted man—at least, I don't think I am," Brian joked.

As they walked away from the tram toward the promenade, two thoughts kept running through her mind.

He knows who I am…

Run away… slip away and run…

She almost laughed out loud at how silly that idea was. How could she run away? She was on a space station. Where was she going to run to? It wasn't like she could jump on a random ship and slip away undiscovered. No matter what happened next, she'd have to deal with it—head-on.

As the two of them made their way through the promenade, they spotted the popular breakfast joint and headed toward it. The shipyard ran a variety of different work shifts, making a place like the Scrambled Egg an ideal place for those who couldn't get enough pancakes or omelets no matter the time.

From the moment she'd left the tram station, Ashurina had maintained a keen sense of her surroundings. She knew she'd likely have a watcher observing her—assessing her to see if she'd been made…or worse, turned. But as they neared the restaurant, she saw something else, a pair of individuals doing their best to appear like they weren't observing her and Brian. She glanced at them casually, determining if they posed a threat. The woman looked athletic, her shorts exposing toned legs like she trained hard. The man next to her looked muscular— not like a bodybuilder, but like the kind of guy who could run probably just as hard as he could grapple with someone on the ground. What gave them away wasn't their clothes or their looks—it was the slight outlines under their shirts near the waistline. They were armed.

When Ashurina walked into the diner with Brian, the place, which was usually busy this time of day, seemed somewhat empty. Two women chatted as they sipped coffee at one table. A man and a woman casually ate at another table. Two lone individuals were seated at the breakfast bar, reading something on their Qpads, drinking coffees.

Brian smiled warmly and directed them toward a table in the back corner of the eatery. As they sat down, a thought settled in her mind.

Damn, I've finally been made. They discovered me...but how?

Like a flying object headed straight for her, moving too fast for her to dodge, she lamented the situation unfolding before her. She was out of moves—no, she still had one. Her tongue instinctively moved to the roof of her mouth. Then she panicked. She'd gotten comfortable; she'd gotten lazy. She'd lulled herself into a sense of invincibility—she hadn't attached the membrane, her fail-safe, in more than six months.

How could I be so stupid? This is why we have the protocol, she chided herself.

Then she heard a voice from long ago, her Ani instructor replaying his tired trope: *Always assume today is the day you'll be caught.* She could practically feel his scorn.

Damn it! This can't be happening. I've been so careful over the years, she thought as the humanoid waiter approached and illuminated the digital menu built into the table.

"When you're ready to place your order, just highlight what you'd like or modify a menu item and hit the order button. Server 003 will bring your order once it's ready," the Synth announced.

If you live a lie long enough, you'll eventually make a mistake.

Now that they were alone, Ashurina stared at the man sitting across from her, waiting for him to make the next move. Then he spoke, his warm smile contradicting the piercing nature of his eyes—eyes she doubted missed much.

"I must say, Ashurina, I hope I'm not being too forward, but I find you to be a stunningly beautiful woman."

Play it cool. Go with the flow and see where it leads.

She blushed at the unexpected comment. That wasn't what she had expected him to say. She adjusted her demeanor and coyly played along. "You're not so bad looking yourself, Brian. Did you stop me from going to work and clear my schedule to see if you could score a morning booty call or is this really about an interview for a position with DARPA?"

The man chuckled briefly before letting out a slight sigh. "Oh man. If only it were that simple. I will admit, it is good to finally talk with you. I feel like I've known you for a while."

She canted her head to the side. "Oh really? That's interesting, Brian. Have you been watching me from afar? It's not nice to stalk a woman, is it?"

She watched him as he took a sip of his coffee, looking at his facial demeanor, his eyes. It was a subtle change, but she saw it. The playful banter, the kind words, the various approaches he had been running from the moment they'd met. He was exactly what she feared—a fellow spook. Recalling how he moved, the smoothness of his arms, the pace of his walk, the air of confidence exuded by every fiber of his being—he wasn't just a spook, he was dangerous. A trained killer like her.

Brian opened his palms on the table. "I suppose you're right—observing from afar isn't very nice. It certainly hasn't really gotten either of us what we want. I suppose it's time we came clean, start with a fresh slate, don't you think?"

The question should have caught her off guard, but the signs flashing around her told her the jig was up. He'd just confirmed it—they knew who she was.

"Hmm, that's an interesting comment. I'm not sure I follow," she countered as she twirled some hair around one of her fingers, adding, "Maybe you should go first. You know, get us moving in the right direction."

The warm, disarming smile she'd seen moments ago evaporated. The man sitting opposite her now had a new mask—one that said he was a man on a mission, bent on accomplishing it.

Then Brian leaned forward, closing the gap between them. "How about we skip the foreplay and just get down to business?" he asked. It wasn't a question. "You've assumed the identity of Ashurina Hamoud, a woman who *happened* to hold the same work history and credentials as you. Keeping your first name makes it hard to slip up; I get it. It also made it easier for us to eventually catch up to you. What we can't account for is how you arrived on Earth to assume your new identity. That actually gave our analysts a real run for their money. The real Ashurina disappeared for a week, then out of the blue...there you are. You took some time to get to know the city and people of your assumed identity. Once you felt comfortable with starting your mission, then you left for the John Glenn.

"When I look back on it, you approached the JBR mission just like I would have—observe the employees until you find your mark. In your case, it was Burt Schumacher. Burt was perfect. He'd be the most likely mark to fall into your honeypot. Like a good operative, you used your sex appeal and likely skills. Poor Burt never had a chance. Once you seduced him back to his place, you gained access to his device. Once you were in, and with Burt wrapped around your finger, you steadily gained deeper access to JBR, and eventually to so much more. Does this sound about right? Is there anything I missed in that synopsis?"

She struggled to keep her mouth closed. Ashurina sat there dumbfounded as Brian recounted with astonishing accuracy what she had done to Burt and JBR.

Brian must have seen the look of surprise on her face. He added, "I'm sure you're wondering how long we've been on to you, but that doesn't matter. What I can tell you is this, I've been hunting you for a long time—and now I've found you."

She squirmed slightly in her chair, uncomfortable with the way he said *hunting*. It gave her pause. He really was a killer...

Swallowing hard, Ashurina tried to speak. "If you've been 'hunting' me, as you put it, what are you going to do now that you've found me? Mount me on some wall like a trophy?"

Brian laughed. "A trophy wall? No, it doesn't quite work like that. You don't have to believe me when I say this, but it's the truth. I don't want to see you tortured; I don't wish you any harm. Here's how I see things—you're a soldier, a tool being used in this interstellar war. I don't blame you for doing what you did. If the roles were reversed, I'd have done the same thing. But here's the deal—you've been caught. That means your part in this war is effectively over. You've been removed from the board. You're no longer a threat to my people."

Ashurina felt beads of sweat forming at the base of her skull and near the top of her hairline. The way Brian had so casually and seamlessly laid everything out disturbed her. If she had to guess, she'd say he'd done this a few times.

Then a thought occurred to her. *He's already caught some of our people. I wonder how many he's managed to turn...*

Brian snapped his fingers. She'd snapped back from her own thoughts, but her fears continued to manifest in her mind. He looked into her soul with those grayish-blue piercing eyes of his as he spoke. "The question you need to ask, Ashurina—and this is something only you will know—is what can you offer the Republic in exchange for either your life or potentially your freedom?"

"Are you really implying that if I provide you with information of value, there's a possibility I could walk away from this with a new lease on life?"

Brian canted his head as he sized her up before responding. "That's exactly what I'm saying. Life has value. Your life has value. The information you know also has value. I'm interested in what you have to trade for your life, and perhaps for your freedom. Who knows? Maybe you even have a family. I'd hazard a guess that if you do, you'd want to try and gain their freedom as well. The question is what information do you have to trade that we would be interested in?"

The mention of trading information for the lives of her family nearly caused her to burst into tears. She knew if Dakkuri found out she'd been caught, her family's lives would hang in the balance—their survival would depend on whether he felt she'd talked or gone out like a hero, using her suicide membrane to take her captors out with her.

"I can see by the look on your face that you're contemplating my offer. I'll help make it a little easier to decide. When I get up and leave, the offer leaves with me. You'll be apprehended and given a very *public* hearing. I don't know who your handler is, but I can assure you of this— he'll see your public trial. I'll make sure he knows you talked and gave them all up. I'd wager if you have a family, he'd make sure they paid for your betrayal."

Fear shot through her body as she blurted out, "You wouldn't dare!"

"Dare what?" Brian asked with a raised eyebrow.

"You wouldn't try to get my family killed. That's not how the Republic operates. You aren't Zodarks."

Brian laughed at her comment. "You mean we aren't like your organization? The Mukhabarat? Oh, we know all about how cruel your organization is, and we also know what they do to the families of people who talk. Trust me, if I was to walk away from this table, I would leak to the press how we captured a high-ranking operative for the Mukhabarat who had infiltrated the John Bentley Reactor company. I'm pretty sure your handler would be able to figure out it was you, and once he knew that, your family would be as good as dead."

Ashurina wanted to lunge across the table and strangle the life out of this cruel man. Taking a breath in, she steadied herself and weighed her options.

"How did you know I have a family?"

"I didn't. But given how you responded to the insinuation of them dying a horrible traitor's death—you kind of gave that away."

"Damn you, Brian," she replied before she said some other choice words.

He shrugged, unfazed by her emotional outburst. If she had to guess, he was enjoying himself, which made her want to punch him all the more.

"I like that about you, Ashurina. You're sweet and seductive when you need to be and you're piss and vinegar when the time calls for it. Hell, if you'd been born into our society, you'd have made a hell of an operator in my outfit. I wish those were the cards you'd been dealt, but they weren't. So that leaves us where we are. Am I going to get up and leave empty-handed, or are you going to play ball and come work for me?"

Seething with anger, she almost choked on her saliva at his final words. Not seeing many options, she pressed for more detail. "Let me get something straight, Brian. You're wanting me to come work for you? As, what, some sort of double agent? Or just spill my guts about everything I know? What are you asking for?"

She saw him ponder her answer for a moment before he replied. *Maybe I caught him off guard...*

"The way I see it, you've got three choices to make and you don't have a lot of time to decide. The first, you tell me nothing. You'll die for your cause like a good soldier. Your family's just collateral damage, their only crime having been that they were related to you. But they'll serve a purpose in this war—a warning to others who may betray their nation."

"Nice sales pitch. I'll bet you recruit a lot of people with that line," she shot back, glaring at him the entire time.

Holding his hands out in mock surrender, Brian countered, "Hate the game, don't hate the player. This is the life you and I signed up for. Your second choice is easier. You cooperate. You tell me everything you know and answer all my questions truthfully and honestly. Just so you know, we have machines and ways of knowing if you are lying, so don't think you'll be able to string us along for months or years before we figure it out. If you're lying, we'll just leak some reports to the media about your capture and cooperation."

"Nice, gotta love blackmail."

Ignoring her comment, Brian explained, "Your third option is a lot riskier, but it's also the option that'll gain you the most personally if you choose it."

"Let me guess, this is the option where I flip. I become a double agent and now swear my allegiance to the Republic?"

Brian smiled, not adding anything to what she'd said, which confirmed her assumption.

Ashurina blew some air past her lips in frustration and resignation. She was still coming to grips with the situation. Then a thought occurred to her, and a plan began to hatch.

Turning her charm back on, she said, "Thinking about the situation, you're right. We're spooks. We know the rules of the game and how things work. If I refuse to cooperate, you'll just torture me until I eventually tell you what I know. I'll likely last a few days or a few weeks, but in the end, I'll break. Everyone breaks…"

She paused, staring at Brian, who knew he had her right where he wanted her. She knew the choice she had to make—so she made it. "That leaves option two or three. Both risky, but one carries a substantially bigger risk should I get caught. While the very thought of betrayal is anathema to everything I believe in, it's also the path that lets my family continue to live, so long as my cover isn't blown."

"I had hoped you'd see it that way," Brian replied. "This game we play is tough—one wrong step and it's game over. My people didn't think you'd go for option two or three. I had to remind them, you're a soldier, just like us. Once you'd been given some options, you'd choose the one that served you best. That's human nature. I also told them you're an engineer. Engineers see problems, then they find ways to solve them. You were presented with a problem, and you worked to solve it."

She smiled coyly at his analogy. What she hated most was that she knew he was right.

Fine, he has me where he wants me. Let's see if they're willing to deal or just all talk…

He must have sensed she was about to say something. He caught her off guard when he held a hand up, declaring, "Ashurina, let me ask you something. What's your price?"

Lifting an eyebrow, she countered in surprise, "Price? I've only lived among your people a few years. There are some idiosyncrasies I still have trouble with. Why don't you explain what you mean by that more clearly?"

She saw him smirk briefly, but he wiped it away as quickly as it had come. "Hmm, that's a fair question. Let me rephrase. I'm assuming there's something you want beyond just keeping your cover intact so your family stays alive. If you're going to agree to work for us, then I'd wager there's something else you'd like to get out of this deal. Hence the question—what's your price?"

Damn, this guy is good. He's been steps ahead of me the entire time, she thought to herself.

"Ah, thank you for clarifying. I'd be lying if I said the thought hadn't crossed my mind. But as you said, Brian, let's skip the foreplay and get down to the details." She saw him smile, so she pressed on, knowing this be her only chance to extract something of value to her. "The way I see it, Brian, I have something you want. Like detailed information about the Mukhabarat, who we are, and where we're actually from—hint, it's not Sumer. But I have a need, something that, in all honesty, I don't think you could deliver on no matter how much I tried to help. So I'm hesitant to ask for something I know you can't provide."

"You're asking about your family, right?"

She nodded, not saying anything.

He looked past her, like he was deep in thought, trying to figure out what to say next. When he looked her in the eyes, she knew her request was beyond what the Republic could offer her.

"Ashurina, here's the deal. I think you've been honest and straight with me up to this point, so I'll be equally frank with you. The request you made isn't an uncommon request. Before the war with the Zodarks and the unification of Earth, this was how the game was played. But you've asked for something that has too many unknowns to even know if it's even a viable option. I don't want to promise something we can't achieve. So how about this—when, not if, we learn more about where your family is, we can reexamine this and see if a viable option could be found. In the meantime, here's how this is going to play out.

"To keep your family alive, we need to maintain your cover. I'd wager you might have some sort of countersurveillance team that monitors you?" When she nodded, he continued. "That's what we figured. So until we know more about how that works, we're going to covertly transfer you to another facility where we can begin a proper debrief that doesn't compromise your cover. As we're speaking, a call is being made to JBR and your supervisor, letting them know that, as of now, you have been reassigned to work on a classified DARPA project JBR will announce they just won. Once we've relocated you, we'll help you send your handlers a note alerting them that you've been recruited to work on a highly classified project even your coworkers don't know about. You can sex it up however you want, but make sure they know it may take you more than a few days to figure out how to covertly communicate with them on a regular basis.

"In time, once we know more about your countersurveillance team, we'll start to let you make more regular public appearances. I know it's a lot of information to take in, but we don't have a lot of time to get things rolling if we're to keep your cover intact. If you'd like, we can talk more details once we're on the shuttle. It's been a while since we entered the diner. It's time to move. Are we good?"

"Uh, yeah, I suppose we are. You're also right—we need to move. I'll have to write a detailed contact report about this meeting as soon as possible. If the watchers file a report without me sending one in myself, then they'll assume I'm compromised. I'll be a kite, cut loose and cut off until I'm retired."

"Retired? That's kind of crude way of saying you've moved on to a higher plane of living, isn't it?"

She laughed at his comment. She wasn't sure what would happen to her next. What she did know was that if she wanted to keep her family alive, to have any chance of reuniting with them one day, then she'd need to play along.

Who knows? Maybe...just maybe...I can still be of value to my people. It will just require a little more creativity.

Chapter 36
The Code

Zodark-Controlled Territory
Alfheim, Sirius System

Alfheim—a planet NOS Heltet had never cared to visit. Yet here he was, standing in the frigid air. A slight wind howled as wisps of snow swirled around him and the thousands of Zodark warriors assembled for the judgment. The commander of the Alfheim force, NOS Griglag, a member of the Blood Raider Clan leadership, nodded slightly, letting him know everything was ready to proceed.

Heltet hated this aspect of his people's culture. The Frocking, as it was called, was a brutal punishment handed down by the High Council and enforced by the Groff's Laktish for grievous acts of disobedience by a military commander or member of the Clan Leadership Council. It was a severe punishment, not taken lightly. The decision to issue such a punishment was often debated for hours, sometimes days, before it was rendered.

Stepping forward to the center of the hastily built stage, NOS Heltet looked at the soldiers and tribal representatives of the Blood Raider Clan. Then his eyes settled on the tribe of warriors standing directly in front of him—the Kushan tribe. The offending tribe that had caught the ire of the Council—they were the reason he'd been sent to this frozen, desolate backwater planet.

Bellowing loudly, forcefully for all to hear, he said, "Zodarks, warriors of the Blood Raider Clan! I am NOS Heltet, the Laktish of the Groff." Heltet saw a subtle shift in the demeanor of the warriors standing closest to him. The mere mention of the Groff was typically enough to strike fear into the hearts of even the bravest of warriors.

"By order of the High Council," he continued, "I have been directed to Alfheim to deliver a message to NOS Griglag, the military commander of the Blood Raiders and the tribal chiefs of the clan. Directive 449, issued by the High Council, was deliberately ignored by a tribe within the clan. This flagrant disobedience cannot be ignored. After much consideration, a decision was reached. I stand before you today to announce the punishment and restore complete, unwavering obedience to the will of the Council."

As Heltet finished this last statement, NOS Zada was brought forward toward the center of the stage. Zada stood several meters behind Heltet, flanked by four Groff punishment guards as he waited to learn his fate. The Zodarks of the Kushan tribe stirred as they saw their military commander trotted out in disgrace by the punishment guards of the Groff.

Heltet stood a little taller as he belted out in an authoritative voice, "NOS Zada, of the Kushan tribe, you disobeyed Council Directive 449. The Council has concluded that you are to be issued the punishment of Frocking. This punishment is to be carried out now. Upon the conclusion of your Frocking, should you prove strong enough to survive, the honor of the Kushan tribe shall be restored from this day forward, along with the honor of the Blood Raider Clan. All past transgressions shall be forgiven and never spoken of again."

Heltet heard a few murmurs of surprise, anger, and shock as he announced NOS Zada's fate. As he revealed the Council's offer of restorative honor through the process of Frocking, looks of hope and excitement took hold of the clan's tribes. With no war to fight, the stain of the Kushan tribe and now this sentence against NOS Zada threatened to be an indelible blight on their clan's honor. If Zada accepted the punishment and proved strong enough to survive it, their honor would be restored.

Turning to face Zada, Heltet demanded, "NOS Zada, do you accept your punishment and wish to pursue restorative honor, or do you demand Shokra to be administered instead?"

Zada held his head high, his pride not allowing him to look submissive or subdued. Heltet thought for a moment that he would throw away the Council's generous offer and demand Shokra. Then Zada declared loudly for the clan to hear, "I accept my punishment and the Council's offer of restorative honor for my tribe and clan."

With the decision made, Heltet took a step back, relieved he would not have to order Shokra. Turning to Griglag, he said, "The punishment has been accepted. It will begin immediately. Should Zada survive, this entire incident will be forgiven and forgotten. Your clan's honor will be restored. Should he not, then your clan will have to restore your honor through another means."

Attempting to look stoic, though he appeared more relieved, Griglag declared, "Then it is settled. NOS Zada, you are hereby stripped of your rank and title as NOS within the clan and your tribe. As the clan leader on Alfheim, I speak on behalf of our clan, praying to Lindow that he will give you the will and strength to survive the Frocking. The shame or honor of the entire clan is now on your shoulders."

Griglag made his way to Zada. Standing in front of him, he tore the NOS designation from his uniform; next, he was stripped naked and left to stand there alone and exposed to his tribe and clan, devoid of his rank, uniform, and honor. Griglag made his way to Heltet, who now stood near the side of the stage. Heltet and Griglag stood to the side as the punishers now took charge of Zada.

The Frocking punishment consisted of two phases that challenged a Zodark's physical and emotional strength as well as their commitment to truly achieving restorative honor for themselves, their tribe, and their clan. With a survival rate of less than eight percent, only the most committed of Zodarks restored their honor.

The first phase was a test of one's skills and abilities to fight and defeat an animal from the Zodark home world called the Chuta. The second phase tested one's mental and physical fortitude through a brutal punishment only the strongest minds had the force to overcome.

The punishers led Zada off the stage to a specially dug pit in the ground to initiate the first phase. As Zada approached the pit's edge, a punisher shoved him in. The Zodarks who had stood before the stage now circled the pit as they waited for the Chuta to be brought forward.

A loud call rose from a nearby tent. The Zodarks standing nearby made way for the priest adorned in a bright red and black robe that covered his body from head to toe. When the priest reached the edge of the pit, he brought forth a sword and recited a prayer to Lindow, the god and creator of the universe and all life. With the sword having received its blessing or curse from Lindow, it was tossed into the pit for Zada to prove he was worthy to advance to the second and final phase of the Frocking.

Heltet and Griglag watched as Zada grabbed for the sword. Holding it up, he twirled it in his hand before running through a series of drills taught to even the youngest of Zodarks. He practiced a couple of slashing motions before switching to a few other drills. While Zada continued to put on his show, the punishers moved the cage containing the Chuta. As the wild animal was moved, it howled viciously at being disturbed. Many of the Zodarks observing the cage tensed up and murmured to each other at the sound of the beast approaching.

The Chuta was a vicious apex predator that roamed the wilds of Zinconia. While not the largest animal in the wild, it was arguably the most vicious. It stood slightly above a meter tall on four legs but could extend to two meters when it rose up on its hind legs in a fight. The Chuta's talons were razor-sharp and not easily broken. The slight hooks at the edge gave them the ability to tear bone from an adversary if it didn't cut right through it. If one failed to move swiftly and avoid the swipes of the beast's talons, it could pull its victim in range of its fangs. When a Chuta bit into its prey, it exposed their flesh to a paralytic toxin that could weaken or kill a creature, depending on its size. If a Zodark was bitten, it would usually cause the bite location to lose feeling and sometimes function. If left untreated, it could lead to severe infection, which could be lethal.

Killing a Chuta wasn't easy. Its body was encased in a tough, leathery skin covered in scales that protected it from other predators. Piercing its skin while not being slashed or ripped apart by the beast required a great deal of skill and brute force on the part of the attacker. A Zodark would need to drive its blade deep into the beast's flesh to kill it. Defeating a Chuta wasn't impossible for a skilled warrior, but a moment of hesitation or inattentiveness could easily result in death.

When the cage containing the Chuta reached the edge of the pit, the punisher looked to Heltet and waited for his signal to start the first phase of the Frocking. In a booming voice heard by all, Heltet shouted, "Begin!"

The door to the cage was flung open and the two punishers lifted the rear of the cage, allowing gravity to drop the beast into the pit.

Crashing to the ground, the animal howled in anger as it scrambled back to its feet. In seconds, its head whipped up, and its eyes locked onto Zada. The two of them sized each other up as they began a dance around the pit, looking for an opportune moment to strike.

Seizing the initiative, Zada roared at the Chuta like a wild savage beast. He lunged forward with lightning speed, his sword pressing home his attack.

The Chuta appeared startled by the roar and the speed of Zada's lunge as it failed to evade the blade being driven into its left shoulder. Screaming in pain as the metal pierced through its thick skin and its flesh, it swiped at Zada with the talons of its right paw. Zada pulled his blade out before he could twist it further into the beast's flesh, barely escaping the grasps of the talons reaching out for him.

With the blade removed, the animal withdrew, rising on its hind legs before Zada could launch a counterattack. Tossing the blade from his upper right hand to his left, Zada twirled the blade like the practiced swordsman he was. Circling to the Chuta's left side, he faked a move to his right, causing the Chuta to drop back to a four-legged position. Changing directions, he leapt at the Chuta in a leftward approach toward the creature's weakened shoulder, driving the blade deep into the beast. Twisting the sword in a downward motion as he pulled it back out, Zada broke several bones and tore the creature's shoulder open.

A gush of blood poured from the wound as the Chuta screamed in agony. It lashed out with blazing speed, its talons fully extended, catching Zada's left upper arm and shoulder.

Zada howled in pain and surprise at how rapidly the beast had reacted to his last attack. In the time it had taken him to twist and tear through its shoulder, he'd given the animal just enough of an opening to sink its claws into him.

Withdrawing from the Chuta, Zada stole a glance at his wound. Three one-inch gashes had torn his upper shoulder open, exposing ripped muscle and tendons as bluish blood began to flow.

The Chuta, gravely wounded and angry, grunted and hissed at its prey. Despite its left shoulder losing its mobility, it moved to end this fight, roaring as it reared up on its hind legs. Zada saw his opportunity and took it.

Lunging forward, his life in the balance, Zada drove his blade into the upper chest of the Chuta, driving it deep inside the beast. Leveraging his forward momentum, he allowed his body to slide across the ground beneath the animal as it began to collapse around him. Sliding from his momentum, Zada's blade opened a wide gash across its chest and below, showering him in a torrent of blood as the animal's innards fell to the ground.

As Zada slid out from under the Chuta, blade still in hand, the mortally wounded yet extremely dangerous animal howled in agony and anger as it made a final move against Zada. The Chuta swung with its right arm, talons reaching for Zada's flesh.

Wielding the blade in a swift upward motion, Zada narrowly dodged the talons as his blade severed the paw. The beast cried out in pain, withdrawing the damaged limb as its body curled into a defensive position.

Seeing his moment, the dishonored Zodark leaped onto the creature's back. He drove the sword deep into the upper body of the beast, leveraging the weight of his body to force the blade to cut down the right side of the animal, disgorging more blood and guts from the wound. As Zada's feet hit the ground, he dodged another swipe by the animal's left paw before separating himself from the mortally wounded creature.

Having ravaged the Chuta, Zada moved to the pit's wall, waiting for the animal to bleed out and hopefully die before it could threaten him further.

The warriors watching from the edges of the pit marveled at Zada's skills as a swordsman. Killing a Chuta was no easy feat, especially when you had only one sword. The beast gave a final cry before grunting in acceptance of its defeat. A couple of labored breaths later, it died.

Zada roared in victory before approaching the dead animal. Kneeling next to it, he cut its heart out, holding it for all to see before taking a bite, accepting the animal's spiritual gift. As blood dripped down the sides of his face, he raised his right upper arm into the air, the blood-soaked sword held high as he shouted a cry of victory.

Shouts of celebration erupted from the Zodarks of the Kushan Tribe. A euphoric feeling swept over them as Zada had survived with minimal injury. The likelihood of Zada completing the second phase of the Frocking had just gone up.

Readying Zada for the next phase, the punishers lowered a ladder for him to climb out. As he reached the top, the priest stood there, waiting for him.

Kneeling before the priest, Zada thanked Lindow for deeming him worthy to proceed to the final test. The priest received the sword and motioned for him to stand.

The priest and punishers led Zada to the stage from which Heltet and Griglag had observed the pit. As he climbed the platform, the instruments of the final test were made ready. The pulley device was anchored to the stage, and a pair of brightly multicolored ceremonial cords were laid nearby, waiting for the priest to give a final blessing.

When the priest and Zada had reached the center of the stage, the holy man spoke a loud prayer to Lindow; if it was his will that Zada should be found worthy of redemption, then he should give Zada the necessary strength to complete this final test. If Lindow felt the crime Zada had committed was too grievous to forgive, then Lindow should provide the Kushan tribe and the Blood Raider Clan another opportunity to restore their honor and serve him better.

Heltet filled his lungs with the cool air as he stepped near the center of the stage and addressed the Zodarks standing before him. "The Great and Almighty Lindow has granted Zada the strength to complete the first test of the Frocking. Lindow will now examine Zada's inner heart and mind to determine if he is worthy of redemption and the restoration of his honor. Few people survive this test. The ones that do are the ones Lindow has determined to be worthy of life."

Turning to look at Zada, Heltet said loudly so all could hear, "I present to you the same choice as before. You may end all of this and choose the path of Shokra, or you may place your life in the hands of Lindow and see if you are found worthy. Which will you choose?"

Strength in his voice, Zada declared without hesitation that he would accept the final test.

With the choice made, the punishers ordered Zada to lie down on his belly. His two upper hands were bound with the ceremonial cords and then attached to the pulley device. His feet were bound with the same cords and attached to the pulley. Moments later, the cords were pulled taut as they began to lift his hands and feet off the ground, bowing his body.

When a Zodark's body was pulled into this position, it constricted the lungs, making it nearly impossible to breathe. With Zada's two lower arms unbound, he planted his hands on the floor and lifted, leveling his body. The change in position alleviated the pressure on his lungs, allowing him to breathe once again.

After some time had passed, watching Zada push up for each breath, Heltet turned to Griglag. "How long do you think you he'll be able to hold out?"

Grunting at the question, Griglag dismissively replied, "Likely not the twenty hours required to pass the test."

"You don't think so?" He was a little surprised by the flippant comment.

"You do?" asked Griglag.

"I don't know much about Zada, so it is hard for me to assess the man. Statistically, however, it is highly unlikely that he'll make it," Heltet admitted. "But statistics have been wrong in the past; it could be that he will be one of the ones that survive the ordeal."

"Perhaps. I suppose we shall see," Griglag replied, not seeming terribly convinced. "If you'd like, I can have some food prepared for us," he offered. "No need to sit here for hours on end. We can come back in four or five hours and see if he is still alive or not."

Nodding in agreement, Heltet left the stage with Griglag, heading to a nearby tent where they could wait more comfortably as some food was brought to them. It was highly unlikely that Zada would die during the next few hours of the test. Most Zodarks lasted six or more hours before their bodies gave out. After that, it became a bit more interesting.

While the two of them ate, Griglag asked Heltet about this peace with the Republic, specifically if he knew if this was likely going to be a permanent thing they'd have to accept and adjust to, or if something else was in the works. Since Heltet worked directly for Vak'Atioth, arguably the most powerful Zodark outside the High Council, it was assumed he knew more than even the NOSs who sat on the Malvari

It was a justifiable question. Griglag was, after all, the only Zodark commander staring down Primord and Republic forces daily. Heltet sensed a chance to create an ally with the leader of the Blood Raider Clan. His espionage experience was telling him this might be the right person to bring into his own inner circle. Establishing more internal sources and loyal confidants among the clans was seldom a bad idea— especially a dishonored one.

Holding a hand up to stop one of Griglag's soldiers from approaching them, he asked, "Do you have a more secured place we can talk?"

Griglag smiled at the suggestion. "As a matter of fact, we do. Let's go where we can talk more candidly."

They exited the tent, leaving Zada alone on the stage with the punishers as he continued his struggle to rest his strained arm muscles while not suffocating at the same time.

When they reached Griglag's headquarters building, they sequestered themselves in a secured room intended for sensitive discussions. Alone at last, Griglag felt he needed to explain to Heltet the real situation the Zodark forces were facing on Alfheim. He was unsure if Vak'Atioth or the High Council were being told the truth by the five NOS commanders who sat on the Malvari.

As the situation on Alfheim was explained, it created more questions than answers. Having spent nearly twenty years on Sumer, Heltet had a poor understanding of what had been taking place along the outer fringes of the Zodark Empire. Griglag brought him up to speed on how this obscure backwater mining colony had eventually led to one of the Zodarks' greatest military defeats.

It had originally been the Orbots who'd told the Zodarks about Alfheim. They had claimed there was some sort of unique material on the planet they needed to acquire. No explanation had been offered about why this material was important or even what it was. Then an offer had been made. If the Zodarks would assist them in capturing the planet from a small Primord colony and agreed to garrison it while they developed some mines, the Orbots would provide them with some new technology that would improve their warships' lethality and some medical technology that would cure several chronic diseases they had been unable to cure themselves.

The deal had been struck, and for dracmas, there had been no serious threats against the planet. When the Orbots had alerted them to the Republic's intentions to seize it, a plan had been hatched to use Alfheim as a lure to destroy the human and Primord fleets. Heltet waved off a further explanation of what had happened—everyone knew the results of the battle.

"So, what was so special about this mineral that the Orbots had been willing to sacrifice so many warships to keep it?" Griglag asked, saying the quiet part out loud. "Is it possible the Republic knew something about this mineral that we Zodarks did not, and that is why they fought like devils to take this planet from us?"

Heltet reclined a bit in his chair. "When I came to Alfheim, it was to administer the Council's punishment. Having spoken with you, it has become clear our Orbot allies have deceived us about what this strange mineral is. Whatever it is or does, the Orbots felt it was valuable enough to fight a battle to keep it—a battle that led to incredible losses on both our sides. It explains why the Orbots readily accepted the cease-fire proposal once the Republic offered them continued access to half the mines on this planet. Until now, it made no sense why the planet had been partitioned in two and why we were still being forced to garrison their half of the planet."

Griglag nodded. "I had hoped you could help me uncover what is really going on. If you would like, I have acquired a small sample of this mineral, and I can have it brought to your ship so you can have it studied? Perhaps Vak'Atioth can get to the bottom of this and inform the Council."

"Yes, please have the material brought to my ship. I will inform Vak'Atioth of what you have told me. Once this material has been analyzed, it may provide us with the answers we seek."

Griglag and Heltet left to arrange the quiet transfer of this mystery substance to Heltet's ship before they went back to the tent to dine and wait with the others. The two Zodarks talked for some time about the kinds of topics that filled up their version of small talk: weapons, tales of battles past, and the conquests that all Zodarks go through in their youth to find a mate worthy of their clan.

After many hours had passed, the Lindow priest who had traveled with Heltet entered the tent.

"I would like to inform you of Zada's fate," he announced. Everyone ceased speaking and listened. "After eight hours and twenty-two minutes, Lindow has determined that Zada was not worthy of restoring his honor. He has failed the final test."

Heltet looked at his new friend. "I guess you were right. His honor was not redeemable. Regardless, you have done a great service for the Groff. If you are correct about this mineral, then I will ask Vak'Atioth if he can speak about your discovery of this Orbot deception to the Council. They may deem this worthy of removing the Kushan's stain of dishonor from your clan since Zada has proven unable to do it himself."

A smile spread across Griglag's face at this offer of mediation on his clan's behalf. He stood and beat both upper arms against his chest, which Heltet mirrored.

"Come, bring the barrels of ale," Griglag directed one of his underlings. They drank heavily that evening. The fermented grain from Shwani produced a thick orangish-brown liquid that did not look all that appealing, but it definitely did the trick in terms of inebriation.

Hours passed with the two Zodarks drinking and chatting. Finally, Heltet had to excuse himself. "Thank you for your hospitality, Griglag.

Tomorrow I have a long voyage back to Shwani and the Groff headquarters."

Griglag slapped him on the shoulder. "May the light of Lindow guide you on your journey."

Chapter 37
Why Alfheim

Groff Headquarters
Planet Shwani

Three days ago, Vak'Atioth had received an urgent report from Alfheim, where he'd sent his Laktish, NOS Heltet. The Council had found that an NOS in the Blood Raider Clan had deliberately disobeyed his orders. An infraction like this was typically dealt with through Frocking the offender. All Heltet was supposed to do was read the Council's verdict and administer the judgment. What Vak'Atioth hadn't expected was for Heltet to uncover the kind of information he had. He was glad his deputy had had the forethought to send this report ahead of his own arrival. He was still six days' travel away, which gave Vak'Atioth more time to figure things out.

The situation being described by NOS Griglag, the military commander on that frozen wasteland, was contradictory to what the NOSs on the Malvari had been telling the High Council. Since the Orbots had forced them to accept a peace deal with the Republic, the Malvari's reports had continued to suggest the Republic was, in fact, much weaker than they were outwardly portraying. It was this belief and reporting that had convinced the High Council to let the military prepare to restart the hostilities and plan to invade the Republic. In fact, after preparing to launch this invasion for more than two years, they were nearly ready.

If what NOS Griglag says is true…if what the Mukhabarat has reported is true…then we are about to launch an invasion based on faulty intelligence, Vak thought to himself. *If the military is wrong…then this invasion could be a trap.*

The more he thought about the conflicting information, the more questions formed in his head. Namely, why were they being pushed to resume the war with the Republic now? A restart of the war would either derail or postpone their long-term plans to seize the Orbots' territory and technology. This strategic goal was the entire reason why they'd spent the last two hundred dracmas growing the Guristas Clan from the Sumerian people they'd taken as tribute. The Groff had spent the last forty dracmas assisting the Guristas in building a fleet of warships needed to fight the Orbots, simultaneously creating and grooming the

Gurista soldiers they'd need to capture the Orbot worlds and bring them under Zodark rule.

If the military was wrong in their assessment of the Republic and their allies, it could cripple or destroy their own military. It could mean they'd have to call on the Guristas to assist them, and that would eliminate the element of surprise they'd have against the Orbots.

Until he had better answers, Vak couldn't bring any of this to the Council. One couldn't level an accusation that the military was deliberately manipulating the Council and feeding them false information unless one could back it up with facts. Then there was this other piece about the Orbots and the mines on Alfheim.

He hadn't really cared what the Orbots were mining or what they were doing with it, but the fact that the Republic was also mining those same materials meant there was something more to it. In fact, the Republic was so interested in these mines that they'd not only invaded the planet to seize them; they'd sent their entire military force to recapture them.

If what's in those mines is this valuable to the Orbots and the Republic, then clearly we missed something—but what?

Heltet's report had mentioned he was bringing some of this mineral from the mine for further study. Whatever it was, they'd hopefully find out soon and figure out why the Orbots had kept it a secret from them. In the meantime, he needed to have his people review the military assessments the Malvari was providing in comparison to what the Mukhabarat had been reporting.

If the military is wrong, then not only might the invasion fail, the Republic might use that Gallentine warship to launch its own invasion of Zodark space. Heltet's warning about how this Gallentine warship could drop an invasion fleet on Zinconia had given him pause. If they did restart the war with the Republic, there was no guarantee the Orbots would join them.

Chapter 38
The Burden of Command

Viceroy's Office
Alliance City, New Eden

Viceroy Miles Hunt looked around the room at the four men who'd joined this meeting: the Director of the Interstellar Marshals Service, Reinhard Gehlen; Lieutenant General John Reiker, who was in charge of JSOC; Major Brian Royce, whose team had uncovered the spy and successfully flipped her; and Drew Kanter from Republic Intelligence. Together, the five of them would determine how best to use this double agent while also undoing the damage she'd already caused.

Once everyone had coffee or water, Hunt directed them to the sitting room next to his office. As they sat down, he knew he'd have to bridge the divide between these power brokers and himself. Turning to the man he'd need as an ally, he opened the meeting.

"Reinhard, I wanted to tell you something as we get going. I respect your dedication to the rule of law and your vigorous defense of it," Hunt began. "Sometimes, in our attempts to do the right thing, we inadvertently do the wrong thing. However, in the last few weeks, you've reinforced why you are the right man to lead and grow this important agency."

Reinhard sat a little straighter. Hunt continued, "An effective leader is someone who can acknowledge a mistake and move to correct it. Many others would have shifted blame, but you didn't do that. In fact, you've shown our civilian government the importance of something I teach every military officer and NCO during our leadership development courses—taking extreme ownership of your actions. I'm not sure Rule 909 would have succeeded without your support and, more importantly, your candor to the Senate regarding why this change needed to be made. I know that wasn't easy, but it was the right thing to do.

"I'm glad the marshals, the RI, and JSOC will now be able to work seamlessly together. I believe, in time, you and General Reiker will aid us in bringing the Mukhabarat to heel." The look on Reinhard's face told Hunt that was exactly what he'd needed to hear after a few brutal weeks with the Senate and the media talk shows.

"Thank you, Miles, for the vote of confidence," Reinhard replied, almost choking up from all the praise that had just been heaped on him. "I certainly don't envy your position, and I can only imagine how challenging it must be to lead an interstellar alliance. It must be like herding cats to even try and get multiple alien species to agree on anything."

"It certainly can be challenging," Hunt admitted with a smirk. "Well, your support in replacing Rule 902 with 909 has greatly strengthened my position, Reinhard. As the marshals yield results, it will help me restore the alliance's confidence in the Republic and in me as the Viceroy."

Now that he'd stroked the man's ego, it was time to start talking business. "All right, gentlemen, let's get down to the real reason we're all meeting in person and not via video," Hunt announced. "This spy, Ashurina—how credible is she?"

Reinhard gestured to Drew and Major Royce to field this question. They were going to be her handlers.

Drew began, "Viceroy, once she agreed to our deal, we put her through the same process of vetting her and the veracity of her information as we have used in the past. This process utilizes a series of biometric and biological lie detector tests. Throughout the tests, she's shown a remarkable level of honesty. At first, she wasn't willing to give up any of the names of her fellow spies, but after being reminded of her agreement, she gave us not one but two names—"

"Really? Did they pan out?" Hunt interjected, surprised by the news.

"They did. We apprehended the remaining two operatives who'd been involved in a series of bombing attacks across Earth. They're both in custody. Their interrogations are not only leading to tangible results in the field, they are also helping us verify information Ashurina has provided. It's allowing us to assess her intelligence with a little more credibility. However, what I need to brief you on next is not going to be comfortable."

"Yeah, I figured you'd say that. Go ahead, Drew. Rip the band-aid off so we can see how bad this is and what needs to be done to fix it," Hunt directed.

Drew spent the next hour briefing the group on the intelligence Ashurina had collected. It was as grievous as Hunt had thought it would be. She'd managed to penetrate into some of their most classified projects—projects that were now compromised. The more he heard, the more nauseous he felt.

We made a serious mistake letting Sumer into the Republic so soon, he realized. And then he started to wonder, *If this spy was able to collect this much information about the Republic in such a short time, how much have they collected on the other alliance members?*

A big advantage in space warfare between different alien species was that it was very hard to collect intelligence on each other's home worlds or colonies. A Zodark couldn't just infiltrate the Altairian or human societies or vice versa—hence the humans' deficit of knowledge about the Zodark Empire, the Orbots, or the other races that fought with them. Ashurina was providing them with a window into the world of the Zodarks they hadn't had before.

Hunt looked at the four men waiting to hear what he'd say next. *Heavy is the burden of command...now take command.*

"That was a good brief, Drew. Thank you for leaving no stone unturned. Here's what's going to happen next. I want whatever tech wizards you have to figure out how to triage the leakage from this breach. I'd suggest a parallel system be developed. This way we can leave her traps in place and summarily feed changes to the compromised files—make them look like updates or refinements, anything other than what they truly are. We can't change what they've already seen, so let's let them think we're modifying it to make it better. Include technological changes that outwardly seem beyond our capability, but slide in a new classification level that lets them believe our true capability is really just a misdirect, a measure we've taken to appear weaker than we truly are.

"At the same time, we need to figure out how we use Ashurina to our benefit while not opening ourselves up to a double cross. She's a spy, a damn good one judging by the damage she's caused. Let's not underestimate her again. You've got leverage on her—use it. Make it known if she burns us, if she tries to play triple agent, it's game over. We burn her cover and let her handlers deal with her family back home.

"One other thing—Major Royce, you said she wasn't from Sumer?"

"Yes, Viceroy, that's right. We're still uncovering more about that. All we know at this point is she said they're called Guristas: a separate Sumerian society. We're running with the theory that this is where the tributes taken from Sumer likely end up," Royce explained.

"OK, that actually makes sense. Let's also make this a priority. Find out everything we can about this Gurista society. Maybe those other two prisoners you have in custody will be able to provide additional context or insights to help fill in the gaps left by Ashurina's intel. We knew from talking with the Altairians that the Zodarks had likely been grooming some sort of alternate Sumerian society. This could be it."

For the next few hours, they discussed topics to explore with Ashurina. She had a wealth of hidden knowledge they were eager to learn more about. They also discussed what kinds of information they should feed her.

Could they further misdirect the Zodarks, or potentially get them to postpone a restart to the war? That could buy them the time they required to keep building the ships they'd need to defeat the Zodarks once and for all.

****

When the meeting ended, Hunt asked Drew to say back for a moment. The others shot him a sideways glance, then left him alone with the Viceroy.

When it was just the two of them, Hunt remarked, "Drew, I asked you to stay behind because you and I need to talk."

Drew lifted an eyebrow at the comment. "OK, what can I or the RI do for the Viceroy?"

"First, what is your position within the RI?"

Drew squirmed for a moment before answering, "Officially, I'm the deputy director for operations. I've been tasked to head our counter-Mukhabarat division."

Hunt nodded in approval. "Thank you for clarifying that. Can I task you with something that'd need to stay between you and me? Your superiors couldn't know about this—I'd deny it happened if questioned about it."

Drew hesitated, then countered, "That's kind of a big ask, sir. I suppose it would depend; what are my options should the RI find out I was secretly being tasked by you? They'd likely cut me or, worse, try to prosecute me."

"If that happened, my office would intervene. If that wasn't enough, then I'd intervene."

"Then what? I'd kind of be done in the Republic. A man without a country."

Hunt smiled. The spook was making sure he had another job lined up, ready to go should things not work out.

"If that happens, Drew, I'm pretty certain I could use your skill set for a few problems of my own. The Office of the Viceroy, as you can imagine, essentially has unfettered access and, if necessary, authority across the alliance. You'd be taken care of, if that's your concern."

Hunt saw the man breathe a little easier. *He'll play ball.* "This ask...it's about Ashurina."

"OK, what about her? What needs to be done?" asked Drew.

Hunt reached for the Viceroy tablet. It was a lot more powerful than the Qpads everyone used. Pulling some files up, he transferred them to Drew. He observed him reviewing the files and could see the spook starting to piece it together—the task Hunt wanted him to do but not tell anyone he was doing it. At one point, he looked a little unsure if this was something he even *should* do.

Intervening, Hunt asked, "You have a concern?"

Drew looked up. "If this went south..."

"I know what happens if things turn out badly," Hunt insisted. "But do you realize what it'll mean if they don't?"

"I see your point. If I can, I'd like to point out that this is risky. Placing this as part of the files she sends to her handlers won't be a problem. The challenge is making sure they act on it. If they don't take the bait, Viceroy, you'd better have a plan B ready to go."

A devilish smile spread across Hunt's face. "If they don't take the bait...the *Freedom* will allow us to pivot and come to the rescue. If it couldn't, if that wasn't possible, I'd never accept this kind of risk. So how about it, Drew? Is this a task you can handle for the Viceroy's Office?"

"Yeah, you can count on me. Just make sure that fallback plan is ready. So long as the Orbots don't get roped into this, we shouldn't have to worry about a bridge being opened behind our front lines."
****

When Drew left his office, Hunt was alone at last. If the plan he'd cooked up worked, then maybe, just maybe, they'd cripple the Dominion. The only concern he had was "the unknown unknowns."

He'd heard intelligence about the Zodarks pursuing their own wormhole device. If they figured out how to incorporate that technology into a warship…it'd likely tilt the advantage back to them.

War, like life, is a gamble. If you want to win, you have to play the cards you're dealt.

Chapter 39
Shifting the Balance

Groff Headquarters
Planet Shwani

Heltet was locked in his office, alone at last, reviewing the latest batch of reports he'd received from his Kafarr, Dakkuri. It had taken some time and considerable effort to establish their means of regular communication. It still wasn't real-time or anywhere near that level, but it wasn't taking months to receive each dispatch either. That also meant he was able to ask and receive answers to follow-up questions or issue a new tasking substantially faster.

A few weeks ago, Dakkuri had broken the news that their most valuable deep-cover asset had been picked up by Republic Intelligence. At first, his heart had sunk at hearing the news. She'd managed to infiltrate her way into more than just this John Bentley Reactors company. She'd wormed her way into a whole host of contractors and suppliers to the shipyard and the builders producing the new warships. The schematics of the ships, their weapons and armor specifications were going to be invaluable in a future conflict. The thought of losing her access ached.

Then everything changed. Dakkuri's next report said she'd been interviewed for a coveted position at a place called DARPA. Reading the attached report about this place made his heart skip a beat. He got down on his knees and thanked Lindow for having shown him favor in getting so many of his spies infiltrated throughout the Republic and their alliance.

There was one last report to read before he could truly revel in this achievement. The Yintar comprised the watcher and Kafarr reports on the status of an asset and their loyalty. If doubts were found, then it would call into question any future information that asset supplied. Until Heltet knew what their conclusions were, he couldn't validate this latest revelation.

Heltet retrieved the Yintar file. He'd read the first line when a notification appeared on his communicator—he'd just been summoned to see Director Vak'Atioth immediately. Heltet cursed under his breath.

I'm not ready yet. I need more time.

Grabbing the tablet with the reports, Heltet took off for the Director's office. It'd only taken him one day to learn you did not make the Director wait when you were summoned. An NOS several positions below him had made that mistake—he was now managing an outpost at the outermost reaches of the empire.

When he'd been summoned, Heltet had assumed this would be a private meeting—one where candor could be expressed freely as they discussed next steps. When the door to the office opened as he approached, Heltet realized this would *not* be the private meeting he had expected. Instead, he was greeted by the sight of Mavkah Otro, the head of the Malvari, and several of his deputies and their aides. The presence of these men suggested his summoning was about more than just discussing this latest intelligence coup. Something much bigger was afoot.

Mavkah Otro spoke loudly as Heltet entered the room. "There he is—the empire's greatest spymaster. Please, come join us, NOS Heltet. We have much to discuss."

"Yes, Heltet. You have elevated the Groff once again. Please, let us gather around the circle of decision," Vak'Atioth added boisterously as he directed everyone to the side room next to his office. It was here, in this most secured room of the Groff, that they deliberated the most closely guarded secrets and plans before speaking with the High Council.

Entering the room with the others, Heltet wondered how much of the empire's actions had been decided around this table, which was possibly the oldest circular wooden table in the empire. It was said to be over two thousand dracmas old. According to the legends, it was at this table that Lindow had created the concept of the High Council, the Groff, and the Malvari prior to being called back to the beyond by the gods. The table was considered sacred, which was why all the important information was discussed here, before it was brought before the High Council. When everyone had taken their seats, the meeting began.

Vak opened the discussion as he spoke to Otro. "Mavkah, as you know, Heltet is my Laktish, but more than that—he is responsible for the Groff having achieved something we have tried for many hundreds of dracmas and failed. It is *his* handpicked spies who have infiltrated not just the Republic but the Altairians, Primords, and Tully."

Otro smiled approvingly. He complimented Heltet and Vak for the great achievements the Groff had made these past years during this pause in hostilities with the Republic. He then asked, "What of the preparations to deploy the Ani? Can the Malvari begin the infiltration process to Sumer?"

Vak turned to Heltet, motioning for him to answer this question. It was his network.

"After reviewing the latest report from my Kafarr, the first stage has been completed. They are beginning stage two. Given the time required to infiltrate a Gurista into the Republic, I believe now is the perfect time to start that process."

"Excellent, we will begin the infiltration immediately," Otro replied. "The Ani's role in this next campaign is going to be critical. Since the end of this war, the Malvari began a process of reassessing our performance, particularly against the Republic. The appearance of this previously unknown human civilization and their frankly rudimentary weapon systems caught our forces off guard. There are few navies left in either alliance that still use kinetic weapons in space combat, hence why our ships have been designed to defend against energy weapons. During the final years of the war, we introduced two new classes of warships to help us counter the Republic's weapon of choice.

"Based on our experience from past battles and the initial information your operatives had retrieved, a tactic to defeat the Republic was crafted," Otro began. "We had based the timeline for invasion on the understanding of the Republic's current and projected military strength over a period of dracmas. However, the newly acquired information has called our earlier projections and assessments into question. If the Malvari understands the revelations your asset 114 has uncovered, it would appear the Republic's Intelligence Service had intentionally left false information for your assets to find. This meant the stratagem we used to craft the invasion plans the High Council had approved was based on information that can no longer be considered accurate.

"As anticipated, the Council has asked the Malvari to provide a top-to-bottom update of the plans to invade the Republic. Given the request and the Groff's newly acquired intelligence from asset 114, the Malvari has requested the Groff's help. The invasion timeline and the entry into Republic territory need to be assessed and either reconfirmed or a new invasion point identified.

"The Zodark Empire suffered great losses during the war with the Earthers, culminating in a humiliating defeat during its final battle. We believe this occurred because we lacked the intelligence to know who our enemy was. The Groff have worked tirelessly to fill that intelligence gap. Per this recent report from Heltet's asset 114, if the Republic's realignment of forces to Sumer and New Eden is accurate, and if these warship completion dates are correct, then militarily, the Republic is not nearly as strong as we originally assessed. In fact, these reports indicate they are at their weakest point ever.

"If their weakest position status is now, then *now* is the time to invade—not when they have rebuilt and the success of invasion could be in doubt," Otro concluded.

"Heltet, have you finished your review of the Yintar? That should confirm the Malvari's invasion plans," Vak asked, the expression on his face telling him there had better be a Yintar file with this latest set of reports.

"I received the Yintar report shortly before this meeting. If you allow me a moment, I will review the final summary for you now," he explained and then brought the report up.

I wish I had been told in advance the Malvari were speaking with us this morning. I could have had this better prepared, Heltet thought angrily. Director Vak was notorious for guarding information. It left his deputies scrambling during meetings rather than appearing well prepared.

Retrieving the report, he highlighted the Kafarr Summary. Since he hadn't read the full report yet, Heltet opted to do something crazy but bold—he was going to share with the Malvari the raw intelligence summary and not provide a version crafted by the Groff. As he cast the summary to the monitor, he saw a look of concern and horror wash over the face of Vak'Atioth.

Please, Lindow, don't let this assessment embarrass me or the Director...

Heltet cleared his throat. "Mavkah Otro, I am giving you something unexpected in hopes that this transparency will assure the Malvari of the accuracy of this latest revelation. The decision to wage war should be based on facts, not speculation. In this report, no names are mentioned, just the operative numbers. This is done to protect their identities should even the Groff find itself penetrated by a foreign power. Please, let us read the Kafarr assessment together so you may feel confident in what you must brief to the Council."

The look of admiration on the face of Otro told Heltet he had surprised him, and likely just earned some invaluable respect from both him and the Malvari.

Kafarr 11 Alpha assessment of Watcher 392's report of Asset 114

114 has continued to perform beyond expectations. Since obtaining initial security clearance to work for JBR and subsequent background check to work at the Republic Naval Shipyard, 114 has continued to avoid attracting counterintelligence surveillance.

Watcher 392 was redirected to the Primord planet Intus to support Watcher 391's overwatch of 002's activities. This redirect was authorized by 11 Alpha in preparation to receive Ani assets. 392 resumed overwatch position of 114 following a multimonth gap in coverage.

During 114's overwatch blackout, 114 provided a contact report outlining her recruitment to work at the Republic organization known as DARPA. Info report on DARPA is attached. During 114's new duties at DARPA, a report outlining the Republic's fleet disposition and battlegroup deployments was discovered.

11 Alpha verified the disposition and location of battlegroup near Sumer, verifying the DARPA report. 11 Alpha continues to task 114 with obtaining additional critical information.

It is 11 Alpha's assessment that, despite that overwatch gap, 114 was not compromised during the blackout period and continues to remain loyal and still in play.

Clapping his hands after reading the report's conclusion, Otro spoke boisterously, declaring, "This confirms it, Vak'Atioth. These Republic Chutas had been feeding the Groff false information to appear stronger than they are while they build a fleet to threaten our territory. Your agent, Heltet"—Otro pointed at him—"has uncovered the true strength and disposition of our enemy. Yes, this is the kind of information the Malvari needs to ensure victory in this coming invasion."

The deputies with Otro spoke excitedly amongst each other. Heltet was confused by their apparent enthusiasm. Regardless of how large or powerful the Republic fleet was, unless the Malvari had a means to counter that Gallentine supership, their fleets would still get smashed, just like they had at Alfheim.

I hope this doesn't get me in trouble, but I have to ask…

"Mavkah Otro, I am pleased that my spies are finding you the information necessary to win. But I feel I must ask what the Malvari's plan is for defeating that Gallentine warship their Viceroy commands."

"Excuse me, NOS Heltet—it is not your position to question the Malvari's strategy, let alone Mavkah Otro himself. Understand your place, Laktish," Vak hissed angrily, chastising him in front of Otro.

Otro laughed at the interplay between them. He held a hand up to forestall further remarks from Vak. "It is all right, Vak'Atioth. I am not offended. In fact, I believe your Laktish is as entitled to know as you are. The Groff have done us a great service, so let me share with you what the Malvari have in store for that great ship of theirs."

As a ship appeared on the monitor, Otro proudly explained, "This is the *Nefantar*—our Titan killer."

Heltet couldn't believe this was the same ship he'd seen just a few years ago. With its final transformation complete, it dwarfed anything the Zodarks or Orbots had built in the past.

"The engineers have solved the wormhole generator problem; the bridge is stable and has twice the range of the Orbots. While I'm not ready to reveal the superweapon within, I will say this—that Humtar wreck the Groff discovered all those years ago…turns out, it had a secret all this time," Otro explained. He turned to Heltet with a devilish look on his face. "That Titan you mention…let's just say it won't be a problem for much longer."

From the Authors

I hope you have enjoyed this book. If you would like to continue the action, you are in luck. The next book in the series, *Into the Breach*, is available for preorder. Simply visit Amazon to have the book downloaded to your device as soon as it becomes available.

If you would like to stay up to date on new releases and receive emails about any special pricing deals we may make available, please sign up for our email distribution list. Go to https://www.frontlinepublishinginc.com/, scroll to the bottom and sign up.

If you enjoy audiobooks, we have a great selection that has been created for your listening pleasure. Our entire Red Storm series and our Falling Empire series have been recorded, and several books in our Rise of the Republic series and our Monroe Doctrine series are now available. Please see below for a complete listing.

As independent authors, reviews are very important to us and make a huge difference to other prospective readers. If you enjoyed this book, we humbly ask you to write up a positive review on Amazon and Goodreads. We sincerely appreciate each person that takes the time to write one.

We have really valued connecting with our readers via social media, especially on our Facebook page https://www.facebook.com/RosoneandWatson/. Sometimes we ask for help from our readers as we write future books—we love to draw upon all your different areas of expertise. We also have a group of beta readers who get to look at the books before they are officially published and help us fine-tune last-minute adjustments. If you would like to be a part of this team, please go to our author website, https://www.frontlinepublishinginc.com/and send us a message through the "Contact" tab.

You may also enjoy some of our other works. A full list can be found below:

Nonfiction:
Iraq Memoir 2006–2007 Troop Surge
Interview with a Terrorist (audiobook available)

Fiction:

The Monroe Doctrine Series
Volume One (audiobook available)
Volume Two (audiobook available)
Volume Three (audiobook available)
Volume Four (audiobook still in production)
Volume Five
Volume Six (available for preorder)
Volume Seven (available for preorder)

Rise of the Republic Series
Into the Stars (audiobook available)
Into the Battle (audiobook available)
Into the War (audiobook available)
Into the Chaos (audiobook available)
Into the Fire (audiobook still in production)
Into the Calm
Into the Breach (available for preorder)

Apollo's Arrows Series (co-authored with T.C. Manning)
Cherubim's Call

Crisis in the Desert Series (co-authored with Matt Jackson)
Project 19 (audiobook available)
Desert Shield
Desert Storm

Falling Empires Series
Rigged (audiobook available)
Peacekeepers (audiobook available)
Invasion (audiobook available)
Vengeance (audiobook available)
Retribution (audiobook available)

Red Storm Series
Battlefield Ukraine (audiobook available)
Battlefield Korea (audiobook available)
Battlefield Taiwan (audiobook available)

Battlefield Pacific (audiobook available)
Battlefield Russia (audiobook available)
Battlefield China (audiobook available)

Michael Stone Series
Traitors Within (audiobook available)

World War III Series
Prelude to World War III: The Rise of the Islamic Republic and the Rebirth of America (audiobook available)
Operation Red Dragon and the Unthinkable (audiobook available)
Operation Red Dawn and the Siege of Europe (audiobook available)
Cyber Warfare and the New World Order (audiobook available)

Children's Books:
My Daddy has PTSD
My Mommy has PTSD

Abbreviation Key

AAR	After-Action Report
AI	Artificial Intelligence
BDA	Battle Damage Assessment
BIOS	Basic Input/Output System
BLUF	Bottom Line Up Front
CCTV	Closed Circuit Television
COB	Close of Business
COP	Combat Outpost
CSO	Chief Security Officer
DARPA	Defense Advanced Research Projects Agency
DFAC	Dining Facilities
DAO	Defense Attaché Office
FID	Foreign Internal Defense
FLIR	Forward-Looking Infrared
FOB	Forward Operating Base
FOBIT	Duty assignment that keeps you on the FOB (reference to the Hobbits from *Lord of the Rings*)
FS	Fighter Squadron
FTL	Faster-than-Light
HR	Human Resources
HRT	Hostage Rescue Team
HUD	Heads-Up Display
HVAC	Heating, Ventilation and Air Conditioning
ID	Infantry Division
IED	Improvised Explosive Device
IMS	Interstellar Marshals Service
JBR	John Bentley Reactors
JSOC	Joint Special Operations Command
LT	Lieutenant
MG	Machine Gun
MOS	Mars Orbital Station
MPL	Multipurpose Launcher
MSR	Molten Salt Reactor
NCO	Noncommissioned Officer
NDA	Nondisclosure Agreement
NIP	Zodark-issued neurolink

NOS	Zodark leadership
ODA	Operational Detachment Alpha (Special Forces)
P2	Priority Pad
PA	Public Address System OR Personal Assistant
PCR	Priority Collection Requirements
PDG	Point-Defense Guns
PFC	Private First Class
PI	Playful Idiot, see *Useful Idiot*
POC	Point of Contact
QRF	Quick Reaction Force
RA	Republic Army
RAP	Remote Access Program
RD	Republic Dollars
RI	Republic Intelligence
RNS	Republic Naval Ship
ROE	Rules of Engagement
SAP	Special Access Program
SF	Special Forces
SFR	Sodium-Cooled Fast Reactors
SOF	Special Operations Forces
SOP	Standard Operating Procedure
TF	Task Force
TOC	Tactical Operations Center
UGS	Underground Sensors
UI	Useful Idiot, see *Playful Idiot*
XO	Executive Officer

Printed in Great Britain
by Amazon

28434632R00175